CIANAN PUCKETT

Never Without Sacrifice

The Void–Sleeper War: II

To everyone that's had to sacrifice a dearly held dream in order for another to have a chance at tomorrow.

I see you. I hear you. Keep pushing on.

To Stephen Khounkeo, a young soul who was called before his path had yet begun. Your family misses you dearly, and remembers.

And to Layden Miller. Words cannot describe the loss of one who chose their hour. But know this. Your name burns in the hearts and minds of those you knew.

Your names burn forever as stars in the sky.

Contents

Preface

There are times when we have to give up a dearly held dream in order for another dream to happen. Times when sacrifice is necessary for others to see the next sunrise.

And life? Life is Never Without Sacrifice.

Acknowledgments

To Alana Mekdarasack, whose original inspiration for Khula gave us the beginnings of a badass.

To Scott Bryden, whose Thäoldr may be a deviation from his design, but is nonetheless a crucial character.

To Myrna Jayne, who has believed in me from the time we first met. Who has, time and time again, urged me to keep writing, even when I wanted to give up.

And to everyone who has given me ideas and helped me get this far.

I

Screams

1

1: Dragonmoor

Karos doubled over suddenly, clutching his head and fighting back a scream. His vision went pulsed between red and black, before an image burned into his mind. A clawed hand closed around a shattered Ranger pendant, blood streaming freely from multiple gashes. The imprint was too familiar to ignore- Sardra was in deep peril.

Khula grabbed the man's shoulders, doing her best to steady him as he threatened to topple. When she had got him back to his feet, she touched two fingers together, asking if he was injured. He shook his head and Khula heaved a sigh of relief. A moment passed, and she brought one finger down across a knife hand, before rotating and closing both hands to point at him. The message was simple- what happened?

Taking a breath to steel himself against any further intrusions, Karos let his hands do the talking- he felt that if his mouth opened, only vomit could come of it. "Ranger in serious trouble. We have to go."

Khula shook her head, showing the potion they had been

brewing for the past four hours. "Ranger will have to wait- otherwise we lose Seran." She dropped her hand dramatically to show the severity of the situation and Karos reluctantly nodded. As dear as Sardra was to him, he could not risk the future of all sapient life to run to her aid.

He would just have to hope that others would get her message. "Is it ready?" His hands asked of Khula, indicating the potion. She had amazed him with her knowledge of the apothecary sciences already and had made several suggestions for herbs to put into the mix. Looking over to the man they were trying to save, Karos sucked in a breath.

"As ready as it will be. It has to work. It must, for all our sakes." Her motions seemed hopeful- *a bold choice*, Karos thought to himself. Hope was an emotion he had only felt in brief bursts, but being around Khula... He was not sure what he was feeling, but her presence was the most comforting he'd been around in many a decade, his Rangers included. There was a peace to her, even in the most chaotic moments. It was welcome, especially against the tempest that was his mind.

Karos nodded quickly and drew a vial of the fluid, looking it over carefully. Then, he raised it to the sky and intoned a prayer to Elyrea, the Ancestor of mercy and healing. "Kindest mother Elyrea. Singer to rest of souls departed, chooser of the fallen, I beseech thee to bless this mixture. Give us a sign that we are not lost. I beg of you, aid us in healing this man." Looking to the skies for a sign, Karos closed his eyes for just a moment before moving over to the man on the bedroll. Crouching down, he angled the man's head and shoulders up, propping them against his knee. The man was delirious and Karos feared the worst already. But when his eyes fluttered open, the man let out a soft groan.

"Water…" the man begged weakly, trying to lick his lips even as his body threatened to fail him.

"Soon enough, Artlur. Drink this." Bringing the vial to the man's lips, Karos tilted it back and let the golden liquid flow into his mouth. Artlur sputtered a little, but drank the potion. As soon as he was sure the man would not choke, Karos laid him back down and exposed his body. Artlur had suffered much at their hands and Karos doubted the man could ever forgive him. He had understood the reason for his pain in his lucid moments, but Karos still worried.

Artlur did something then that he had struggled to do since Karos had begun treating him- he took a deep breath. Then another. Karos' eyes widened as he watched the man begin to visibly strengthen. His pulse, which had originally been so weak as to barely be detectable, was now palpable in his neck. His hands clenched and unclenched and most miraculous of all, his sores closed and the pustules of plague withered and fall from his body, leaving gruesome scars in their wake. All at once, he sat up, taking a deep breath. "Warden Ranger, you have done it! I can *breathe!*" He was unsteady, soon collapsing back to the ground, but he continued drawing stronger and stronger breaths.

"Khula!" Karos cried, forgetting that she was standing close by. "You have done it!"

Recovering from the fright of being shouted at, Khula smiled and grabbed a cup of water from the table, quickly bringing it to Artlur. Propping the man up as Karos had done, she pressed the vessel to his lips, allowing him to drink deeply and drink he did. Karos clapped his hands together and shouted towards the other Rangers in the camp. "*Tengarii! Shkali! Shkali!*" The call of victory felt sweet to Karos as he beckoned his friends over to his aid. "Quickly, Rangers. Gather all the Dragon's Pipe, talthras, ynalos, blazefir and tyngfir you can find. We need as much as possible. We have successfully healed Artlur, at least for now."

"How? Warden Ranger, this is wonderful news, but how did you do this?"

"'twas not I, Otho. 'twas Lady Khula. I merely cooked the mixture; she was the one who chose the herbs."

The Rangers then looked at Khula, who had a cheerful smile on her face. Raising her hands, she signed her answer quickly and precisely. "I have always been friends with the Master Archivist of Cúledan. He gave me access to Kingmage Las'Sa'Reeth's notes on the Great Plague. An honor he usually only gives Rangers." She seemed aptly pleased with herself and turned to Karos. She had not given him this nugget of information before. "My parents wished for me to be an obedient, quiet mouse belonging to Magus. I refuse."

Karos, in his surprise and jubilation, cupped her face and kissed her forehead. It was a completely spontaneous move, but it made both their hearts flutter. When he pulled away, Karos turned once more to work. Artlur was resting comfortably and Karos investigated the cauldron, quickly tallying up how much of each herb he had placed into the mixture and checking against the notes they had worked up together. As he wrote up an approximate recipe, he felt a tap on his shoulder and turned to see Khula holding out one written in much neater writing. He grinned and took the parchment from her, placing it down and copying it as precisely and legibly as he could. Once more, he felt a tap on his shoulder, this time slightly more frustrated. He turned again, and she grabbed his hands for a moment, before signing.

"This is not just my work. This is yours as well, Karos."

"Nay, dear Khula. This victory belongs on your shoulders. You have saved Seran."

Shaking her head emphatically, Khula gave a few more signs, this time jabbing Karos in the sternum with a finger. "You are just as responsible. Own it."

This went on for several minutes until one Ranger returned with a large quantity of herbs. "That is quite enough, you two. Karos, if she asks you to take some credit, you answer with, 'yes, milady.' You have been slaving just as hard as she for the last few hours. Now, how do we plan to distribute this?"

"How else but us and our new allies? It must be us. Someone else may get it wrong."

Otho nodded and clapped his hands together, before walking to a tray of vials that had been brought back from Cúledan by the two. Quickly drawing twelve vials, he placed them in a pouch, wrapping them to avoid breakage. That done, he made his way out of the camp, when a gigantic shadow passed overhead. Thäoldr had returned upon the back of his great dragon Namryll.

Back-winging to land, the great beat let her feet press the dirt beneath, before angling her shoulder to allow Thäoldr to debark. When he had, she rested her bulk fully upon the ground, quickly dozing. Thäoldr looked over his dragon for a moment with a mix of worry and love- she was getting old, but still definitely able to move when she needed to.

"Karos! Warned away six caravans and took down three Raider bands. Then, I thought you may have some word- what have you?"

"We may have found a cure- but one of my Rangers is in peril. She left imprints of her location that just now make sense to me."

"Well, it seems as if we have a solution to both that and a problem you failed to mention- spreading the cure. Namryll!" At Thäoldr's command, Namryll let out a great cry that rattled everyone's chests. The call echoed for quite a distance and was soon given a reply- many loud cries reported back, and Thäoldr grinned.

The first to answer soon came into view. A large lance of ten dragons and riders, backed up by twelve griffons and riders. They landed swiftly and Karos had to sprint to cover the precious potion that had been made. Nothing could be mixed in, lest the efficacy of the medicine be compromised. Thäoldr waved to the Lance-Lead, who dismounted quickly and raised an arm in greeting to Thäoldr. "Paragon Thäoldr, I trust the winds have been kind?"

"Aye, Tirian. I have much news for you, but we must wait until everyone is assembled. Namryll called to as many as could hear."

"So... half the continent is coming?" Tirian smirked for a moment, before noticing the Ranger. Instantly, his blade was out and his eyes flashed with fire. "Explain yourself, Ranger. What betrayal are you plotting?"

"Damnitall, Tirian, put that blasted sword away before something stupid happens. We work together with the Rangers now, by my orders. This task is bigger than either of our groups, so you had best get used to it."

"But the things they have done. The Riders they have killed-"

"Were in defense of innocent lives, you fool. The Riders my Rangers slew had forsaken the bonds of honor and become little more than bandits in the skies." Karos interjected angrily, positioning himself to fight.

"You hold your tongue in the presence of a-"

The call of many dragons, which were well-timed, drowned the next words out. Tirian stumbled back, having taken a metallic fist to the face at the same moment. He eyed Thäoldr with anger, but soon realized that the Paragon of Knowledge could kill him with the slightest effort. Sticking his sword into the ground, he put his hands up slowly in a show of surrender before looking to the sky. Another lance had just arrived, landing quickly and carefully. There was less wind at the camp, thanks to the distance they landed from it, but Karos still had to scramble to protect the potion. Taking a breath, the man watched as Thäoldr played out basically the same scene with the new arrivals.

Within the hour, no less than twelve wings had landed. They were briefed upon the accord Karos and Thäoldr had made and most accepted it- reluctantly. They were not so keen to forget almost three thousand years of animosity. But necessity makes strange allies, and they soon took to their tasks, preparing more of the cure with their best alchemical skills and loading them on their magnificent beasts. The dragons and griffons took their new assignment with pride, readying themselves for the task and trials ahead.

When the Riders and Rangers had left, only Karos, Khula and Thäoldr were left and Karos' mood turned grim. "I cannot ask this of either of you- but one of my Rangers is in the deepest peril and I must find them. I can only give the landmarks they passed on their way- but something tells me we will know when we find their location. It is likely that some of my Rangers are already on the way there as we speak- so time is of the essence."

Khula spread her feet into a fighting stance and brought her hands up, crossing her fingers and jabbing to the right in the hand-sign for 'ready.' To die or to live, she would stand by her new friends- Karos alone had already given her something her parents had tried to keep from her- adventure and with it came a pounding heart and a new sense of self-worth. She could feel the primal surge in her mind- she was not to be just some decoration on Magus' arm. She was going to take hold of her life and fight for every moment. This was her time- and none would take that from her. If she died, she died free.

Thäoldr looked over at both his companions. One new, one familiar and both ready to die. Karos, Thäoldr thought, looked like an older brother whose sister was under attack, ready to fight the world, if he had to. Khula, who he had had only a slight introduction to, looked as if this was her way of fighting back against injustices that had been done to her. He could only wonder what things had happened to her in her years. Finally, he decided. Jumping as high as he could, he slammed his fists together. "If today is our doom, so be it. We will face it with honor and fury." Then he waved at the two and climbed into his saddle.

Karos positioned Khula between the two, so she would be the most secure and attached his belt to hers, making sure that if she fell, he would catch her. Gently, he patted her shoulder before calling to Thäoldr. "All secure, Rider!"

With that, they were aloft, the dragon's robust muscles propelling them from the ground and into the sky. Then, her great wings unfurled and began beating the air, pushing the trio into the distance. Taking the landmarks from Karos' mind, Namryll angled her wings, sending them east and north, towards Westerspring.

Karos had a pit in his stomach as he thought of what lay ahead. He could only wonder where they were going, but something was familiar about the image of Sardra's hand. *The Cliff of Abandoned Dreams...* That was a place he was terrified to return to- he had a camp he could isolate himself in when his *þrúnsaal* got to be overbearing, a tactic that had always served him well, even if he knew it was a bad idea to be alone during those times. Something told him that one of those times was coming soon.

Khula, not caring for the pain it would cause, let out an ecstatic whoop as they cruised through the air. Unfolding her arms, she let the wind tear at her garments. She cried out in joy, welcoming the sting on her throat as the winds tore away her whoops. *If this is freedom,* she thought to herself, *then I would sooner die than be caged again! This is wondrous!*

Higher and higher they rose until Karos tapped Thäoldr's shoulder. "Any higher and we may not breathe!" A nod was his reply, and the elf slapped Namryll's neck, letting the creature know to stop rising.

The dragon and her passengers cruised along, flying over the Wyrmspine Mountains as they approached Westerspring. Her powerful wingstrokes blew gale-force winds below and behind her as her onyx scales gave the appearance of a statue gliding overhead. The fields and hills around Cúledan were soon far behind, the Wyrmspine Mountains slowly beginning to come into view. Far below, Karos could see the ruins of the Nexus, still visible even nearly eight thousand years later. *The site of the Rift.* He thought silently. It was an odd thought, but he knew what it meant. *The site of the Rift between the Order and the Rangers.* Taking a breath, the Ranger glanced ahead to Thäoldr, wondering if he'd seen the same thing, and had the same thought.

"The Nexus!" The Dragonrider cried out, loud enough for his passengers to hear.

"Aye!" Replied Karos. Khula tapped his shoulder three times as a way to ask what that meant. Turning his head, the Ranger spoke to her as best he could with the buffeting winds around them. "The Nexus was the sight of one of the largest battles in Seranese history. A slaver fortress-city. The forces of a prominent Ranger at the time were hunting a being called the Dollmaker. If the old legends are true, she was a Ranger. I will tell you more of the tale later. But during the battle, the Order of Gelvrentael and the Rangers fought each other after the Rangers began killing Dragonriders who were allied with the Nexus."

Thäoldr chose that moment to add in a few thoughts about the event. "The Rangers believed they were in the right to kill the oathbreaker Riders. And they were. But the Order, at the time, believed they were the only ones with the authority to kill traitors to their cause."

"And since then, the Order and the Rangers have been in... an *iyz'keð seltri*. A cold war. Without end, but usually without blood." Karos added, prompting the elf in front of him to nod. It was an old tale, and a sad one. One that was told to every Ranger, to remind them that actions have consequences. That one should always, *always* consider the ramifications of what they were planning.

Karos remembered more of the story they'd been told about the event. More than he was willing to share, for certain. How the Kingmage had made his last stand before the gates of the Nexus, and had brought the walls of the fortress down in one catastrophic blow, though he'd been pierced with an incredible amount of arrows. How two Rangers and a scant number of others were the only survivors out of the attacking force, which numbered... *well, if the stories hold true, six Banners of Rangers, one cohort of adventurers, the Kingmage's Own, a quiver from the Scouts, a regiment from the Brotherhood of Dres'Lan, and at least ten Lances from the Order.* So, in all, the attackers had numbered nearly two thousand. Certainly not a large force, but that was all that the groups could spare. And they'd expended nearly *all* that force to bring down the Nexus. *But, ahh, what a battle it must have been.*

But that battle had destroyed so many lives. Karos didn't want to even think of how many slaves had died in the onslaught. He knew the *official* total to be almost sixty thousand deaths from all involved. He didn't know the makeup of the numbers, but he'd done his own homework into the matter a long time ago. It was staggering to consider the losses everyone had endured, all in the name of freedom. But the message had been clear as a bell; *no slaver shall stand against the Rangers.* Which was why it burned at Karos' soul that a slaver fortress had popped up in his own homeland. In Northrealm itself, and he'd never been told *where.* But somehow, he knew the time was coming when it would need to be razed.

But nothing could prepare him for the reality when it came.

As they flew over the Wyrmspine Mountains, Karos got a clear view of both the grasslands that led into the swamps of Nevian, as well as the meadows and kindly hills of southern Westerspring. They were far above the land, higher than the Ranger was comfortable with. In his head, Karos did some mental math to figure out just how lethal a fall from this height would be. Absently, he tightened his belt, but said nothing of his concerns. Taking a breath, he slapped Thäoldr on the shoulder. "We have been flying for some time, mate! Perhaps a bit of time on dirt would be good?"

The elf nodded, having the same thought. Karos glanced behind him to see that Khula was beginning to nod off. *Evidently the thrill has worn off. Or she is just that tired.* Reaching back, the Ranger gently patted Khula's shoulder, startling her back to full wakefulness.

At a command from Thäoldr, Namryll started her gentle descent, making lazy circles down and down until the ground was far more detailed than it had been. Even before they were within a safe distance, the old elf was looking for a safe landing place. Spotting one he liked, he relayed it to Namryll, who let out a rumble of approval. Soon, the landing site was near, and the dragon delicately dropped to her feet on the ground. Her shoulder dipped, and Karos was the first one off, having unbelted and slid to the ground before she even turned to let her passengers know it was safe. He hit the ground, rolled, and the only thing keeping his arrows in his quiver was the force of his roll.

Looking around, Karos picked out the lay of the land. There was a small, spring-fed pond nearby, surrounded by what *looked* like a bunch of young men and women. Immediately, the Ranger groaned, causing his companions to look at what he was watching. Thäoldr moved over and slapped him on the shoulder.

"Come now, it cannot be that bad, Karos."

"Look closer, mate."

Shrugging, the elf focused as best he could on the young people around the pond. They were still about forty spearlengths distant, but that was nothing to the elf, who'd trained to spot details from *miles* above. Immediately, he groaned as well.

"Aye." Said Karos. A tap on his shoulder alerted him that Khula had arrived, and he turned. Quickly, she signed her question, and the Ranger looked at Thäoldr for a moment. "Would you like to tell her?" He asked.

"Oh, please, feel free."

Sighing, Karos began signing and speaking to the younger woman.

"Pehin. A group of the Fair Folk. We can approach, but we have to invoke the Free Waters, otherwise they will try to ensnare us to do their bidding. Rangers learn to be immune to their wiles. What about the Order?"

The old elf grunted and spoke.

"The Order hardly runs into the Fair Folk, but we usually teach people to be careful of them."

Nodding, the Ranger continued along with a sigh. Reaching up, he pinched the bridge of his nose.

"They will try to ensnare *anyone*, and it is usually not for *dark* purposes, but it is *incredibly* difficult to try to reclaim someone's mind once one of the Fair Folk captures them." Shaking his head, the Ranger made sure to be the first to approach the young women. As soon as he approached near enough, they began chittering among themselves in an ancient language that Thäoldr was almost *certain* was an old dialect of Indekari.

"I invoke the Free Waters!" Karos called out. Immediately, the mixture of people began grumbling and shaking their heads. Nonetheless, they opened their ranks to allow the Ranger and his companions through. One glanced at Thäoldr and fluttered her eyelashes as an attempt to get his attention, but the ancient elf merely grunted and continued on.

Khula, however, was having a more difficult time. Two

were walking with her, as close as they dare with a Ranger standing nearby. One tried to grab her hand, and she pulled away roughly. Bringing her hands up, she tapped Karos on the shoulder and grabbed one of his hands for protection. He nodded and put the arm around her shoulder.

This caused many groans of annoyance from the Pehin around the pond, but none of them were willing to disobey the Ancestors. Or displease a Ranger. One Pehin leaned close to Khula and whispered in her ear, trying to entice her away from her guardian. The Ranger hissed a command in the Sk'av'A, and she snarled and backed away once more.

Turning his topaz eyes on the Pehin, Karos bared his teeth in a show of dominance. At first, the young woman-looking creature hissed back, trying to assert her own dominance over the Ranger and his companions. Karos, however, was accustomed to the ways of every type of the Fair Folk, and knew how to deal with an aggressive Pehin. Baring his teeth to the maximum he could, Karos hissed louder and growled. The Pehin returned the gesture and flexed her ears, so Karos rolled his shoulders back and took in a deep breath, making himself bigger and more imposing. Then, he took a step forward. He'd been keeping solid eye contact with the Pehin for some time. His own eyes were burning, but he knew hers had to be screaming with pain now.

She blinked. Then, she backed away, stopped hissing, and put a hand over her eyes, signaling her defeat. Nodding, Karos made a sharp hiss that lasted less time than a heartbeat, and nodded to Khula, who'd watched the entire thing. She nodded in return, showing that she'd understood the lesson.

"You cannot give them an inch," Karos said a moment later, "or you had best say farewell to the world you knew." Another

Pehin stepped between the Ranger and the pond. Thäoldr was already at the pond, having scared the Pehin away from him by simply charging a spell. Certainly, the creatures were foolhardy, but when someone went for a weapon of any sort, be it steel or spell, they knew to back down right then and there. They were silly, not stupid. "Look big, sound scary. Or, in your defense, find another way to intimidate them." He hissed at the Pehin that'd stepped between them, and she immediately covered her eyes and backed away. Satisfied, Karos reached the pond with Khula in tow, and both of them refilled their waterskins and drank from the spring gratefully.

Thäoldr let out a yell behind them as several of the Pehin approached Namryll, as he was on his way there.

"Shoo! Go away, little idiots! You cannot ensnare a dragon! Numbwits!"

Almost immediately, the Pehin scattered before flowing back toward Karos and Khula. The Ranger shook his head and finished refilling his waterskin. Khula watched one approach and let out a loud hiss. The Pehin puffed up her chest, doing her best to look alluring and busty, expecting that to help her ensnare and therefore enslave Khula.

But they didn't expect the force of will the woman had. Locking eyes with the Pehin, Khula realized what the creature was trying to do. That she was the target of something trying to take away *her* control over herself. She realized the Pehin was trying, as so many others had done, to exert its control over her. To take away her freedom. In that moment, a black rage overcame Khula. Her vision wavered and red pulsed at the edges. *Somehow*, Khula abruptly hit the creature with the full force of her thirty years of torment and pain. Every whip she'd endured from Magus and his friends. The moments she'd cried herself to sleep from some pain or other that her parents or her husband had inflicted. Every single time she'd wanted to slit her wrists, every time she'd wanted to leap out a window. The anger when Magus had killed her beloved friend and lover, Crelsthan. The sorrow when she'd miscarried Crelsthan's child. The unadulterated *rage* she'd used to inspire her to poison Magus to sleep so many times, so she could slip away unnoticed.

The Pehin let out a yelp as she collapsed to the ground, chest heaving. Khula stood defiant, her eyes shining with anger at the creature that'd tried, *like so many others*, to exert its will over her. Her hand went to a rock before Karos gently grabbed her shoulder. She nodded gently and took a deep breath as the anger, pain, and utter black rage washed away from her. Turning, she looped her waterskin tighter and followed Karos, leaving a devastated Pehin behind to be tended to by her incredulous kinfolk. The trio found their way back to Namryll, who was staring down a Pehin. As the trio approached, she backed away submissively, as if they all had come to respect the right of these visitors to be in the area.

They broke their fast at that time, after Thäoldr had built a small fire. Karos was the first to shuck his pack and take out his cooking pot, a kettle, and his precious kuksa cup. Pouring the majority of his waterskin into the kettle and pot, Karos glanced at Thäoldr, who was already cutting slices of dried meat and dropping them in the water. A moment later, Karos added some dried vegetables to the mix, along with a powder made of dried broth. The water assumed a brownish color, and the smell of stew soon filled everyone's nostrils.

"It will be some time before the vegetables are tender,"

Karos remarked, earning a nod from his companions. In the meantime, he put his kettle near the fire to heat, and searched his pack for- *oh, where is it?* A moment later, he let out a triumphant shout and pulled a small burlap bag out of his pack. Khula quirked an eyebrow at the noise, and the Ranger passed the bag to her.

"Take a sniff!" He instructed, and when she did, she was enraptured. It was a fine tea, she assumed, and made from such herbs and even a few spices as she'd never known. Holding the bag close, she took another breath through her nose, not willing to let the stuff go. When she finally passed it to Thäoldr, she glared when he gave it a sniff and shrugged, as if the tea did not impress him. He looked at her and shrugged again.

"Rangers have the best tea, this I do not deny. But what I would not do for a pint, right now."

The woman let out a gentle chuckle at the elf's words. Truly, the tea was wonderful, but his wishes for a pint made her think of the last time she'd had a fine wine. *Before this mess started,* she realized. Sighing, she watched as Karos filled a small mesh bag with the tea and plunked it into the water in the kettle. Then, the trio waited for a while as everything cooked.

As Kjetta descended to the western horizon, the air was pleasantly warm. The glow of the fire lit each face with warm, orange light, hiding the colors of their skin, making them all the same. The Ranger, sitting still and quiet, watchful and calm. The Dragonrider, imposing and impressive, simply listening to the sounds of the evening. And Khula, the Lady, out of her element but learning fast that she enjoyed this far more than the trappings and safety of court life. This time she'd spent away from it all was filling her heart and mind, reminding her of what she *could've* had so long ago. What awaited her if, or when, Magus found her again. The thought soured her slightly, and she realized it showed on her face when her companions stared.

Bringing her hands up, she signed quickly.

"Bad memories."

Karos grunted, and Thäoldr nodded. Both had experience with such things. Karos, though far younger, had seen almost as much as the much older elf. It had broken both in far more ways than the woman would, or could, ever know. Neither was annoyed at her, though. Neither was anything less than sympathetic. They were both teachers and understood what it was like to have one's life turned upside down in a heartbeat. Both knew pain, even if for different reasons than the woman sitting with them.

For a moment, the woman felt *so much* smaller than the two men sitting near her. A glance at Thäoldr, the scars decorating his body, the white beard, the bald head. The tattoos speaking of Ancestors-only-know-what he'd been through. He sat so regally, as if he were a noble himself, and dragon-saddles were his throne. She decided in that moment that he carried a quiet dignity about him, and it impressed her to ponder what he'd seen. He was *refined,* in a way only she could understand or respect.

Karos... she thought for a moment as she considered the Ranger. If Thäoldr was grace and poise, Karos was... at first, she didn't have the word to describe the man. He was nearly the antithesis of Thäoldr. Certainly, their height was similar, but that? That was it. He was brutal and quick, which she'd seen already. Untidy, and yet, not *unclean.* He always looked as if he'd just stepped out of the brush, and even though she knew he bathed, smelled of soil, pine, patchouli, and sandalwood. Not an off-putting scent, but the woman couldn't explain why he *always* smelled of it. And there was more. Where Thäoldr was meticulously groomed, Karos seemed to have twigs laced into his beard. *Almost as if he put them there*, she thought for a moment. Decorations not unlike the beads in Thäoldr's. Looking the man over, she realized an additional detail on him. His right eyebrow, about halfway along it, held seven bone rings looped through the flesh. How she'd never noticed it, she did not know. *Always something new with him.* Where Thäoldr seemed, well, *regal*, the Nolvern man, for lack of a better word, was purely *feral.* The juxtaposition was... nearly breathtaking.

When the food and tea were finally ready, Karos served everyone, and they began to eat. The stew was scrumptious, if a bit thin, but they knew it would hold them over for a few days. No one was too good to ask for seconds, and the Ranger was quick to supply. Soon enough, they were sated and Karos was cleaning his supplies before making his way back to the spring to refill his waterskin. The night was still young, and the trio began to wonder if they wanted to make more progress toward Sardra's rescue tonight, or if it would be better to relax, to give themselves rest for what was to come.

2

2: Westerspring

The screams echoed for a few minutes through the *tengjäv*. The first one shook Fae to her bones, made her nearly leap from her skin. *Kiri!* Immediately, she was on her feet from the nap she'd been taking, rapier in hand. Rushing out of the sleeping cave, she hot-footed around the *tengjäv* until she found the wild elf doubled over, clutching her head and shrieking. Sheathing her blade, Fae held out her hands and approached.

"Kiri!" She cried out. "What is it, my friend?"

When Kiri finally ran out of breath, tottering and collapsing, Fae caught her gently. "Alador!" She cried out as loud as she could, only to find the other Ranger clutching their head as well. *By the steel. What magic is this?* Looping Kiri's arm over her shoulder, Fae half-dragged her to a chair and set her in it. Sweat poured from the wild elf's face, her eyes, usually serene, were wild and unfocused. Grabbing her wrist, Fae felt her pulse. *Racing.* She was heaving and gasping. *Fuck.* Without thinking, the woman grabbed the first cup her hand hit and tossed the contents on Kiri's face- by pure luck, it was the right thing. The frigid water splashed the wild elf, causing her to gasp and cry out.

"Sardra!" She yelled as she came back to reality. "Sardra is in peril!"

"One of your Rangers?" Fae said, already making mental calculations for what she would need to bring, thinking on the kit they'd given her. She didn't know how far the jaunt would be, but if a Ranger was in peril, well... *I must aid how I can.* Kiri nodded and Fae took a breath.

"Right," Fae said a moment later, "Where are we bound, and what do I need to bring?"

Kiri shook her head for a moment, finally completely coming around. "Not your problem, Fae. I have another thing you need to do, though." She said, taking another deep breath to steady herself. Hobbling up into the main cavern, Alador shook their head and stepped over to the others.

Raising their hands, Alador began signing to Kiri. "I cannot get involved, Kiri. Not yet, at least. But you and I both know." Kiri nodded. She'd known for some time. She'd known, in fact, longer than Alador had. Longer than any of her friends had.

Once she'd steadied up and shaken off the pain, Kiri looked at Fae. But the wood elf was quicker with her questions, concern furrowing her brow.

"What in the name of the stars was that about, Kiri?" She asked.

The wild elf took a breath and pulled her Compass out, tracing the stone spearhead with her finger. "This is our symbol. Of authority, of station, everything. It is also our key to any Ranger places. As well, it has a bit of secret magic. If crushed, it will cut the hand of the wielder, and when it reacts with their blood, sends a flare to any Ranger nearby, warning them that their fellow is in absolute peril. We do not do it without reason, and I cannot remember the last time it happened."

"So what am I supposed to do? Sit and watch? Kiri, though we have not long traveled together, I would hope you understand me more than that." Fae said, reaching for the pack they'd given her. Alador was quicker, though, intercepting her hand and holding up one of their own, a single finger pointed up. A moment later, they were signing.

"Her path diverges from yours here, Fae cos'Criux. You have other tasks. Perhaps it is time to assemble Dire Company once more?" They signed, eyes a-twinkle with roguish mischief. *That one knows something,* Fae thought with an absent nod. When they released her hand, she shrugged and pulled the pack on.

"Well, there is nothing to say our paths cannot meet again, of course. I have a feeling of where I need to go." With a smile and a wink, Fae loped through the *tengjäv* and headed out on her own adventure.

Kiri and Alador looked at each other for a few minutes, sitting in silence and enjoying each other's company. She was younger than they were, by far and away. But they had seen similar sights, done similar things. But both knew- this next task would be her last. Whether by choice and going into reclusive relaxation or death, neither knew. Both had their suspicions.

Finally, Kiri coughed into her hand and smiled at Alador.

"Farewell, *ka teljt.* May the winds always be warm on your face." Alador smiled and signed a response, and the two broke company. Kiri grabbed her own pack and headed up the cave toward the exit, following in Fae's footsteps. As soon as she slipped through the rock door and closed it behind her, the wild elf was off on the trails once more.

Using her knowledge of Westerspring, she got a general idea of where Sardra might be, and headed off. Taking a gentle lope at first, she bounded over the hills and fields, waving farewell to the forests she'd known for... *ages, at this point.* Waving farewell to her past. For fell or good, this chapter in her life was ending. *So let us see where the next one begins.* Tightening her pack straps, the wild elf took off at a dead run, the wind whipping her hair and comforting her as she ran.

Waving farewell to Littlebrook-Once-Besieged, she felt a pang in her heart. *So many innocent people.* Sighing, but not letting the memory slow her, she threw a salute and kept on. The trails of destiny were clear in her mind, and she moved along at her best speed. Many friends' last stands lay between her and where she was headed, and something told her to visit as many as possible. *It will be important,* she realized. As she crossed the border into Sheffrith County, the wild elf stopped in a meadow to rest, take a meal, and take in the scents. But it was only for a few hours, then she was off again.

At her best speed, she knew it would take a few days to reach Sardra's location. Where, she hoped, the dokk would be waiting in good health, if not good spirits. *If not,* she mused, *someone's blood will join hers on the ground.* As she moved through the wildlands, she occasionally felt the need to trail her hands along the tall grasses, stop and smell a flower or two. Such things were life for a wild elf, a life she'd long ago forsaken to be a Ranger. *But perhaps I will return to that life,* she thought, smiling to herself. Her cloak flowing out behind her, Kiri wandered the wilds for quite some time.

Part of what guided her was her own intuition. Part of what

guided her could be considered fate. But what kept her on the path was the wardstone, the Ranger Compass, around her neck. The blessing, carved into the stone in the Sk'av'A runes, was such that a Ranger would *always* find themselves where they were most needed; even if they didn't know they were needed there. In that way, a Ranger could *never* lose their way. Even if they never ended up where they intended to go.

Drifting along as would a seed in the wind, Kiri found herself nearing the site of an old battle. Even as she approached, she could feel the old spirits, the energy that'd gone into the battle. Even from her distance, she could feel the emotions of the world around her turn sour. Steeling herself, she trod the ground where many died, in stories she'd been told long ago. Stories she'd passed down to countless other Rangers in her time. Stories she'd nearly died in. Chuckling as she wandered the battlefield, Kiri lost herself in trying to read the land, the old scars.

Then she was off again, heading away from the setting sun and into the oncoming dark. *How fitting,* she thought to herself, *that I go towards the distant darkness.* The same darkness that lurked in her soul. In the soul of every Ranger, she knew that much well. Every Ranger had the capacity for limitless kindness and unquantifiable evil. As she strode through the fields and meadows, she pondered on many things of that sort. Many questions and potential answers, all leading up to this point. Some involving her, some involving others.

At length, Kiri's thoughts turned to her most "successful" Tenderfoot. Her dearest *valtagt,* though she saw every Ranger as her children. Every one she ensured had enough to eat. Enough to drink. Someone to write to when they felt low, someone to advocate for them when needed. They fought and died alongside her, and she was always the one to mark their graves or their deaths. In her journals, which spanned millennia at this point, there was always a few pages of names; those of Rangers she knew well who had gone to the Path. But this Ranger wasn't one of those fallen. This was the Warden Ranger. Karos himself, her most "successful" project.

As she moved along, she pondered the young Nolvern man. He had become a fearsome fighter with his beloved bastard sword, Northrage. His seax knife, one of the few remaining links he had to his childhood home of Coldforge. His bow, Ravensong, a constant companion carved from the limbs given by Eldest. Karos had been a decent Ranger even in his first years. He had a tendency to find secret paths, hidden things, and lost people. Indeed, he was even a capable tongue, having talked more than a few bandits out of desperation-based-hostility by offering not only comforting words, but also his own supplies. *Something he learned from Alador, no doubt,* she mused. But there was far more to the man than even she knew.

He kept to himself for the most part, having never taken a lover. At least, that she could remember. There were years when she'd not traveled with him, especially before he became Warden Ranger and she one of his Talons. But he never spoke about lovers. Never really spoke about his sexuality. But the few times she plied him with calm, careful needling, he'd revealed himself to be *anegidara,* or *pansexual* in the common tongue. He'd occasionally commented on what he found attractive in a potential lover, be it some physical attribute, or more often with him, some other Aspect of their Being.

If anyone breaks through to him, she thought, a smile creeping across her face, *they will have someone who will go through lifetimes to find them again.* That much she knew. Someone like

Karos didn't fall in love with a *person.* He fell in love with *souls.* Inwardly, she wondered if Fae might be interesting enough to break through to the man. She seemed his sort, and from what she'd talked about with Karos, may very well be someone he would wander with. Was she headstrong? It seemed like it, and if what she'd learned about Dire Company was true, she had a penchant for the dramatic. *Of course, our dear Warden Ranger has his own.* Chuckling, she found a memory, long locked away.

It'd been *ages* since she'd thought of that event. An ambush, long-planned against her, Wastan, and Karos. But somehow, they'd kept the element of surprise. Karos, posing as a crippled youth, hobbled into the enemy camp. At first, they didn't recognize him as a Ranger, and in truth, he wasn't. At the time. The young man had made his way up to the leader of the bandits under the pretense of giving him "tribute" to pass through their lands. When the bandit extended his hand, Karos made it look as if he were handing over a coin pouch. In reality, it was a pouch full of blast powder around a dark-stone. The moment the bandit reached for it, the young Nolvern slammed the pouch into the ground, creating a terrific *bang* and a sphere of utter darkness. Within moments, he emerged from a chaotic fight with the bandit leader, bloodied and swinging at anything near him.

The enemies fell before him without him even drawing his sword, which was impressive. Later, they learned that those particular bandits were a lesser group from a greater evil. Karos insisted on hunting them, but was convinced, with great difficulty, that he was far too new to combat to be useful. So they continued his training elsewhere. He'd pouted for some time, but eventually moved on. Smiling gently,

Kiri remembered how the man had retained his fiery nature throughout the years. When he'd finally become Warden Ranger, in fact, it was by setting up the craftiest series of *accidents* against a bandit group who'd seized a tollgate. With clever traps and crafty machinations, he'd whittled down a massive enemy force, embarrassed and harassed them until he was near-faint from hunger, and by then, other Rangers had arrived to help.

He'd survived that trial, and by showing his innate cleverness and indomitable spirit, had proven, even without the ability to use Pathway magic, that he was a serious contender for Warden Ranger. Then, after the passing of Thorvan Koza, he'd been ushered into the position after orchestrating a raid that freed... *how many was it again?* By investigation, observation, and pure will, he'd crushed a force of slavers and freed their captives. Smiling, Kiri remembered that fight. Certainly, it'd been brutal. Brutal, indeed, to the point of horrific with how Karos, losing his weapons at some point, utilized Sk'av'A phrases defensively and *ljas'atuk* offensively, to terrible effect. The slavers came to fear him before they died.

Moving along, Kiri passed through the battlefield and kept her pace up and shifted through the wilds with all the sounds of a passing shadow. Every creature that beheld her, fell or good, ignored her, realizing her intent lay elsewhere. Bandits considered accosting the lonesome Ranger, but thought better of it when they spied her pace, not to mention the single talon necklace sitting next to her Ranger pendant. In their souls, they knew it would be a *grave* miscalculation to think that this Ranger, above even others, was *alone*, let alone less dangerous. So they let her pass.

A delvoranth family lumbered across her path. The gray skinned, colossal creatures took no notice of the Ranger, save for wondering in their primal mind if she had treats for them. But as she cleaved a path across the wildlands, they realized she must be on a mission for survival, and elected not to beg. So the next few days went, flashing by as the scenery did, until she began to see water. Specifically, the waters of *Laghe Valorii*, visible for many leagues in every direction. She'd taken a route to avoid Hollyhead. As much as she would've loved to stop in the city, such was her urgency. And here she approached, altering her speed to a slower, more careful gait.

Moving around to the north and down through the Forest of Memory seemed like the best option. So she shifted her course, slipping into the glowing trees. Adjusting her shimmercloth cloak, she blended in with the scenery, moving like a shadow through the trees. As she picked her path, trudging secret ways only she knew, movement caught her eye. Instinctively, she dropped low, shifting next to a pile of fallen branches and leaves. *Right into the arms of her tracker.* A hand went over her mouth, another around her waist.

One quick vertical jerk, curling her torso as she did so, Kiri threw off her supposed attacker. But before she could see who it was, they were *gone.* Frantically looking around, she kept her guard up, using her senses *other* than sight until she felt movement behind her once again. *So fast!* Dropping low, she tried a leg sweep, only for the figure to flip over her leg. Luckily, they didn't come down *on* it. *So they do not mean to harm me, it seems.* As the figure came down once more, Kiri lashed out with a cleverly timed fist, catching them in the stomach. Her reward was a gasping heave, and the slippery figure stopped moving long enough to cough out a compliment.

"Exactly as expected." The figure chuckled. Standing to their full height, the figure stepped out of the shadows, and Kiri's heart sang.

"You pronking *bitch!*" She cried out, throwing her arms around the figure. "By the Ancestors, where... how? How have you been? All these years? Rúwia!"

"Shh, Kiri. You are still in danger. I come to pass news, and ask for in return." The figure whispered, pulling back their hood to reveal patently feminine features. But the glint in the eyes was anything but. A freeborn stood before her, a wild elf like her, but at the same time, this one was something... something *far* more. "You know the news I bear, for you have felt it in your heart. For some time now. But I ask, what of Guidestar? I long to see his face, see the man he has become. I have heard things. Incredible things." They continued, looking Kiri in the eyes.

"He is well. He serves in Thorvan's place, bless and damn that man forever. His soul rests, and I hope he was able to find forgiveness." Kiri replied, a hint of sadness clouding her animated face. "But what of you, my old friend?"

Rúwia smirked. "I have become more. *The Sadja Seranis,* the trees and creatures, call me now. It was only by grace of what they have given me, that you did not immediately fell me, for you were always the more skilled combatant, Kiri." The lithe form chuckled gently and patted the other elf's shoulders. "But, I am forgetting myself. I know you have little time. Young Sardra is in the depths of peril. But I can deliver you closer than you could get in a day. I must not see her *yet,* though. She must not know of me until the time is right. Take my hand." Nodding, Kiri took the strange being's hand. The being that had once come to her, desperate and grief-stricken at the loss of her tribe, only to hunt down the ones who had been responsible for it. The being that had been mortal at one time, and ascended above even the considerable possibilities of their race.

Within moments, they'd traversed *leagues upon leagues*, seeming to fly through the forest. Within a few minutes, they were in another forest, and a familiar, bulky form laid low, hiding in the brush, waiting. Waiting for what, only Kiri and the *Sadja* knew. Releasing her hand, Rúwia vanished once more, leaving Kiri to slip over to her friend, her battle-sister. Reaching out, she grabbed Sardra's shoulder.

The dokk nearly shrieked up a lung.

II

The First Battle

3: Westerspring, Elsewhere

Magus fumed as the spy spoke. "You mean to tell me you simply watched as *my wife* ran away with that... Ranger? And a Rider as well?" He was ready to strike something, anything, but the man speaking to him held up a warning hand.

"You contracted me to watch, Magus. Not to act. There were far too many to fight and I prefer my head where it is. Now give me my money and begone." The words carried the insinuation of a threat, but Magus knew he was not in a position of strength. He could barely make out the shadows moving in the cavern's darkness and knew there were at least six rogues watching and waiting for their chance to cut his purse- and his throat. Sighing in defeat, he extracted six platinum Sereim coins- a king's ransom for the information he had been given- and placed them in the gloved hand that was being held out. The hand closed around the coin.

"Now then, if our business is done, we have elsewhere to be."

"Of course, Jerut. I look forward to our next meeting."

As he made his way out of the cavern, Magus raged. He would not let Khula get away this easily. His plans for her would not be derailed, especially not by a shiftless Ranger. But that the Riders had intervened on behalf of the Ranger was strange indeed and brought a new level of trouble, but Magus had been preparing to take on the Rangers for some time and not just with The Red Lance. He had contacted- or had he been contacted by- an elf who claimed to have the power to destroy all his enemies. The power to cross Seran in an instant, which not even the Kingmage could do. Magus scoffed. *The Kingmage... his power is nothing next to that of my friend.* Placing his hand upon a talisman, he signaled to his friend that he was ready to rejoin him.

Far from where Magus stood, Vaelyn was working in vain, creating more of the plague that he knew would bring the world into his grasp. He grinned as a stone near him glowed. It was inscribed with oddly shaped letters, ones that came from another world entirely. Tapping the stone, he backed away from the table he'd been working at and strode to a cleared area with a strange sort of circle drawn into the ground, ringed with the same strange letters as found on the stone. With a quick array of hand movements, he brushed as many of the tattoos covering his arms as he could. A pillar of black flame erupted from the center of the circle and the strange letters glowed. Slowly, the black flames parted and Vaelyn could see what was on the other side- grasslands for miles around and a cavern. Through the image stepped Magus, dusting himself off as the portal closed behind him.

"About damned time, Vaelyn. Anyone could have seen that."

"Then perhaps Magus- *and stay with me here. Do* not call for a portal anywhere near where other folk may be? Our need for secrecy outweighs your need to look fearsome."

"Of course, Vaelyn, of course. Now, are we ready?"

"Aye. If that prisoner is correct, the Warden Ranger is coming, as well as the Paragon of Knowledge. We will deprive both the Rangers and the Riders of their best in one fell stroke. They will provide little resistance once we parade the bodies of their leaders through the lands."

"So you think. When have you last encountered the Rangers, Vaelyn? You seem to know little about them."

"I do not concern myself with those fools. They will die soon enough."

Not exactly an answer, thought Magus, wondering just how far gone his friend was. He felt a twinge in the back of his mind and a voice crept into his consciousness. *Kill him when he ceases to be useful. Then you will have his power!* Magus had to remind himself that that was not how power worked in Seran. The voice quieted down for now, and he sighed gently.

"Very well, Vaelyn. Now about our prisoner. Is she awake?"

"As always. It is as if these Rangers sleep not. Damn bitch has been nothing but trouble, already cost me an eye." Vaelyn turned to Magus, revealing the destroyed eye socket where his azure eye had once rested. Raising a hand up, he touched the spot gingerly. A sigh escaped from his lips, one that quickly turned to a cry of anger. "I will kill her at a snail's pace and savor her agony!"

"Of course you will, Vaelyn. But not before her friends get here- the more witnesses, the more people know to not cross you." Magus nodded slowly, making sure his hands were completely visible while he spoke to his volatile accomplice. When Vaelyn had calmed sufficiently, he continued. "But let us remember, it is wise to leave some alive to spread the tales of our conquest."

"Indeed." Vaelyn grunted, signaling an end to his talkative mood. He returned to his table and continued the work that Magus' summons had interrupted and waited for the inevitable triumph. An odd thought popped into his mind, only to be quickly shushed, but it rang in his head for a few moments. *When did we last eat?* He could not remember- not that it mattered at all. *We are all-powerful.* He could feed himself whenever he chose and right now, he chose not to.

Magus, however, was famished. Off he went, exploring the cave in search of stored foods. Soon enough, he was rewarded with meats hanging from hooks, breads and cheeses in various stages of being eaten and cool water in a cave stream near the back. Quickly allowing himself a prime cut of meat to roast over a fire, he began cooking himself a steak from what looked like a deer. Then, he grabbed some dried meat and a block of cheese, using his belt knife to cut off a few slices. There was a lack of spices, which upset him somewhat but he knew one could not have it all.

When the meat had been cooked to his liking, Magus pulled the steak from the cooking-pan near the fire and placed it on a platter with some bread. Once he was satisfied with the meal, he ate.

Vaelyn, on the other hand, was busy at work, perfecting the last batch of plague. He had already protected himself against it as per the Void-Sleeper's instructions and had given the same precaution to Magus. In the back of his mind, though, he knew that Magus' uses would be few once he had Khula in his grasp. For a moment, he thought about disposing of the man right here and now but realized that his endgame would be unattainable without the man. Sighing, he resigned himself to allow Magus to continue living. Looking at the last batch of plague through the crude microscope he had constructed, Vaelyn smiled. *Perfect. This will serve well and kill many.* He half wondered about removing the magic that protected the dal'Korin from the plague- after all, they were traitorous snakes and had to be watched with care. *But,* his mind reasoned, *we need an army to conquer Seran.* After a moment, he thought, *bah, to the void with the whole damned planet! I will kill everything in due time!* It was as if he had forgotten his goal of conquest at a moment's notice. He took a breath and steadied himself, the fluctuating lines in his vision resolving some. He glanced up- was someone there? Had the Ranger escaped her cage? He would not put it past her but after a moment he remembered he had sealed the cage with magic. The only way she would escape that cage is if he freed her.

Standing slowly, he steadied himself against the table before wandering over to where the cage was. The Ranger watched him silently, her eyes tracking his movement with perfect acuity- even in the cavern's darkness she resided in. Sneering at her, he watched as she provided no resistance- indeed; she was *meditating.* How maddening that she was enjoying some peace while in captivity. Vaelyn felt a rage build in his stomach and he began shouting at the cage, slamming his hands against the bars, screaming complete gibberish. But the Ranger did not react in the slightest. The more he screamed and raged, the more serene she seemed to grow—until a smile crossed her lips.

"You may scream until the sun burns out; it shall not distract me." Sardra had resigned herself to inaction now. She knew there was not much she could do, so she bade her time. But every movement Vaelyn made worried her- not just because he could slay her at any moment, but because they showed a severe crisis in the man's head. He was quite far gone, to where his hands seemed to cast spells of their own. His skin was pale, nearly translucent, and she knew he had not eaten in quite some time, judging by how many times his belt was snaked around his waist. One could only guess what was ailing him.

As Sardra studied him, Vaelyn grew more and more agitated, until he finally stormed off to clear his head. She smirked slightly, emboldened that she had got such an angry response from her captor. She had to be careful, though- after all, he could kill her at a moment's notice. Studying the lock on her cage, she reached out with her mind, using the magic of the Sk'av'A in furtive whispers- but nothing could budge the lock. *What form of magic can defy the Sk'av'A,* she wondered to herself, *and what toll is it exacting on that man?* She sighed and leaned back against the cage bars, trying to reason things out in her mind. *He has not slain me, which is what I would have done. Perhaps he knows little about Rangers?* The thought stopped her for a moment. Perhaps he really did not know about the Rangers. *His mistake.*

"That damned Ranger!" Cried Vaelyn as he stormed into the cavern he used for his supplies. "Staring at me silently, judging me. Who does she think she is?"

"Why are we not torturing her for information? Surely she would know where the Rangers hide themselves and their total numbers."

"Do you think me a fool, Magus? I have already attempted torture, and she has resisted well."

"Perhaps your methods need work. I happen to be excellent

at interrogation. Give me an hour with her and she will sing."

"All you know is how to take advantage of women. She is far beyond your power." Vaelyn nearly shouted at Magus, his face contorted with anger. He still had not calmed down and was therefore dangerous. Magus made a mental note to tread lightly, lest he end up on the receiving end of his friend's unpredictable rage. "Why are you just sitting there? If you think you can interrogate her, then go to it!"

Magus eyed Vaelyn severely as he chewed on his steak. "I am eating, Vaelyn. Do not act as if I am your underling- we are equal partners in this endeavor." Slowly, he made a show of breaking off a piece of bread and cheese before bringing it to his mouth. He chewed slowly, taking his time to enjoy the food and watching for Vaelyn's reaction. It was, as expected, volatile. He brought his hand to slap the food away from Magus, only to stop before impact- what was that noise? A clattering, banging- and breaking glass. Vaelyn nearly jumped through his skin and bolted to his lab. When he saw what had happened, he let out an inarticulate shriek of rage. His bottles of plague- every single one, were shattered and strewn about. They had wasted his work! Elsewhere in his lair, he heard things getting destroyed. Making use of his Void magic, he opened a portal to one of the other rooms, trying to catch the perpetrator.

Sardra grinned widely and grabbed a torch down from its sconce, throwing it into a massive pile of what looked like a fine powder. *This should do some damage!* She thought to herself and dropped back into the shadows. The cacophony soon began as the flame touched off the items in the pile, setting off an enormous explosion that nearly knocked her flat. As a scream of rage tore its way through the lair, Sardra smirked and shifted herself into the least visible spot in the cavern. She had already tried to exit, but there was that damned dragon right outside. She had taken a risk and now she would just have to keep herself from getting slain- or captured again.

Magus seemed completely unconcerned with the chaos in the cavern. He reasoned Vaelyn was already working to deal with the situation, so why would he need to? As he heard Vaelyn screaming, he chuckled to himself. *My friend certainly has a short temper.* Finishing his meal, he rinsed the plates in the cave stream like a good peasant and placed them near to the fire to dry. Then he wandered to the front of the cave and pressed open the door. "Talakath, we have a captive loose inside the cave. What would you suggest?" In response, the beast lazily opened one whirling eye to regard Magus.

I do not like this man, Talakath said to Vaelyn, distracting him from his fury. *He seems dishonorable.*

"Well, you had best accept that he is working for us, Ta-lakath." He had stopped mid-stride to take his dragon to task, not expecting her words. "Now be silent unless you have something useful to say."

Talakath grumbled, annoyed. She did not like this path that Vaelyn was taking, or this madness that she could feel consuming him. Reaching into the distance, she sought others of her kind- there were only two black dragons that worked for the riders- one now, her progeny Namryll. Try as Vaelyn might, he could not sever the connection between mother and daughter, leaving the two able to talk freely without his knowledge.

She felt for her daughter's mind, reaching out as far as she could in a panic. When she felt the connection, she sent the only thought she knew she could get away with. *Help!* She sent an imprint of her location with the thought, giving her daughter a concrete trail to follow. She had been planning this for a while, but only now did she realize Vaelyn was lost- completely lost. Nothing could save the man from the damnation he had brought down upon them and she hoped she could at least save herself- or at least the world. There were far too many people who did not deserve what Vaelyn was doing to them, and it was time to put a stop to it.

The message sent, Talakath relaxed, stretching languidly. *If only I could reach that Ranger,* the great black beast thought to herself, *I could give her a way out.* But alas, the Ranger evidently thought her to be a foe. A pity it was, for one could have no more dangerous an ally than a black dragon.

As he stormed through his cavernous home, Vaelyn fumed. *How did that damned Ranger escape?!* He could not see any way she could have slipped from his grasp- the door to the cage was still in place, the bars unbroken- but he had not noticed the stones had shifted. Perhaps it was too minor a detail for his addled mind? Storming back into the cave he had placed her cage in, he began looking it over, first normally and then using magic. But his magics found nothing- no trace of any oddity. In due time, he would realize why- but by then, it would be too late- the magic of the world had forsaken him when he drew power from the Void. Reaching out, he touched the vast dimension, seeking to speak to the Void-Sleeper. *I ask for your wisdom, oh most powerful of beings.*

A terrifying cacophony of voices answered him, echoing in his mind, creeping into every corner of his thoughts. The voices were all distinct, but unified, as if being spoken from many mouths. *What is it, child?*

I am not a child! Vaelyn's reply was angry as he spoke, and he quickly realized his error.

I have existed for longer than your species has had words. My anger has burned longer than the stars in your sky- the stars your primitive races believe are memories. You are a child. The voice hit with unexpected force- and Vaelyn felt his body attempt to shrink away from the voice in his head- but he knew it could see him. He wondered to himself if it was male or female and soon tried to backtrack, remembering that the creature could hear every single thought. *Your thoughts are laughable and archaic. There is no male or female in the void. We simply are.* An immense pressure exerted itself on Vaelyn's mind and he felt as if the thoughts alone would crush him. *Now explain why you have contacted me.*

My captive has escaped. Immediately, Vaelyn regretted his words as the pressure increased twofold. He screamed, clutching his head and trying to gather his thoughts through the pressure being exerted. *She is dangerous and could cause our plan to fail. I need to find her.* The pressure lessened somewhat with that revelation, though the voice did not sound too pleased.

You would have been wiser to begin with that. But I cannot help you- I can only see beings that have touched my realm. You must find your lost captive on your own. Do not contact me again unless it is for something useful. The connection was severed, and the pressure vanished from Vaelyn's head, leaving him dizzy. He stumbled through the cave for a moment, before realizing he was bleeding from the ears and nose. Shaking his head, he stumbled to his bathing cavern to clean up, before collapsing to the floor. The world seemed to fade in and out for a few moments before the darkness welcomed him and he remembered nothing else for a few hours.

Sardra used her time wisely, setting up as much to be destroyed as she could— avoiding Magus to the best of her considerable abilities and setting the whole place up for more mayhem. To her great displeasure, though- she could find no useful gear to don. Her primary captor relied far too much on magic, it seemed. Idly, she wondered if he was breaking down- if his body was collapsing in on itself and he was soon to become a *lok'vi*, one of the strange magic spirits that listlessly roamed Seran. With the power she had seen so far, that was a frightening outcome, though she couldn't know that his mind would never survive it.

When Magus went searching for Sardra, he found nothing but traps. Evidently, the Ranger had been quite busy indeed, aggravatingly so. *How did she get out? I am certain Vaelyn's magic would be more than enough to contain one.* But there was the evidence in front of him. She had escaped and was busily causing difficulties. His surprise mounted when he stumbled across Vaelyn laying on the floor, evidently unconscious by some method yet unknown. Shaking his head, Magus rolled his ally onto his back and crouched to listen for his breathing, but could barely tell if he was. *Is he even alive? He told me that the Void gives powers never seen on Seran... Perhaps he is a walking corpse?* After a moment, Magus pushed that thought from his mind- Vaelyn was alive. He could see his chest rise and fall- but it was strange. He'd not seen the elf eat in the entire time he'd known him. Sighing, he propped Vaelyn up against a wall in a sitting position. Then, he went his own way, trying to spot the Ranger. *Oh, the pain I will cause her when I catch her...* He grinned as he moved along, completely missing the pair of ice-blue eyes peering out from the shadows.

As soon as Magus moved past her, Sardra darted from the shadows towards the door to the outside. *Dragon or no dragon, I have got to get out of here.* Reaching the door, she gave it a cursory glance and a check for traps- nothing. Bracing herself for what was likely to come, she pushed the door open and slipped around the jamb, trying to ease her way out into the open and past the dragon. What greeted her was a pair of whirling eyes. She froze, her heart sinking. *So, this is where I die.* The thought echoed in her mind as she readied herself for the blow that would undoubtedly come to send her to her ancestors and the family she had not seen in at least two centuries.

But the blow never came. Instead, the dragon blinked and angled her head towards a thick copse of trees. Common tongue issued from the dragon's mouth. "Run. Regroup, get your friends. You may need an army to avert this evil." She then angled her head back down and closed her eyes, giving Sardra the best chance at survival she had had in a while.

"Thank you." Sardra dared not say more, lest the dragon's helpful mood dissipate abruptly. Taking off at a dead run, she wound her way towards the grove, keeping low and running on her hands and feet to give her a lower profile. When she reached the trees, she sought out the most hidden place and secreted herself away. Then, she positioned herself to watch and wait. She had no weapons other than the ones the Ancestors gave her, and she was on high alert.

Vaelyn came to near nightfall, blearily opening his eyes and trying to function. He could barely remember what had happened, apart from a pounding in his head and a voice echoing around. His eyes darted back and forth, and he wondered where he was. Slowly, he pulled himself to his feet, trying to collect his thoughts. Once he was standing, he felt quite unstable, so he braced himself against the wall and called out. "H-hello?" His legs threatened to give out beneath him, but that was a minor thing compared to the utter confusion he was feeling. His head was buzzing now, which was an improvement from pounding, at least, but still distressing. His confusion tripled when he saw a man approach.

"Damnitall, Vaelyn. I think our captive escaped!"

"Captive? Who are you talking about? Who are you?"

"Vaelyn, do you not recognize me? I am Magus, your ally."

"Ally, yes... to what end? What is going on?"

Magus raised an eye at the confused elf before sighing and shaking his head. "We are poised to take over Seran, and you have lost your wits. Idiot!"

All at once, Vaelyn's mind came back to him. He snapped an arm out, catching Magus by the throat and drawing him close enough for Magus to smell his breath. "I would pick your words more wisely, Magus. Do not think yourself indispensable to me." With that, he threw the man away from himself.

Magus stumbled backwards and shook his head. "Then keep your mind about you, Vaelyn. These distractions will do us no good." Collecting himself, the man strode away from Vaelyn, leaving the elf to his thoughts.

Vaelyn snarled impotently as he watched Magus walk away, still somewhat unable to move. When his legs finally responded, he made his way towards the exit, slamming it open to awaken his dragon, nearly shrieking out a command. "Talakath. Find me that damned Ranger!"

Talakath rolled her eyes and shifted slightly before sniffing the air. A lie crossed her thoughts, hidden from Vaelyn. *Protect the Ranger*, came a voice to her mind, and she responded in turn to Vaelyn.

I do not smell her. She is either long gone or has not left the cavern. Nodding, Vaelyn stormed back inside, failing to hear the dragon's thoughts. His work with the Void had so eroded his connection to the beast and his goals so monstrous that not even the black dragon could willingly stand by him. Talakath wondered to herself how Magus justified working with the elf. How could the man ignore just how horrible his goals were? Then, she remembered- Vaelyn had offered him power, both over Seran and the woman he obsessed over. Such things were a great motivator to an already warped mind.

Sardra took in a breath, feeling her body carefully, looking for the ribs she was sure were broken. Oddly enough, they all seemed solid- she could feel no grinding or popping, no matter how hard she touched the spots of pain. Exhaling in relief, she relaxed a little, and the curiosity came back to her. *Why did that dragon aid me?* Was her first thought, sitting at the forefront of her mind. *Are dragons not completely loyal to their riders?* This brought much of her knowledge of the Dragonriders into question. For years, she had thought the dragons subservient to their rider, but- a voice that was definitely not her own interrupted her in her musings.

We are equal to our riders in thought... but Vaelyn forsook our bond when he began dabbling in the Void's magic. The voice was pleasant enough, though Sardra could feel the pain- evidently the dragon had some regrets, either for her actions, or the actions of her rider. *He has become more monstrous than I have ever known, and I can follow or aid him no longer. But I cannot openly defy him. That is up to you and whatever aid you have coming.*

Sardra's blood ran cold as she thought of what may happen to whoever was coming to her aid. Repeatedly, the feeling of heat, the terrified squawk let out by Tyfa, the vision of charred wings falling to the ground, tore through her mind and she let out a yelp. *We must warn them of his power. He could slay them all the way he slew Porrik and Tyfa. We cannot let him destroy them!* She relayed her thoughts as best she could to Talakath, who agreed readily. Reaching out, the dragon touched the mind of her daughter and passed along the feelings and the images from Sardra's mind.

The Ranger took a breath and glanced to the sky, looking for whoever was coming to her aid. Her anxiety mounting, she drew back further into the trees, searching for any caches the Rangers had left in the area. She needed weapons and gear- her armor and overtunic would provide enough protection when bolstered with magic... she hoped. Finding nothing, she sighed, wondering if her captors had destroyed any caches- or if the Rangers simply had not explored this region yet. It was hard to say which reason it was. When she returned to her vantage point, Sardra positioned herself low to watch the entry of the cavern she had escaped from. As she watched, she monitored the dragon, just to be safe, as she was still not sure of the creature's loyalties.

Talakath shifted slightly, her eyes whirling as she felt Vaelyn's internal struggles. He was going further down the path of the Void and it was claiming more and more of his mind. All Talakath could do was watch in mixed sorrow and horror. Her mind was made up though and she had cast her lot, unbeknownst to her rider. She would serve the light for however long she had left. Resting her head on the ground once more, she let her eyes slide closed. She knew she was dying, and she welcomed it. She was a dragon at her largest and all she wished to do was sleep. Even the idea of flying was becoming tiring to her, but she knew her work was not done yet.

Vaelyn began pacing back and forth after he had gotten the worst of the mess cleaned up. He was still livid, as the damage that damned Ranger had done would set him back weeks, if not months. But it was not as bad as having to start from scratch- he wasn't sure if the Void Sleeper would be as understanding about the delays. Already he could feel the twinges in the deepest reaches of his consciousness, the fluttering at the edge of his vision. It was coming back, and he was not sure how strong it would be this time. He had to work fast while he was still lucid. As he tried to run back to his lab, he felt his foot catch on something. He pulled hard, trying to break free, but the more he struggled, the tighter the grip on his foot. Touching one of his tattoos, he unleashed a blast of fire towards whatever was trapping him- to no avail. Touching more of his tattoos, he made the flame more and more intense, trying to burn his foot free. The stone refused to give and he grew more frustrated.

Magus heard the shrieking and stormed through the cavern, trying to find the source. When he finally found Vaelyn after half an hour, he could barely keep from laughing at the elf's plight. Vaelyn was stuck fast and swearing up a storm as he tried every spell he knew to blast himself free and Magus moved to approach, before feeling something catch his leg as well. Realizing he had gotten himself into a trap, Magus fought back panic and took a breath. Slowly, he worked his boot back and forth until his foot popped free. Looking at Vaelyn, he called out. "Stay calm, Vaelyn."

"Do not tell me to stay calm! I am trapped, and this is enraging me!"

"It is an old Ranger trick meant to keep people from getting too aggressive when talking. Calm down and work your foot forward and back." Vaelyn snarled at the man, but followed the instructions, rocking his foot back and forth in his boot. Finally, his foot popped free of the stone prison with some pain and the elf swore, before landing flat on his face. This was the last straw for Magus, who was hit with a rolling wave of laughter. Trying to steady himself, the Knight-General placed a hand upon the wall- for less than a second, as the wall was searing hot. He swore as he instinctively yanked his hand away, quickly patting the heat away on his trouser leg. "Damnit, Vaelyn, how long have you been blasting away with your flames?"

Panting, Vaelyn glanced up at Magus before speaking. "I have been trapped here for thirty minutes!"

"Aye, and you are the same one who said the Ranger is no threat. Consider this a learning experience. Living Rangers are always a threat and a great one at that." He shook his head and bent down to retrieve his boot from the trap. One solid tug and it came free, allowing Magus to inspect it for damage. When he found none, he nodded and slipped the boot back on, quickly looping the leather around the toggles to secure it. Then he looked about. "I have never been in this part of your cave, Vaelyn. What secrets do you hold here?"

"You do not need to know yet, Magus. Withhold any further questions and begone, back up the tunnel." Vaelyn snapped at his compatriot before pushing open a stone door and vanishing inside the room. Once inside, he closed the door behind him and leaned back against it, listening for Magus to vanish up the pathway. When he was sure Magus was gone, Vaelyn strode to his worktable and slammed his fist down.

Fool, he chastised himself, *you should have known better than to store any vials of plague in the main cavern. This setback will cost us.* Shifting quickly, he opened a chest to reveal the reagents he had been using to create his masterful work. Looking them over, he extracted just enough of each to create more of the last batch and smiled. The exact measurements were still in his head, so it would be easy enough to replicate. She had merely delayed the inevitable.

Magus stayed at the closed door for a moment, judging by himself whether to burst into the room and demand answers. Glancing up to the scorched and partially melted wall, he found his answer- upsetting Vaelyn would likely result in a painful death and that was to be avoided if possible. So, he trudged back up the passageway and slipped around the tapestry that hid it. Idly, he wondered just what had possessed him to run full tilt toward the hanging without knowing what was behind it. It had worked for him this time, at least, and that was enough, but more care would have to be taken in further endeavors.

Sardra sighed as she watched for activity around the cavern. *Nothing. Either they are busy with my gifts, or I wasted precious time in placing them.* Moving further back from the cave, Sardra ducked behind a fallen log and felt around for any food she could recognize- she was hungry and the beating she had endured had done little to change that. Finding a handful of mushrooms, she looked them over, searching her mind for what they were. Settling on the most likely option, she took a nibble of one- pleasant enough, though she knew that pleasant taste could hide powerful toxins. But the mushrooms were ones she recognized as non-poisonous and she settled herself down to eat.

She nearly jumped through her skin when a hand landed on her shoulder.

5: Westerspring

The dokk fought back a scream as the hand landed on her shoulder. Turning swiftly, she bared her teeth and readied herself for a scuffle. What she found instead were the kind eyes of Kiri Topalin regarding her. Heaving a sigh of relief, she threw her arms around the elf and squeezed her. "Kiri, I thank the Ancestors it is you. But damned if you did not give me the fright of my life!" After kissing the woman on the cheeks, Sardra finally stepped back. "I take it you received my warning?"

"Aye, and I have no doubts that the Warden Ranger is on his way as well. Now, what is your plan?"

"Honestly, Kiri, I am unsure. My weapons and pack are all destroyed... apart from my claws and teeth, but we will require much more than that for this foe. He commands a fell magic the likes of which I have never seen. However, the Lifesong seems to have an adverse effect upon it. We may use that to our advantage."

"Well, that is good news, at least. How came you to be here? I thought you were with Tenderfeet?"

"I passed them off at *Ca'e Möratuk*. Then, a Lance of the Riders of Gelvrentael arrived, mentioning something about a pact between one of their own and Karos. I could hardly believe it. But sure enough, one of their riders ferried me to Dragonmoor, where I intended to meet with Karos... Things did not go as planned." She sighed gently and shook her head. "The names Porrik and Tyfa; we must remember them for all time. The bastard in those caves mercilessly murdered them. As a warning, he has a friend- the General of the Red Lance, Magus Kefarion."

Kiri sucked in a breath. If Magus was working with someone who Sardra was identifying in such a way, things were already bad. "So, what must we do, Sardra Woodstrider?"

"We must hold his attention. Keep him distracted until Karos gets here with whatever aid he is bringing. I know more Rangers saw your warning and I would hope that they are on the way as well. But it will take time."

Nodding, both women stood and began incantations to protect each other, as suggested by Sardra. In the Lifesong, they chanted to themselves. "*Skin of stone, spirit of wrath. Keep us on the victorious path.*" As they spoke, their hands shimmered with light and they placed their hands on each other's shoulders, giving the protection of the Lifesong against magical attacks. When the ritual was complete, they once more faced the cave and began walking towards their destinies.

The first hint Vaelyn and Magus had that something was wrong was when an explosion caved in the front door and emerald-green fire blasted through the tunnels. Reacting purely by instinct, Magus dove into a pool of water and Vaelyn raised a shield of black flames, protecting himself from the worst of the inferno. Rushing out, the men saw two women, glowing with magic, standing against them, defying them openly. Vaelyn snarled, his face turning into a wicked grin. "You fool."

"You stand in defiance to the Ancestors, Kingmage and the Rangers of Seran. You have committed crimes against the world and her people. You stand sentenced to death."

Vaelyn screamed his defiance and touched a few of his tattoos, firing a spell in his mind. Immediately, a geyser of jet-black fire erupted from his hands. The women seemed unfazed by the show, placing their hands to their sides.

In time with each other, they began a chant, watching as the black fire washed over them. "*Flames of the Ancestors. Fury of the Ancestors. Purge the fell elf. Purge the insanity.*" They slammed their palms out, causing pillars of blue and green flames to surge forth toward Vaelyn and Magus.

Magus timed the spray and leapt out of the way, ducking and rolling to avoid catching fire. When he came up to his feet, his sword was in his hands and he took up a fighting stance. Kiri turned to face him, her daggers at the ready, twirling easily in her hands. As Magus approached, the woman popped her neck and brought her daggers to the ready position. "On whatever honor you have left, Magus Kefarion."

Then Kiri charged, daggers flashing in the cold light of the moons.

Sardra eyed Vaelyn severely, and he likewise glared at her through one eye. She noticed something odd about him, about his form- he was not breathing. There was no rise or fall to his chest, even with the exertion of great magic. She could feel her own breaths coming easily, her heart's pace picking up as she readied an offensive Phrase. "*Raging winds, breath of the world, strike my foe!*" Her cry was powerful against the growing storm of magic and she twirled her hands around and around, one above the other. At first, the effect was hard to see, but soon enough, a tornado erupted from her palm and she pressed it outwards, causing it to grow as it screamed towards her foe.

Vaelyn laughed at the attack before touching three more of his tattoos. Opening his magical pathways quite wide, he blasted more dark flames towards Sardra. When the flames were sucked into the tornado and extinguished, he let out a scream of rage before blasting away at the tornado. Soon enough, it was reduced to a gust of wind and dissipated, and Vaelyn once more faced Sardra.

Sardra wheezed, realizing she was overdoing it with the Sk'av'A phrases. She could feel the pain in her throat that came with overuse of the Lifesong and quickly realized that she would need a new tactic. Closing the distance with Vaelyn as swiftly as her legs would allow, she slammed her body into him as he was focused on incanting another spell. He fell backwards, and she quickly recovered, her claws at the ready.

Laughing, Vaelyn touched the only tattoo on his arms that looked different, causing a blade of black flames to shoot from his arm. Bringing it close, he angled it in front of his face protectively, seemingly unfazed by the heat it was producing. Grinning, he closed the distance with Sardra, making a wide slash to take her head. It quite surprised him when his blade was stopped by her clasping the flat between her palms.

Sardra grunted, feeling her hands burning. It was luck alone that allowed her to catch the blade, and she was not sure how long she could hold. Thinking fast, she delivered a harsh kick toward Vaelyn's groin and was rewarded with a squeal of pain and the blade being yanked away. Shifting her mindset from using the Sk'av'A to pure pathway magic, she drew multiple circles in the air. Then, drawing her hands across one circle, she summoned a weapon of her own. "You are not the only one with the knowledge of mage-tools, Vaelyn." She snarled as she brought the weapon to bear and, in the back of her head, prepared another spell in her left hand. Parrying a clumsy blow from Vaelyn, the dokk let out a sharp cry and threw her hand outward, sending a pulse of lightning towards her foe.

Vaelyn barely dodged the lightning, off-balanced as he was by the parry, sending his blade wide. With another scream, he leapt towards Sardra, sending a flurry of thrusts and slashes to off-balance the woman. To his growing fury, she remained calm and collected, meeting his blade each time. Clearly, he had underestimated this Ranger, and he half wondered if the others would be this annoying to slay. Charging his sword with more Void energy, he finally caught a lucky swing and was rewarded with a pained yelp and blood on the ground.

Superficial, thought Vaelyn, *but promising.* Attempting to drive home his advantage gave him no luck, however, as Sardra redoubled her efforts and began closing more gaps that she had left open.

Sardra grinned as she watched Vaelyn grow more and more frustrated. His attacks became clumsier, and she realized he was losing his grip again. Driving home her advantage, she went on the offensive once more, intending to keep him off-guard long enough for help to arrive. A quick glance told her that the injury she had sustained wasn't all that serious, but there was a persistent sensation of heat in the wound. *A concern for later,* she reminded herself as she pushed the thoughts away, focusing on the bigger problem- the maniacal elf.

As Vaelyn faltered, his mind screamed. He was the Paragon of War. *There is no reason this Ranger should be able to keep up with us.* But she was keeping him on the ropes, not giving him a chance to recover. He grew angrier as he realized he was faltering, and desperation crept in. What if she gained a critical advantage? *No!* His thoughts screamed; *I cannot die! I am invincible!* With a snarl, he leapt at Sardra, bringing his blade across to flay open her chest. She blocked easily and threw it wide, giving the woman too big of an opening to ignore.

Grinning, the woman pressed her advantage, coming in with a slash meant to lay open Vaelyn from collar to waist. But the blow never struck. Sardra recoiled, sure she had struck- but nothing had happened. Cursing, she dropped back and shifted, watching her foe's blade come in again and again, repelling it. This time, she drove in closer, coming to slash upwards from Vaelyn's navel. The attack rewarded her with a gasp and a grunt, but when she looked to see her strike, her blood ran cold- her enemy had suffered no injury.

Vaelyn had felt the impact, felt the searing burn of magic through his pathway nerves, but when he reached down, he felt no blood, no torn skin. Grinning at that revelation, he swung his free hand up and caught Sardra by the throat and lifted her. He was about to crush her throat when her mage-blade collided with his own neck. Immediately, his grip faltered, and he dropped her, both of them coughing for a few moments. Glaring, Vaelyn touched more of his tattoos, forcing his pathway nerves to allow even more magic to flow through them. To his surprise, there was no palpable change in his blade, but he felt more and more energetic. When he had recovered from the coughing fit, he stood once more and came on the war path towards Sardra. His sword came from one side and he opened a jet of void-fire from the other, giving her no chance to dodge.

Sardra saw they hemmed her in on both sides and took a gamble. Her magic was still holding, so she dove through the pillar of black flame. The heat clung to her fur for a moment and it almost felt as if her skin was going to boil off. But just as abruptly, the feeling was gone, and she was in the clear. Grinning, she brought her palms together and spun a circle, once more sending energy down her pathway nerves and firing off a succession of fireballs towards her enemy.

Kiri and Magus danced in a deadly fashion, though they kept their distance from each other. Occasionally, one would push an attack and everyone could hear the ringing of steel on steel, but they were effectively at a stalemate for now. Kiri was a practiced hand at stealth and *ljas'atuk*, but Magus was the General of the Red Lance. He had seen enough battles and watched the Rangers and how they fight, enough to know that he needed to stay far away from the elf's cruel daggers. He had known that taking the dokk hostage was a mistake, but he hadn't been around to tell Vaelyn off for it, and now here they were.

Kiri stepped in closer, testing Magus' responses. He moved quick, but not quick enough to catch the lithe elf. His sword arced down and her right dagger flashed up to catch it while she danced the rest of her body out of the way. Then she twirled in close and gave a vicious stab with her left dagger. As expected, Magus slipped away at the right moment, leaving the dagger to tear uselessly at the air. Then Kiri dropped back and flexed her neck, popping a few vertebrae. She was nowhere near winded, but the fight between Sardra and Vaelyn had her attention divided.

Magus seized the opportunity, driving in a stab meant to gut the Ranger and end the fight, but he was met with a hearty clout to the back of the head. Stumbling forward, he sank his sword into the dirt and flipped over it, landing clumsily on his back. Grunting with annoyance, he threw himself back to his feet and grabbed his sword, shaking his head to clear the fog caused by the pommel of the dagger. Kiri did not mean to kill him, which was a pleasant nicety. One he would not hesitate to turn into her last mistake. A moment later, it dawned on him- she was *toying* with him. She could have easily slain him and, with half the effort she was showing. But she seemed to make a game of it. With this realization fueling his ire, he almost let anger guide his blade, before realizing how foolish that would be.

Kiri watched the dawning knowledge as it showed on Magus' face. Letting out a playful laugh, she twirled her daggers and faced him once more, letting one arm stretch out with the dagger at the end and the other arm hold back near her cheek. An obvious challenge in her eyes, she shifted, carefully circling Magus. When her foe was once more standing steadily, Kiri twirled her daggers around in her hands. "You are fighting a battle you cannot win, Magus Kefarion. Give up now, while you still have your life."

In response, Magus charged. Feinting to the left, he waited to see if Kiri would go for the bait. Instead, she drew back and brought her daggers back around. When he gave a slash, she forced his blade up and away, before twisting up and under with her other dagger to slice open his arm from wrist to elbow. Predictably, the man shrieked and dropped his sword before clutching at his flayed arm. Anger clouded his judgment for a moment and he charged at Kiri, swinging his functioning fist wildly as his right arm hung uselessly at his side. "Damned sprite! I will have your guts!"

Kiri moved nimbly around her opponent and delivered a stunning blow to the back of his knee. As he fell towards the ground, the elf helped him along with another knock to the back of the head with the pommel of her daggers, forcing consciousness out of his body for a time. He struck the ground without knowing it and stayed there. Kiri surveyed her victory for a moment and nodded, before dropping a healing potion next to the man. It would at least ensure the wound closed, though he would have a permanent reminder of his folly. Turning to face the other problem plaguing them, the Ranger took a deep breath and readied a slew of spells in her mind. Touching her hands together, she charged the first one, a simple stream of fire meant to distract the foe from being able to concentrate on larger spells.

As Vaelyn pushed another attack, he found himself doused in bright flames; the heat washing over his skin and searing pain shooting through his pathway nerves. He faltered and scrambled backwards, desperately trying to get out of the way of the searing pain but could find no escape. Snarling, he leapt at Sardra, trying to drag the flames towards her. In his distracted state, he failed to notice the savage slash until he realized, passing his right flank to his left shoulder. The pain tore through his body and coupled with the pain of the flames; he was quite ready to be away from this assault. Stumbling back, he conjured a ball of black fire and threw it onto the ground, causing inky darkness to envelop the area. Instead of pressing the advantage he assumed he had by attacking, he chose the smarter option and ran.

Back into the safety of the cave, where he used as much of his magic as he safely could to erect a barrier. The exertion left him panting, or at least he felt like he should be, but nothing seemed to happen, no matter how hard he focused on breathing. His energy seemed to return, albeit slowly, and his heart rate calmed. *This is getting out of hand. The plan must advance!*

The voice came to his head suddenly, startling him. He whirled, expecting to see one of those damned Rangers pursuing him, but there was no one. Wandering the halls of his cave, he shook his head. *Die! Kill! Die! Kill!* The words echoed endlessly in his brain. Was it better to end it now before his enemies could succeed? Or would it be better to fight to the last?

Sardra looked at Kiri and nodded solemnly. Focusing their energies together, they began chanting in the Lifesong. Their words climbed into the sky, burrowed deep into the ground. They reached into the primal energy of the world, taking what they needed and offering their body's power to the world-spirit. The surrounding ground cracked and crumble, with clods of dirt beginning rise into the air. The two joined hands and focused on the barrier that had been erected. As one, they pushed their hands outward, sending a surge of energy to batter the barricade, causing it to shudder and shake, as the surrounding cave began to collapse. *This cave holds secrets that are an affront to the Ancestors.* The thought crossed both minds, *and it must be obliterated.* More and more energy they poured through their bodies until both felt faint. In one moment, a colossal bolt of lightning screamed down from the clear skies above. There was a rending crash, an ear-shattering *BOOM*, and for a moment, both Rangers were blinded by a flash bright enough to make Kjetta jealous. Nevertheless, they kept pushing their energy, hoping their bodies would hold out long enough to render the entirety of the house, everything in it, and whatever madness the elf had wrought into dust.

Sardra fell first, dropping to her knees and spitting up blood, heaving out her breaths as her body fought for precious energy. Kiri lasted a little longer, but soon enough she too was kneeling on the ground, her head spinning and her heart pounding in her ears. After a few minute's recovery, both looked to see what they had wrought. The mouth of the cave was a crater, though everything behind the barrier was still intact. Cursing, Kiri stood up and helped Sardra to her feet. The women glanced at each other and planted their feet, standing shakily but defiant, ready to try again, ready to send another barrage of energy, when they heard a warbling cry. A massive black dragon, nearly the size of Talakath, winged into the area. Peering intently, Sardra could just make out the forms upon the creature's back and her heart leapt into her throat. "Kiri! Karos comes! Karos comes!"

Talakath, who had been dozing some distance away from the cave, answered the dragon's challenge, evidently unconcerned with the massive explosion that had just taken place.

Kiri and Sardra both threw up their arms, signaling to the passengers on the black dragon, though their spirits were dampened when the creature landed near Talakath. Something told Sardra, however, that this was a good thing, and she calmed slightly. Grabbing Kiri's shoulder, she waved for the other woman to follow her and took off towards the landing site. Kiri loped along behind her and they cleared the distance in short order.

Striding up to Karos, Sardra greeted him by slapping him

across the face. "What in the name of the Ancestors took you so long?" After a moment of glaring at him, her face broke into a toothy grin and she threw her arms around the man. "Damnitall, Karos, you are a sight for weary eyes. Now come, there is trouble afoot. Mind not the dragon, it is our ally."

Karos blinked slowly as he took in all the information. "You have been in this enemy's company. What have you learned?" He waited for her answer, wondering just what new terror would rise from it.

Sardra did not disappoint as she spoke. "I have learned that this creature, who goes by the name Vaelyn, uses a type of magic I have never seen before. He slew a Rider and their griffon- Porrik and Tyfa- with the greatest of ease and a blast of black fire. Destroyed my weapons and gear, but underestimated my abilities, which cost him dearly." She took a breath before continuing, her eyes sharp. "I have learned that he is the progenitor of this plague. He dabbles in things the Ancestors themselves find blasphemous and his works defy life itself." She spat out a clot of blood and sighed, knowing she had taken more than a few years off her life with the exertion she'd underwent.

Karos sucked in a breath and was about to speak when he was interrupted by Thäoldr, who seemed extremely perturbed. "What was that name? Speak it again, for lives hang in the balance."

"Vaelyn."

Thäoldr's blood turned to ice. Visions of many fell things passed over his mind, but confusion drew itself on his face. He opened his mouth for a moment, realized he had not decided what to say yet, and closed it again. Karos' voice snapped him back to reality.

"What is it, Thäoldr? Who is Vaelyn?"

"Vaelyn is an incredibly old name... a very hated name among the Riders. But to me... he was a father. If he has something to do with this... damnitall. The bastard is using Mirror Magic." Sizing Karos and his Rangers up, Thäoldr eyed them severely. "We must put an end to this. Now. Step not one foot toward that cave unless you are prepared to die... for chances are high we may not leave here."

Sardra grinned at the old elf. Taking in his measure, from the scarred face to the artifice arm, she chuckled for the first time in many days. "Well, Master Thäoldr. A Ranger always stands ready to die for the good of Seran. So, you are in good company."

Thäoldr nodded and turned to Khula, perking an eyebrow up. "And you, young mistress? Do you cast your lot in with us, for life or death?"

Khula stood defiantly in the presence of Ancestors. *Yes, Ancestors is the right word,* she thought to herself, *for any of these folk could turn the fortunes of the world however they see fit.*

Raising her hands, Khula crossed them over her chest and knocked her wrists together in the show of defiance she always saw the Rangers do. Grinning at Karos, she watched as he did the same, followed by Sardra and Kiri. Thäoldr grinned and picked up the gesture as well, his bracers knocking together. Then they made their way toward their destiny. Only one knew who would not survive, and they did their best to hide that knowledge until the time was right.

Only one of the assembled crew knew their time had come. That they had passed along all they could in this life, and the great clarion of the Ancestors was calling them to the

Path. To their next home in the Afterworld. Even through the trepidation they felt, knowing the moment of their doom was approaching, and fast, they knew they would make *such an end as* to be remembered forever. They knew their time. Perhaps not the exact time, or the method, but they knew it would be a sacrifice. *Their* sacrifice, that turned the fortunes of their friends, and their world, for the better.

In their mind, the condemned recited a phrase, one that had always brought comfort to them in dark times. One of the Verses, passed down by the High Ancestors to mortalkind, to give hope and guidance through all things.

In life and in death,
there is no certainty.
Though you may not greet tomorrow,
tomorrow will remember you.
As such, you must do your best
to protect the tomorrow
that you may never meet.

Pondering the verse as they walked, the condemned went further toward their doom with glad heart. With a mind full of love for their companions. As they tread the path, part of their mind wondered if it would hurt. If their last moments would be a memory of pain, or if what task they were on would be an adequate anesthetic. Part of them didn't care. As long as they gave their all for their friends, they could go to the Path with their head held high.

One of the group had theirs suspicions that things would never be the same after all this mess was said and done. Inwardly, they worried about their place in it all, wondering if they had made the right choice. Or if the choice had been made long before they ever had a chance to understand it.

But onward they walked, though fear threatened to take their heart and breath. They'd seen who was lying prostrate on the ground a few spearlengths away, and a rage boiled within them. A black rage. Moving closer to the two they knew, the courageous one kept their rage in check. *For now.* They felt in their stomach that a moment would come when they would be able to unleash that rage. When the years up till now would be worth all the pain, the suffering, the heartache, and the loneliness. When they would, for the first time, be allowed to exact revenge on someone who had dominated their life for so long. Hounded their every step. Harmed them every chance they got, in every way someone could harm someone without slaying them. *But my time comes for vengeance.* The thought echoed in their mind, louder than their drumbeat heart. Their feet plodded along, courage and fear fighting for mastery over their body, but nearly indomitable will keeping both at bay.

One of the group was in shock. Someone they'd been told a thousand times was dead was *here. Alive.* And unleashing fell magic against the world they loved. Someone who they'd loved beyond their own family. Someone they'd looked to for nearly a millennium, who'd taught them nearly everything they knew. Who'd shaped them into what they were today. Blinking, the person strode along with measured steps. Inwardly, they wondered exactly how this reunion would go. But they knew in their heart, mind, and soul, there was only one way this reunion *could* go. There would be blood. And by the end of it, there would be at least one corpse on the ground. Wincing as the energy in the air caused a painful thrill through their body, the figure clenched their fists for a moment before relaxing them and laying one hand on the hilt of a jet-black sword.

One of the group was ready to prove themself. To show the

others what they could do. To prove to themself that they truly had what it takes to stand next to giants; even though they'd proven themself time and time again. Their eyes ranged the surrounding area, taking in every detail with the keenest of stares. The crater that'd been left after the powerful blast. The ruins around the rim. The two black dragons, who seemed not to care for the struggles of the small beings near them. The barely visible barrier keeping the insanity within the cliff face protected from whatever they could throw at it. And finally, the surrounding friends. The figures walking alongside them, old friends and new, bolstering their resolve and making them ever more eager for a chance to prove themself. To show their elders how it was done. On they walked with light, ready step, their hands held loosely at their sides, where a keen eye could tell that the muscles beneath were tensed, ready to explode into violence at the signal from their leaders.

The last one of the group was calm. Collected. Each variable in their mind was being measured and weighed. Each avenue of attack was being considered. In their mind, they were recounting the events of the past year. Reviewing the information that'd led to this point. Pondering, even as they walked toward the unknown, possible death, where this all would lead in the end. Their eyes ranged restlessly, their mind working out the details to their plan. The solution to the puzzle ahead of them, and the best way to take down what they understood from recent talk, to be the unquestionably most dangerous foe they'd ever face one-on-one. Their right hand hung loosely at their side, occasionally clenching and unclenching. Their left hand rested on the pommel of a sword, fingers gently draped on the cold steel. On they walked with measured, confident step, their boots leaving barely a dint in the grass and dirt as they tread the road to destiny. As they moved along, one Verse came to their mind, a piece of wisdom passed down from the High Ancestors, and it almost felt directly to them, for this very moment.

Courage is not
simply fighting.
It is loving what you have
more than hating your foe.

This one did not hate their foe. In fact, they didn't even know them. But they knew what their foe stood for. What they planned to do. *That* is what they hated. What their foe represented. Was planning. What they *were*. But nowhere in their mind was there hate for a being they'd never met, never seen. At least, not yet. Not until the foe proved themself worthy of the *energy required* to hate. For now, they were an unknown menace, one who had sentenced countless innocents to death already. One whose actions had likely claimed some of their own. Some of their friends and family. And that? That could not be forgiven. But that didn't necessarily require *hate*. Just defeat. Just that the foe be cast down from their loftiest of plans to crash mercilessly into the jagged rocks of failure. *At the hands of myself and my allies.* They would prevail. They *had* to. The other option?

Death. Death for all they held dear. All they protected. All they'd worked toward in their centuries of life. And that? That would not do.

4: The Skies Above Westerspring

Namryll slowed suddenly, looking back and forth as images flooded her mind. A presence she had not felt in many centuries was making itself known to her, confusing her. *Mother?* Sprang the thought to her mind. Her mother was reaching out to her in desperation, but there was no hint of pain or torment to the message. What was happening? She back-winged abruptly, throwing her neck back and calling out a challenge, leaving her passengers scrambling to stay on her back. Then, just as suddenly, she took off, flying as fast as her body would allow, as Thäoldr tried to push through her panicked thoughts to speak to her.

"Namryll! Namryll!" The dragon responded by flying faster. There was confusion tearing through her mind like a tornado, blocking out anything else. Pulling his straps tighter, he barely heard Karos' cry over the wind.

"Thäoldr! What on Seran is happening?"

"I do not know! Namryll has just gone wild! Hold on as best you can!"

Khula fought down panic, swallowing a terrified scream

as best she could. A thought came into her mind and she tried to ignore it at first, thinking that there was no way it could work. But when the thought persisted, she relented and accepted it, before pushing her thoughts outward. She had been taught of the ability of mind speaking, though she had never practiced– but there could not be a better time. Focusing on the magnificent beast between her legs, she closed her eyes and breathed slowly. Slowly, she became more aware of the world around her and less of the two men shouting. She whispered a thought in her mind repeatedly. *Calm. Breathe. Calm. Breathe.*

Thäoldr felt it first, having the closest connection to the great black dragon. The powerful wingstrokes began to relax and slow from the frantic pace they were setting. The beast's breathing began to even out and stabilize. Her thoughts still pounded in his head chaotically, but one seemed to call out the loudest and it was not Namryll's. *You bear passengers. Passengers who are less able to fly than you. Calm. Breathe.* And it was working. When they reached a sane speed, Thäoldr glanced behind him. Karos was barely strapped down, though he did not seem that concerned, but Khula. Khula seemed as if the entire world was gone from her mind and she was focused on only one thing. He was uncertain, but in the back of his mind he wondered if Khula was the one speaking to his dragon and calming her down. How she was doing it, he had not the faintest idea, but he was glad for it.

Karos shifted slightly as the dragon slowed her frantic pace. He too was curious what caused the sudden change, but knew to keep his thoughts to himself for the moment. He felt Khula in front of him, her breathing slow and even. She was obviously elsewhere in the moment and the Ranger felt it would not be wise to interrupt her. Taking a breath, he surveyed the land rushing past, looking for any familiar landmarks, but nothing looked familiar enough to identify from above. In that moment, Karos realized just how small his perspective of the world was when he could only see from the ground. *If the Riders worked with us... our scouting abilities would become beyond compare. It would only serve the people better if we joined forces permanently.* In the old legends passed down from the time of Elkin Var, they whispered that the Riders and Rangers worked together, though Karos did not know how much credence to give such tales. For as long as he had been alive and many centuries more, the two groups had been at odds, but times could change, as his new alliance with Thäoldr showed. Distracted by these thoughts, Karos hardly noticed the white-knuckle grip his hands had on the belts, keeping him on the dragon's back.

Namryll listened to the girl speaking peaceful waters through her mind and, in doing so, found she could recognize more and more of the area in the vision. She was still deeply shocked that her mother had even spoken to her after so many centuries, especially after the Order had claimed her to be dead. *Could this be a trap?* She wondered, ever on guard. She was a black dragon and an old one at that- one did not get to be her age by being foolish. Black dragons were hated and more often than not for good reason, though there were ones that served the light. Most, however, were nearly insane and completely evil.

Khula opened her eyes slowly and for a moment, she saw double- not just from her eyes, but also from Namryll's. She was confused for a few moments, trying to figure out what was happening. A voice came into her mind and she could identify it as if she had always known the owner– it was the dragon. *Thank you, young one.* The creature let out a great sigh and Khula pushed a breath out as well.

Then, it was over; the connection faded away, and she was just Khula once more. *There is nothing about being me that is demeaning,* she pondered, *for I am my woman.* The realization came to her as the dragon dropped below the clouds. *I am powerful.* She smiled as the thought echoed in her head, again and again. Abruptly, she let out a whoop and threw her hands to the sky.

Karos grinned as Khula let out a cheer and patted her shoulder gently. Taking a breath, the Ranger leaned close. "How are you holding up, Khula?"

Turning her head, the woman spoke, her voice ringing clear even with the wind. "This is wondrous! I have never felt so alive!" She grinned at him for a moment before turning back. A few moments later, she was coughing terribly from the exertion of speaking, and Karos winced slightly at the sound.

Thäoldr gently slapped Namryll's neck and gave her a silent command to descend. He was feeling quite hungry and his legs were nearly numb from the saddle, so he could only imagine how his passengers, who were not accustomed to riding, were feeling. Idly, he wondered if he should show off before chastising himself. Now was not the time for antics. As the great black dragon descended, he turned to make sure Karos and Khula could hear his words. "We are going to land and break our fast for a short time. My legs are nearly saddle-numb and I imagine yours are as well, and I am quite hungry."

Khula nodded, having completely forgotten about food in the time they had been flying. Her belly rumbled as she thought of food and she turned a shade of pink.

Karos shrugged; as a Ranger, he was used to eating small meals, few and far between. But it would be nice to get a full belly for the first time in a week.

As the dragon lazily drifted towards the ground, she watched the surrounding ground change from the plains and forests of Dragonmoor to the blue grasslands of Nevian. As the group wound further towards the ground, a group of houses came into view. This was Elask, one town that sat along the border between Nevian and Westerspring. Karos watched the activity as they approached, a few dal'Korin running to- his heart dropped when he saw what. A host of dal'Korin troops sat along the border. "So, the scout reports were accurate..." He murmured to himself.

Immediately, three battlemages in the Neviani contingent threw up defensive wards- *An oddly hostile gesture*, thought Thäoldr, *especially against a dragon of Namryll's size*. When Namryll touched down, the leader of the contingent came forth.

"You and your passengers are not welcome here, Dragonrider. You must leave now."

"We merely seek to stretch our legs and get a meal. We mean no harm, honored scale-kin." He moved to slide off the dragon's neck to better speak to the dal'Korin and was met with an enraged hiss.

"I will say this once more. Begone from our lands, Dragonrider. We have nothing for you here."

Karos took a breath and leaned forward to whisper to Thäoldr. "It may be best for us to depart, Thäoldr. Let us cross the border into Westerspring, and if you wish to taunt them, you may."

Upon hearing Karos' voice, the leader of the dal'Korin hissed once more. "You are doubly unwelcome in bringing a Ranger onto our soil. Begone or be treated as the threat you are!"

"The Rangers are only a threat to those who make an enemy of the Empire and the people living within and when last I checked, the Scala'Dun were still beholden to the Empire. Do you have something to confess?"

"No, Ranger. But your kind are not welcome here. Begone immediately." The lizard-man hissed through clenched teeth.

Nodding curtly, Karos glanced up to Thäoldr- his hand was resting upon one of the many tattoos etched into his artifice arm. Evidently, he was ready to engage. When he saw the glance from Karos, Thäoldr nodded and moved his hand away from the tattoo and issued a silent command to Namryll. The dragon spread her great wings as far as they would beat — powerfully in a show of force, simultaneously pushing herself off the ground and bowling over the nearest of the dal'Korin. Karos and Thäoldr, having expected the blast, remained upright, standing proud in defiance of the Neviani contingent. A moment later, Namryll settled back down and allowed her rider and the Ranger to clamber back on and belt down. Once they were settled and secure, she let out a cry and took to the air once more.

She rose slowly and for fun let out a gout of jet-black fire. The heat was intense enough that most of the assembled troops had to cover their faces and the message was obvious- the Riders and Rangers combined was a not a force to trifle with. Namryll took to the sky with ease, before winging her way north. Her great wings carried her well across the border until they were safely in Westerspring.

Karos noted that the Neviani contingent stayed back a suitable distance from the border town, but it was troubling to him they had been so hostile. Were they not affected by the plague that had struck? Karos searched his memory to see if the dal'Korin had indeed been immune, but the knowledge, if it had been there, was buried under more pressing concerns, like the survival of the world. The troupe landed near Holdrin, and the dragon allowed them to climb down to the ground. Karos dropped first, moving to help Khula from the beast's neck. Thäoldr patted Namryll on the head gently before throwing a leg over the saddle and sliding down her foreleg to the ground, his boots causing a few flowers to kick off pollen. Once on the ground, he glanced to Karos, who was already inspecting the area for unseen dangers. When none presented themselves, the Ranger nodded and tossed his pack down gently, taking a seat next to it. The countryside smelled of flowers and fresh-cut grasses, which made all three wonder how close the nearest farm was. Namryll, however, was unconcerned with such things and quickly took to dozing in the sun, her eyes sliding closed as she basked in the warm blue glow.

"Gelvrentael be praised. The winds have been kind to us," began Thäoldr, "but I fear great peril awaits us."

"Indeed. But come what may, we will be ready."

They broke their fast solemnly, each wondering what the future held. Karos thinking of what evil had befallen his Ranger, wondering who Khula was going to be and wondering how long the pact between Riders and Rangers would last. Khula wondering what could be worse than the plague they had already seen; the violence that had been directed towards her all her life and the loss she had never known. Thäoldr's thoughts wandered frantically, wondering if this person they were chasing caused the plague- and who they were. There were few Riders that allied with black dragons and fewer still with the size of this beast and then there was Namryll's panic. Something had disquieted his dragon, and something capable of that could only be extremely dangerous.

Khula moved set down the waterskin Karos had handed her and spoke to him in hand-signs. "What do you expect to find?"

"Someone who wishes us all dead. Someone willing to make an enemy of the Rangers and the Riders of Gelvrentael. Someone with nothing to lose." Karos' hands spoke quickly, showing his thoughts. Khula shook her head in wonder. Someone willing to make an enemy of two of the most dangerous groups in Seran... that was definitely not a good thing.

"What of the Red Lance? Could we not call them?"

Karos shook his head emphatically. "The Red Lance would never help a Ranger, even one with the authority of the Kingmage." He dropped his hand to show how severe an error that would be. "And with Magus on the loose, I would be reticent to trust the Red Lance."

Khula nodded quickly, having forgotten that Magus was still out there. Even that struggle seemed small compared to what she had already accomplished- and what still lay ahead. Shifting uncomfortably at the mention of Magus, the woman took a breath and looked at Thäoldr. "What do you expect we will find?"

"Answers." was the only reply that came from the metal-armed elf between bites of stew. Again, he praised Gelvrentael and Vil'cav for the supply cave he had raided near Jorun's Watch. The Riders had shown incredible foresight in setting up the caverns so all Riders could access them.

Khula shrugged and plucked a lump of *pul'gra'an* being offered by Karos. She was unsure of what to think of the strange-looking food, but when she took a bite, she was amazed. It was quite flavorful and not unpleasantly textured. Eating the lump quickly, she found herself quite sated – *though some tea or wine would not go un-thanked;* she thought. But alas, where they were in the wilds, such comforts would not be possible. Instead, she took another pull of the waterskin Karos had handed her.

Karos chewed on a lump of *pul'gra'an* thoughtfully, trying to collect his thoughts in between bites. What first came to mind, was a question when he had made these particular lumps. They were still good, of course, but seemed a little stale. *Ah well,* thought Karos, *it could be worse.* Then, other thoughts entered his mind, plaguing him with scenes of destruction and death. He sucked in a sharp breath and both his companions glanced up at him.

"What is it, Karos?" Thäoldr, of course, spoke quicker. He seemed the least concerned though, but it would be rude for Karos not to answer.

"I am not sure... A warning it seems in my heart and against something that feels all too near. But no sense does it make and no reason or rhyme. I would need to consult with a *Wol'jalar,* but the nearest one is many leagues away." *Cryptic enough,* thought Thäoldr, *at least, to be annoying.* He shrugged slightly and watched Karos for a few more moments. "When I first set out on this quest, the wol'jalar, or fate-Watcher of Ca'e Möratuk, did a rune casting for me. And what she foretold was war. I wonder just how weak the lands have become... and who will take advantage of that."

Thäoldr didn't like that line of thinking at all. But in his soul, he knew the wisdom of it. The lands *had* grown weak. Unconcerned with their own safety, merchants and caravans rarely set night-guards. When bandits came upon them, they were often surprised to disaster. Sighing, the old elf played with his ear tips quietly, scratching the flesh against itself. Shaking his head finally, he spoke.

"It will not do. If we are in a weak state, especially after this plague and whate'er else may come, well... Too many innocents will die."

"Aye," Agreed Karos, shaking his head as well. "And that will leave us further in peril. Woe that these black days belong to us, and yet," he paused for a moment, listening to everything around; the way he set his brows and closed his eyes, Khula half-wondered if he were reading the winds. "We are the best to have our hands in it." He finally said. The Sage of Wind nodded slightly in agreement.

"Of course, that does not discount our young friend here! Already, she is shaping up to be far more than a noble could dream!"

Everyone let out a chuckle at the mention of Khula, who'd already shown such strength and courage, far beyond many of her type. *Her type,* thought Karos, *who so willingly hide behind the bodies of my people.* Reaching out, he patted the woman on the shoulder. She smiled gently and ducked her head in thanks.

They stayed there for some time, chatting and eating some of their rations. Karos picked at his pul'gra'an occasionally, Khula snacked on a few lumps he'd given her, and Thäoldr offered her some stew from his supplies. Smiling, she accepted, though at first she looked around for a vessel to hold a portion in. Karos unlooped something from his pack and handed it to her. It was a strange wooden bowl; cup? She wasn't sure which it was, but Karos took the initiative and filled it with the stew before handing it and a wooden spoon to her. Then, he passed the vessel back to Thäoldr.

Chuckling at the seemingly endless preparedness of the Ranger, the old elf finished off his portion of the stew and absently handed a sizeable chunk of bread to Khula. She nodded her thanks and soaked some of the stew with it and ate quietly. Occasionally, she would chuckle gently at some thought or another, and both men watched, almost transfixed, as their newest friends came to terms with what was going on around them. Looking to the sky a moment later, Thäoldr made a near-silent statement.

"Might rain later."

Karos looked up to the sky as well for a moment and shrugged. He could read the winds and the clouds just fine, but in his mind, the Riders had such a deep connection to Ara, the Ancestress of the Sky, that they could understand the slightest wisp of cloud. It was fascinating to learn about their relationship, though he'd made many assumptions himself. *Always something new with that lot,* he mused about the Riders. Returning his gaze back down to Khula, he watched as she ate for a moment, and then looked off into the distance.

"Storm gathering." He said without thinking, and both the noblewoman and the dragonrider looked the direction he was staring.

"I see nothing." Khula signed after setting her food down for a moment. But one look at the others told her what she needed to know. It wasn't a literal rainstorm. It wasn't something that could be seen in the clouds. But a storm was coming. Sighing, she nodded gently as she realized the truth in what Karos was saying.

"How many will it wash away?" Mused Thäoldr a moment later, and Karos nodded. The two were evidently off on some mental adventure, leaving Khula in the here and now. Sighing, the woman went back to eating her food, somewhat ruffled at the lack of explanation she was getting at the moment. As she picked up her food once more, she looked at her dress. The beautiful blue and red linen and silk were both stained beyond saving, and at first, it made her sad. But a moment later, she realized it to be a point of pride. *I am leaving behind all the trappings of nobility.* Though, with a smirk, she looked at the two men, and realized she needed far better clothing. *Perhaps once all this calms back down?* She mused for a moment.

Soon enough, their rest had ended, and they were back in the sky upon dragon-back. With Namryll's thoughts of her mother guiding them and Karos' images of landmarks giving them pointers to look out for, they flew over the landscape.

As the sun fell over the horizon, Karos could not help but be transfixed by the sight. The deepening blue sent a thrill through his body, one unlike he had ever felt before. Seeing it from this high up was something he had never done, and it fascinated him the way the sunset played across the clouds. All too soon it was over and the sun was gone, giving an incredible view of the stars, the star-paints and the family of Ni'la. Khula glanced skyward as well, having drank in as much of the view of the ground as she could. Whispering just loud enough to be heard, but not enough to harm her throat, Khula posed a question to Karos. "Name to me the star-moots you know."

Grinning, the Ranger pointed to his favorite constellation, that of Veljra's bow. "That one is Veljra's Bow, with my name-sake, *ca'e Karostrun*, at its peak." He traced the constellation with a finger to show her the shape and Khula nodded.

"I have heard of that one before. Is it really that sacred to you Rangers?"

"Being born or chosen when the moons bracket Veljra's Bow is one of the rarest honors a Ranger can be given in life. It shows that the Ancestors themselves bless their skills and have honed them in the Afterworld." Glancing to see her expression, he chuckled.

"I was not born under such auspicious signs. If memory of what my parents told me serves, I was born in the middle of a rainstorm."

"Are there no legends about that?"

"With the Rangers, there are portents to all things. Being born in a rainstorm it depends on the season and the timing of the thunder. I drew my first breath at a crack of thunder that was said to be heard for one hundred leagues in all directions— though much of that was hearsay. All the folk who remember my birth are long dead, by at least three centuries." He sighed gently, and a tear made its way down his cheek unbidden. Shrugging away the sadness, he glanced skyward again, this time pointing out another constellation.

"That one is Elras, the Guardian Archer. It is said—"

Khula interrupted him, her voice still carefully measured. "That when Kingmage Ywelin called upon him and his great bow, he turned his back on him. As retaliation, the Kingmage placed him in the stars to watch over Seran forever, never to sleep or know the comforts of home. I have heard many of the stories... but I could never see them— at least when my parents knew."

Karos nodded, impressed at her knowledge. He was also incensed that her parents forbade her from learning the constellations, especially considering it was among the most important pieces of knowledge passed down by the Rangers. After all, if one were lost, they need only look at the sky to find their way home. Orienteering by stars was a considerably basic skill and for someone to not be taught, showed that their family planned for them to never leave their home, never really do anything outside of their own town. It was sickening to the Ranger who valued freedom above all else.

Khula smiled at Karos, her lips parting long enough to form another question. "Would you name me another?"

Karos nodded and smiled, wondering just how Khula had gotten used to flying so quickly. She seemed perfectly at ease, even when Karos' own stomach was turning and he was wishing for the feeling of dirt beneath his feet once more. He kept such things private and pointed out another constellation. "That is Mara-gith, the Serpent."

"She is the firstborn of dal'Kiyr, the incorruptible. She is said to watch over the lands of Seran and alert her mother whenever an innocent life is threatened and whenever a life is ended without just cause." The answer was not Khula's whisper this time. It was Thäoldr's voice. "dal'Kiyr is also the mother of all dragons in Seran. Blessed be her family and her name."

Karos chuckled at Thäoldr's interruption. He was right, of course, and Karos realized it was likely a holy symbol for them. After all, from the little he had known of them, the Riders venerated dal'Kiyr as a god-ancestor, much the same as the Rangers did Veljra. Taking a breath, Karos called forward. "Thäoldr, where are we now?"

"Just crossing over the Hollyhead reaches. Another day or so, and we will be nearer to where we need to be."

And so the night went, with the trio flying through on the back of Namryll, the Last Shadow. They passed like shadows in moonlight, noticeable only to the keenest of eyes. One such pair of eyes watched with interest, wondering what was taking an elf and two humans on such an urgent task. A moment later, though, other movement caught the attention of the watcher, who descended on silent wings, talons outstretched, to capture a weasel that had made the misjudgment to scurry through the area.

The winged creature thought little else of the dragon. They had escaped its notice, which suited it fine. Then again, such things were often below the notice of dragons, especially dragons of the Order. So the creature passed the night with its snack. A few birds went about their nightly tasks, and bats screamed for their food, searching in the night. Raccoons trundled along, searching for good scrounging.

And so it went until Kjetta began to crest the eastern sky. At first, the change in the lighting was imperceptible, just a slight change to the tinge of the indigo sky. Then, as the trio flew on, their rumps growing saddle-sore and their legs saddle-numb, the brilliance of Kjetta began to bloom. The horizon became thirty different shades of iridescent blue, each one creeping upward and filling the sky in turn. Finally, dawn broke and the radiance of the Ancestor of the Sun, racing across the sky in his chariot, was laid bare.

When Namryll finally touched down again, they'd left Hol-lyhead hundreds of leagues behind. Karos was still utterly amazed by how far and fast the dragon was capable of flying. As soon as he'd slid from her neck, helped Khula to the ground, and watched Thäoldr safely disembark, he began massaging feeling back into his legs. Khula had a harder time of it, her legs flatly refusing to hold her up, so numb were they. Shakily, she managed a step before they gave out and she dropped to the ground. Cursing, she pulled herself into a seated position and followed Karos' example. Thäoldr, having long been accustomed to what a saddle could do to a rider, was stretching and walking in circles to stimulate bloodflow.

"Try walking, mate." He said to Karos after a moment of thought. The Ranger shrugged gently and stopped kneading his calves, before standing up and taking a few not-so-confident steps around. Quickly, the numbness turned to pins and needles, and as he walked more, resolved into the normal non-feeling of blood-sated flesh. Nodding, he made his way over to Khula and helped her do the same.

"Well, Lady Khula has little of her own rations, I wager, Thäoldr. I have little fare myself, at least little that would make a true meal. I will be back in a few hours. Be a mate and get a fire going, would you?"

The elf grunted and headed toward a small copse of trees to gather wood as the Ranger plucked his bow from his back, strung it, and sauntered off into the distance. As his figure retreated from sight, Khula thought she could hear Karos whistling some jaunty tune, though she wasn't sure what tune it was. When he vanished into the scenery, she looked up at Namryll before walking to where she was certain the dragon could see her. Then she reached up and patted the great neck. The dragon let out a friendly rumble and turned her head slightly, one massive opalescent eye settling on Khula. *Why do you risk yourself so?* The dragon thought at her, and the woman blinked at the question. The answer was obvious, at least in her mind.

Because I am tired of others having power over me. The woman took a defiant pose as she thought at the dragon, fists on her hips. As if she thought she could fistfight a creature that stood taller than most houses. As if she could outfight a creature that could turn her to ashes and scatter them to the wind.

Namryll let out an amused chuckle. *Little lady, someone will always have power over you. Whether it be the power of love, the power of friendship, or the power of domination, someone always will.*

And I will fight it until I cannot fight anymore. I accept love. I accept friendship. I will fight till the end of my strength if someone tries to dominate me again. It has happened enough in my life. She let out a snarl as she thought those words, staring defiantly into the opalescent eye. It blinked slowly, as if considering her words.

"Nearly to the eastern shore of Laghe Valoria. We should be able to see something, anything, soon." Thäoldr said, rousing Karos from his inattentiveness. He wasn't sure where the last few days had gone, which terrified him. But the company he was in assured him that it'd went fine, and all was well. Taking a breath, he looked around.

A few moments later, Karos nodded and blinked the moisture back into his eyes. Unlike Thäoldr, he did not have the advantage of - what were they called? Right, 'goggles.' He had no goggles to protect his eyes, so he was reduced to blinking like a madman. Khula seemed to suffer the same problem and her eyes were growing quite red. Peering outward, Karos picked through the gloom, searching for the subtle signs that would give away their destination.

What he found was a massive dragon, dozing indolently near a destroyed cave entrance near the Cliffs of Abandoned Dreams. Elated, he realized he saw two forms pointing excitedly and focusing as much as he could, he realized he could see who it was. Kiri and Sardra, already on the offensive. No doubt they had already been here some time and had engaged whatever foe awaited.

Karos did not need to say anything, as Namryll had already spotted the massive dragon and angled herself to approach. With a challenging bugle, Namryll folded her wings and dropped to the ground about fifty yards from the other dragon. Her landing kicked up rocks and dust and her riders slid off her neck in rapid succession. First Karos, then Khula, who was caught and helped by Karos, and finally Thäoldr. All three looked ready for whatever was to come.

Thäoldr touched a few of his tattoos, both on his flesh arm and his artifice arm, preparing himself for an onslaught from the black dragon ahead of them. His mind went through several rounds of disbelief as he realized he recognized the dragon that faced them. *Talakath.* The name made his spine run cold. Immediately beginning a defensive incantation, he sought to protect himself and his companions from the beast.

Talakath merely turned to regard him with lazy eyes.

6: Westerspring

M agus came to with a dull throbbing in his head. He was not sure how long he'd been out but judging by the beginning of Kjetta's rise into the sky, it'd been a while. His arm still screamed with pain and he wondered exactly what happened. A glance at his arm and the ghastly wound thereof caused the memory to rush back to him in a searing blast and he fumbled around for a moment, reaching for anything he could steady himself upon. His left hand bumped an odd shape on the ground and he quickly closed his hand around it- *glass*. Picking the object up, he looked it over- a potion that looked to be one of healing. Yanking the cork open, he poured the mixture into the gash on his arm, uncaring what the effect would be. He was happy to realize that the torn flesh began to reknit itself and soon enough the wound was closed, though a terrible scar remained. Flexing his fingers, he tested the strength of his arm by picking up his sword, and it seemed steady enough to satisfy him. Growling, he realized that the Ranger who injured him so must still be out there. Slowly, he climbed to his feet and surveyed his surroundings, wondering what exactly was going on. It was then he became keenly aware of the thrum of intense magic, the roaring sound of dragon-blown fire and the chanting of a group of voices. *This bodes poorly,* the man thought.

Slinking towards the sound of the voices, the man peeked over a rock. He shuddered to think what would happen if he got caught by the group. Looking them over, he tried to put a name to each face. There was Karos, which angered him greatly, an old, artifice armed elf he could not recognize, the dokk they had captured, and that damned elf-wench. Finally, his eyes settled on the last one and his rage boiled over, nearly blinding him. His first instinct was to seize Khula, to punish her for her insolence in running away, but he quickly realized what a grave error that would be. Taking a deep breath, he clenched and unclenched his fists, trying to work out the anger he felt at the girl. *How dare she! How dare my betrothed traipse around with this group!* He seethed as he watched them, before realizing that he'd best calm down. If he went after them, it would not end well. If Kiri had put him down with so little effort, there was no telling what Karos, who had been in Khula's company, would do. *Bide your time and temper your anger. Strike when the time is right and reclaim your bride.* The thoughts screamed through his head, his breathing finally slowed, and his heart stopped pounding in his ears. As the red lessened from his vision, he realized what the group was doing.

A chant was being raised and a spell prepared to take down whatever was stopping them from advancing into Vaelyn's sanctuary. Magus was unsure of what was going to happen, but even he could feel the raw energy being summoned and knew that he did not want to be anywhere near that when it went off. He was confident in Vaelyn's abilities, though, and knew he would need to stay close by to aid in his victory. Slipping further away from the group, he headed for one of the secret entrances to the cave. He was not completely sure why he was doing this, as he felt he owed no allegiance to Vaelyn apart from a business relationship, but something compelled him to re-enter the cave and reunite with Vaelyn. Sneaking his way through the different caverns, he found Vaelyn in his hidden tunnel, feverishly working to protect his work and knowledge, from the different reagents used to the tomes worth of notes he had on the subject, written in a strange language not even Magus could recognize. Clearing his throat as he approached, the man made himself known. "Vaelyn. What are we to do? There are three Rangers and one Rider."

"Kill them! Kill them all! Rend their flesh and burn their souls!" The answer was worrying to the man. It was delivered in an uneven pitch and the look in Vaelyn's eyes was not one that Magus had ever seen. The elf was clearly losing his grip on what little sanity he had left. Obviously, the time was fast approaching where Magus would have to part ways with this maniac. Sucking in a breath, he backed away from the manic elf and slipped back up the corridor, searching the cave for any weapons that would allow him to stay at a distance from the foes outside. Shaking his head as he found nothing, Magus sighed and watched through the barrier as the Rangers prepared their attack. It was like this that he wished he'd studied the magical side of things more in his youth, because perhaps then he could lie down some measure of protection- or level an attack at the ones facing them. Watching the movements of the ones casting, he realized a pattern. The three in front, the dokk and the two elves, were charging their spells up as high as they can. The male elf was moving his hands along a few tattoos spread out across his flesh and artifice arms and Karos– the name alone angered him– was standing in the back, chanting. What he was chanting, Magus could not make out, for there was quite a distance between them, but the effects were quite visible; the sky was darkening, and lightning was building. The charging of the air caused moisture to accumulate and soon enough, rain fell. *A perfect backdrop*, thought Magus, *to decide the fate of Seran.*

Karos continued his chant in the ancient tongue of the Lifesong. His words touched the world's core, shaking loose primal energies that had been bottled up since the time of the First Tribes. Around him and his allies, rocks and dirt rose. *"Bring to me the life of the land. Bring to me the anger of all creatures. Bring to me the rage of the righteous. Bring to me the sorrows of the lost. Bring to me the burning cold of the North. Bring to me the heat of the flame."*

The chant was repeated, over and over and as it was, the energy built palpably. He was set, ready to die if he must, but ready to kill. His use of the Sk'av'A, though, was based less in offense, for his mind could not grasp using the Lifesong for cruelty, as did his contemporaries. This was because of his upbringing and the ways he was taught– that one must protect and bolster those who need aid and raise their weapons only as a last resort. The rain picked up as Kiri's voice joined his.

"Focus on the cry of the eagle. Focus, on the call of the Raven. See with the eyes of twylan. Shake the ground with steps of the giant. Bring to bear the might of leviathan." As Kiri spoke, she traced out the form she intended her spell to take. The energy continued to build, and a bolt of lightning slammed into the ground with a deafening blast. More lightning arced between sky and ground as the air became more and more charged. Kiri could feel her hairs standing on end. She looked over at Sardra and barely held her composure.

The dokk's fur was standing on end, with little bolts arcing between the hairs. She was a ridiculous sight, her fur fuzzed out to where she looked akin to a cloud. Kiri took a breath and continued her chant, quickly regaining her composure. Pressing her hands to Thäoldr's left shoulder, she let her energy flow through him, even as it continued to build.

Sardra's voice added to the terrible symphony as her compatriots continued their chanting. "*Voice of world, tongue of life. Anger born of righteous strife. Power drawn from Ancestors above, hope of those yet to come.*" The lightning picked up, and the rain had become a torrential downpour. Bolts of white plasma blasted downwards, rending trees and sundering rocks. The world itself was growing impatient and between the three Rangers, it seemed as if the energy was enough to tear them all apart. Sardra growled, baring her teeth as she spoke. She knew what would happen if they failed. She had seen how easily Vaelyn had slaughtered a powerful beast and brave rider. *Porrik. Tyfa.* Her voice echoed in her mind, barely audible above the sound of her heart pounding its ceaseless melody in her ears. *I give this gift to you. Your spirits give my anger reason. Your sacrifice gives my fury voice.* Reaching out, her hands crackling with barely constrained energy, she put one hand on Thäoldr's right shoulder. The bridge was made, and her energy flowed into Thäoldr's form while continuing to build. Her hair sparked and sizzled, catching fire and extinguishing itself moments later. Her eyes glowed bright violet, both with magic and with unadulterated fury. *This is for those you have slain! This is our answer to your evil!*

Thäoldr's mind went wild as the energy thrilled through him. His magical pathways glowed first, forming searing blue traces beneath his skin. His eyes were next, shining with the colors and facets of a mystic opal, the heart of the Ancestors. His silver beard shimmered with the colors of the night sky. He could feel the energy awaken his body in a way he had only felt once before, when he'd first connected with Namryll. His artifice arm shuddered and come apart, breaking into a liquid form. After a few moments, it shifted back into the recognizable form of an arm; but gone was the clumsiness of the smiths who had crafted it. Gone was the metallic creaking that accompanied every movement. He could feel every single touch through it, as if it were biological once more. As the energy burned its way through him, he felt as if his body was changing, growing stronger every heartbeat. His precious scars burned away in searing pain. His head suddenly felt itchy as hair that had not grown for over a millennium sprouted and grew long. Reaching up with his artifice arm, he brushed a few locks into his view and was amazed. The color was that of the nebulae above, with the stars themselves captured within. But there was still more to come. He could feel his body screaming against the energy, threatening to collapse upon itself. Every breath felt like he was breaking apart and every heartbeat felt like a mountain was erupting from his chest. Then, all at once, his other thoughts were silenced. *We are here together, Thäoldr.* Instinctively looking towards his dragon, he saw the beast glowing.

His eyes were keener now than they had ever been, and he could make out violet light edging each of Namryll's scales. The magnificent beast moved over to the group, glowing with the fury of Kjetta himself. Her wings had ceased to be flesh and bone and were instead made of the sky themselves, glowing brightly and reforming. The torn flesh wound itself tight, repairing damage that had been done centuries ago. The scars and old wounds upon her body sizzled and close, one at a time. A bright point of light erupted from her empty left eye socket, quickly forging itself into a new eye that whirled with the colors of Ancestors-heart. She called out a challenge that deafened and terrified even her mother, as her body became new- and charged with energy beyond what she had ever dreamed.

Thäoldr, too, felt his mind become something more than he had ever imagined. He felt as if he could see three steps ahead of his comrades, plan for the very tiniest of details, and imagine the scenario in seconds. Then another scene popped up and another. He could scarcely focus on one and solve it in his mind before another brought itself into his mind. He hyperventilated, unsure of what to do with these thoughts. They were coming so fast and with such energy. Then, he felt a hand on the center of his back. *Karos*, he thought to himself. He barely had time to brace himself before he felt another blast of energy pulse through his body. His pathway nerves glowed different colors, some he had never seen before. His body seemed to flicker between transparency and solidity. Taking a breath, he focused his mind on the task ahead and drew his sword, pointing it towards the barrier. Every fiber of his being screamed with energy as he formed the pathway in his mind. Pushing the energy from his core, down his arms and into the sword, he formed a clear pathway into the world for the massive amounts of energy that were coursing through his body.

Lightning crashed down in a terrifying maelstrom of energy

and the rain pelted down, threatening to drown them even as they stood erect. All at once, everything went dead silent and for Thäoldr, time seemed to slow to a crawl. He was pushed out of his body and stepped away, watching as a point of light formed at the tip of his sword, Ill-Blood. The blade glowed, with light pouring from cracks that formed on the onyx surface.

Then, Thäoldr was slammed back into his body and a beam of light, more intense than he had ever seen, blasted from his sword. There was a terrible sound, akin to the eruption of a world-forging volcano, and the beam struck Vaelyn's barrier. At first, it did not seem as if anything had happened. But quickly, cracks formed in the barrier as it tried to absorb the energy it was being pummeled with. The Rangers continued to pour their energy into Thäoldr, and he found every breath becoming easier and easier. Then, with a sound Thäoldr could only think rivaled that of the creation of the world, the barrier exploded. The beam of light broke and with it, the blade of his sword shattered into many pieces, which scattered themselves in more than a few directions at great speed. Thäoldr himself was pushed back as if by the hand of dal'Kiyr itself, and forced and the air from his body, leaving him quite unable to remember how to breathe for many a moment. The Rangers supporting him were pushed backward as well, barely holding their ground. The blast blinded all and none came from it unscathed.

Karos was the first to recover, though recovery may not have been the best word. He was somewhere between conscious and out cold, his vision constantly flickering between blackout and perfect clarity. He blinked hard, but that only seemed to make it worse and in a moment of clarity, he saw the result of their efforts. The cliff wall and the cave had almost completely collapsed, and the barrier was nowhere to be seen. Magus, who had been hiding within, was revealed to the world and he looked more terrified than he had ever been in his life. Vaelyn was visible, having just barely protected his precious work against the onslaught. But his home was gone. All his possessions, his weapons, and everything he had not protected with magic were simply gone. The crater in the cliffside had dug in about twenty spear-lengths, forming a round bowl in the barrier's shape. The rock was burnt jet-black and smoked heavily and they could see here and there the glow of molten stone.

Thäoldr pulled himself to his feet after a moment. Taking one look at the destroyed sword in his hand, he moaned sadly. "Ael'Varum..." His closest companion, save Namryll, had perished in saving the world. But somehow, Thäoldr knew the worst... the worst was yet to come. Steadying himself, he moved his hands, flexing his artifice arm. It had cooled significantly, but still reacted more naturally than ever before. He still felt as if his mind was in a state of sensory overload and everything was happening too fast, but, he could process it as if it were his natural state. He took a breath and found that his chest ached as if he had gone thirty rounds in a fight with Kervig, one of his Lance-Riders. Touching his chest, he half expected it to be caved in, but it was still steady and strong. His heart was racing, he could feel warm liquid trickling from his ears and there was a constant pounding in his head that would not go away. His vision pulsed with his heartbeat and he felt it had crushed as his entire body under a dragon. He had to remind himself to keep breathing, and he wondered if he was dead and just seeing things as he made his way to the path. He was shocked back to reality as Karos' arm landed clumsily on his shoulder. He turned to look at the man and realized that he felt like Karos looked. The Ranger's face was bruised, blood flowed freely from his nose and there were cuts and abrasions all over. He looked like he had lost a fight with a vivacious cleaverback.

"Thäoldr! Come! It is time to end this! Sardra! Kiri! Rouse yourselves and follow me!" Brandishing his sword, the Ranger stumbled out to meet his foes, for the first and last time.

Sardra heard nothing but a ringing in her ears. She saw Karos say something to Thäoldr and then turn to address her and Kiri, but the words were completely lost to her. Pulling herself off the ground, she flexed and stretched, her muscles abused by the explosion and her consciousness returning with a vengeance. One hand moved up to clutch at her skull, while the other readied itself, claws extending. This was shaping up to be a painful, if interesting, day.

Kiri alone seemed to be unaffected by the harm that had been caused. She seemed unconcerned with the hellish, blasted wasteland they had created and readied her daggers, stepping forward to follow Karos. A glance to Thäoldr told her all she knew; the older elf knew, as did she. She would not be joining them after this. Thäoldr's eyes softened for a moment with a silent apology, before steeling themselves for the task ahead. Kiri charged ahead of Karos, once more charging the surrounding air with protective wards. There was only so long they needed to hold, she realized. She could tell her hour of doom was approaching, but she felt no dread or fear. In her mind and heart, she knew she would once more enjoy the company of all she had lost as she made her way along the Path towards Veljra's hunting grounds. Twirling her daggers, she popped her neck. A flick of her wrists sent Magus hurtling through the air out of her way and she called out. "*Vaelyn!*"

Vaelyn turned to regard the woman. She was fast becoming a nuisance. Touching his tattoos, he began blasting her with flames and grew enraged when she simply strode through them. She seemed none the worse for wear and when she got into polite range; the woman held her weapons at the ready. "As I told you before. I sentence you to death." He let out an enraged shriek and formed a mage-blade, intending on ramming it through her chest. It was blocked by the daggers and thrown wide. He was clever now, his mind clearer than ever, but she was just as quick. She would leave an opening for his blade only to deflect it with her daggers, dancing around him to enrage him further. She was extremely mobile, but he was the last Paragon of War. None could stand in his way.

She fought hard, her blades ringing with the promise of unending pain as they clashed against the mage-blade. But she knew her time was running out. She could feel her motions, which up till now had always been sure and swift, slowing. Openings formed where they would, and she felt the mage-blade bite into her arms and legs. She was quick enough to keep it from the goal Vaelyn had in mind, though. *Just a few moments more*, Kiri thought to herself. A quick glance told her that Karos was looking, and the fire in his eyes said he was finally lucid once more. Stepping back, she pushed the blade away from her one last time and her daggers went out wide. She felt the bite of the mage-blade as it tore through her armor and into her flesh, the searing pain cutting through her body. Her breath came ragged, and a hand grabbed her throat, drawing her in closer to Vaelyn's face. "You fool. You cannot best me."

"No," she sputtered, spitting in the elf's face, her lifeblood splattering on and clouding his remaining eye, even as the light died from Kiri's own eyes. "But they can." With one last effort, she pushed her remaining energy out of her body and into two forms. Thäoldr, a new friend and companion and Karos, her beloved adopted child. Then, she fell backwards, released by Vaelyn's hand, and struck the ground. She felt no more the air of Seran and passed onto The Path, to be greeted by her family, not just the children she'd buried and the husband she'd lost, but the Rangers she'd trained and comforted, some even on their dying breath.

Thäoldr cried out as the woman died. "Kiri! You fool! What were you–"

Karos' voice sounded distant, angry, and more dangerous than Thäoldr had ever known. "She knew what she was doing." It almost sounded like someone other than Karos had spoken, for the voice was too low. But it was Karos' mouth that moved. He blinked hard, a brainstorm happening in his head as his mind rewired itself. Pulling himself to his full height, he suddenly seemed as if he was ready to kill the Ancestors if they got in his way. "Thäoldr. I have an idea."

"It had best be a good one."

"You told me some time ago that your artifice arm contains gems that slowly bleed off energy. I do not think you remember mentioning it."

"What of it?"

"Abryx can house vast quantities of energy and this shard..." Reaching into a pouch, he removed a glowing necklace. A star, shaped from star-steel and clasping a single shard of Abryx, sat in his hand. "Contains the pain of all my three-hundred years. Put into it your anger, your fears, your hatred. Let them all go. I will give you the time you need."

Tossing the necklace to Thäoldr, Karos gripped the handle of Northrage. In his mind, he had a stinging one-liner to say to Vaelyn, but he realized he had nothing to say to the mad elf. He had just slain the closest person Karos had to a mother in three centuries. He deserved no words.

"Karos, he slew Kiri in moments. What makes you think you will be any different?"

"Do not worry about me, Thäoldr. Focus on the abryx." He brought his sword up, the flat facing him, and turned to where the edge was pointed toward his enemy. "I have something to work through." His steps seemed to resonate in the ground and as he approached Vaelyn, he let out a cry. "Topalin!"

Vaelyn barely had time to react. He had just cleaned she-elf off his blade when a crazed man approached and called out a name. A sword flashed down and he only just got away. Calling his mage-blade back up, he swung it at Karos. The blade passed inches from the man's head, sailing harmlessly into the air. What happened next, Vaelyn could barely understand. "*Force Unrelenting!*" Karos slammed one palm into Vaelyn's gut and, though there seemed to be no impact from the hand, he felt himself slammed backward by many feet. He barely kept himself upright and as he steadied himself, he saw the crazed man come in for another attack. Reaching out, he sought to get the man to skewer himself on the mage-blade and winced as the man's sword slammed his own blade away. The sword then moved in and sliced at him. He felt the blade slice, felt the searing agony as the weapon cut through his form- but there was no torn flesh, no blood on the ground. Grinning, he charged a blast of mage-wind and slammed his hand outward.

Karos flew backwards, landing hard and quickly recovering. He had forgotten that he was fighting a practiced mage and had gotten lucky that the man had only used a blast of wind to gain some space. Bringing his sword up, the man angled his neck until his vertebrae popped. He was going to fight this enemy until time ended, if that is what it took.

"Rage unrestrained!" Once more, the Ranger closed the distance with his enemy, his body charged with the power of the Lifesong. Slamming himself into Vaelyn, he knocked them both to the ground, his sword flying away ; the mage-blade sputtered and vanished. On top of Vaelyn, Karos quickly locked his legs around the elf and began pummeling him for all he was worth. The elf hadn't had the time to put up a defense and suffered the indignity of repeated punches to the head. Once again, though, he felt the impacts, the pain of the bony flesh striking him– but no bruises formed, no damage became apparent.

Vaelyn had taken enough of this. Taking in a breath, he slammed his hand outward, catching his foe with a magically charged palm-heel strike to the chest. The man flew backward, landing in a crumpled heap. Vaelyn approached, once more charging a mage-blade to ready himself to end the aggravating man.

Khula shook her head finally, having felt useless this whole time. She was watching a battle between people of such power that she could be erased from the world in an instant if that was their intent. But something about this group gave her strength and when Kiri fell at Vaelyn's feet, she knew she must do something. Picking up a rock, she smirked. How odd that the first thing available to her was the thing she needed most. Readying herself, she coiled her arm back and sent the stone sailing through the air. What Karos needed right now was for his enemy's concentration to falter and falter it did, as stone after stone sailed towards that foe.

Vaelyn was not sure what was happening at first, when he felt the sudden impacts on his body. They were powerful, but nothing he could not ignore- for a moment, at least. But when a rock struck him square in the nose, he rounded angrily. Throwing Karos back with another blast of mage-wind, he used the Void to close the distance between him and Khula. "Impudent girl! Magus! Your toy is over here!" He raised his hand and struck her across the face, and received a blast of searing agony as claws raked his back and spine. The woman he had struck eyed him defiantly, even as blood ran from her nose, before delivering a powerful punch to his face. He turned long enough to deal with whatever had struck his back; Sardra, of course. He went to end her once and for all, before he felt a dagger tear into his thigh. Squealing, he stumbled away from the two women, clutching at the point of pain, though there was no wound to be found.

"I am no one's toy. I am Khula, free lady of Seran. I defy you and Magus, and I cast my lot with the Rangers!" With a yell, she went to charge after Vaelyn, with her dagger at the ready. She was unafraid of dying at this point, and anything would be better than going anywhere with Magus. Sardra caught her arm and pulled her away at the last moment.

"Come away, milady Khula. Let Karos have his revenge. I believe he and master Thäoldr have a plan. We have enough to worry about." Turning the woman to face the other threat that had been coming, Sardra took an offensive stance. She was unarmed against the General of the Red Lance, but she had someone to protect, someone to keep safe while Karos and Thäoldr dealt with Vaelyn.

"I suggest you stand out of the way between me and my property, *bitch*." Magus grinned as he leveled what he thought was a stunning insult. His sword flashed in the gloom as he approached and he watched for Sardra's response. *She must know her folly*, Magus thought to himself, *for one facing the General of the Red Lance can only meet with their doom.* When he looked at Sardra, he did not see the danger he was in. He saw a young dokk, obviously out of place, though she wore the garb of Rangers. He had not spent enough time to know who she was, of her place in that organization, so he assumed she was beneath him not just in station, but in skill. In addition, she was unarmed and thus easy prey for him. He would beat into her a respect for his position and a fear of men, and he would see the fear in her eyes before he killed her. But every glance brought his eyes back to Khula, distracting him. He had to get her away from this rabble and instill in her the values her parents wanted. He had to dominate the girl once and for all and would stop at nothing until he accomplished his goal.

What happened next was nothing short of a ballet on Sardra's part. Every time the sword came at her, she would gracefully flow around it and deliver a skilled blow to Magus' body. His armor made it difficult to cause him any injury, but that she could keep him off-balance was enough. As the sword flashed in her direction, Sardra danced, giving Magus no satisfaction. He grew more and more annoyed as he realized that, yet again, he had underestimated his foe. She looked no older than thirty, so he was confused- did the Rangers not age? The thought of this made his blood run cold as she slid a hair's breadth away from his sword's tip, leaving him swinging at the air.

Sardra grew tired of the game finally. Reaching out, she caught Magus' sword by the flat of the blade, before gingerly wrapping her hand around it enough to give her purchase- without slicing her hand open. Then she gave a quick vertical jerk and a backward yank, intending to remove the sword from her foe's hand. It worked- barely, and she cast the sword away before dashing in. Using her momentum, she closed the distance with her foe and gripped one arm before giving a sharp tug, pulling Magus into a bent position. In the same moment as he was bent over, Sardra delivered a sweeping kick across his legs to send him into a flip and land him on his back. She then threw her legs around his arm, one over his neck and the other over his chest and dropped backwards, applying an arm bar to keep him occupied with fighting her. If her luck came through, she would dislocate his elbow and remove him from the fight quickly.

Magus fumed. He was not as used to grappling and this type of fighting. Sure, he could throw and take punches with the best of them, but this Ranger seemed to have other goals than trading blows in proper fashion. This *bitch* would not outdo him, and he prepared himself for his next motion. Driving his feet up, he curled Sardra on top of herself, yanked his arm out and twisted out of the hold of her legs, before pushing to his feet and backing away. Searching for his sword, he found nothing and turned back to Sardra. This time, he would simply pummel her into unconsciousness and death. Bringing his fists up, he closed the distance as quickly as he dared to reach his foe and began a quick series of jabs to test her.

Sardra had simply had enough of Magus' antics. As he came at her throwing fists, she dropped underneath his clumsy attack and charged her fist with magic. Then, she struck him in the stomach, his armor cracking and giving way to her fist and knocking the wind out of the man. As he stumbled back, her claws flashed out, cutting his armor away. Then, she drove in for the kill, striking him again in the stomach, just below the ribs, then in the throat to keep him off balance. He gagged and gasped for air and she grasped at his head, intending to snap his neck. But the blow never landed and a sound akin to that of tearing fabric could be heard. Sardra landed on the ground, knocked cold from a blast of magic that struck her from behind. "Magus, you idiot! Take your prize and be done with it. I will finish these fools!"

Karos had had no luck up till now finding an opening in Vaelyn's magical defenses. His sword back in hand, he had been getting steadily pushed back for the last few minutes and finally dug deep. With a cry that rocked the world around him, he rushed in as Sardra fell to the ground, unconscious. "Enkar Raaz Diigan! Topalin! Elruviel!" His sword flashed as he swung it tight and unleashed a flurry of slashes, stabs and strikes. He was growing sluggish, he knew- after all, he had been taking a steady stream of magic attacks through his body and even with his malformed pathway nerves protecting him from the worst of the pain, it was taking its toll. In the back of his head, he whispered a thankful prayer that his nerves had been malformed from birth- else these attacks would have been lethal by now.

Vaelyn gave a terrifying laugh as the Ranger attacked. He was so far beyond Karos' abilities now that even as the blade cut into his form; he felt nothing. *I am a god! His blade can do me no harm!* Reaching out with an effort of will, he blasted into Karos with a steady stream of lightning. His surprise increased when the man flicked up his sword, allowing the enchanted artifact to take the brunt of the assault. In response, Vaelyn increased the energy he pushed through his form, opening his pathways to their absolute limit, intending to destroy the sword and kill the wielder.

Karos heard the crack first and thought it appropriate to run a stab, thinking it was something in whatever damned armor was protecting Vaelyn, but when he went to move, an explosion knocked him back. He landed hard, barely dodging as more lightning blasted towards him. He knew the minutes were precious, and so he drove himself back in, his axe now in hand. The Ranger, the three-century-old fighter, was not planning on letting Vaelyn off easily; especially after what he had done to Kiri. Gripping the haft of the axe, he dug his feet into the ground and leapt towards Vaelyn. "On your guard, bastard!"

Vaelyn barely had time to react as the crazed Ranger dove in once more. Lashing out with his mage blade, he intended to make quick work of the man on his second assault. Once more, though, he was thwarted by the sheer tenacity of the Ranger. Around the mage-blade he came, his axe swinging down powerfully in a blow that would have severed any mortal's arm. *I am beyond him!* In his assumed triumph, the Paragon of War had completely forgotten about the still very alive elf working with increasing amounts of magic.

Grinning, Karos turned as his axe shattered in the face of a blast of lightning coming from Vaelyn. The man felt a moment of sadness for his weapon, but when he looked to Thäoldr, who was glowing once more- and had an odd sort of grin on his face, he knew that it was time. Dropping back a ways as another blast of lightning came towards him, he took the brunt of it, once more feeling his consciousness fighting to remain in his body. Then his companion let out a challenging cry.

"Mulrah Vaelyn! I, Thäoldr Sagewind of the Riders of Gelvrentael, issue forth a challenge for the position of Paragon of War!"

Vaelyn whirled, his stream of lightning stopping as he moved to see what Thäoldr was on about. In that moment, Thäoldr, who had been charging the abryx shard in his hand for a good twenty minutes, crushed the gem in the palm of his artifice arm. This released the energy stored within in a terrible maelstrom, which Thäoldr directed toward Vaelyn with a blast of mage-wind. As the energy approached, Thäoldr added his own blast into it, discharging the power that had been building since the Rangers gave their own to him. The sky exploded with lightning and a bolt screamed down to strike Vaelyn with a force equivalent to the fallen star that created the Star-Lake in Northrealm. The very air seemed to be afire as a blast wave rippled outward, flattening trees in its wake. Letting out a primal scream, Thäoldr touched as many of his power tattoos as he could, bringing the energy up even further.

Karos was thrown nearly into the lake, some hundred spear-lengths away. Rendered nearly unconscious by the blast, he could only watch impotently as Thäoldr blasted Vaelyn with everything he had. "Take it all," screamed Thäoldr, "my hopes, my loss and all my sorrows! Burn in everlasting fire, burn until the sun dies, and the world grows cold!" In that moment, he wished for nothing more than this elf, who he had once seen as a father, to die a thousand deaths. To be forgotten by the Ancestors and cast off The Path, to walk alone throughout eternity.

But the Fate-Weavers had had other plans in mind. Vaelyn shrieked as his body glowed, the energy penetrating his body through every pore, every opening. Then his form broke down. His mind yammered and screamed, unsure of what was happening. For a moment, he believed he was ascending, before it became obvious that something was terribly, terribly wrong. He was fading! Becoming a magical spirit! In anger, he screamed out a spell, unsure of what it would do at this point. Then, with a rippling explosion of energy, his body shattered into crystals of light that dissipated into the sky. Everything he had ever been drained from him in moments and he forgot everything, including his own name. He was *angry*, but could do nothing about it. Shrieking unintelligibly, he tried to escape the damning light that consumed him. Slowly, it faded and Vaelyn realized he could *see*. Not just what was ahead of him, but what was to the sides and behind. He could see everything and- and who was that elf standing before him? He looked angry and rather young.

It enraged Thäoldr as he realized what had happened. In one last act of anger, Vaelyn had taken from him many things he had held dear. His sword to begin with and now his tattoos, scars, and even his artifice arm. He flexed the flesh arm experimentally, feeling the crackling of energy, the stiffness of bone and muscle that had never been used. "Damn you, Vaelyn! Damn you!" He raged for a few more moments, before realizing- *Karos! Sardra!* Both had sustained incredible injuries through this fight and would need aid. Running to Sardra first, he looked around for Magus, knowing the man to still be a threat. *Too late.* He realized that the man was gone and had absconded with Khula.

"Damn! Sardra! Sardra, awaken now! You are needed!" Slapping the woman's face, he worked to get her to come around, before realizing it would work better to use a healing spell. "Thäoldr, come to your senses," he murmured under his breath, "and use your head." Moving his hands in a geometric pattern, he formed a pathway between his body and Sardra's, letting the healing energy flow into her. When her eyes opened, he smiled and propped her up. "Come on then, lady Ranger. We had best get moving. I saw Karos running up the cliffs. We had best get after him."

Hauling Sardra to her feet, Thäoldr called out to Namryll. The dragon swooped in to grab them both, but Sardra waved the dragon's claws away. She needed to get her legs back after all this, and the best way to do that was to run. She took off towards the cliff, following the rapidly retreating form of Karos, wondering why he was rushing up the way into the fog. A moment passed and her blood ran cold as she realized his intent. These were the Cliffs of Abandoned Dreams, and there was usually only one reason someone came to these cliffs.

Karos had felt failure in his bones and knew he could blame only himself. He had gone up the cliffs to die.

III

Travel and Cure

7: Westerspring

"**W**ARDEN RANGER!" A voice cried out over the wind that threatened to tear it from the owner. "Step back from the cliff's edge!" The voice was a command- a feminine voice speaking with the authority of centuries.

Another voice soon joined it, this one speaking with the authority of eons. "Belay your intent!" *Veljra.*

"You do not command me, Sardra Woodstrider!" Karos looked over the precarious edge of the cliff he stood at. It was a far fall- far enough to be lethal, no matter who you were. *Perfect,* thought the man, *a fitting end for one who has failed so many- and so much.* The foggy drop called to him, and he was unsure if he could resist anymore.

"No! I do not! But I am your friend, Karos anrak'Lyvan! And as your friend, I beg you, turn back while you still can! Do not take to The Path yet!" Sardra was closing the distance at a dead run- if she had to, she would fall with him- just so that he would not die alone.

The other voice called out once more. "You have a woman

out there who loves you more than a lover ever could! Who has risked *everything* to be with you! She needs you now more than ever!" The voice boomed above the wind, echoing into the distance.

"She is gone, Veljra. Taken by Magus and I have no trail to follow, no path to seek her out. I have lost her and failed her. Just as I have failed you- and all of Seran."

"You have only failed her if you give up the chase." She was closing the distance too, anger in her voice as she did. This was not the time. This was not the place. Seran needed Karos now more than ever, and there was only one way she knew to show him. She cast her hand out, throwing a powder into the fog- slowly, the fog lifted, to show *thousands upon thousands* of lights, reflecting from places so far away that Karos was not sure he'd ever seen them.

"What am I to do, hunt all over Seran?"

"If that is what it takes. Look below- look at the lights. All of those are people you have saved. People singing your praises, Warden Ranger. They know what you have done, they know you have saved them. All over Seran, your Rangers distribute the cure YOU created. That YOU found-"

"That Khula found!" He retorted, edging closer to the precipice. *End it, now!* The dark voice called out in his mind, overpowering all other thoughts. He fought it back, but knew it would soon win. *You are not fit to live if you cannot save one woman!*

Veljra's eyes flashed dangerously. "You save that one woman. You have survived countless trials. The only reason that voice plagues you is because it is afraid. Afraid of what Khula is to you! Afraid that you will silence it! You have never failed a task I have given you. You have shouldered each burden without complaint and without fuss. Now I beg of you, Warden Ranger Karos anrak'Lyvan - Guidestar Waking-Fire; Guidestar of Clan Lyvan; Captain Highest of the Rangers. I beg of you- turn back from the edge." Tears had formed in her eyes as she called out to one of the Heroes of Seran. The man who had turned the tide against a plague that threatened every life on the planet. The Ancestress felt the tears and smiled wryly. *This is a first. An Ancestress crying over a mortal.*

"He has an army of knights to protect him. He has the authority of the Red Lance!"

"And you have the authority of the Ancestors! The might of the Rangers always by your side! The Red Lance is nothing!" Sardra cried, her voice a shrill bark against the wind. She was judging the distance between her and him- calculating how fast she could reach him if he dove. She edged closer and closer. "He fears you. Fears what you will make Khula into. He is goading you, Warden Ranger! He is begging you to show yourself and show him he cannot take anyone from you!"

"But I have no leads- no path, no trail." He shook his head, tears running down his face. Few things had ever made him cry- but this insult, losing his dear friend Kiri. It had all come crashing down upon him and he could bear it no longer. He watched the lights beneath- saw each one from afar and tried to remember how it felt when they had created the cure. How elated he had been when he realized Khula and he had saved Seran. The anxiety of realization- that worse things were coming. The quiet confidence given to him by Thäoldr that they would face the odds and beat them. For the life of him, he could not remember that feeling right now. All that remained was black despair, threatening to claim him and everything he had experienced.

"You are a Ranger! Forge your own trail however you must, Karos. You faced down Vaelyn when he struck her, when he slayed Kiri, even with your sword and axe shattered. You endured his assaults until you lost consciousness and even then, you held on until the bitter end." Sardra's words were loud enough that his ears were ringing, even above the deafening gale. She stood proudly, near enough now that she was confident; that she could do what had to be done; that she could stop him from taking his own life. She could see the tears in his face- smell the caked blood from his wounds. This man had saved her life more times than she cared to admit- and she hoped he would let her save him- just this once. She watched him carefully again, judging the distance and preparing herself to leap and knock him away from the edge- if that became necessary. "Karos, *ka teljt.* The sharpest blades failed to cut you down. You waded through a maelstrom of magic energy and survived. Please, I beg of you as a friend- do not let your *prúnsaal* be what wins."

Far and away- though not as far as Karos thought, Magus had dragged Khula into a cottage. Shouting at the residents to leave, he threw her onto the bed. "I am going to take what you owe to me- and there is no one to stop me now! You are *mine!*" His eyes were filled with an insane fury as he realized he was so close to his goal of dominating Khula. He would not just have his way with her- he would break her to his will. Reaching down to her shivering form, he tore the dress from her body, rendering her naked and helpless before him.

Glaring, Khula spat the blood in her mouth at his face- the only thing she knew she could do. "*I will* never *be yours, Magus.*" She coughed up more blood and spat it onto his face as best as she could, trying to at least get some form of an attack in. Her words enraged the man, who slapped her across the face as hard as he could and roared at her.

"You belong to me! You have *always* belonged to me! You were promised to me the moment your parents birthed you, you ungrateful cunt!" He slapped her- again and again, intending to beat any resistance out of her. But her time with Karos had taught her much- and right now, she was conserving her energy. She would strike back at the right moment, and then it would be over for this bastard. For now, she just had to survive.

Magus began removing his clothes when the door to the house was forced open. "Get out of my house!" Cried the man as he brandished an adze. A poor weapon at the best of times- but this was not the best of times. Charging the larger man, the peasant raised the weapon above his head to strike and was immediately doubled over by a blow to the stomach. Then a hearty clout to the head assisted his fall to the ground, before Magus picked him up by his shirt.

"Do not dare interrupt me again, peasant, or it will be the last thing you do!" He hissed into the man's face and threw him bodily from the house. Then, he turned his attention back to Khula, who had seized a chance and grabbed a hunting knife. Laughing, Magus stood between her and the door. "And what do you think you can do with that, Khula? You are no warrior- you have no skills. You are weak, defenseless, and subject to my will." Closing her eyes for a moment, Khula remembered what Karos had taught her of the thrown knife. This one was not balanced that well; but it should at least fly. She opened her eyes, a new fire burning within them at the thought of her friend and mentor- and she threw the knife expertly. It flew true but caught just under where she wanted it to. Instead of putting an eye out, Magus was rewarded with a deep gash to the cheek. He yelped in pain and crossed the distance between them quickly before backhanding her, sending her to the ground. Reaching down, he grabbed Khula by the throat and tossed her onto the bed like a rag doll before undressing himself the rest of the way.

He was ready for this- he had been for so long, ever since he had seen the woman she had become. Originally, his plan was to wait until after he and his friend had conquered the world, but he felt that consummating here would serve better to break her. No Ranger to save her, no one to hear her cries. He would own her, body and soul, if it was the last thing he did.

Khula curled up, her legs tightening and her arms crossing over her chest defensively. She knew it was a poor defense against Magus and as the bruise growing on her face showed, fighting him was pointless. She was glad, though, that she had gotten a shot in at him and disfigured him. In the back of her mind, she begged Karos to come rescue her, to be her savior once again. But somehow, she knew- even if he was near, there was not enough time. She would forgive the Ranger. But Magus- she would end him.

Magus approached, his hands grasping at her thighs to peel them apart and allow himself entry. If she had come willingly, he would have been kind- allowed her body a chance to prepare itself. But her screams would be music to his ears. He readied himself and forced himself upon her, reveling in the feeling. Khula winced and held her breath, determined not to let him hear her scream. When he began his assault and the pain began, though- the shrieking tore from her throat, ripping it open more and more. Now she was not only bleeding from her body, but from her throat as well.

Karos felt something deep within him. Some fire raging back to life. Some spark burning bright, catching kindling after being fanned desperately by a soul lost in a deep, endless night. He closed his eyes and reached out to search for Khula, using the birds and the beasts of the land. Their eyes became his as he searched for some clue. He was a Ranger, a pathfinder of the highest order, and if he was to rescue his friend, then he would need everything he could bring to the table. A moment later, he opened his eyes- and stepped back from the edge.

Veljra clapped and Sardra breathed a sigh of relief, before running to the Warden Ranger and throwing her arms around him. "Thank you." She whispered, burying her face in his chest. "Thank you, Karos."

Karos gently patted her shoulder, and when she released, she saw the fire in his eyes. He had purpose once more and he would see it through, no matter what it took.

Veljra spoke, breaking the silence. "What have you seen?"

"One league. A small farm on the road a distance from the Woods of Spirit. A raven saw him dragging her in." His voice dropped dangerously and Veljra nodded.

"I cannot meddle in this affair, Karos Waking-Fire." Veljra used a term that none other had used in over three centuries. A term from when the Lyvan clan had adopted him and his family, when they had seen his future written in the flames. Karos shot a glance at her, his eyes steely with intense purpose. She nodded, and he looked at Sardra.

"If you come with me, there is a chance neither of us will see tomorrow. But it must be done. We must rescue Khula from this fate." Sardra nodded and clenched her fists, her claws drawing blood from her palms. Karos continued. "In your presence I swear, Veljra. I will not rest until I see Khula safe."

"Heard and witnessed, Guidestar Waking-Fire." She smiled and vanished from Seran once more, going back to her plane.

"Heard and witnessed!" Cried Sardra, and she grinned. This was her Warden Ranger again, standing proud with the intent of rescue in his mind and grim deeds written upon his face. A booming voice startled them both as Thäoldr, looking for all the world like he was back in his youth, rose on Namryll's back.

"Heard and witnessed!" He cried and looked over at both. "I was waiting to see what you would do. Had you jumped, you never would have reached the bottom, brother Guidestar." Thäoldr grinned, his teeth white and even. He missed his scars and his artifice arm terribly, but it was comforting to be whole once more. Even if that bastard Vaelyn was the reason for it. "Now come, jump on, both of you. We shall clear the distance in mere moments."

Both Rangers nodded and took a running jump, landing behind Thäoldr on Namryll's neck and shoulders. The great dragon folded her wings and turned the bulk of her body, dropping towards the ground for a few hundred feet before opening her wings and gliding away from the cliff. Then, she rose quickly and soared over the tops of the trees in the Forest of Spirit, down towards the lonely cottage. Letting out a powerful roar, the dragon closed the distance and dropped quickly. Within a few minutes, they had cleared the distance that would have taken much longer, even at Karos' best speed. Namryll landed and Karos was the first off her back, dropping the three spearlengths from her shoulder to land and rolled before popping back up to his feet. His sword, shattered though it was, would make a good enough weapon for this task.

He closed the distance between him and the cottage, stopping when hailed by a peasant family. "Be warned, Ranger! Magus of the Red Lance is in there and is harming a girl! He threw me aside like I was nothing!"

Karos merely nodded and strode quickly to the door. Bracing back on one foot, he slammed the other into the latch. As he did, he called out in the Sk'av'A. "*Kajaat ne elvyklar!*" In response to the dual-pronged assault, the door was torn asunder, splinters flying into the cottage.

"Peasant! How dare you intrude again!" Seethed Magus as he heard the door collapse, little realizing the door's demise was not due to an impact. In that same moment, fueled by rage and the Sk'av'A's primeval energies still seething in his body, Karos let out a terrible scream, brandishing the remains of his sword. In one meteoric leap, Karos sent himself across the room and struck. Magus let out a cry and tried to protect himself with his arm, only to cry out in pain as the shattered blade sank deep into his shoulder. Karos twisted the blade and yanked it out, causing further trauma to the region.

"I am Guidestar Waking-Fire! Your time has come, Magus!" Magus, his attention now focused on Karos and not what should have been his moment of triumph, tore himself away from Khula and leapt on Karos, one hand moving for his neck. But Karos was quicker, slipping out from under the larger man and give him a good slash across the chest for good measure. Grunting in pain, Magus forced himself to his feet and turned, letting out a flurry of punches and kicks meant to slam Karos around. As a kick aimed for his head came in, Karos threw up an arm- and wordlessly used the Sk'av'A to plant his feet into the floor itself. Magus, expecting the lighter man to be thrown, was quite surprised when Karos stood firm- and even more so when Karos grabbed his leg and drove the shattered blade up to the hilt in his thigh. Magus howled and reached down, yanking the blade and tossing it aside. It landed near Khula, who seized her moment. Seeing Karos fighting for her had rekindled her fire, and she did not intend to stand idle. Magus slammed his leg down, neatly dislocating Karos' shoulder, and closed the distance. Karos did not have time to uproot and was yanked upwards along with a section of the floor and slammed against the wall, with one of Magus' hands wrapped around his neck. Magus began squeezing, intending to crush the man's throat and end this.

"I own her! I have always owned her! Her entire life belongs to me, which means her body belongs to me, you worthless fucking peasant!"

"She... belongs... to... no one!" Karos choked the words out as he desperately searched for his hunting knife. His hand hit the familiar handle, his oldest companion. It was from his childhood, and had been kept lovingly maintained all these years, waiting for this moment. Fighting the urge to panic, Karos tightened his grip on the handle, and he snapped it out of the sheathe to bury it in Magus' arm, but the man was far too enraged to notice. Weakly, the Ranger tried to twist the blade, only for it to snap off in the enraged man's arm. Karos felt his vision wavering, black edges coming inwards as his brain fought for oxygen. He wondered how much longer the delicate bones in his throat could avoid collapsing when he saw his newest friend moving from the bed.

Khula had endured plenty at this point. *Too much have I endured at Magus' hands! This ends now!* Spotting the broken blade Karos had been using, she leapt from the bed Magus had attacked her on. *One chance. One moment.* She would be free, but only if she could manage it. Grabbing the sword, she closed the distance. The sword came up. With a mighty cry, Khula mustered every ounce of strength; born from fear, born from pain, anger, all of it. She had frozen up when Magus had attacked her and now her body screamed for vengeance. But now, even more than her own health, her friend, her ally; the man who had helped her discover herself; was in danger of being slain by the man who she had learned to hate. On top of all that? Her *freedom*, the taste of which she'd only just learned; The wonderful aroma of being under her own power, for the first time in her life; that was now under threat. Already, Khula had decided that death was preferable to having to submit once more to Magus; *no*, she thought, *to anyone!* That rage, fueled by fear for her friend, defiance in the face of potential powerlessness and submission to someone else, and untainted by thoughts of kindness or mercy, or even the thought of how she would answer Karos if he asked for an explanation, pushed her into an action that she'd never considered. A plan she'd never had the courage to even formulate, an attack she'd never before had the daring to dream. At that moment, something awoke in Khula. Something that'd been slowly realizing itself. A sun that only now crested the horizon, spilling brilliant light into what had before been darkness lit only by the occasional torch. From then on, her ship was *hers* to captain. Her trail was *hers* to blaze. And only *she* would decide who helped her, who guided her, and who shaped the seas and landscapes she would negotiate.

This. Ends. Now! She thought, giving action to plan.

Magus had almost entirely forgotten about Khula, his rage at Karos' intercession blacking out her cry of defiance, when, with the handle and broken blade of the sword Northrage, she made the last point she'd ever need to make to Magus. As a result, he lost all interest in Karos, in Khula and in life and fell- dead before he even hit the ground, the Ranger's broken sword having sunk through the side of his head, right up to the hilt. He twitched in his death throes and Karos, now untangled from the floor and the man attempting to strangle him, collapsed to the ground, nearly falling onto Magus, coughing as he struggled to get air through his agonized throat.

When he could finally form words again, Karos spoke between pants and coughs, struggling to his feet. He was still unstable from the attempted strangulation, his brain still recovering and fighting for every gasp of air. "Khula... I have no words to tell you how... how sorry I am." Karos choked on his words, tears flowing down his face from his near-strangulation. He was about to speak more when she closed the distance and kissed him on the forehead, gently wiping the tears from his face.

"You came back for me... that is all that matters now." Her voice was barely a whisper as she spoke, hardly audible even though Karos was right there. She threw her arms around him and sobbed into his shoulder. For the first time, he knew what to do and reached up her back, pressing her close with his good arm, as the other hung limp at his side. Her body racked with silent convulsions as the pain, the torment, everything she had just endured poured out. The raw emotion threatened to overtake her, and they stood for some time, just holding each other, each pretending that they had not just been at the end of their rope, at the very end of desperation.

Finally, Sardra stepped through the door and spoke.

"Karos... Milady Khula. We have an urgent summons from the Kingmage himself." Karos nodded slowly and Khula released him. Moving his working hand up to her face, he wiped away her tears and smiled, before pressing a tender kiss to her forehead. Then, he turned to Sardra.

"Sardra, would you mind moving my left arm? It seems to be... out of place." But before Sardra could react, Khula had seized his dislocated arm and twisted it. With a pop, it jarred back into place, causing Karos to gasp and wince. Then, he experimentally flexed the fingers in his hand one by one. They all seemed to work, which was good enough for him. Then he turned to Khula. "Thank you." Again, he pressed his lips to her forehead and looked her over. "Ancestors, but you look a fright. Come, let me give you some clothes from my pack." Before he had finished speaking, he dropped his pack to the floor and opened it, removing a pair of trousers, boots, and a tunic. He thrust them into her hands and turned away so she could dress herself. Sardra smirked and walked outside, moving to Thäoldr's side to wait for the two.

Khula felt like it would be some time before she would feel clean again, she knew. In time, she would make her peace with what happened- but she would never forgive the dead man at her feet. Finally dressed, she reached down and yanked what was left of Karos' sword free before presenting it to him. He took it silently and sheathed it, before Khula wrapped an arm around him and they walked out of the small house. The lady wondered if she could ever look her parents in the eye after this- after what they sanctioned. Somehow, she knew she could not; she preferred it that way. She would deal with them in time, but for now, her mind was on the task ahead.

8

8: Westerspring

"**I**t is here we must part ways for now, Karos. I must investigate Vaelyn's research and ascertain the truth of his work. In doing so, I hope to find a true cure for this plague." Thäoldr began brushing his hand through his hair. He looked quite young now, and it was hard for him to truly grasp what had happened in those ultimate moments. They had come back to the cave to pay their respects to Kiri, upon who Karos had used the Sk'av'A to give a proper funeral by cremation. Then, the four of them looked over the devastation they had wrought, and Thäoldr had realized that his task was not yet done. "My Riders have already begun distributing your treatment as best they can, but your Rangers will be needed. Call all you can to me, and I will enlist their aid in creating a true cure."

Nodding, Karos examined the elf one more time. He looked quite regal, especially now that his hair and beard had stopped glowing and had assumed a more normal blonde hue. Each had played their part in the cataclysm and had been punished in their own way. With one last look at the charred spot of ground where Kiri had been cremated, he whispered a prayer to the Ancestress. "Veljra. Watch over her, teach her what you will. Comfort her, give her love. These things I beg for my dear companion. She will serve by your side with honor and ferocity." Kissing his palm and raising it to the sky, he let out a cry. "Kiri Topalin! Walk well and be with Veljra! We will remember you!"

Sardra let out an ululating howl for her departed friend and moved in behind Karos. "Come, Warden Ranger. The world awaits." Then she strode off, waving at Khula to follow her. "Come along, Lady Khula. We must make haste if we are to reach Karnost at any speed." Grinning, she popped her fingers and set off on the trail that led away from the Cliffs.

As Karos spared one last look to where Kiri was cremated, he smiled as he realized something; through the devastation, life was taking over once more. Shifting, he tightened the straps on his pack and took off after his companions. The road was ahead, and all that was left behind here was sorrow. But he walked with a lighter step than before, knowing that Vaelyn could no longer threaten the people of Seran. He was a *lok'vi* now, a magic spirit, and had lost what was left of his mind. He was a threat only to those who could understand his rantings, but there were few who could. Confident that Thäoldr would monitor what they left of him, Karos set his thoughts ahead.

Thäoldr waded into the depths of the blasted cave, wondering just what he would find within. Sifting through the rubble, it surprised him to find an intact chest bearing the wards of Void Tongue. He remembered more than he had let on to the Council of Wind and it fascinated him to see that the old knowledge would prove useful once more. Opening the chest, he peered in. "By the Ancestors..." There were hundreds of scrolls and tomes, samples of different bloods and vials of what Thäoldr instinctively recognized as the plague. It was all coming back to him, his early years and the sessions he'd sat and listened to Vaelyn, then his mentor, as he spoke of things to come and how he would make Seran a completely fair land once more. He showed him the alphabet he had gleaned from the Void Sleeper, spoke to him in the tongue of that dark realm. It had been locked away by the Council for the protection of all and he had accepted that necessity, but now the time had come to open the old secrets. Dragging the chest to a table that had survived the onslaught, he delved into the work, looking through what must have been centuries of research, all wasted on death.

As the hours wore on, the trio made their way through the countryside. They had made a brief stop in the Woods of Spirit, reflecting on the lessons they had learned recently. Placing their trust in the spirits, they had drunk deep of the Spring of Strength and the waters rejuvenated them, giving them what they needed to carry on. A few leagues out of the Woods, Khula tapped Karos on the shoulder, causing him to turn. Her hands worked quickly, giving him a question to ponder. "It is past midday and I have not eaten for at least two days. Before we stopped at the Spring, I felt as if I could not go on, but now I feel I could traverse the distance alone. What magic does that spring contain?"

Karos pondered the question for a few moments as he sifted through years of rumors and facts in his head. "It is said that the Spring of Strength is both food and drink, containing precious energy for the body. The Old Scholars say that a past Kingmage created the Spring, though their name escapes me for the moment. It is said to have a source of power buried beneath it, causing the Spring to give life energy to all who drink of it, that even when their bellies are empty and they are on the edge of starvation, they will find the strength to carry on. They say four full cups to be enough to keep an ogre on their feet for a day at least." Karos grinned as the information came rushing back to him. It had been some time since he had last visited those woods and the Spring, so he'd cataloged the information about it away until it was needed. He was planning to say more when Sardra interrupted him.

"Mojhannar was the Kingmage who discovered the Spring."

"Ah! Thank you, Sardra. I cannot believe I had forgotten that."

Sardra smiled at her Warden Ranger. He seemed different now, so much more than when they had begun this journey. Gone was the meek man who doubted everything he did, replaced with a calm, collected Ranger. In the back of her mind, she wondered just how much more he would change before journey's end. She knew she had changed as well, but in what ways, she could not tell yet.

As the day wore on, the three approached the low wall of a small town. Instantly searching his memory, Karos allowed his face to brighten. "Ah! Elday's Rest. Hopefully, we may find some good news here." Picking up his pace, Karos approached the town, keen eyes searching for anything that could tip him off to fell happenings.

"You there! Stay away! The town is ill with plague never seen! We received just enough potions to stave it off thanks to a Rider and a Ranger. We do not have enough– Oh! Master Karos. 'Twas Ranger Ulivar, who delivered us from peril, as well as a Rider whose name I do not know. I find it strange, your Rangers working with Riders, after all the talk of bad blood. What do you make of it?"

"Well, milord, it means things are going to change and for the better. Come, I have a Lady in need of succor and rest. We have been on foot for many leagues."

"Of course, Warden Ranger, of course. Come, the Inn still has supplies. Just... mind not the smell of burned flesh. We found that by keeping the fires going, it burns off the worst of the stink... I wish it were unnecessary, but sometimes fate is unkind." Waving the group onwards, he turned to lead them through the town.

"Pray tell, did Master Berram survive? If memory serves, he and his wife made the most wonderful honey-cakes."

The man responded with a sad shake of the head, taking a few moments before he spoke. "Berram was one of the first we lost, because of his advanced age. His wife followed not long after. We pray The Path is kind to them."

"That is quite upsetting to hear. He was always a goodly half-ling. What of the inn proprietor? What was his name... Lorden? Lorren? Lyrren? It has been many a year since my last visit to your town, milord."

"Lorvin, good sir. And aye, he made it through. But he was none too pleased about how long it took aid to arrive."

"You must realize you were not the only town stricken. Everywhere I went, there were the dead and dying. Sardra, what about you?"

The dokk perked up slightly, raising an eyebrow. "Nay, I cannot say I saw much. I made my way to Eldergrove with Porrik, bless his memory. They were quite untouched, by whatever miracle. Milady Khula? What of you? What have you seen?"

The woman responded with the simple hand-code as always,

not daring to use her voice and start coughing up blood here—they would likely throw her on a pyre, thinking her infected.

"Cúledan was quite problematic. Apart from the nobility and gentry being holed up in Castle Vigilance, there was hardly anyone alive."

Nodding, Karos glanced up at the man, suddenly realizing how rude he had been. "I apologize, milord. What was your name again? You are familiar with mine, but I do not recall yours."

"Nor should you. We have never met. But I am certain all know your name, Karos Warden Ranger. I am Hulmren Wyngart. I own the butcher shop here in town."

"Ahh, many thanks, Hulmren. I am in your debt."

"Nay, Warden Ranger, I– and all of Seran– are in yours. The Riders tell that you found the cure."

"Lady Khula Tallam found *a* cure. But Thäoldr Sagewind is convinced that its effects will be temporary, so he is poring over everything he can to find a true cure. The only reason we left his company is that the Kingmage has sent for us. Which reminds me, Sardra. What delivered the message?"

"A pretty young eagle by the name of Cavarn. Quite talkative. He did not bear the stripes or the vestments of one of the Kingmage's birds, which makes me wonder if the Kingmage was trying to keep attention off him."

Karos nodded and smiled as Hulmren led them up the road to a tavern and he glanced up at the sign, reading it over as they approached the door. *The Golden Stewpot,* he rumbled in his mind, *an interesting name.* They were not in a pleasant part of the town, though with all that had happened, there would not be a *nice* part of town for some time. As the Stewpot's door opened, it confronted Karos with a wonderful array of aromas. Fresh linens, hot cider and stew, gravies, baked bread. It was nearly enough to make him stop short, were it not for the three other people behind him. Entering the establishment awkwardly, he realized that all sounds had stopped, and all eyes were on his troupe. Unsure of what to say, he moved away from the door and stood there waiting for the rest of his party to enter, scanning the room as he did. There were quite a few faces he recognized, at least, and that comforted him... but not nearly as much as he would like.

"Warden Ranger Karos! This is a treat! Come on, get the rest inside. You are letting the warm out!" As soon as the group was inside, the door shut, and the latch clicked. Karos immediately felt trapped and panicked internally. Then a hand touched his, and he looked down, not sure what to expect. The hand was Khula's, and she gently dragged him further into the tavern, waving brightly at the folk who stared. She led him to a table off in the corner where his back would be against a wall- and he would have a clear view of the door. How she had guessed what he was looking for, Karos could not understand, but he appreciated the gesture. Waiting until Sardra and Khula had taken their seats, Karos gave one last look around the Stewpot to ensure no threats would arise- at least for now. When he was content, he lowered himself into his seat and placed his hands on the mahogany table, looking between his companions.

"If our pace holds, we should make the border of Nevian and Dragonmoor in about a week's time. Khula, I apologize for this, but you must do your best to keep up. We cannot afford to slow. If we must, one of us can bear you across the more troublesome parts, should we end up in Nevian."

Khula glared for a moment and signed back her retort

emphatically.

"If you still believe me to be a defenseless flower, I will gladly prove otherwise. I can make the journey, Karos. It is you who must forgive me for being only human. I am not a god walking Seran as you are used to traveling with."

Letting out a bark of laughter, Sardra patted Khula on the shoulder gently. "He meant no offense, young lady. There is no need to chastise him in such a manner. But he is also wrong- we have time to take breaks to rest because Ancestors know what awaits us at the end of this road. We must face our tasks with clear heads." She shot a glare at her Warden Ranger and glanced up as a young maid approached their table. She bore the scars Sardra knew to mean that she had survived the plague and, even with her injuries, she looked wonderful.

"Welcome to The Golden Stewpot, honored guests. I am Tässa, I will serve you. What may I bring you?"

Karos pointed to Sardra and Khula, indicating that they should speak first.

"A bowl of pottage would do me wonders, milady Tässa." Sardra's desires were simple enough when it came to food. Pottage or Hunter's stew was usually enough to keep her happy, along with- "And a mug of cider, please." The girl smiled as she took Sardra's request down and looked to Khula, who had signed her request. Tässa looked confused for a moment before speaking.

"I apologize, milady. I do not speak the hand-signs."

Karos, who had been watching Khula as she spoke, nodded, and cleared his throat. "She requested lamb stew and a glass of your finest wine." Khula nodded, before gesturing her thanks to Karos. He smiled in return and when the maid looked to him, he spoke once more. "I would like a bowl of pottage as well, please, and a mug of cider as well."

The woman nodded and moved away, and Karos leaned into the table. "We may be wise to keep to the road as little as possible. We know not what may await us." The two women nodded, concurring with the Warden Ranger's observation. "But perhaps a horse for lady Khula? I do not doubt your abilities, but it is at least 200 leagues from here. You may try as much as you can, but you are not built as we are."

Khula nodded and sighed, before putting her hands up to sign. "Allow me my pace and to make that request when I will. Do not decide for me. Remember, I killed the last man who tried to decide fate for me."

Nodding sheepishly, Karos continued. "I apologize, Khula. I am not used to dealing so closely with folk other than my Rangers."

Khula nodded gently and continued. "Do not underestimate me, but I believe you know to not underestimate anyone." Then she put her hands down, looking him over. *He is far too used to traveling alone.* She decided she would make it her mission to travel with him as much as possible. She was his friend and felt it her duty to keep him on the best path.

Sardra grinned approvingly at the girl's willingness to take Karos to task. She was already making a fine addition to their traveling troupe, and it was refreshing to have someone else to challenge Karos' assumptions, not just about himself, but about others. "So, what do you make of this summons, Karos? It does not just involve us, but likewise Khula and I am told by Cavarn that the Kingmage sent for Khula's family as well."

Khula flinched at the mention of her family. She was an only child and had very few fond memories of the people who raised her. Shifting her focus back to Sardra, she watched the she-dokk as she spoke.

Sitting up suddenly, Karos cried out as his mind struck a vein of inspiration. "Sardra. I am going to run outside for a moment, I have an idea. Thäoldr needs Rangers to aid him in creating and distributing his cure. I just had a moment of realization- Carwaan! Carwaan should be nearby!"

Sardra resisted the urge to clap and nodded slowly.

"Of course, Carwaan the Great would aid us well. Perhaps he is with kin in the area?"

Grinning, Karos shot from his chair and slipped out of the Inn. Once outside, he placed his fingers between his lips and let out a piercing whistle. Many inside the in clapped their hands to their ears, crying out in pain, but Sardra and Khula seemed unfazed. In fact, Sardra chuckled at the reactions of the folk around them and shook her head. When the whistling had stopped, everyone looked outside in mixed shock and annoyance, with a few scattered folk grumbling.

That died away when they saw Carwaan.

The massive great raven landed lightly near Karos, letting out a series of croaks and caws. He was quite talkative today, for there was much that had transpired in the past few days. He hopped back and forth rapidly and head-butted Karos gently, rubbing his head against the man's stomach, before letting out a soft croak.

"No, Carwaan. I am not going anywhere, my friend. I did not mean to scare you." He could feel the creature's disquieted mind, the emotions running through its head. The bird was worried about him, saddened that he had been driven to the edge once more. Gently, the creature closed its beak around one of his fingers, tugging gently until he placed another finger atop its beak. Tenderly, Karos stroked the creature's head with his thumb. Khula interrupted him, tapping him on the shoulder and he glanced up to see her hands moving.

"What is this incredible creature?" Wonder filled her eyes as she beheld Carwaan. She could hardly find the focus to sign; such was her excitement, and she came around Karos to see the magnificent beast better. As she did, Carwaan untangled himself from the embrace he held Karos in and made a show of backing away.

"This is Carwaan, chieftain of all Great Ravens. He has been my guide and companion for many years and serves the Rangers. He is more intelligent than most beasts and can recognize and vocalize the faces and names of all Rangers and more than a few folk."

The great raven regarded Khula with intelligent eyes, blinking occasionally. Then he looked back at Karos. He croaked out a single word, looking between the two. "Who?"

"That is Khula, Carwaan. Khula friend."

"Khula friend?"

"Aye, my friend. Khula."

The bird hopped to-and-fro for a moment, excited to meet someone new. Then he let out a sharp caw and poked at Khula with his beak. She nearly yelped, jumping back slightly.

"He will not harm you, Khula, be not afraid. Here. Give him some of these." Reaching into one of his pouches, he extracted a handful of dried highberries, pressing them into Khula's hand. Nodding, she took the berries and extended her hand to Carwaan, who immediately plucked a few berries from the pile. As he ate, the great raven made a pleased sort of croaking noise, before digging through the pile of highberries. Emboldened by this display, Khula reached out to pet the creature, running her fingers over the gold stripe running down his head to his tail.

"See? He is a wonderful creature."

They sat there for some time, feeding the raven and talking to him, when Karos finally shifted his focus from teaching Khula about him.

"Now, Carwaan. Listen." Immediately, the bird's head turned to regard Karos, the eyes watching him unblinkingly. When he was sure he had Carwaan's attention, Karos continued to speak, slipping in and out of the Lifesong without thinking about it.

"Carwaan, *ka teljt*. You must seek out all *Tengarii* you can. Send them to *Qayzar'haftalo Thäoldrii*. He sits near the shores of *Laghe Valorii*. Two *qayzarii* are with him, great black beasts. They will not harm you."

Carwaan bobbed his head as Karos spoke, quickly memorizing everything he was told.

"Now be off, my friend, and may the winds carry you to a warm sun!"

The raven pecked gently at Karos, croaked at Khula and then was off, hopping into flight and spreading his great wings to their eight-foot span. Within moments, he was over the top of the buildings and Karos gave a salute to the creature, placing his fist over his chest. Then, he led Khula back inside the Golden Stewpot and back to their table, waiting for her to seat herself first. She was extremely excited as she signed to him, her hands flashing quickly.

"He is such a beautiful creature..."

"Indeed. Long has he served... some say he is older than I am and has been with the Rangers since the childhood of Thorvan Koza."

Smiling as Tässa made her way back to their table, Karos

shifted slightly, bracing himself further against the wall. The woman placed the drinks before them and stood back, bowing slightly before backing away.

Khula focused on her wine, gingerly taking a drink. She was not expecting much from it, given that they were nowhere near a capitol, but she was pleasantly surprised. *A good vintage,* she thought to herself, *quite pleasant.* Glancing to her companions to see them already drinking deep of their cider, she chuckled gently. She did not enjoy wine as much as her parents or Magus had, but it seemed to be safer than water in most places.

When Tässa returned, bringing their food, Sardra looked longingly at the bowls of pottage. It had been almost a week since she'd eaten last and she could feel her stomach's protests growing ever louder. Once the food was in front of her, she discarded almost all formality- apart from waiting until all were served- and began digging into the rich stew happily. Karos was not far behind, working at his meal with a deep hunger born of self-imposed starvation. Khula was the only one among them to eat with some decorum, after placing a napkin in her lap. But after a few moments, she was hungrily wolfing down her lamb stew, having suddenly remembered that it had been quite an ordeal since she had eaten last.

Tässa watched them eat for just a moment, shocked that such heroes had so little in the way of table manners. Glancing up at the innkeeper for support, she readied herself to say something when he waved her to move over to him. Once she was in polite speaking range, Lorvin shook his head gently. "Do not pay them any mind, Tässa. They do not intend to be rude; it is just the way of the Rangers to eat with so little thought and decorum. After all, it is said that to discipline themselves, a Ranger will often go a week or more without eating." The woman's eyes widened as she gave thought to that fact.

"Why, that is terrible. How do they even function?"

"It is said that instead of food, most Rangers draw nourishment from the dew and the warmth of the sun, though they eat small snacks on the road. I remember when I was an adventurer, back in my youth, I happened across a Ranger and he shared what they call *pul'gra'an* with me. A single lump smaller than your fist could keep me on my feet for almost three days. Long have I been trying to replicate their recipe from what I tasted with little success." Lorvin chuckled gently and shrugged slightly. "So, their lack of propriety is understandable. After all, would you not eat like a starved wolf after a sevenday of no food?"

"I am ashamed to admit that I have, master Lorvin. After I recovered from the Plague, I was insatiable for more than a few days. Sadly," the girl sniffled slightly, "I do not seem to have the same charm as I did before, nor can I use magic quite as well."

"But you had such pride in your little spells. Have you any idea what happened?"

"I have none."

Karos had been listening unintentionally the whole conversation and finally interjected. Making his way over, he cleared his throat.

"You say your magic has been affected after your bout with the Plague?"

"Aye, Master Karos."

This was troubling to the Ranger, and he wondered if it had anything to do with the cure they had come up with. Nodding slowly, he stepped away and back to his spot at the table, gently tapping Khula on the shoulder. She came up for air from her ravenous feeding and looked at him.

"Khula, remind me, what herbs did we put in the curative potion we created?"

"Karos, for shame, can you not see the girl is starvi-"

"Sardra, hold your tongue for now. Chastise me later, this is important. A girl has mentioned that her magical abilities have waned since her affliction, and something in my mind believes it may be connected to the cure."

"But-"

"Sardra, this is something that *must* be investigated. Think of it, how many folk of Seran depend on magic for daily tasks, even to survive?"

Sardra's hands shot to her mouth as she realized the gravity of the situation. "I see what you mean, Karos."

Khula was glad for the interruption, though, as it gave her time to clear her mind from the past few days. Nothing had gone well for her, but that was beside the point. She needed other things to think about, other things to occupy her. Thinking hard for a moment, she pictured each herb and began signing.

"Dragon's Pipe may be the culprit."

"What makes you say that, Khula?"

Her hands worked at a dizzying speed as she explained something that, to his great surprise, Karos had never learned.

"Dragon's Pipe damages the magical pathways for quite some time, stunting their regrowth. It may take a full year to recover."

"And in that time... Khula. Do you know of any method to speak across distances?"

"I was attuned with Namryll while we rode. I could calm

her."

"I need you to speak to her again. Relay this information in its entirety. Carwaan will bring all the Rangers he can."

Karos' face went a terrifying shade of white as he realized just how critical of a discovery this was, and it meant that the cure Khula had created could fail much sooner than expected.

Khula focused her mind, piercing through the veil of pain and anger. She reached out as far as she dared and then pushed a little bit farther. It took considerable effort, but she could touch Namryll's mind, startling the dragon awake.

"Namryll."

Yes, young one?

"I bear a message from the Warden Ranger. Aid is coming, but time is short. Thäoldr must find his cure soon, or all is lost. He believes our cure is not enough."

I will inform him, young mistress.

9

9: Westerspring

F ar and away, Thäoldr's work took on a fevered pace as he double- and triple-checked each piece of information.

"Damnitall. I run into dead ends everywhere I go. Everything Vaelyn had written was a mess. What little makes sense soon devolves into gibbering inanity and cursing all who walk Seran."

Thäoldr, Khula sends word. Rangers are coming, as many as can be summoned in a short time. But she also cautions that we must make all haste. Karos believes their cure insufficient; more so than we do.

"Nedah. Time is against us, Namryll."

Another voice chimed in, a deeper, sorrowful voice.

Perhaps I may be of help, young Thäoldr.

"Talakath? What would possess you to aid us?"

To make right what was wrong.

Thäoldr could not argue with that, and he was thankful that the beast had chosen to come to their aid. As he sifted through the seemingly endless scrolls, he found himself looking at them with new understanding, as Talakath gifted what she knew. With his knowledge growing, the ancient Rider understood just what he was up against.

"He used Mirror Magic, the bastard. But he was a fool. He must not have thought I would be here."

Grinning, Thäoldr found what he was looking for- a basic counter to the plague that had been created. *He calls it a 'virus' and denotes the meaning of a plague that is alive. Fascinating.* He took a breath and looked over the reagents that would make up the counter, thinking that there must be some nearby. The chest seemed to hold an incredible amount of space within, so Thäoldr searched as much as he could until he found something that seemed important. A leather satchel with a label of 'do not discard' tied to it. Immediately, he removed the satchel from the chest and laid it open to reveal jars of every reagent that seemed possible.

"Thank dal'Kiyr. Now let us see what we can brew."

Striding over to Namryll, Thäoldr went through his saddle-bags, quickly pulling out a small chemist's set. It was not exactly standard equipment, but then again, Thäoldr wasn't a run-of-the-mill Rider. Unpacking his kit, he began looking over each of the reagents and reading off the instructions left behind. *Evidently Vaelyn had planned for this to be used on folk who willingly followed his madness,* the elf thought. Bringing water up from the stream in what they left of the cave was easy enough, but when he went to touch his tattoos, he groaned slightly, remembering that they were gone.

"Damn you, Vaelyn."

Sighing, the elf resigned himself to using vocal incantations and tracing the magic's path into existence to start his fire on the fuel he had found and assembled. Once the fire was crackling happily, he placed a small cauldron of water next to it to boil. He felt a tickle in the back of his throat and grunted before a coughing fit overtook him and he realized the stakes had just climbed. He was infected, and he thought of the reason- Karos had once said his artifice arm, and the magic required to use it, would protect him... but he no longer had his artifice arm, which meant that protective magic was no longer coursing through him.

As he fought to regain control of his body, he coughed up a clot of blood and sighed, before turning back to his work. *More reason to sort this problem,* he thought to himself. Sighing, the ancient elf looked over what he had to work with. Nodding thoughtfully, he pondered the recipes in his head, going over each and every option that Talakath had gifted him the knowledge of. Taking in a deep breath, he began his work.

Quickly selecting the first of the reagents, he cut them into the pieces suggested by the recipe. There was death-shade, sarashal, spiderthorn, talthras. *Mix well the talthras with the blood of a black dragon, separated into the four humors. Black bile being the first. Well, that is an interesting addition and quite quaint, considering that the humoral method was abandoned almost ten centuries ago.*

"Namryll."

I hear your thoughts. How am I to aid you?

"I need to collect a small quantity of your blood, that I may separate it into the various humors."

Of course. Do you have a vial at the ready?

Thäoldr moved quickly, grabbing a larger vial and making his way to Namryll. Carefully, the dragon drew the claw of one foot across the opposing foreleg. This drew a good quantity of blood from the dragon, which Thäoldr quickly gathered in the vial. *Now how am I to separate the blood into the humors? I do not have the time to let this vial sit.*

As if she were waiting to answer, Talakath spoke in the elf's mind.

Inside Vaelyn's chest, you should be able to find a small wheel connected to a crank by gears. He called it a centrifuge. It has slots for seven vials of blood. He spun it as fast as he could for ten minutes to separate the blood in the vials.

"Many thanks, Talakath."

Seeking the item, he looked it over. It was a strange device, but then again, it came from a mind dabbling in magic far beyond the world of Seran, so anything was to be expected. Taking the vial and placing it in one slot, he turned the crank. To his wonder and surprise, the wheel spun and the faster he turned the crank, the faster the wheel turned, until the vial was a blur in his eyes. Faster and faster he turned before he realized his arm would grow tired long before he reached the time. With a sudden burst of inspiration, he threw some magic into the centrifuge and removed his hand. Sure enough, it kept spinning at the rate it was meant to. Grinning, he mixed the other reagents into the cauldron, checking his measurements on every single one. It had to be perfect, else innocent people would die needlessly.

"Namryll, Talakath. I am afraid to ask this of you, but I have a feeling we will need quite a quantity of blood from each of you."

I stand by your side, Thäoldr, as I do in all things. Namryll's reply was reassuring and gave him hope.

I pledged to make right this wrong and should I die in doing so, I welcome it. My rider dishonored my name and the name of the Riders of Gelvrentael. Talakath's response worried Thäoldr slightly, but he was glad for the beast's willingness to give her life for the cause. It was a courage seldom seen in black dragons. Honestly, it was a courage seldom seen in *any* creature, and Thäoldr knew it. But from a black dragon, who were usually the most self-serving of all dragon breeds, the most chaotic, even... It was something else entirely.

When ten minutes had elapsed, Thäoldr quickly dispelled the enchantment he had placed upon the centrifuge. It slowed to a stop, and the elf beheld the fruits of his labor with a fair amount of joy. The blood had separated into four distinct parts, which Thäoldr knew from his studies were not different substances, but merely parts to a whole.

"The black bile, as it used to be called and is rather known as the agent by which scabs form. It is called a clot." He murmured to himself as he drew each of the substances off into their own vials. Adding the clotted blood to the cauldron, he watched as it bubbled and changed colors. Then he glanced at the recipe once more. "Add next the phlegm." He was unsure of what this substance was at first, but a quick look back into the old things he remembered gave him the answer. The white substance, of which there was little. Pouring it into the mixture, he nearly gagged as a stench of decay flowed upward. "Followed by the yellow bile." This one Thäoldr could recognize easily. The scholars of the Healing Halls called it 'serum' and said it was the liquid in which the blood flowed. Pouring that in, he held his nose for a moment before he began coughing once more. Spitting out another clot of blood, he took a breath and shook his head. He could feel himself having trouble breathing, and he knew time was running short. "Finally, the blood, added with the venom of a spintki."

Shaking his head, Thäoldr added both reagents into the

mixture and looked at the result. The liquid had turned blood red and had an odor of death, and he was wary of it. But knowing his time was short either way, he threw caution to the wind and filled a vial, allowing the potion to cool before glancing at the instructions- drink as fast as one can. Sighing, he held his breath and downed the vial in one shot.

Immediate regret followed his actions. Thankfully, he did not have to think about the taste for long, as it overloaded his senses and he lost consciousness. He did not notice the sun rising in the east, or the carrion birds gaining an interest in his unmoving body.

He found himself falling through... nothing. If falling was the right word. The sensation was there, but nothing else. *How can one fall when there is nothing around them?* He wondered, trying to make sense of the absolute darkness he seemed to be careening through. But even as he felt the sensation of plummeting through the darkness, he also felt the reassuring ground beneath him. The two sensations fought each other, confusing the elf as his mind fought against what was going on. *Did we mix something wrong? Is this death?*But there was no feeling of fading, no slowing of breath or heartbeat. He was simply *falling.*

Closing his eyes, Thäoldr tried to will the sensation away. Tried to reach out to something, *anything* to bring him back to reality. He heard Namryll's voice, but she sounded leagues away. Far enough away, in fact, that he couldn't make out her speech. Blinking, or at least thinking he blinked, the elf tried to reason with his mind, with his body. To wake up and see everything around him again. The sun beat down on his fair skin, baking what was exposed as the elf lay insensate. But he didn't know what was going on outside of his mental prison.

Namryll watched her rider, concern sending yellows and reds through her opalescent eyes. A quick glance to the sky told the black dragon that carrion birds were taking an interest in his body, thinking him dying or dead. Craning her neck, she let out a challenging bugle, loud enough that the birds, though high above, got the hint and scattered into the distance, frustrated. Then she extended a protective wing over Thäoldr, placing him in a fleshy tent as he fought with demons she didn't know a thing about. She could feel his mind wrestling with... *something.* It was something dark and evil. Something cruel and wicked. Something from far beyond their world, and yet so terrifyingly close. Even as Namryll tried to reach out to Thäoldr's mind, she found *something else* blocking her from being able to reach the elf.

Inside the darkness, Thäoldr wrestled with his own thoughts, with his own mind, trying to win back control of himself. For hours unknown to him, he fought with what he *thought* was himself. But little by little, the elf began to realize he wasn't fighting something he knew. He wasn't fighting something familiar. This was a presence he'd never known, never felt, and never realized before. But it was *powerful.* Powerful beyond anything he'd ever felt, and the elf wondered exactly how he could wrest himself from such a grasp. *But you must fight!* A voice broke in, unfamiliar and yet so tantalizingly dear. A feminine voice, slicing through the fog and the darkness.

The voice came again, and with it came a pinprick of light, seemingly so far in the distance as to be unreachable. But Thäoldr fought with the utter lack of sensation everywhere and tried to move toward the light. But there was no movement. No sensation of walking, running, or even crawling. The light grew.

Then a voice called out. The most awful, ear-wrenching voice Thäoldr had heard in his long life. At first, it was nothing but a screeching, screaming noise. So the elf focused on the noise, distracted from the light. *You will be lost here forever!* It called to him, trying to force him to give up. But he fought it with all his might. Fought the urge to give in and just stop trying.

But the other voice beckoned once more and the light grew brighter. It was still far, far away, but the voice was growing stronger. More insistent. Bolder. Slowly, Thäoldr felt some sort of movement other than falling. This time, he was moving toward the light, as if he were being pulled. But then something caught him from behind, and he felt as if his consciousness, not his body, were being stretched. Fought to be dragged two different ways. And it *hurt.* He let out a soundless scream as they dragged his consciousness from what seemed like every direction, stretching and threatening to tear him into pieces.

After what seemed an eternity to the poor elf, something won. Suddenly, the pulling from one direction stopped, and he felt himself being pulled inexorably toward the light. Even as he was, Thäoldr felt a surge of utter terror as the light closed in. *What if the light is the wrong way? Without knowing what it is...* He tried to shake off the crippling fear as he was pulled toward the light. Toward something he didn't know.

Then the light was extinguished as something got in the way. A black rage boiled within Thäoldr at the loss of the comforting... *comforting? A moment ago it was terrifying.* Without knowing it, he blinked. Once more, he was fighting between two other consciousnesses. One felt familiar. Dear to heart. The other felt like an anchor tied around his neck, dragging him down, deeper and deeper into the black. He began choking, drowning in nothing as it dragged him further into the depths of the black.

Suddenly, a firm hand slapped Thäoldr on the back. He coughed and spewed the nothing from his lungs, from his throat, into the utter nothing around. With a soundless scream, he heaved breath back into his starving lungs. *What torture is this?* He wondered as unknown hands hauled him from the depths. Something was trying to eradicate him. Something else was trying to save him. And here he was, poor mortal, caught in the middle of this titanic struggle.

A comforting pressure met the bottom of Thäoldr's body, and he lay there quietly for a time. Focusing through the mess of emotions running through his mind, the elf tried to make sense of what was going on. He was being tortured, that much he could work out. But when it seemed as if he could go on no further, something... *something* saved him. *What is the purpose of this torture*, he wondered. *How long have I been unconscious?* Another thought that plagued him. He didn't know what was going on outside, didn't know that his dragon was shielding him from unfriendly eyes.

He was about to try and marshal his strength and return to his body, or at least try to, when searing pain ripped through his consciousness. Every nerve felt as if it were being seared to the core. Every moment was a lifetime of agony as some consciousness directed incredible rage toward him. *Toward me.* Another soundless scream tore its way out of the elf, but he refused to give into the pain. Though he hadn't the slightest idea of what the consciousness wanted, or was trying to force him to do, he knew one thing. *I... must... resist!* And so, for what felt like an eternity striving against a will that somehow Thäoldr knew could crush his mind with the slightest of thoughts, he focused through the pain. Pain was an old friend of Thäoldr's, and he knew it wasn't real in this instance. It *felt* real enough, but there was that hint at the end of each pulse. That subtle promise that *if you comply...* But again, the Sage of Wind didn't even know what the malicious consciousness *wanted* from him. Even without that knowledge, though, he knew in his core. *I must not give in.* Even against the searing pain, the feeling of being ripped apart, inch by inch, the elf held strong.

And then the pain stopped, ripped away in an exultant feeling of relief that left the elf gasping for breath. His mind calmed down from the agony, and if his heart felt anything, he wagered it would be calming back down. A coolness flowed over him, soothing his aching consciousness, his burning nerves. *Is this the work of the other?* He wondered, trying to put a name to the consciousness that was helping him, and half wondering if it was just another side of the same coin. *I will take what I can get,* he reasoned, and lay there, giving his body time to calm down and accept the gentle coolness.

Namryll watched as Thäoldr's body convulsed. She couldn't push through to touch his mind. To see what he was warring against. Her opalescent eyes whirled. Red, orange, and yellow sparkles shining in the deep pools of her eyes as she watched, helpless, as her rider thrashed and contorted. A soothing pressure abruptly weighed her mind down, and she looked up to see Talakath staring her down, green and blue waves flowing through her eyes. *Calm. He needs you calm, even if you cannot actively touch his mind, my daughter.* The pressure increased, even as Namryll instinctively fought the calming waves. *You cannot help him but by your presence and pressure. Nothing else you can do.* Again and again, the dragon sent calm, peaceful thoughts to her daughter. Trying to keep her from worrying herself to death, which was entirely possible at the moment. *Focus, Namryll. Focus, Last Shadow. You must be calm. Let the river flow around you, let it carry you. Do not try to master what is infinitely your greater. Even the great boulder knows to let the world carry it to where it must be.*

It worked. A little, at first, but the whirling colors in Namryll's eyes began to slow. Her massive heart, beating far faster than it was ever meant to, began to calm. Her breathing evened out. Soon enough, her eyes returned to their deep, passive indigo coloration, and with the pressure her mother kept on her mind, the dragon was soon lulled to rest. Talakath took up the watch over her daughter and her rider, occasionally glancing at Thäoldr's body and wondering what the elf was fighting. Something in her heart, though, gave her the answer. *The Void-Sleeper.* She shuddered at the very mention of that ghastly name. A creature of such evil, such keen malice, was able to turn her rider completely mad. *And if Thäoldr isn't careful, it will claim his mind as well.* Exhaling a soft sigh, the gargantuan black dragon laid her head on her forepaws and watched her daughter and her rider. Inwardly, she wondered if Vaelyn could've been saved from his path. Even as she wondered that, though, she found that she didn't care. *He made his choice. And it was his end.*

Content, the black dragon gave a gentle puff of air to a dandelion that was ready to spread its seeds. The tiny pappus of each seed caught the puff, breaking them loose from the head of the flower and sending them into the air. Idly, the dragon watched as the tiny seeds drifted on the wind, sailing higher and higher and dispersing outward. There was little other movement, even as the sun beat down on the two dragons and the elf one sheltered. Sighing gently, Talakath looked over at her daughter. There was so much she wanted to say, so much she needed to say. But she knew in her heart she wouldn't have the chance. It was rare for a dragon to outlive their rider, but... with a casual glance over to where the floating cloud of energy that *had* until recently been Mulrah Vaelyn, she wondered if she really had. But in that moment, purpose set into her mind. If she could find a way to help... *even at the cost of my life, I will set this right.*

Back in Thäoldr's consciousness, things had taken a turn for the worse once more. Now, instead of drowning, burning, or being pulled apart, he was being frozen. Little by little, he could feel his temperature dropping to agonizing levels and staying there. Even as he fought with the pain, something in his mind told him to endure. That he *must* endure, even to the end of his strength and sanity. Clenching the teeth he had in his consciousness, the elf did his best to fight through the utter, biting cold that seemed to permeate his very being. A single thought popped into his mind, and he would've laughed if he were conscious. *After all this, I need a stiff drink.* That thought buoyed his mood for a bit.

But then the pain returned double, as if one of the beings vying for his mind was angry that he'd *dared* find humor in his situation. Another soundless scream. Another silent, agonized wail. But still the elf held on to his mind and the secrets within. Some other voice from far and away told him he *needed* to hold on for as long as he could. That it would be worth it in the end. But his own mind fought against even that idea, wondering how much more he could take. *How can I fight this, when I do not even know what I am fighting?* The cold crawled further up his legs and arms. Or at least, that's where he felt it crawling. His fingers ached abominably, his toes seared with cold. But still he held on.

Doggedly, Thäoldr tried to think of happy memories. Something to distract him from the agony he was facing. Sorting through his twelve centuries of life, the elf revisited old times. The birth of his daughter, Cirhael. *How elated we were to see her for the first time, especially after our love's labors.* He'd been as good a father as he could be, or at least he hoped so. But duty had always been first in his mind, even if Cirhael and her mother were first in his heart. He'd already been making a name for himself in the Order, and he remembered his wife fondly. She'd been a strong woman, to the last. Wistfully, he drifted through his memories until he settled on another one.

Cirhael being chosen by the chalice. Her blood causing the liquid inside to flare up in brilliant sparks, signifying that she, like her father, was destined to be a Rider of the Order of Gelvrentael. And then, the absolute joy when her dragon, Briem, had chosen her, and the aftermath of that hatching. The agonizing years where he'd been forced to hand off her training to others, while duty called him away to other lands. Searching his memory, the elf tried to remember if it was during that time he'd gotten his favorite scar. A scar that, like most of the rest of the decorations telling his twelve century story, was gone. *Damn you, Vaelyn. Damn you forevermore!* He cried out soundlessly, his rage threatening to take the forefront of his mind. Quickly, he fought it back down and focused on the happy memories. The memory of flying with his daughter for the first time popped into his head, and he couldn't help but feel his heart swell. *Oh, how nervous she'd been.* Even with the training she and Briem had gone through, Cirhael was still so nervous that Thäoldr could still see how white her knuckles were on the flight belts.

And then, as if the other consciousness' anger surged to new heights, the cold became so deep, so utterly rabid, that the elf couldn't focus on anything but the pain. For what seemed an eternity, he was trapped as chills and aches wracked his body, his sensitive areas searing with icy fire. But he fought through it, fought for every inch of his sanity, even as a being far more powerful than he could ever hope to be clawed at every corner of his mind. *Powerful,* he thought, *but I am Thäoldr Sagewind, and I am indomitable!* In a moment of incredible defiance, of impossible courage, an unbridled flame burst out of Thäoldr's mind. Everything went brilliantly white, and he could hear one consciousness shriek in incomprehensible agony and rage, while another, soothing consciousness laughed in a sound like water trickling over rocks. He kept up that defiance as long as he could, until suddenly, everything was extinguished. All three consciousnesses, his own included, went silent, and everything, though already black, went somehow *blacker,* and Thäoldr could think no more.

10: Westerspring and Dragonmoor

Once rested and ready to fly again, Viktor and Helve rode as Alvarath and Vu'Locav made a leisurely southwestern drift towards Dragonmoor and Starwatch Keep. As they caught the occasional updraft or downdraft, the two dragons lazily watched each other's back. It was about midday when they neared a tower in the wilds of Westerspring and a dragon called out a challenge to them, which the white and red echoed in kind.

He is requesting that we land and stop for a briefing with the Master of the Watch here. Vu'Locav drawled to Viktor as the two dragons winged around the tower, descending in a rather lazy, if safe, flight pattern. As soon as they'd landed, a man dressed in flying leathers and wearing a gold shoulder rope stormed out of the tower.

"Flame it and scorch it, I do not know who your Lanceleader is, but when I figure out their name, their neck is min-" The man paused as he observed the two riders and the dragons, *clearly* not of the Order. A half-giant strode up to him and spoke rather impertinently.

"Whate'er the need for this briefing is, we must be swift. I have things to do."

"Excuse me? *Initiate,* you will-" The man puffed out his chest and pointed to his shoulder cord.

"Initiate? You must be quite the addled man if you think I am with the Order of Gelvrentael. No disrespect to the order, but I am not one of your lackeys," Viktor said calmly, doing his best to maintain an even composure against the man's blustering. The urge to pick him up and set him at eye level was maddening, though Viktor knew it would not do to insult or humiliate such a person. He recognized the gold shoulder cord- this was a Premier of the Order, one of the most skilled, and indeed dangerous, people possible.

"Then why in Ara's name are you flying with dragons? Hmm?" The man tried to look bigger, and Viktor sighed.

"*Clearly* you have not heard of me, so I will forgive your insults. I am Viktor Budstyn, son of Calem, son of Ulfric, current of the line of Mastersmiths of The Dragonforge of Coldforge. This is my Forge-Second, Helve Uhfalo. And these dragons are blood-pledged to my line. This is Vu'Locav the Balefire, and Alvarath the Frostwing." He said carefully, introducing himself as some of the folk of the Order had taught him. "I greet you in kindness, and ask again to be swift with your request, for I have a delivery to make to the Kingmage and his sister." He finished with his task and watched the Premier's eyes change. Immediately, he was almost.. *deflated?* Perhaps at losing the chance to yell at an initiate? Who knew? After a few moments, though, he puffed himself back up and nodded.

"Right. Well met Viktor, Rider of Vu'Locav, and Helve, Rider of Alvarath. *I am Prem-*" He stopped for a moment and took a breath. Immediately, his puffing stopped, and he looked *even more* deflated. Mumbling something under his breath, the man nodded. "Yes... of course, Orith." Glancing away for a moment, the man sighed. "My apologies, *Craftmaster*." He used the term appropriately and respectfully. Certainly, he could kill them both in an instant. But after speaking with his dragon, he knew they could do far worse to him, especially if he was rude, to their annoyance. "I am Jorgin, rider of Orith. Premier and all that. I apologize, but have you not heard?"

"Heard?" Viktor said.

"There is a plague going around, the likes of which have not been seen in our history. Please, come into my Watch. Orith will find your dragons some food, and I will likewise find some for you as I give you the briefing." With a nod, Viktor half-crouched to walk through the stone door, and everyone followed him. Once Viktor had arranged himself at a table, Helve followed suit, and then the Premier took a seat. "Right. Plague. Littlebrook-Once-Besieged is all but decimated. There're hundreds of towns I have not heard from. Riders I have heard nothing from in weeks. Something fell is going around, and I have only been lucky enough to avoid infection by way of my isolation with my Lance."

Viktor sucked in a breath and winced at the thought of a plague decimating Littlebrook. *Such a nice town. That is indeed a pity.* "Very well. We are bound for Starwatch to deliver a great blade and spear to Kingmage Harthos Harrolsen and his sister. Are there any places we should avoid? What path should we take?"

The Premier scratched his chin for a moment and took a breath. "I would avoid all Watches unless they call for you. Towns and hamlets the same. Rest only in the wilds. But be careful of fell folk or ruffians. The Rangers are about, and that never bodes well."

"What is the great friction between your people?" Helve asked, unprompted. Normally, the Premier would take the woman to task for speaking to him, but then he remembered before. She could destroy his entire life without raising a blade.

"It is a millennia old hatred," began Viktor, to the surprise of the Premier. "It started at the siege of the Nexus, where the Rangers and Scouts felled dragons that had aligned themselves with the Nexus."

"Rather than..?"

"Rather than allow the Order to take care of traitors, as it should be." Jorgin said rather gruffly. "They spilled dragon and rider blood despite their low station, and that is unforgivable.

Viktor scoffed gently, but said nothing for now. The Premier continued. "And they were unapologetic, even going so far as to challenge the Riders there if they felt they were in the right. Which, they were *not*, given their ways."

"Save for the fact that the dragons and riders of the Order were late for the party." Viktor grunted. "And since then, there has been a cold sort of war between them. Proxy battles here and there, but no *outright* bloodshed. Mate, I suggest you forget that shit, it were millennia before your time."

"I would, *Craftmaster*, but it is a thing of the Honor of the Order." Jorgin snarled gently, and Viktor blinked.

"How many of your Order are cold by the cause of this plague, Jorgin?" Viktor responded, his tone even and calm. "How many men, women, and children that your Order claims to protect are now dead by this plague?"

"I fail to see–"

"A number, Premier." The Mastersmith demanded. After a moment of muttering and thinking and talking to Orith, the man had the answer.

"Around five hundred-thousand in Dragonmoor alone, according to estimates. It is difficult to get our numbers, but dragons say the dead of the Order number in the thousands. At least forty percent our numbers, perhaps."

"Ask the dead if that honor matters. Stand in their ashes and ask the ghosts of hundreds of thousands of souls, your own kin included, if honor, or in fact, that event, matters in the fucking least." Viktor snapped. There was an uncomfortable silence afterward. One that persisted for a few minutes.

They ate in silence, with Jorgin still unwilling to answer. Viktor and Helve, though, had their own answer. Honor didn't matter at a time like this. *Survival* did. *If this Premier was unwilling or unable to see that,* mused the Mastersmith of the Dragonforge, *perhaps they are not as clever as we first were led to believe.* When Viktor and Helve finally left the tower to wait for Alvarath and Vu'Locav, they could hear the Premier speaking to his Lance. "I need you to seek out every Ranger you can. Tell them you come in peace, and that you are at their disposal for the duration of this crisis."

"Are you certain?" spoke one voice.

"Fuck's sake, I am certain. Would you ask a mountain if it is stone?" The Premier barked. Within minutes, the Lance streamed out of the Watch and waited. Viktor and Helve saddled up when their dragons landed, and were back aloft within a few minutes and on their way. As they flew over the green country, the two friends continued their lazy flight, wary of the plague, but unknowing of whatever other dangers awaited.

When night approached, they'd just crossed the bordering Wyrmspine Mountains into Dragonmoor, and found their way to a cave, big enough for themselves and the dragons, to rest. With a sigh, Helve found herself far too keyed up to sleep. Pacing back and forth, she debated the things in her heart. The things in her head. Her red hair flowed over her shoulders, her silver eyes shined with annoyance. Rage. Impatience. And... *want? What do I want?* She asked herself.

With a glance over at the peacefully dozing Viktor, the woman *realized*. Chuckling, she wondered if the big oaf would even notice her trying to woo him. Debating the intelligence of such a move, the woman shrugged and decided to try something simple at first. Walking over and settling in beside him, she leaned her form against the Dragonsmith's bulky frame, crossed her arms over her chest, and did her best to try to sleep.

"Need something, Helve?" The half-giant grunted gently. *Oh, so he is not asleep*, she realized with a start.

"Rest. Comfort. The Premier's words put me off me coals a bit." She muttered. Snuggling against the massive man, she tried to make it obvious that she wanted physical contact with him. Alas, he was somewhere else in his thoughts, and instead offered a flight cloak to her as a blanket.

"If plague makes it to Northrealm, we will deal with it then." He said tiredly. Wrapping the cloak around her with one arm, the man nonetheless didn't make any moves to embrace her. Annoyed, she snuggled against him regardless and found herself drifting rather quickly into a dreamless sleep.

When she awoke, Helve found herself still curled up against

Viktor. Still wrapped in his flight cloak, which she mirthfully reckoned she could use as a tent. He was asleep, and definitely more than a little. Snoring like an angry bear, twitching occasionally. But his right hand sat near the haft of his forge hammer, cocked to bring it to bear. *No doubt an old adventurer thing,* she thought. Taking a breath, she glanced out of the cave to see what looked like snow falling. *Is it winter?*

Those are ashes, said Vu'Locav sorrowfully. *Many people nearby have died and their corpses are being burned for safety.* Helve winced and realized just how small her problem really was. How insignificant she must be, complaining about a lack of affection while others were burning their loved ones. Their spouses, their children. *No.* Said a voice rather sharply. *Pain is not for sport. There is no winner at pain, and one person's is not less than yours, nor is yours less than theirs.* The dragon said gently. *You long for something you think you cannot have. They long for something they have lost.*

Nodding, Helve made up her mind a moment later. Shaking Viktor gently, she tried to rouse the massive man. In response, he snored louder. *What do you wish to do?*

I am going to make him talk to me. She said a moment later. *Actually. Fucking. Talk. To me.* Gently, she pulled away from the man and threw the cloak over him before beating on him. Again, he snored and grumbled, but didn't wake. At least, not until Alvarath let out a bellowing call.

Instantly, he was on his feet. Hammer at the ready, he shoved Helve behind him protectively, though he knew she could easily defend herself. His feet naturally planted themselves at the width of his massive shoulders, and he angled himself to take a blow. "Easy!" Helve shouted. "There is no peril."

"Then why- Alvarath, you *git!*" He said before breaking into laughter. "What is the urgent matter?"

"*Me.*" Said Helve, sticking her thumbs in her belt and staring up at the man. "*I* am the *matter* right now. Come." She commanded, and somehow, the burly half-giant meekly obeyed, following her as she walked to the back of the cave. Throwing down his cloak, she set up a quick spread of food and wine before ordering him to sit.

"What is wrong, Helve?"

Where to begin, thought the woman. *Where to begin.* Taking a breath, the woman looked at Viktor while she prepared a slice of cheese and chunk of bread to eat. Pondering her words carefully, the woman swallowed her cheese and took a breath. "What do you see when you look at me, Viktor?"

"What do you mean?"

Scoffing, the woman shifted herself and looked at him once more. "What. Do you *see*. When you look at me, Viktor?" She was making a show of trying to seem sultry and inviting. Angling herself so her fair framed her face, shifting so her bust moved. She did everything she could to make Viktor aware of what she was playing at.

"I see what I have always seen. The most competent and capable Forge-Second I have ever known or seen. I see my friend and colleague. Red hair, silver eyes, all that."

Rolling her eyes, Helve tossed her hair back over her shoulder and blinked up at Viktor. "Do you ever think about things *other* than work?" Already irate, she was almost to tears. "Or do you just lament your past so much that you are unwilling or perhaps *unable* to see a future?" She wanted to storm off. To saddle up Alvarath and fly into the distance to clear her head, but she knew that was likely the worst possible idea right now.

"I mean..." He paused for a moment to try to grasp at thoughts. At words. *Words*, he realized, *that would likely be a lie.* "Why do you ask?"

"Why do I ask?" She nearly shrieked at the half-giant, causing him to do something incredibly out of character. He *flinched. Winced.* Not out of fear, but because he knew he'd stepped in something he wasn't prepared for. Was no way ready for. "Why did I bring three bottles of Nilaetha Thirty-Three Four-Thirty? Why did I insist on tagging along with you when I *know* for a fact you are more than capable of carrying both weapons, and conducting yourself before the Kingmage and his sister?" She paused for a moment, taking a breath and huffing "Why, you... you..." At first she couldn't find the words, the *insult* she wanted to throw at the man. Was he being intentionally oafish? Was he leading her on? "Are you *really* forging square horseshoes right now?" She finally shouted.

Again, Viktor was just confused as could be. "Helve, there is no need for such words. What have I done to upset you? What have I done to anger you and make you bandy such rude words? Do you dislike me for something I did not notice and have just been holding onto a grudge?"

"Your steel has been in the fire so long you have gone past straw and are now at white!" She cried out at him, wanting desperately to reach up and shake the half-giant until he *saw* her. Actually *saw her.* Tears in her eyes, the woman finally gave into her urge and stormed off. Not far, mind you; she wasn't stupid from rage. But far enough that she could clear her head and be out of Viktor's sight for a moment while she did. The dragons, though, they could easily keep watch for her.

And little did they know that a rock guardian, a Sendweln, was watching as well. As Helve stormed along the mountain path, occasionally looking back to make sure she could still find her way, the creature ambled down from its own home. "Something the matter, little lass?" The creature said in a gravelly, yet genial voice. A friendly, calming voice.

"Not that I wish to share with a stranger," she said, turning to see the source of the voice. "Oh! My apologies, honored guardian." Wiping the tears from her eyes, the woman made a show of clearing her head and bowing respectfully to the rock creature.

"Oh, think nothing of it, dearie." The creature said. "Come, tell me your troubles." As it spoke, the creature arranged itself on the mountainside in a way that it found comfortable and stared down at her. Even through the rocky face, she could see the onyx eyes, glittering with kindness, curiosity, and unknown depths of intellect.

Sniffling slightly, the woman arranged herself on a small stone and pulled a knee up to her chest. "Long have I wished for my friend to see me as more than just that. Long have I wished to be more than just a Forge-Second to Viktor, my oldest and closest friend. But the oaf refuses to see my interest!" She complained, her voice carrying only a few dozen feet.

"Alvarath." Viktor said after Helve stormed off. "What in the name of Seran has gotten into Helve?"

That is something you must suss out, old friend. Vu'Locav and I have sworn to silence. Was all the dragon said. *She is safe, though.* Both dragons rumbled with laughter as they felt the utter perplexity in Viktor's mind at the moment. Pacing back and forth, the half-giant tried to sort out what was going on. She'd seemed a bit offended when he offered to repay her for the wine. Offered to give her *something*.

Perhaps it is her monthly? He thought.

I would not *ask that if you value your knees.* Vu'Locav said quite pointedly before going back to silence. That much confused Viktor even more. She's always been upfront about when she needed to clear her head due to thoughts from her monthly piling up. So why would she be offended *now* if he asked?

Pacing more, Viktor resigned himself to just wait until the woman returned.

"And you have been at his side for *how* long?" The Sendweln, which Helve had come to know as Uiuth, asked. "And he has not noticed you wearing his favorite scent. His favorite *color*? Are you certain he is worth the frustration?"

"Do mountains grow overnight, or do you have to watch their splendor day by day, century by century?" She asked in return, and the creature nodded sagely.

"You speak as one of us," Uiuth said softly, their face crinkling into a rocky smile. "Truly, you have lived." Reaching up with a stony hand, the creature scratched its chin, sending a shower of sparks down as it considered what to say. What advice to give this tiny being. Contrary to belief, such things were not beneath them, and in fact, creatures such as Sendweln and Giants, even enjoyed giving advice on such things as relationships to the *younger* races. "What about asking one of his kinfolk?"

"A giant? Would they not dismiss me out of hand?" She asked, wondering truly if such a question would be enough to interest a giant.

"When it involves one of their kin? Absolutely." The Sendweln chuckled and stood before offering a massive hand for Helve to step into. "Come, I will bring you to one."

"Very well." She wasn't worried; she'd heard enough of giants to know they weren't dangerous to other people... Unless you were in a hurry. They had a reputation for taking half a day to say hello, and another half to say goodbye.

But given that she needed to clear her head, Helve knew that some time up-slope would be welcome. So, when the Sendweln deposited her on its shoulder and started up the mountain, she got comfortable and continued speaking.

"Oftentimes he speaks of his first wife, Seldred, whom he lost to sickness ages ago."

"Did he ever see a mind-healer?"

"I doubt it. He is a man. They do not process grief well, it seems, and instead of getting help for it, choose to cling to old memories." Shaking her head, she sighed gently. Soon, though, the rhythmic thumping lulled her to sleep.

When they arrived at a giant's homestead, the Sendweln awoke her gently and tapped on the door. "Oi!" The creature called.

"Who is there at my door, at this hour, only saying 'Oi' as a way of greeting? That is not the most pleasant way to introduce oneself, you know."

"Uiuth." The Sendweln said.

"Oh! Rock and stone, river and stream, Uiuth. It is good to hear your voice, though you sound as if you are in a hurry. That is not good. Come in, come in, and let me put on the kettle and the tea. Moss and lichen and sandstone, yes?"

"That would be pleasant, Hovar. But just for me. For my

guest, here, how about something along the lines of lavender and mint?"

"Oh, you have a guest, that is always wonderful, always welcome. Lavender and mint, that is an interesting combination, good for the nerves, good for the mind, and decent for the stomach. Something tells me your friend is having troubles with those things right now, so yes, I will put on the kettle."

As the Sendweln opened the door, Helve got her first proper look at the inside of a giant's home. It was a splendid, massive affair, meant to fit the thirty-foot person comfortably and give them ample space to amble. She knew they didn't usually move fast, as it could prove lethal with the wrong step. But given that the sun had moved almost a quarter of the sky in the time the *greeting* took, she wasn't sure about the wisdom of speaking to it. But when the scent of tea hit her nose, the woman instantly disregarded her reservations. Allowing herself to be seated in a chair made for *smaller* people, she looked at the giant and the Sendweln as they seated themselves.

"So," began the giant. "Tell Hovar your troubles. Lay upon me your sadness and let us come to a conclusion that would benefit you the most. I am all ears, as you younger races sometimes say, and I have no doubts that Uiuth is willing and ready to listen as well. If I walk away while you speak, do not mind, I can hear you, I am just preparing the tea is all. Tea is such a wonderful thing, especially to have while discussing troubles and sadness, for it warms the body and the heart and can aid in washing away tears and terrors. Lavender is good for the nerves, to calm and quell the fears and the anxieties. Mint is refreshing and kindly to the senses, and always seems to help my stomach when I am nauseous." He paused for a moment and continued droning on in a pleasant, if long-winded manner, adding comments about self-discovery and healing. Pathways entered the mix somewhere, and before long, Helve was almost too confused to answer. But when Hovar finished his epic speech and looked at her, she remembered why she'd agreed to come.

"Well... I fancy a friend of mine. He is a half-giant of the Bludstyn clan of Northrealm; err... Nolveris. And he just... just seems to look straight through me, and I am unsure if it is worth my heartache to continue trying." She said with a gentle sniffle, trying to sort out the thoughts in her head. When the tea was brought out, she said her thanks to the giant and watched as he ambled to another kettle and poured a much larger cup for the Sendweln. Then, he sat down with his own cup and settled on a rather comfortable looking chair.

Then he started talking. Suggesting this and that, offering advice, though it was hard to tell what was advice and what were old memories and stories. Even as Kjetta descended into the western sky, Hovar was *still* talking, and honestly, Helve wasn't certain if he was even on the same topic anymore. But she did her best to pay attention, regardless.

But when the night came and Hovar was still blustering on, she knew she couldn't keep her eyes open. Drifting to sleep, she mumbled an apology to not seem rude. Both the Sendweln and the giant chuckled, and Helve was certain Hovar was still talking whilst she slept.

11

11: Westerspring

Fae took off from the *tengjäv* at speed. First, her plan was to check on the guardsmen at Littlebrook–Once–Besieged. So, through the Summerdusk Forest, she sprinted, taking only the time to fill her waterskin and take a small buck rabbit to make a small stew for the guardsmen, hoping they were still alive. Taking the fur as well, she did her best to make use of the organs before moving on. Given her knowledge of the Summerdusk, it wasn't difficult to find her way through the area.

Her heart sank, though, when she saw the armor sitting next to a pyre. As far as she could tell, there were suits from each of the Townsguard, including Captain Idorick. Cursing the cruel fates that allowed him to expire, the woman made her way up to the pyre and said a quiet prayer of hope. Taking a breath, she sighed and left the pot of stew for whoever survived, and made her way through town. The stench... as long as she lived, Fae would remember the stench above everything else she'd ever smelled.

Shuddering, the woman made her way out of Littlebrook–

Once-Besieged, hoping it would find a way to come back. To survive in some way, and thrive. With a sigh, she picked up a patchouli bloom and ran the flower beneath her nose, making sure to get the oils on her skin so she could forget the scent of rot and death. Burning corpses was a scent she knew she could never escape. But that of the rot, she hoped she could leave behind.

Three days on foot had her closer than she liked to a territory usually held by govlim. While she didn't necessarily *like* the creatures, she likewise didn't hate them. Just... held a healthy distrust of them, for many were conniving and sometimes cruel. *But then again, the promise of a hot meal and pay could sway many people's alignment, if offered at the right moment.* With that thought in her mind, the woman nodded. It would not do to prejudge those she had never met.

And so, her first week out from Littlebrook had her run nearly over a govlim who was sitting on a stump. Quieter than most of their people, though clearly not asleep, the govlim shouted at her. "Careful!" Though there was no hostility in the obviously feminine voice. Just... caution. Opening one eye, the govlim regarded her for a moment.

"You know, I could hear you a mile away, adventurer." She said, looking Fae over as she opened her other eye. Reaching up, the govlim adjusted herself and popped her back before scratching her chin and sighing.

"Sorry," Fae replied with a bow. "Jus' not used to folk being out this far from a town."

"And where would you put me? Most Govlimi are not exactly welcome in big people's places. Or even small people's places." The woman said a moment later, quirking an eyebrow at the wood elf. "Not like you elves, welcome everywhere."

"Almost everywhere," Fae offered, "some places in Nolveris still are not friendly to elves."

"Friendlier than they is to Govlim." She retorted.

With a sigh, Fae nodded at the woman and chuckled gently. "I am Fae. You?"

"Taryth. Well met, Fae."

The two stayed in each other's company for just a few minutes before Fae had to make tracks once more. With a sigh, the woman once more delved into her own thoughts. *Why are Govlim unwelcome?* She couldn't help but wonder about that fact; but at the same time, she'd met plenty of Govlim in cities, working odd jobs–

–there it was. *Odd* jobs. She'd never seen a govlim doing more than just little jobs here and there, nothing one would call lucrative or realistically supportive. Without even having to *remember,* she saw the *gobnhaus,* as people called them. Roughly eight families to a one-room house, and it was *by design.* Not by the design of the Govlim, mind you. No, but by design of the *'higher'* races. With a snarl, Fae realized she knew where she could track such edicts to. The High Elves of the Indeka Islands.

Of course. Sighing, she hoofed it along to find the High Road once more, making her way along. It was a pleasant enough day, certainly, but her thoughts had put a cloud over her head. Glancing around a few minutes later after her introspection, she realized she was back on the road, and about three hours from a small river town. With a shrug and a wink to no one, the woman adjusted her course and headed along at her best speed. Though she'd been absolutely floored by the abilities of the Rangers to sprint and continue sprinting for hours, she didn't go for that route. Instead, she took off at a gentle lope, letting her legs stretch as she jogged along.

By the time Kjetta was descending into the west once more, Fae had crossed the distance to the town of Wolf River. Reaching the gate, the woman rapped her hand on the solid wood and waited a few moments.

"Identify!" Shouted a voice.

"Fae Cos'Criux. Captain, Krygan-Shawv Adventuring!" She replied.

Immediately, the gate swung open and three guardsmen, all bearing crossbows trained on her, waited a few moments. "Who is with ye?"

"No one. I came on my own. What are the happenings?"

"In, quickly. There is a Ranger distributing cure. Town square. Go nowhere else until you have had a dose, or you will end up on the pyre." The lead guard commanded, and of course, Fae was quick to obey. After all, she knew she'd likely been exposed at this point, and it wouldn't do to die of plague. As she walked through the town, the woman made note of the whispering voices and the furtive glances from townsfolk hiding behind windows.

As she reached the town square, Fae raised her hand when a Ranger called out. "Has anyone not had their dose?"

"Aye! Just got here, Ranger!" She shouted. The Ranger nodded, beckoning her forward, and handed her a vial of a strange sludge.

"Drink it, do not smell it, and try to avoid letting it hit your tongue." Quirking her eye at the instruction, the woman shrugged, popped the cork from the vial, and downed the contents.

And regretted it until the day she passed onto the Path. She could *feel* the texture of the stuff as it oozed down her throat. *Smell* the putrescence and death within her mouth, and even without it touching her tongue, the scent alone made her start gagging. Doubling over, she made a valiant attempt to avoid vomiting the disgusting substance, and when she felt it coming up, a hand went over her mouth. Then someone elses hand clamped hard over hers. "Swallow for all you are worth." The voice commanded, and she obeyed. Screwing her face up in agony as she worked her throat, she only *just* managed to avoid the stuff coming out her nose and mouth.

Then, a pint of beer came into her hand. Without even thinking, she started chugging it to get the taste of the bilious substance from her mouth. When she'd finished the pint, only then did she look around. "Lucky I had no ill intent." Said a voice, "else I could have had you in a bad spot." A tavern keep looked her over. "Do you always drink without asking who handed you something?"

"Only..." She took a cautious breath to try and gauge how she felt. Her stomach was calming quickly, likely due to some medicinals in the pint. "Only when I have ingested... something like whatever foulness that was." She managed before sagging to her knees and heaving. The tavern keep was beside her, rubbing her back gently.

"Keep it down, lass. You need that foulness to survive the plague." The keep said gently. "Else you will end up like my wife and child."

Shooting an apologetic glance to the havlai man, Fae nodded and gulped hard. A few more times and her stomach started settling. Shuddering, the adventurer looked around at the different people in the town square. Every one of them looked about a heartbeat from vomiting, but were recovering.

Meanwhile, the Ranger stood and watched for anyone else that needed the potion.

"Now. Be off to your homes with renewed hope for tomorrow!" The Ranger cried out, and the people slowly disbanded until only Fae and the Ranger remained. Raising a weak hand, she motioned to the wandering warrior, and raised an eyebrow.

"Mate." She began, before having to swallow hard again. "What in the name of fuck was that? Pure shite?"

"I am fair certain that drinking pure shite would have been more pleasant, friend. Lilia. And you?"

"Fae. Cos'Criux. Well met, Lilia." When the Ranger drew back their hood, Fae got a good look at the feminine features. Gentle, not overstated. A bit of stubble here and there, as if she were born male, or had some unfortunate problems with her body. Either way, Fae wasn't about to judge- or ask. "I would like to ask what is being done for the Govlim, Lilia." She said a moment later, unsure why she mentioned it, but strangely happy she did.

"Everything we can. Govlimi have a natural mistrust for bigger people, but we at least take the time to learn their language, so they are a bit warmer to *Tengar*-types." The woman said with a chuckle. Throwing her hair back over her shoulder, the woman nodded and patted Fae on the shoulder. "Now, if you need a place to stay... what is your quest, Captain?" She asked a moment later, noting the small double-bars on Fae's armor that denoted her rank in the Krygan-Shawv Adventuring Guild.

"Rest would be wonderful. And my quest currently is to make for the last place my Dire Company was seen, Dahal in Khataar." She said rather simply. The Ranger nodded gently and tugged her along to one of the inns near the edge of town. Glancing up at the sign, she memorized it, in case she needed to remember it later. *Gwendlyn's Bed and Board.* Simple enough name.

When they entered the Inn, though, it was anything but simple. Lively; incredibly so, in fact, with adventurers of every stripe within. There were a few dal'Korin, and a few of their much more rare, larger cousins, a species whose name she couldn't remember. They were burly, taller than the dal'Korin, and more often than not, worked as Paladins for local temples. There were a few martial artists, a few swordsmen, and Fae realized the Ranger was leading her to a table with folk that looked; looked rather like her. Not wood elves, mind you, but the way they sat, their swords near and at the ready, and the air around them crackling.

Spellswords, like her. Clapping her hands together, the Ranger spoke. "Well met, fellows. I present Captain Fae Cos'Criux of Dire Company."

"Oh! Dire Company, eh? Good lot you are. Good lot indeed." Said one of the adventurers. Another nodded appreciatively, and one grabbed a chair from an empty table.

"Have a seat, Fae. I am Klurgan, Captain of The Tricksters. That is Errol, Captain of The Acrobats. We have a few other captains here, but this table specifically was given for us Spellswords. And yes, we can tell." Klurgan, a massive orc, said with a wink and a nod.

"Oi! If you are introducing people, dinnae fergit me!" Shouted a voice from almost below the table. Huffing and puffing, a govlim clambered up onto a seat high enough they could be seen. Wearing what looked like a dagger to normal-sized folk, they were nonetheless rather intimidating.

"Treshkin. At yer sarvis." The govlim affected a bow, his ears wiggling.

"Ah yes, Treshkin, who may very well be the most dangerous of all of us." Said Klurgan.

In the company of her type of people, Fae fell into chatting gaily. Everyone shared stories of their exploits, their company's strengths, and such. "I take it you lot got the summons?" Fae finally asked. A few faces went dark. None, though, went darker than the dal'Korin Spellsword Hes-Fal-Garan.

"Aye." Hes-Fal-Garan said softly. "My people are, once again, being nothing short of fucking daft." With a sigh, he downed another pint. "They are, once again, listening to the whisperings of the Dark Ancestors and ignoring the light. Further proof that power corrupts."

"So, what do we do?" Asked another adventurer.

"Our very best, I wager." Hes-Fal said in response with a chuckle. "Kill my countrymen and those they have fooled until the Scala'Dun realizes what a fucking pointless idea it is to wage war upon the Empire?"

"Hear, hear." Said Klurgan, and everyone raised their drinks. "To the poor bastards we cannot save."

"Cheers." Said Fae gently, before taking a sip of her own drink. In the back of her mind, she wondered just how many innocent people would die before a conclusion to the current mess was reached. An adventurer she was by trade. Not a soldier or a general; in fact, she wasn't even certain that in her two-hundred-something years, she'd ever heard of the Empire fielding a standing army. There were whispers, of course, of the Nolvern having their own force. But everyone else? They relied solely upon volunteers and such.

Whether that was wisdom or folly remained to be seen. But given that the Kingdoms were offering hefty sums from their coffers to adventuring groups to become a makeshift army? Folly was more likely in Fae's mind. Nonetheless, she did her best to enjoy the company of other adventurers, eventually going so far as to mingle around the other tables. She found other captains, their lieutenants, and of course, regular adventurers.

She even found a few newly-christened adventurers, eager to show off their certification papers from Krygan-Shawv. As an old hand, though, she was quick to caution them against being overly proud of themselves. Pride was often a gateway to recklessness, and new adventurers were hard enough to train. They took her words to heart as best they could, and she moved on, scanning the room occasionally for any newcomers, any threats, and such.

She didn't fail to notice the shadowy figure in the corner, smoking a pipe and watching her. With a stiff nod, she acknowledged their presence, and they hers. That was the extent of their interaction; at least, at the time. When she made her way to one of the wenches, the woman tapped her shoulder. "Oi, sorry lass. How much for a room?"

"That would be eight doreim, milady. Though across the street is the 'venturer's Den, which may be cheaper, if a bit squalid." She offered kindly, leaving Fae to wonder if they had any rooms available.

"D'you have any available?"

"Sadly, nay. We are booked quite until the end of the season, I am 'fraid, milady." She said gently, before moving off from the conversation. Shrugging, Fae slipped away and headed for the door, checking to make sure she had all her things. After all, she'd seen plenty of rogues in the Inn, and wanted to make sure none of her gear got lifted.

Heading across the street to the Adventurer's Den, she slipped inside to see... pretty much what she expected. It wasn't *squalid*, by any means, but cluttered? Absolutely. There were adventurers dozing, talking, arguing. A few checked their supplies to make sure they had everything for the days ahead. Making her way to the proprietor, Fae dug in her coin purse. "How much for a bed for... two nights?" She asked.

The man looked her over for a moment. He seemed a rough type. Not exactly ugly, but definitely not handsome. Scarred, one eye covered with a patch. When he spoke, his voice was like sanded paper to her ears. "Rank?"

"Captain." She said, half wondering why it mattered.

"Three Doreim for a private room. Five Aureim for a barrack."

"It is just me."

"Five Doreim for a private room. One Doreim for public lodging. Four for public lodging and insurance against an idiot trying to steal your things."

Was that a threat? A promise? She wasn't sure, but Fae was certain of one thing; if anyone tried stealing her things, it wouldn't end well for them. Palming over the four silver coins just to be safe, she followed the proprietor to the nook he'd assigned her. As soon as he was gone, she stripped her boots and tied them together with a special knot she always used. Then, she tied those to her rucksack and the rucksack she looped over her left leg, knowing that if anyone tried taking it, she'd wake in an instant. Her sword she kept within arm's reach, still on her belt, and glancing around to make sure no one else was looking, she tucked a field knife under the straw pillow.

The place was clean enough, and there was an odd sense of security that came from being around other adventurers. It wasn't like sleeping in an inn back on the Islands, where everyone was snobbish and snooty. No. *These* were her people. The young-looking Nolvern man dressing a wound in the corner and grumbling. The old Khataan, gray in the muzzle, rocking in a chair. The dog-like Dokk warming by the hearthfire. There were adventurers aplenty, including a few monastic monks. She could feel the presence of other spellswords, obviously dozing.

Thinking ahead, she placed a ward rune on her gear, so that if anyone but her grabbed them, they'd get burns beyond what they'd think possible. Then, Fae did her best to drift off to sleep, finding comfort in the uncomfortable lodgings. Finding peace in the clutter and dim light of the Den. Hostels were often her favorite lodging, for she could overhear everything that went on around her. Everything she needed to hear.

Sighing, Fae drifted into a dreamless sleep.

IV

Distant Drums

12

12: The Wilds of Westerspring

The time had come to get back on the trail, and Karos had paid for everyone's meal out of the coins he had collected. He had overpaid, as was his custom, and left before anyone could protest, taking his companions with him. Soon enough, the road stretched out before them and Karos hummed one of the old wandering songs he had learned as a child. Anymore, it was not in fashion, but it provided comfort to him as they trekked across Westerspring. It was a pleasant day, but soon enough, the sun was falling behind the western horizon.

Khula was nearing the point she could walk no longer when she heard it on the wind- music and merriment. Perking up, she glanced ahead and around until she saw a point of light some distance away, surrounded by larger shapes. Tapping Karos on the shoulder, she pointed it out excitedly.

"Sardra, what do you make of it? North by northwest, just off the road."

Glancing in the direction, Sardra gave her hunter's eyes a chance to adjust and focus. When she spoke, Khula could

183

hardly contain her excitement.

"gah'Drin caravan. I make out ten wagons and twenty adults in the main circle. Five and thirteen in the *edja* circle. Perhaps they may give a place for Khula to rest and us to catch up on news?"

Karos nodded, barely visible in the gloom. Shifting his pack to be more comfortable, he changed direction from pure east to follow the branching road northeast towards the caravan. His stride was long, but his companions kept up easily and soon enough, they had arrived.

As the trio approached, one watchman cried out, holding a bow at the ready.

"Who goes there? Advance and be recognized!"

"Rangers! Karos Lyvan and Sardra Woodstrider, with lady Khula Tallam as company!"

"Well, why did you not say so earlier? Come, come!"

Turning to his clan, the watchman relayed the information to the excitement of all. The trio made their way into the ring protected by the wagons and found themselves among a jolly group. A few were playing instruments and Khula could make out the delicate sounds of a hand-harp among them. Looking back and forth with wide eyes, she drank in the rich colors of the caravan.

"Hail, Clan Helvaraith!"

A cheer went up from the throats of all the assembled folk and the Rangers smiled, going between each person and greeting them. When they finally reached the clan leader, they bowed, and he bowed in return. Exchanging pleasantries and greetings, they made themselves comfortable in each other's presence and talked.

"Warden Ranger, to what do we owe the honor?"

"Well, Haldwygg, I come bearing ill tidings and a quest. A plague grips Seran and both my Rangers and the Riders of Gelvrentael are hard at work distributing a temporary solution, while Thäoldr Sagewind works to create a true cure. A great evil has been vanquished, and the Kingmage has summoned myself and my companions to Starwatch-in-Karnost. This I ask of you- for the time being, keep close your clan and stay away from cities. I believe your lifestyle affords you protections from this plague, but I would rather not test it."

Shifting uncomfortably, Haldwygg looked the Rangers over, taking in their measure. Karos seemed larger than life, something beyond mortal. Sardra looked regal and dangerous, capable of taking on any foe. *These are dangerous folk*, Haldwygg reasoned, *and I had best be polite*. To his absolute horror, several of the clan's children ambushed the Rangers and began tugging on their clothes and begging for treats. Haldwygg's face went white. He was used to Rangers visiting his clan, especially Earlaine, but to have two guests of such stature- and a Lady with them?

"Children! Leave our guests alone! They are far above your station!"

Karos chuckled at the man's panic and spoke gently as he handed each child ten gold coins.

"We are above no one, dear Haldwygg. They are doing no wrong, merely being children."

"Of course, Warden Ranger. Many apologies."

Karos smiled slightly and patted the man on the shoulder as the children ran away, gleefully pocketing their treasures. Glancing over to Khula, who was still dealing with a small crowd looking her over, he chuckled. Switching into the tongue used by the gah'Drin clans, he barked out a quick set of instructions. Quickly, the children dropped away to leave Khula alone, going about whatever it was they were doing when they arrived.

"You know our tongue, Warden Ranger. Few outsiders choose to learn it."

"We expect Rangers to know all the major tongues, Haldwygg. We train for a century and not everything we do is fighting."

"Of course, milord. I apologize for not knowing... I do not talk to Earlaine and the other visiting Rangers enough to know."

"Speaking of Earlaine Goodheart, where is she?"

"Last I heard, she was off with Aygwn performing reconnaissance. They are not due back for another half a day."

Nodding, Karos shifted the focus of the conversation off his Rangers and onto the Clan. Looking Haldwygg dead in the eyes, he watched for the man's reaction as he spoke.

"And what of your clan, Haldwygg? Any interesting happenings of late?"

"My wife took to The Path many months ago... I still miss her, but such is life. Llornywn and his family have another young one as well. Eldyg's oldest just left the Clan for his Rite of Passage. Not much else has been happening of late. With what you have said, we have been fortunate to avoid any troubles."

Nodding, Karos looked over the adults gathered there, and then to the children as they played. This was a wonderful clan, and they all worked to better each other's lives. It was pleasing to see, especially for the Warden Ranger, who saw the horrible things the races were all capable of. Sometimes it brought him close to tears and other times to unrelenting rage. Now, though, seeing the different races that made up Clan Helvaraith getting along so well, he was filled with hope. As he watched the surrounding faces, some looking upon him in awe, he made a decision that would change the Rangers forever. Reaching up, he slid his mask down to reveal his face. Sardra, who had been watching out of the corner of her eye, arched an eyebrow.

"Warden Ranger, what of the Writ of Masking?"

"I have long thought of that, Sardra. It is my thoughts that people cannot trust a face they cannot see."

Shrugging, the dokk pulled her mask down from her face to reveal her even white teeth and curved fangs. When both Rangers had removed their masks, the assembled folk gave soft gasps and chittered among themselves. Not knowing quite what to do, Karos reached up to touch his *litik'röka*, the silver-threaded scar on the left side of his head. It took him another few moments to realize that he and his companions were still standing. Shaking himself out of his stupor, he found a spot and dropped his rump to the ground, crossing his legs in front of him. Sardra followed suit and Khula was not long after, having slipped closer to Karos to see him better. This was the first time she had seen him without his mask, and it took her breath away. He was scarred in multiple places, but it did not seem to detract from his handsomeness.

Shifting slightly, Karos looked over the Clan as they sat chatting and eating. A moment passed, and he remembered why he had approached.

"Haldwygg, I hate to impose, but I must ask. May we shelter here for the night? I fear lady Khula can barely keep her feet beneath her. We have been walking since Elday's Rest and before that, Laghe Valoria. She has done admirably, but I feel rest would help her greatly."

Haldwygg nodded kindly and stood slowly, stretching out to his full, imposing height of over three quarters of a spearlength. Gesturing to his own wagon, he spoke directly to Khula.

"Milady Khula, I invite you to take to my wagon to rest. I have drawn the lot for watch tonight and having slept all day, have no further use for it for the rest of the night."

Karos stood next, deftly aiding Khula in her own ascent. She nodded tiredly and stumbled a little, just standing still, so Karos carefully walked her to the wagon. By the time they had reached the steps, she was so weary that she could barely see, let alone walk, and she repeatedly fell against Karos. Finally realizing her condition, the Ranger picked Khula up in his arms and pushed the door open. As he stepped into the wagon, carefully angling so he would not strike Khula against anything, he wondered at the rich colors and decorations within. Something in the back of his mind realized that if he were to ever have a permanent home, this would likely suit him. After all, being inside cities always made him and indeed all Rangers irritable and nervous.

Carrying Khula back to the good-sized bed, he gently placed her on it. She shifted around for a few moments while trying to get comfortable on the feather-stuffed mattress. Karos watched her for a few moments, before realizing that she distracted him. Shaking away his thoughts, he examined the interior of the wagon for a moment. The mirrors reflected not only the inside of the wagon, but, as expected, showed him his haggard face, set with stubble that had grown out of control around his goatee. The table was solid enough and there was a small basin and pitcher of water next to it. A ledge jutted out from one wall, across from a rather beautifully adorned chest. Another chest sat next to it and Karos could feel the life within. It was a mimic; a tame one at that, meant to confuse robbers and protect what the owner kept dear. Reaching out to the mimic, he heard the beast give out a low growl. When he touched its top, the growl turned into a snarl- just for a moment, until the creature, in its simple mind, realized that the man was not a threat.

"You are an interesting creature, *ka teljt*." Without thinking, Karos switched his mind into the Lifesong, speaking to the creature with the primal tongue instinctively understood by all beings. "Perform your duties well, *ka teljt*. Protect all who rightfully enter here." Multiple lanterns hung from hooks in the walls, though all were cold right now- after all, unattended lanterns would spell doom for a wooden home and possibly everyone inside. As he stepped out, he pulled the door back into place and made his way down the steps gingerly.

When he was finally on the ground, he stepped back over to the crowd, which was dispersing. The adults were herding children into wagons and extinguishing lanterns to go to bed, and soon only the watchers were left. They sent those who had been on the perimeter when Karos and his friends arrived to their wagons to sleep while the new shifts took their places. It was all done in an orderly, practiced fashion, which gave Karos comfort. As he watched, Sardra took a position with some of the others, giving her body as backup to their guards.

Making his way through the camp, Karos came across an enormous field where the horses had gathered around each other. Some were dozing and others were grazing, seemingly disinterested in the events of their human friends. One, seemingly sensing that someone new had arrived, turned its head to regard Karos. The Ranger looked the beast over. The clan took care of it well, groomed it, and had a fair bit of decoration woven into its mane. It was a beautiful beast, nearly twenty-two hands high and boasting a dappled coat. Nodding slowly, Karos backed away- it was obvious the creature did not want its herd disturbed.

Making his way back to the fire, Karos took a seat where Haldwygg had been sitting earlier and stared into the fire, quickly losing track of time. Many thoughts flooded his mind as he recounted the events of the past few days. They weren't making for Klwynspell-Three-Corners, as was his usual method of entering Dragonmoor from Westerspring. Instead, they were making, by his choice, for the Old Morwes Ranger Road, one of the many hidden paths his people main-tained in secret, to aid their free movement throughout the lands. He'd not told Sardra about his plan yet, but the Warden Ranger assumed that the canny dokk had long figured out the general idea. Sighing, he stared into the fire, watching the flames dance in the night.

Sometime after midnight, Karos pulled himself to his feet and produced his kuksa cup from his pack. Winding his way over to the cauldron next to the fire, he peered in. *Kaffa*, he thought to himself, *and it is gah'Drin strong, as it should be.* Nodding, he ladled some of the black liquid into his kuksa, hung the ladle back where it went, and went off to find where Sardra had perched herself, bow in hand, eyes watchful. It took a bit to find the younger dokk, as she'd concealed herself well. But he'd been the one to teach Sardra her skills, and knew *exactly* how to find her. Walking up to the dokk from behind, he let out a whistled chirp to announce himself. He more than anyone else knew all too well what happened when someone, whether accidentally or intentionally, surprised the dokk.

It wasn't her fault, he knew that. *Oh, do I know that.* It was a quirk of her upbringing, if it could be called such. From the age of five until her liberation at the age of fifteen, she'd been a slave. Certainly, she'd been used for work, as she'd always been stronger than most, but she'd also seen other... uses at the hands of her former masters. Karos shuddered gently just thinking about what the poor girl had gone through, and how it had so efficiently killed what she *could've* been. What she'd become though? That was something fearsome, though Karos wondered if she regretted her decision. Looking the dokk over, he realized she'd been staring at him for a few minutes.

"Something on your mind, *katryg teljt?*" She murmured, taking the kaffa he absently offered to her, even as her words jarred him back to reality.

"Hm? Oh. Just... far and away."

She smirked slightly. She knew that look all too well, especially when he was drifting into the past. Taking a long sip of the kaffa, she blinked, nearly coughing at the strength of the stuff. The urge to gag passed and she drank a bit more before speaking again.

"I know that look, Karos. None better. You are thinking about the past again. What has you distracted right now?" She asked, her voice not giving a note of her curiosity.

"I was thinking..." He began before pausing, trying to consider his words. Did he really want to tell his closest friend that he was thinking about the fact that her family had been cruelly ripped away, and for the first three months he'd known her, he had to constantly remind her that her name wasn't 'Bitch,' as she was used to being called back then? "About our past." He smiled gently at the dokk, trying to be as gentle as possible about the phrasing.

She was having none of it.

"Oh?" She cocked her head at him. "Let me guess. You are remembering how we met. Or what I was able to tell you about my life when you finally pieced my mind together again." Her voice was almost bitter, as if the thought of him reliving those times, and by extension reminding her, was enough to sour her mood. Perhaps it was. After all, who looks fondly on ten years of being beaten, whipped, and worse? Who looks fondly on ten years of backbreaking labor and constant use and abuse?

"I did not want to say it." He said apologetically after a moment. Casting his eyes down in apology, the Warden Ranger refused to look at his student for a moment.

"But it was there. Come on then, Karos. What were you remembering? Certainly it has merit if you remembered it just now." As she spoke, Sardra leaned her bow against the wagon she hid in the shadow of. Then she reached out and grabbed Karos' forearm lightly. The memories caused her pain, certainly. But she knew they caused him as much, just for different reasons. "We do not need to go back there, old friend."

"I was remembering the first time I startled you." He said, without a hint of emotion. *What is he hiding about that memory?* She wondered as she looked at her elder.

"And how I nearly took your throat?" She retorted gently. It wasn't a fond memory, but it *had* taught them both a valuable lesson. Karos had learned that startling her was a critical error, especially where their rapport was still being weaved. She'd learned that he was *far* more skilled in combat than she had been, as he'd nearly effortlessly subdued her. The only thing that'd kept her, at the time, from going back to *that* place mentally was his constant reassurance. He'd *talked* to her through everything, even as he held her in a chokehold for both their protection. Reassured her, even as she left gouges in both his arms from her claws. Whispered strength and compassion to her, even as she struggled and fought to bite at him, to end him.

In the end, she'd worked herself into exhaustion, and it was at that point that the Ranger, then only a little while past his Tenderfoot years, had shocked her to her core. Instead of *making use* of her for her defiance, he'd gently laid her on *his* bedroll, pulled the wool blanket up to her shoulders, and told her to get some sleep. The lesson for that day had ended with that scuffle, and the Ranger hadn't wanted to push her further. He, throughout the entirety of her first year with him, had fought tooth and nail to show not only the Rangers, but *her*, that there was far more to the terrified, nearly dissociated dokk girl than either believed. When she went to the dark places in her mind, he'd always been there to coax her back out. When something startled her, prompting her to lash out in utter terror, he'd patiently talked her through it. *Everything I am, I owe to that man.* She thought to herself as she stared at her mentor, her closest friend and ally.

Where even other Rangers would've given up, and even some tried to convince Karos to give up on her, he stuck with her. Learned as much as he could about her without touching her. Piece by piece, *he*, and no one else, had put her mind back together. Where it would've been *far* easier to just take her to Mount Wounds-End and foist her off on one of the mind-healer teams there. He'd sat patiently with her as she cried herself to sleep, expecting a beating at any moment. *Ancestors, he taught me how to deal with the things my body was doing.* She wondered about that sometimes. *How and when did he learn of the female body?* He'd taught her as much as he, a man, could about everything her body did. And he'd taught her everything he could about what was going on in her mind. Pieced her shattered psyche back together, minute by minute, hour by hour. Patiently, he'd sat through the night, sometimes more than a few at a time, just talking her down from flashbacks. From going back *there.* He'd held her warmly as she sobbed herself nearly catatonic, just whispering kindness to her. *Ancestors, he put off my martial training more than a few times because he saw how uncomfortable it made me.* Often, Sardra wondered just *why* he'd given so much of himself to her, and how much of herself he'd taken on.

And then, when she was mentally whole again, he'd taught her the life of the Ranger. Given her incredible skills, even as he sharpened his own. Inwardly, the woman wondered just what he could've been had he not been saddled... *no,* she thought, cutting off that line of self-recrimination. *He was not saddled with me, but by his own choice.* Turning her serene, icy blue eyes on her mentor once more, the Ranger considered her elder. He was tall for his kind, standing just over three-quarters of a spearlength. She'd seen him naked several times, and though he was an impressive specimen, she'd never had any interest in knowing him carnally. Smirking, she remembered when they'd both made that agreement. The tension had been awkward beyond words until they breached the topic one day while he was teaching her about such things as *consent* and *love.* Two words she'd forgotten the meaning of. Truly, they loved each other, but they knew they could never possess one another romantically or carnally. It just didn't feel right to even consider, and she knew he felt the same.

Reaching out, Sardra put a hand on Karos' shoulder and squeezed firmly. Leaning her head against his, the dokk touched her forehead to the man's.

"Talk to me, Karos." She said a moment later, before taking another sip of the kaffa he'd brought her. "Tell me what ails you, my brother, my mentor."

"We are still in the dark. There is so much we do not know. We are stumbling in the darkness, praying for some glimmer of light. But what if we are too late? What if there is no point to all of this?"

"Karos Lyvan. Guidestar, Warden Ranger, Captain of our kinship. We are never too late, not with your leadership. Who led the raid of Salrin Hills? Who led the battle of Knost? Who has outfought *every* enemy that has come his way, no matter their skill, numbers, or power?"

The man gave a pained smile as an answer and sighed. *Certainly, this feels like those old battles. Proving myself against impossible odds, and coming through. But there is so much I do not know.* Wincing, he reached up to his *litik'röka*. Sardra cocked her head before reaching out to comfort the man.

"What is it?" Sardra asked.

"The energy in the air. It is... all wrong, and it hurts. Ancestors, I cannot imagine what it must be doing to you, who can actually *use* and *feel* magic." Rubbing his head, Karos answered as the shooting pain suffused through his head to become a pounding headache.

She chuckled gently and shook her head before responding.

"I feel... an odd sensation to the magic in the air. It tastes, well, wrong. As if contaminated by something, or soured. I wager Master Thäoldr would have better words for it, though, and likely some wise, ancient knowledge." Her words did little to comfort the man, even as he tried willing his head to stop aching. The silver threaded through the ancient scar seemed to be afire, seemed to sear his skin. Sighing, he shook his head.

"Remind me to look into the Old Tales about Laf'Sa'Reeth and the Great Plague. I remember Thäoldr mentioning 'Mirror Magic,' perhaps there is something at one of the *tengjävi*. Maybe if we stop at one, we can find some answers." He said after a few moments. Sardra nodded and patted his back before handing back the empty kuksa. With a grunt, she signaled the end of her talkative mood. Karos nodded and took the cup, drifting back to the cauldrons to draw a fresh fill and drink it himself.

The night wore on, the four moons above drifting lazily in the sky. Silently, Karos looked up and recounted the name of each moon. *Kyrgin*, the closest and least pock-marked. *Tazka*, the second-closest, larger and more scarred. *Ulzi*, the third-closest, far more scarred and quite a bit bigger than the other two. *Ni'La*, the furthest and biggest, standing as an imposing guardian against anything that may come from the stars to threaten their world. Inwardly, he said a prayer to each of the Ancestors of the Moons by name, silently thanking them for the light they gave, as well as guarding the world he stood upon.

13: Westerspring, Near Vaelyn's Cabin

Thäoldr came to sometime during the night. Judging by the position of the moons, it was about fourth watch. He had a taste in his mouth worse than anything he had ever had, but that was a paltry concern as he realized what was happening. Pulling himself off the ground, he looked at the potion, which had cooled. The embers of his fire had only recently gone out, which he was thankful for. Moving quickly, he transferred as much of the potion as he could into the vials he had. He knew he would need more soon— *Where are those damned Rangers?* He calmed himself quickly, remembering that as fast as the Rangers moved, they still took time to close great distances. Shrugging slightly, he reached out to Namryll and Talakath.

"How far are the nearest Riders?"

The closest are nearly a day away and you will not like who it is. The Watchmaster at Jorun's Watch. Namryll's response was simple and he wondered just how the dragon knew.

"Reach out to his dragon. Tell him it is a matter of utmost importance and supersedes all other tasks. If he speaks of ill riders, tell him we may have a cure, but it is critical we get all riders we can. Namryll. Bespeak-"

Over three hundred dragons drowned his next words out in a great windstorm. How they had arrived without either of the black dragons noticing, he did not know. As he mused, a voice called from above with perfect clarity despite the distance.

"Thäoldr Sagewind! I bring three hundred strong riders and the same in Rangers. We are at your disposal!"

Thäoldr could not believe his luck for a moment and let out a whoop of incredulous joy. Waving the dragons to land, he watched as the group that blackened the already dark sky set down. They had illuminated themselves in friend-fire, so he could easily identify them even at this time of night.

"What is the occasion? The last I heard, the Council thought me mad and seditious for working with the Rangers?"

"When the Paragon of Healing falls ill with a fell plague, you throw out thinking anyone mad for working with anyone."

Thäoldr recognized the voice- Amrilyn Sarthon. His heart leapt as he realized she was one of his Lanceriders. On her own, she had gathered a massive force and tracked him down. When she dismounted her dragon, a dal'Korin Ranger followed her, and Thäoldr could barely contain his joy.

"Damn you, Amrilyn. Took you long enough!" He mocked anger at first, before embracing the woman tightly. "We have much work to do, sister. And you, Ranger! I am quite glad you have come." He noted as he released Amrilyn.

"When the Great Ravens sing that the blood-feud between Ranger and Rider is ended, we are duty-bound to aid however we can, Thäoldr, Sage of Wind. I am Ku'Sao'Raan. I bring with me three hundred of my best Rangers to honor the pact made between Ranger and Rider. More will come."

Thäoldr could barely contain his glee. Not only were the Riders and Rangers working together, but they had come when they were most needed. Taking a breath, the elder Rider looked over the assembled army.

"We have to make a cure for this plague. The Warden Ranger has done well to give us time, but I feel I have found a true cure. Listen close, Rangers, and gather all you can of death-shade, sarashal, spiderthorn and talthras. Spintki venom we have in ample supply, but if we can find more, do it. Riders, we must take the blood of a Black Dragon to create this cure. Talakath the Bold has volunteered every drop of her blood into undoing what her Rider, *damned be his name forevermore*, has wrought." He looked over the Riders with a grim expression on his face, so that they understood the gravity of his instruction. He was telling them to bleed a dragon dry, to kill it in the name of the lives of all folk. "Glory to you, Talakath, for your blood will save the world."

I am ready, Thäoldr.

Even though he knew the dragon was willing, those words still shook him to his core. Grabbing as many vials as he could to contain the blood, he motioned to the riders.

"Ready your brewing kits and if you do not have one, try to find one quickly. We will need all we can. Rangers, should you have alchemy kits to spare, I would appreciate their use."

As one, the assembled Rangers dropped their packs and quickly extracted alchemy kits of varying sizes, including collapsing cauldrons. When everyone had their things assembled, Thäoldr waved to some of his Riders, instructing them to bring along vials of their own. They approached Talakath reverently and watched as the dragon drew a claw across one of her main veins, gashing it wide open. Her blood flowed freely out, and the riders brought cauldron after cauldron to receive it.

The army went to work quickly, with Rangers quickly reading over the recipe and passing it along, teaching others as they went. Soon enough, the air was rank with the stench of the cure, and many folks, both Rider and Ranger, had to pull masks on to keep from gagging. Thäoldr walked from cauldron to cauldron to inspect their contents and nodded. The group had picked up the recipe quick enough, and he felt it should work. It had to. Motioning to a few riders who had nothing to do, due to them not having alchemy kits and being newer riders, he brought them over and began showing them how to construct a basic basket to hold the vials that would contain the cure. They took to the work with great enthusiasm, ready to do their part to help everyone else.

As Thäoldr stood over a pair of Rangers who were working feverishly to assure the purity of their cure, he tutted and spoke some advice.

"You will have better luck crushing the sarashal, rather than cutting it."

The Ranger glanced up at the Rider, nodded once, and followed the instruction before passing it along to the nearest other Rangers in their strange Sk'av'A tongue. As he listened, the ancient Rider realized the tongue was not that dissimilar to the Mage-Tongue the Riders used. It sounded *incredibly similar*, in fact, and Thäoldr made a note to talk to Karos about it. Walking along, he inspected each and every cauldron, nodding and speaking to everyone, guiding them and occasionally warning a Ranger or Rider as they started to mix wrong, or add the wrong ingredient. *When we have this perfected, only then is it acceptable to add to the recipe,* he thought to himself. Unbeknownst to him, the Rangers shared the same sentiment, though they were doing what they could to ensure the cure's efficacy.

As a sudden thrill of... pain? Energy? Thäoldr couldn't put his finger on what just happened. He let out a cry, dropping to one knee as a feeling of being hit by a lightning blast ran through him. One hand hit the ground to steady him, and when he went to take a deep breath, he noticed his chest not moving. *Did I die? Have I been dead and just not noticed?* Panic made his heartbeat a deafening drumroll. Sweat poured from his face as his body continually wracked with electric feelings, as if every nerve were on fire. Glancing at his hands, Thäoldr noticed a faint glow and cracks forming in his skin. *What?* Blinking, the elf looked again- the glow was gone, but the cracks remained, looking more like old scars than fresh wounds.

When the cry went up, a Ranger immediately bolted over to the rider, but was waved off. Shaking their head, the Ranger helped Thäoldr to his feet and looked him over.

"By the Ancestors, man," said the Ranger, "when did you last eat?"

"I suppose... a little over a few days ago?" The Sage of Wind replied.

It has been a week, came the voice of Namryll, concern coloring her voice.

A week? Thought Thäoldr to himself. Then, a moment later, his stomach groaned and the realization hit him. He was dreadfully hungry. *Starving, even.* Looking at the Ranger, he cocked his head.

"I will sort it, Ranger. I need you focused on the task at hand." He finally said.

"As you say, Sage of Wind." The Ranger replied curtly, squeezing the elf's shoulder. For a moment, Thäoldr thought their voice sounded quite familiar. Regal, with a tinge of roguishness. Not at all gravelly or harsh like most Rangers. *And they knew my title.* Though he supposed it may have been passed along in talk, that didn't quite sit right. "But we need you alive."

Taking the advice to heart, Thäoldr excused himself from the small army, making his way over to Namryll. Unpacking his mess kit from the saddlebags, the Rider quickly set up a small cooking fire, before realizing he'd not had a chance to resupply *anything* at this point. Sighing, he called out to one of the Riders.

"Amrilyn!" He cried, and the named Rider came sprinting over.

"Aye, Sagewind? What do you need?" The woman said as she approached.

"Food. I am famished, and by Namryll's reckoning, I have not eaten in a week." He replied with a grumble.

"By dal'Kiyr's talons! Have you forgotten the lessons you taught me?" She accused him, and he grunted. Chuckling, she called over her own Searla, a magnificent gold Sonorus dragon. When she arrived, Amrilyn went to work unpacking her own rations as quick as she could. "It is not a hot stew, I am afraid, old friend. But some cheese, bread, sausages and what the Rangers call trail mix. Nuts and berries."

Handing the elf a cheesecloth bag, Amrilyn let out a gasp as Thäoldr, with nowhere near the decorum he usually showed, opened it and wolfed down every scrap of food, crumbs and all, in *moments. He really is starving,* the woman thought with a pang of pity. Without even looking at him, she handed over another ration pack, which was also ravenously eaten. *How many does he need?* She wondered, looking at the elf. His arms seemed... somewhat wasted, as if a week had done him far more damage than he realized. Blinking, she leaned close and whispered.

"Thäoldr, are you well?" She asked, her voice barely audible to even the elf.

"I do not know." Was all he said and refused to comment further.

When Thäoldr's hunger had finally been sated, Amrilyn promised him she'd look after preparations. Then she made him swear to get some rest and try to recover, to which he protested. But with mental pressure from Namryll, he was soon fast asleep.

As the work went on, Talakath continued refreshing the wound to ensure the supply would hold. She could feel herself fading, though, and knew she would pass soon. Resolutely, she held to her course. *It is my duty to die for the greater good.* Her claws grew weaker as she gashed open the wound again and again, her onyx blood flowing and being caught as readily as the Rangers and Riders could in their cauldrons to be spun and siphoned. Her breaths slowed as her body, panicking about the loss of blood volume, began to give out. Even as the massive black dragon fought the rising alarm in her frame, her mind remained calm. Resolute, as she faced her death with dignity and grace. The flow of blood became a trickle. The trickle stopped, and Talakath knew– the time had come. Her heart slowed– slowed– and finally stopped. She took one last breath, and raised her head, letting out the strongest cry she could– a victorious scream, louder than any had expected from the dying dragon.

Feeling her mother fading, Namryll let out a bugling cry. Not of alarm or worry, but of pride. *Go to your eternal rest now, dear mother. Your sacrifice will save all. Sleep now forevermore.* Her call echoed throughout the land, audible as far away as Jorum's Watch. Far and away, other dragons and griffons picked up the sound, wondering exactly what had caused such a sound. Wondering what sacrifice had prompted the call. Thäoldr, connected at the very core to his dragon, felt the swelling of pride in Talakath from Namryll. Of joy in redemption of her mother. And a moment later, his soul suddenly burst into a new fire as his dragon passed along her renewed dedication. Her renewed hope burned brightly in both her and her rider. Eyes burning, the two renewed their pledge to each other. To their world. To dal'Kiyr, their Ancestress and most beloved leader.

With one last look around, Talakath's eyes closed as her blood volume was depleted and gathered. Her last thought was of pride; in herself, in her daughter, and in the Riders she had helped. With a final breath, the hulking form ceased moving and Talakath, black dragon of dal'Kiyr, and oldest dragon on Seran, passed into the Afterworld to reunite with the dragon mother. The last of the Ancient Dragons, finally gone to rest after all these years. After millennia of toil, the last of it under an ever-maddening disgraced Rider.

The assembled dragons and griffons let out a keening cry that rose higher and pierced the very heavens. The Riders paused in their work and looked to Talakath before raising praises to her as a send-off. As the unearthly noise filled the air, Thäoldr looked to the east. The blue light of Kjetta was growing, and the flaming orb crested the horizon. *Kjetta rises! The Ancestor of Day blesses our efforts!* His heart leapt to his throat and he let out a cry.

"We banish the darkest night! A new day rises!"

The Riders of the Order of Gelvrentael let out a victory cry, pausing in their work to clash weapons together and rattle their armor; at least, those who wore steel. The Rangers looked up to the dawning sun silently, whispered a prayer to the Ancestors and to Talakath for her courage, and went back to work. The general consensus among the Rangers was; *we will celebrate when the task is done.* So on they worked, letting the Riders have their victory cries. There was still far too much to do for the Rangers to be content. Far too many innocents were in danger of gruesome death.

Victory had not come yet, though hope was burning higher with every passing minute.

The hours wound on and after a full day of cooking; the cure was ready. Vial after vial was filled and corked off and the baskets were loaded. Rangers loaded their packs with as much of the cure as they could carry and were off. Dragons, griffons and riders soon followed suit, preparing to take off with a mass amount of the cure. It was the single biggest gathering of power in Seranese history, and Thäoldr felt it was time to ride. Loading his own dragon with the cure, he grinned as he watched each person take off. It took a full half hour for the area to clear out, but Thäoldr felt it was a good way to end the work. The Rangers were all on foot, heading in the directions they knew they needed to go, and the Riders would go further on the air, to the worst-hit cities, hoping to find survivors to cure. Thäoldr had his own direction to go, and he knew where he would be of the most use- Ormere Keep, the great citadel of the Order of Gelvrentael.

Namryll turned her magnificent head to her mother, and a tear rolled down her cheek, unbidden. When Thäoldr had mounted, she rose into the sky before unleashing a blast of flame, hotter than anything she had ever tried or managed. Hotter than the black fires of the Void, and purer than the light of Kjetta. She sustained the flame for many minutes until she was certain that she reduced the hulking body of her mother to ash. *A worthy sendoff for a dragon, to be certain.* Thäoldr looked on for a few moments and raised a salute to the immolated dragon and whispered his thanks.

Then the two of them began flying south and west into the new day they had helped create.

14

14: The Wilds of Westerspring, A gah'Drin Caravan

As Kjetta began his ascent into the sky, burning away the night, Khula was still restless. She had at least slept, though, and that was good enough. Kicking her legs over the side of the bed, she blinked the sleepiness away from her eyes and examined her surroundings. She had barely been awake when Karos had carried her in here, so she'd not gotten a very good look at the inside of the wagon. It was painted lively, with red walls and gold highlights. There was plenty of room for the man and his wife. They were old enough that their children must have struck out, at least by Khula's reasoning, though she wondered where the man's wife was. A picture hanging on the wall, obviously painted with great care, made the woman remember the sad reality. Haldwygg's wife was obviously on The Path, given the small shrine that was in the wagon, and Khula nodded slowly. Making her way out of the wagon and back into the open air, she stretched her arms and back, yawning away her exhaustion.

"Ah! You are finally awake. Are you rested, Khula?"

Karos, of course, seemed as if he had not slept- and that it didn't matter. Truth be, he had sat staring into the fire for a good portion of the night, not talking to anyone. Even Sardra had placed herself in a hidden spot and waited the night away. But Karos seemed to think that if he slept, bad things would happen. Khula signed a question at him, her hands working quickly even through the fog in her head.

"Have you had any rest at all, Karos?"

He grinned slightly and ignored the question, instead asking her one.

"Are you ready to face the road, milady?"

Realizing she would get no useful answer out of the man, Khula nodded slowly and made a show of adjusting the straps of a non-existent pack. After a moment, she signed once more as her stomach rumbled gently. As her hands laid out her request, she arched her head to vaguely point at the large tent that was set up to the east, where the sounds of merriment and smells of food were coming from.

"May we get food first?"

Karos grinned slightly and waved her on.

"Go on then, Lady Khula. Fill your belly and see if they will give you some food and a pack." He said.

She smiled and curtsied to Karos before making her way over to the food tent. When she entered and saw the folk gathered inside, she could not help but smile. They all seemed so lively and were dressed in bright, cheerful colors, which was a wonderful change from the dull garb worn by her friends. Making her way up to Haldwygg, she curtsied and moved her hands up to speak, hoping he was fluent in sign language.

"Many thanks for allowing me to sleep in your wagon, milord Haldwygg."

"I apologize, milady. I do not speak the hand-signs, though one of my clan members does fluently. Algord! I require your help, my good man!" Haldwygg called out.

A younger man glanced up from his food, quickly swallowing the mouthful he had. Shifting from the table, he moseyed up to where the Clan Leader was and looked both Haldwygg and Khula over.

"Aye, Haldwygg? What do you need, sir?" The young man said.

"You speak hand-signs, do you not?" Asked Haldwygg.

"Aye, sir. Do you need my services?" Answered Algord.

Nodding, Haldwygg pointed at Khula, who repeated her gestures.

"She thanks you for allowing her to sleep in your wagon while you were not using it." He said, translating with perfection.

Smiling, Khula curtsied once again. Haldwygg gave a small smile as well, before looking back to Algord.

"You are most welcome, milady. Algord, you may go back to your meal, sir. I have no more need for you." He said matter-of-factly, though not with a lack of gratitude.

Bowing, the spritely man slipped back to his seat at the table and resumed eating his breakfast. Khula made her way to the far end of the tent, where the clan's cook was preparing plates for everyone. She stepped up and curtsied again, before signing once more.

"Many apologies, but I must ask if I may have some food?" Her signs prompted nothing more than a look of confusion from the cook in the tent. Sighing gently, Khula readied herself to speak. Unbeknownst to her, Algord had been watching her motions from afar. When the cook looked confused, he called out.

"She wants to know if she could have some food, Veryl." He called out to the cook.

"Oh! Well, why did you not just say, miss?" Veryl asked, eyeing the girl with some suspicion.

Gently, Khula tapped her throat and made a universally known gesture, one meaning 'hurt'. Veryl nodded and chuckled gently.

"What a wonderfully strange world we live in. Here you are milady. Enjoy." He said with a smile.

Handing her a plate of food and utensils to eat with, the large man ushered her to sit at the table with everyone else. Wisely, she made her way to sit across from Algord, just in case she needed to speak with anyone. The young man smiled broadly at her and took a long draught of his cider.

"So, you only speak in hand-signs?"

With a voice that was barely a whisper, Khula gave her answer.

"Hurts too much to speak with voice." What little Algord could make out of her voice was raspy and near-silent.

Algord immediately regretted making her speak, as he could see the pain in her eyes. Nodding slowly, he put his hand to his chest and performed the hand-sign to apologize. Khula smiled and shook her head, instantly signing a response.

"You could not know unless you asked."

Nodding slightly, Algord went back to his food and Khula began eating hers. She was in the company of folk who ate with some manners, which gave her spirits a boost. The terrible things her parents had told her about the gah'Drin melted from her mind as she sat among them, realizing that they were people, not unlike her. They were kind and their mode of dress gave her joy- surely; they weren't as poor as her family had said?

Looking over at her nearest table mates, she quietly judged the makeup of their clothing- it was much finer than the garb Karos had given her and it looked both durable and comfortable. With how much time this folk spent on horses, she reasoned that clothing being both durable and comfortable were musts. Eating, she carefully picked through her meal, which comprised sausages, root vegetables, eggs, and a chunk of bread.

A small meal compared to what she had been used to, but she was alright with that fact. Spearing one sausage with her fork, she used the knife to cut a chunk off, eating thoughtfully. The sausage was wonderful, tasting of pork and sage. Quickly finishing the first sausage, she moved to the vegetables, which were quite pleasant, being seasoned and fried. Then the eggs, made in the scrambled fashion. Even the bread was pleasant, and Khula realized she would have to eat with the gah'Drin clans more often.

Back at the embers of the fire, Karos stretched and performing small exercises meant to get his heart up to speed. Just because he had not slept didn't mean he hadn't rested, and his body had entered the Ranger Trance while he sat staring into the fire. Quickly enough, he was awake and strode to where Sardra was in the Trance. Gently patting her shoulder, he spoke to her.

"Sardra, it is time to awaken. Come now, dust yourself off. The road awaits."

Slowly, Sardra opened her eyes, focusing in on Karos. It took her a moment to remember where she was, but Karos did not mind. They were safe enough for sure. But with most of their weapons destroyed, it would not do good to be caught unawares. Taking stock, Karos looked over his weapons. He had the hilt and part of the blade of Northrage, a knife that was rent in two and an axe with a broken head. Sighing, he touched the bow he hoped was there- and let out a sigh of relief. His quiver, which sat on his hip, was full of arrows and his Ravensong was still in one piece, so he was not completely dependent upon *ljas'atuk.* It was not preferable, but it would at least last until he arrived at a *tengjäv* and managed to get a hold of something more. Slipping his pack off, he flipped the buckles to open the top and quickly sorted through his things. He had a few bundles of food left- *not enough for the trip ahead, unless we hunt, or Sardra and I simply do not eat.* Enough bundles of kingscress to ensure they would not be without pure water for some time. That was always a good thing. His alchemy kit was looking a little barer than he'd like, but given the circumstances, it could be forgiven.

Sardra shook herself awake as Karos sorted through his belongings. Stretching herself out, she yawned and scratched behind her ears gently.

"What is the situation, Karos?"

"Well, we have two weapons between us- your claws and my bow. And that is the start of the good news."

"Of course it is, Karos. When are things ever simple?"

Chuckling, Karos gave a full rundown of the gear he had. Silently cursing himself for the oversight, he wished now that they had stopped at a shop in Elday's Rest. That would have made things a lot easier for the journey ahead. Closing his eyes for a moment, Karos thought to his map, before realizing that the skin was still on him. Quickly plucking it from his belt, he cleared his mind before focusing on where he was.

Slowly, the ink on the magical map shifted from showing the continent and closed in on their location, showing the nearest 30 leagues. Sure enough, there was a *tengjäv* and even better, it was in their intended path. A quick prayer was sent, and Karos packed his bag back up and belted it shut. Then, he slung it onto his back and tightened the straps as best he could before looking to Sardra.

"All is not lost, Sardra. There is a *tengjäv* about ten leagues due west. If memory serves, the Watcher is..." He paused for a moment as he searched for the name, sifting through three hundred years' worth of Rangers he had met, watched die or heard of their death and those who had not finished their Tenderfoot stage. "Damnitall. Burwyn. Aleius and Burwyn. Now I remember."

Sardra chuckled at her Warden. It had to be difficult remembering the names of every single Ranger he had ever met, and she felt for the man. *Karos must have quite a lot filling his mind on the regular.* Little did she know the truth of her curiosity and how it would affect her if she knew. Her own mind was quite cluttered, to where sometimes it was hard to form a coherent thought- it was times like that she and other Rangers depended upon *dra'la'thel*, the mystical herb smoked by their kind. Reaching out to tap Karos on the shoulder, she made the sign for 'pipe', to give him an idea to help himself. His face brightened, and he gave her a grin.

Working quickly, Karos pulled his pipe from one of the many pouches he had belted across his chest. With it came a small bag of *dra'la'thel*, and the strange minty scent caused a thrill to run through Sardra's spine. She loved the stuff, as all Rangers did, and lamented that her own stash had perished with the rest of her gear. Putting the plant matter into the pipe, Karos retrieved a small item from yet another pouch– a small wooden stick that seemed to always glow with heat. Gently blowing on it, he coaxed a flame from the emberstick and put the flame to the *dra'la'thel* in the pipe. Taking a few puffs to ensure it had ignited properly, he let the smoke into his lungs before passing the pipe to Sardra, who took it gratefully. Already, he could feel his mind's focus increasing. His racing thoughts calmed down, and he could almost feel his muscles reacting quicker. Even his vision seemed clearer. Exhaling the cloud of smoke, he grinned slightly. He had needed that. Throwing his head from side to side, he popped his neck loudly as Khula made her way back to the two.

"I am ready, dear Rangers. Are you?" Her hands spoke as she approached them. Karos nodded, quickly followed by Sardra and the trio made their way to where Haldwygg was eating his meal and preparing to get some rest.

"Good Haldwygg, I thank you so much for your hospitality and kindness to us. May the roads be ever kind and all odds in your favor."

Shaking the man's hand, Karos deftly transferred a pair of platinum coins into Haldwygg's palm and closed the man's fist around them.

"Do not look until we are far away."

Once he had said that, he turned and waved to his companions. The road awaited them once more, and they had their next destination. If luck held, they would arrive around mid- to late afternoon and would have time to stop to allow Khula to rest if needed and even get a bath in. *I feel a bath would do wonders for her spirit,* thought Karos as he sauntered along, his own spirits high. Sardra passed him the pipe again, and he took a puff before passing it back, a grin forming on his face.

This was the life he enjoyed- being able to wander free, with but one goal on his mind. Nothing walled him in and the only task ahead was to arrive at Starwatch-in-Karnost and speak to the Kingmage.

This was the life of a Ranger. Aid where you can and roam. *This is the best life to live,* thought Karos, and he knew Sardra had the same thought in her mind.

By the end of the next day, they'd made the *tengjäv*. Where normally she'd have been half-dead on arrival, Khula was finding herself *somewhat* more able to tackle such distances. Her body, under the most extreme stress a Seranese person could endure, was adapting. Adapting fast, even. Already her legs, which were *abominably sore* at this point, had carried her through a ten-league march without further complaint. Her feet, though sore and probably blistered, were hauling along as best they could. So when they finally reached the *tengjäv* and the promise of rest became real, Khula wobbled with every step until one of the Rangers helped her.

Sardra was at her side, expertly looping one of Khula's arms over her shoulders and taking most of the woman's weight off her feet. Karos was up ahead, staring into what seemed to be an unyielding stone wall. Quirking an eyebrow, the woman looked at Sardra for a moment, then at Karos, angling her head to ask what the wall was. Grinning, Karos untied his Ranger Compass from his neck, touched the runic symbol engraved on the front, and pushed it into a slot in the rock. There was a loud CRACK, *and* a seam appeared. Bracing himself against the wall, Karos shoved, and the rock gave way, swinging wide to reveal a torch-lit passageway. Waving at the two to precede him, Karos waited until they'd passed and shut the door with a resonating *WHUMP*. From somewhere inside, a voice called out.

"Who enters?" The voice cried.

"*Karostrun anrak'Lyvan, ia Sardra Öd'Lirklar, ia Khula Tallam!*" Karos shouted into the depths as he caught up to Sardra and Khula, the former of whom was basically carrying the latter. Slipping up on Khula's right side, the man looped her arm over his shoulders just as Sardra had done on her left, and together they hauled the woman down into the main cavern. Her eyes adjusted quickly, and the woman soon beheld the inside of an *Oskin-Tengjäv*.

A roaring fire dominated the larger part of the main cavern. Around it were many tables, set with clean dishes and cups, waiting to be filled and eaten from. The two Rangers carried Khula to one of the tables, and no sooner had they sat her down in a chair then they were attending to her. At first, the woman winced and tried to push Karos away when he moved to untie her boots. There was no malice behind the motion, just pure instinct, born from the trauma she'd endured. Glancing up, the Ranger met her eyes, nodded once, and stepped back. Wincing, Khula did her best to remove her boots, and though she knew Karos would try nothing, she just could not allow a *man* to undress her. Not anytime soon. Pulling her boots off, she gasped as the air hit her torn, tenderized feet. Tears sprang to her eyes, but in a moment, the pain was forgotten as Karos brought a stool, sat at her feet, and began rubbing a tyngfir salve into her feet. With care that belied the normal intensity and aggressiveness she'd seen in the man, he massaged her feet one by one, working the salve in and providing desperately needed relief to the woman's muscles.

A soothed gasp escaped Khula as Karos worked his hands over her feet and calves, kneading the protesting muscle and working out knots and cramps that'd formed over the past few weeks. At this point, she wondered if she would ever feel normal again. As Karos sat and worked on the woman's legs, Sardra came over with a kuksa, a wooden cup filled with a tea of braceroot and stahal leaf. Bringing it to the woman's lips, the dokk issued a gentle command.

"Drink." She told the woman. Khula complied immediately, taking a hearty draught from the cup. Almost immediately, her body began to relax. The worst of the cramps in her body worked themselves out, and she took a much easier breath than she had for a few days. Carefully, Sardra took Khula's hands and wrapped them around the cup. "Keep drinking that. I will prepare some food."

Food? Khula thought to herself. Certainly, she'd eaten at the gah'Drin caravan they'd left the day before, but she'd long ago accepted that food was a luxury. But when Sardra brought over a wooden tray laden with wedges of cheese, Ranger bread, sliced fruit, nuts, both roasted and raw, dried, sliced sausage, and a sight which made Khula's heart leap into her chest, a *heaping* bowl of calcanna, a traditional Moriani food. Quickly, Sardra set the tray on the table next to the woman, bowed gently, and stepped away. By then, Karos had finished his ministering to her feet, rinsed his hands, and bandaged her aching appendages. Then he took a seat on the other side of the table. Reaching up, the man touched his shock of black hair as if he were forgetting something about it. Or something that went on it. He shrugged a moment later and gazed almost longingly at the tray of snacks and food.

Khula waited a moment, wondering if things with the Rangers, which she was still becoming accustomed to, were like things in her home. That is, the *menfolk* ate first, while the *lowly* women waited their turn. But when Karos didn't move toward the food, and in fact turned his attention away from it, hunger overcame caution. Reaching out, Khula grabbed a piece of sausage, a bit of Ranger bread, and shoved it in her mouth. The bread wasn't the most pleasant she'd had; it was grainy, as if they'd found the coarsest-ground flours they knew. It tasted faintly of corn and grain, and was remarkably dense. *Is this the type of bread Rangers eat? There must be some advantage to it,* she wondered. It wasn't vile, by any means, but the idea that it was *anyone's* first choice of food shocked her. But she was hungry enough to not care at all, and soon took another round piece, this time layering cheese and sausage atop it. Then, with glee, she attacked the bowl of calcanna.

Calcanna is an odd sort of dish. Incredibly simple to make, it has been a staple of Moriani cooking for uncountable thousands of years. Consisting of mashed potatoes mixed with leek and cabbage, usually made with a bit of cream and spices, it is a well-loved dish even in other lands. Rangers adore the mixing of flavors, and have taken to dipping pieces of *tengbrök* into the mash to flavor up their otherwise bland and grainy bread. In Northrealm, calcanna is called by a different name; gefkarys, but the recipe is basically the same. The main difference between Dragonmoor and Northrealm as far as this dish goes is that in Northrealm, Avira's leek is substituted for normal leek, despite its overall grainier taste, as Avira's leek grows much more readily in the frosty realm.

With the Rangers doting on her, Khula had an easy time forgetting how sore she was. How much her body ached. How her spirit was wavering. She was fighting to keep from breaking down, especially in front of her friends. Fighting as hard as she could. But to have people treat *her* as if... *as if I matter.* It threatened to overwhelm her at every moment.

Khula took her time eating, savoring every bite of the food, in case she never got it again. But she knew she needed time alone. *Alone. No Rangers, no one at all.* There were things she had to think about. Things to consider. Looking at Karos, the woman set down her spoon as she finished her food, and raised her hands.

"Where may I bathe… and sleep?" She asked, signing to the man.

"This way, my friend." Reaching out, the man helped Khula to her feet, which had gone blissfully numb. Together, they walked through the *tengjäv*, with Karos pointing out the different areas. Angling a finger to their right as they went down into the cavern, Karos indicated the armory cave. Then, to their left, the reading-room. Ahead, the sleeping cavern, and as he led her down a narrow passageway, Khula could hear the splashing of water. The smell of soap-sand. Fresh linens. As soon as they crossed through the doorway, the woman gasped.

There was a massive rock pool, fed from above by a small waterfall, and draining to some unseen far below. Water, time, and feet wore the pool smooth, but despite that, she could see a deep purple bowl beneath. *Amethyst?* She wondered to herself. The bottom of the pool certainly *shined* like amethyst. But the odds of such a thing being natural were incredibly minute, or at least that's what she thought. She was about to ask Karos a question when she realized he'd vanished. Shrugging, she slipped out of the clothing Karos had given her and made her way to the pool. Unknown to her, her skin of burnished gold was covered in healing bruises, traces of dried blood, and she still felt… unclean.

Slipping into the pool, Khula sucked in a breath as the water stung tiny cuts and different painful spots on her body. Warming her aching muscles and skin. Wading into the pool until her red hair floated around her, Khula did her best to relax. Dunking herself under the pool a few times to soak her hair, the woman wondered at the tingling on her skin. After her lungs began to starve, the Moriani noble made her way to the sitting area of the pool, settled herself... and cried as the last few weeks finally came crashing down on her. The constant aching. The pain, not just from her body, but in her mind, her soul. Her entire life had burned around her and she'd been *helpless.* Helpless to change her own path. Helpless to save herself. *Until that moment.* She almost snarled as she remembered. The black rage that'd overcome her. The years of torment and pain that'd led up to that point. And then? The adrenaline coursing through her veins, through her body as she leapt into action to save someone else. The incredible rush she'd felt when stabbing Magus through the head. And finally, the euphoria she'd felt when the realization hit... *I am free!*

It was still overwhelming, though. Cripplingly so, and she continued sobbing. It wasn't just Magus. Wasn't just the Rangers. There had been so much change. So much trouble in such a short amount of time. And then to have been hiking across the length of Westerspring and into Dragonmoor? *How have I survived all of this?* Somehow, the woman knew anyone lesser than her would have died long ago. But it went deeper than that. *How much of this can I take?* Sighing, Khula cradled her head in her hands and sat there, just listening to the splashing of the water. So many conflicting emotions were blasting through her mind that she couldn't even keep up.

She shrieked as a hand touched her shoulder. Leaping

backward, further into the pool, she twisted until she saw who it was. Who she thought was attacking her. *Sardra.* The dokk threw up her hands, one forming a fist and rubbing on her own chest in a circular motion.

"Sorry! Sorry, Khula! I did not mean to startle you!"

Chest still heaving, Khula nodded slowly and took a breath. Somehow, she found herself able to master her utter terror and calm herself down. Looking at the dokk after a moment, the Moriani woman began signing.

"What do you need, Sardra?"

The dokk smiled gently and settled herself on the edge of the bathing pool, ice-blue eyes watching Khula.

"I wagered you needed companionship at this point. I could hear you sobbing through the *tengjäv*, but I wager you cannot be around Karos right now." She said, her voice gentle and nonjudgmental. Khula nodded stonily, her eyes staring elsewhere as she sat. "Well, I understand. Not for the same reasons, but I understand."

"How can you?" Khula whispered, barely loud enough for Sardra to hear, even with her keen ears.

Sardra gave the woman a tender smile, even if she knew Khula was looking away. While she pondered her answer, the dokk woman went through her two-hundred years of life, focusing her thoughts in on the ten years before she became a Ranger.

"I was... enslaved. From the time I was five until my damsel age." Sardra finally said, looking over at Khula. She had the woman's *full* attention from the moment the words left her lips. "I was a plaything for every desire of evil men; and women, too, sometimes. *Every* desire. I learned my *ljas'atuk* against other slaves; there are still hints of it in my fighting now, even with what the Rangers taught me." Pausing for a moment, the dokk turned her head, so the light brought the various scars on her head and muzzle into sharp relief. "Not all of these are from my service as a Ranger, Khula." Reaching up, the dokk touched some of her scars, gently running her clawed fingers along them. "They whipped me every time I refused someone my body. Every time I refused to fight. Every. Time. So yes. For different reasons, I understand your pain."

Breaths shaky, Khula raised her hands to sign another question. A more personal one. One she'd been wondering for a while, and especially now when the dokk laid her story out bare. She'd heard a little. Enough, honestly, to know that this question was valid.

"How did you survive?" She asked with her hands, looking the dokk directly in the eyes.

Sardra's eyes flashed. Suddenly, there was no doubt who Khula was talking to. She wasn't a scared dokk child, pulled into a world she never understood. She wasn't a confident Ranger, forging her own path. This was Sardra Wood-Strider, laying herself bare before a noble she hardly knew. Because she felt they had common threads.

"The fire inside me burned hotter than their brands could ever hope to. Throughout my life, my trials and triumphs, my weak moments and failures, a voice spoke to me. Constantly whispering strength. Whispering hope. Urging me onward. It was this same voice that commanded my first strikes when I broke out of captivity. This same voice that pushed me to fight on until I escaped. That guided me, a terrified fifteen-summer-old child, out of bondage and into the waiting arms of the Rangers."

She grinned, showing exquisitely clean incisors and canines.

"I have a brand burned onto the back of my neck. Many of my friends helped me deface it. Many of them sliced it out of me, but it always grows back. So I wear it as a badge to show other slaves that they, too, have hope."

A deep, gravelly voice suddenly spoke, nearly sending both women scrambling.

"And you have done well, Sardra Wood-Strider. You have kept that torch burning and ignited it in so many others."

Both women's heads whipped around to see who the intruder was. At first, neither recognized the burly urok, standing high enough that the shadows enveloped part of his face. *Or is that by choice?* Sardra wondered. A pair of twinkling blue eyes watched from what seemed an impossible height.

Khula studied every detail she could see of the stranger. The cloth that, at first, looked like a slave's garb. An adze shined dully from a loop on his rope belt. Powerful green arms, manacled at the wrist, crossed over a massive chest. A collar, partly hidden in the shadows. This was a slave who escaped. *Escaped? Or fought his way out*, wondered Khula. He was decorated with more scars than even Sardra had on her body. And he felt *old*. Impossibly old. Looking at Khula for some idea who this was, the woman found the dokk slack-jawed. Evidently, this was someone who commanded the Ranger's awe. The figure grinned, showing even, carefully tended teeth and tusks. *An orc, for certain. A recently freed slave?* For some reason, Khula found herself unable, unwilling, even, to meet his eyes.

The orc reached down and touched Sardra's head gently, which seemed to break her out of her stupor. She shuddered gently and blinked once more. Then the figure turned to Khula. At first, his hand moved toward her, but then paused and returned to his side.

"No, no. The time is not right, the wounds are still too fresh."

For a moment, Khula hadn't the foggiest idea what he meant. But then she realized, quite suddenly, that she'd curled up into a ball, as far from the orc and the Ranger as she could. Her skin felt as if it would slough off if anyone touched her. Her bones felt like they were made of jelly, and she just wanted to be away. Far away.

"Khula, you are safe. Breathe, girl." The orc said, his voice somehow gruff and warm at the same time. But she couldn't bring herself to look at him. At anyone. When she felt the Ranger's touch, she tried to recoil even further. But Sardra wouldn't let her. Instead, the Ranger wrapped her arms around the woman, holding her close.

"Whisperer-Of-Hope. I fear she is not in a condition to be near any male." Sardra finally said as she read every detail of Khula's body language. "Or really anyone." The orc nodded gently and stepped back. Far enough back, in fact, that a lot of the pressure threatening to drown Khula ceased. She took a gasping, deep breath.

"I am the voice that guided you, Khula. The urge to carry on, despite what was done. The hope that things would get better. It is by my will you were delivered to the company of Rangers. By my suggestion, you slew your abuser. I am Pohgrak. Whisperer-Of-Hope. Ancestor of the unwanted and abandoned. The torch carried by all who escape slavery."

Khula was quite beyond her ability to process things, such was the pain she was carrying. The Ranger cradling her could feel the tension in every part of the woman's body. Every wracking sob. Everything. Finally, Sardra looked up at the

Ancestor who was trying to help and shook her head.

"You cannot help right now, Pohgrak. Please. She will speak to you when she is ready." Sardra said after a moment.

"I understand, Ranger. I will remove myself until she is ready." With that, Pohgrak walked out of the bathing cavern and through the halls of the *tengjäv* until he found a spot he thought pleasant.

Karos was there, in the reading room, when a massive orc clad in the garb of a slave wandered in. Raising an eyebrow, the Warden Ranger shifted to his feet.

"Here, friend. Sit, allow me to aid you as I can." He said, moving to gently guide who he thought was a recently freed slave to a chair for rest. In return, he got a chuckle and a kindly pat on the shoulder.

"Karos," he said, "You are always the kindest you can be to those you see as needing your aid." The Ranger blinked as the orc addressed him by name.

"You know my name, but I am unfamiliar with you, friend." Karos said, his voice somewhat cooler than before, as if he were expecting trouble.

"Oh, you know me, even if you do not know my form." The orc grinned and sat down in one chair as he spoke. The wood creaked under his bulky frame. "I am the hope you give to those oppressed. The freedom you offer to those enslaved."

"Pohgrak." Karos said, immediately casting his eyes down and moving to kneel. One of the gargantuan green hands picked him back up.

"No, Warden Ranger, you need not bow." Pohgrak said, his voice cheery and warm.

"To what do I owe the honor, Whisperer-of-Hope?" Karos

said a moment later.

The burly orc Ancestor considered his words for a moment. *What am I to say?* He pondered for a few moments. Looking the tanned Nolvern man over, Pohgrak finally had his answer.

"I was trying to give hope to one of your companions. Khula Tallam. But by Sardra's words, she is... beyond my aid right now." He said ruefully. Karos nodded as he spoke.

"I fear she will not respond well to any man at the current moment," Karos answered, choosing his words carefully, "for it was by a man that she was harmed. Harmed for many years." Sucking in a breath, Karos recounted a bit of what Khula had told him. Pohgrak listened intently, steepling his fingers in front of his face and watching as Karos' face ran the gamut of emotions he felt at recounting the tale. When he finished, Karos gave one final thought. "I will give her the tools she need to *never* need me again."

Pohgrak considered those words for more than a few minutes, sitting in silence and watching the Ranger's face. The way he drew himself to his full height, and that, for just a moment, this human, this *Nolvern mortal*, stood taller than he, an Ancestor. The orc smiled as he saw the unquenchable fire in the man's topaz eyes. There was a reason Pohgrak loved this man as his own kin. There was a reason, one only *he* knew, that he'd guided Karos all these years. Still watching the man, Pohgrak noted how he was standing. Chest out, shoulders back. A stare that challenged Pohgrak; *and anyone who would deny his path,* thought the Ancestor, to *try to* change his mind. To force him to recant his ideals.

"Everyone should be their own master," Pohgrak finally said. "On that we agree, Warden Ranger Karostrun anrak'Lyvan. Last of your surname, first of your title. For you to give others the tools to not need you is the utmost of deserving honor."

They stayed in the *tengjäv* for another three days. Karos searched high and low in the armory cavern to find a new set of weapons. A bastard sword, this time made in the style of the gah'Drin wanderers. A long, slim blade, wood handle, silvery steel crossguard with a single adornment; an oak leaf, directly in the center on both sides. The *tengjäv* keeper was sore to lose that sword, for it had belonged to a dear friend.

"That is the sword of Alhan Tu'Garyig. He saved my life many times, once at the cost of his own. Treat that sword well, Warden Ranger Karos, for it is all I have left of my closest friend." Said the keeper solemnly, before handing the blade to Karos reluctantly. The Warden Ranger nodded slightly. Then he belted the scabbard on, sheathed the sword, and looked through the rest of the weapons for his secondary.

Something caught Karos' eye. A strange-looking axe; *or is it an axe?* Sitting almost hidden behind a war axe. It called to him, in the deepest parts of his soul. Seemed as if it were *meant* to be wielded by him. Reaching out, the Ranger took the axe and examined it with a perfectionist's eye. A leaf-shaped blade, coming out from an expertly mated haft, and a dense, square head on the back. As he pored over the blade, he spotted several holes through the steel. Taking the weapon in his right hand, he tested the feeling and balance of the weapon. *Or is it a tool?* Glancing over at the Keeper, he quirked an eyebrow and gave the weapon a few experimental swings.

"What is this? Such a strange design, and yet... It calls to me." He finally said, before shifting the weapon to his offhand and again testing the feeling. *No matter what hand, it feels as if it were made for me.* Swinging a few more times, he nodded. It moved perfectly in his hands, felt as if it were... *almost more natural than Northrage.* Dropping the weapon into his axe frog, the Warden Ranger waited for the Keeper's answer.

"It is a tomahawk. Specifically, this is the Windsong, carried by Warden Ranger Galrajh, over five thousand years ago. Fourth Empire. If memory serves, this was *the* weapon he was using during the charge of Dularin Gate." The Keeper said, and when Karos glanced over, he realized the Keeper was thumbing through different parchments. "According to these notes, it was the final product of the Forgesinger. As such, the axe possesses an... odd quality."

Quirking an eyebrow at the Keeper again, Karos pulled Windsong into his hand once more and looked it over. It *seemed* to be a fairly simple weapon. But the idea of an 'odd quality' echoed in his head. Finally, he spoke.

"What 'odd quality' are you speaking of, Keeper?" He sighed as he spoke.

"Well, give it a swing, and do it like you *mean* it." The Keeper answered.

Nodding, Karos took a stance and swung the tomahawk. A thrill ran through his arm, and he *thought* he could hear a fluting sound. Shaking his head for a moment, he began swinging the tomahawk once more. This time, he moved through an aggressive drill routine, shifting it from hand to hand, as if he were fighting multiple opponents. As he did, the fluting sound became more obvious. More audible. And much more melodious. As he fought through invisible enemies, the music of Windsong became apparent. Even as he moved, the blade began to glow, and as he became more aggressive, more concerted, the tomahawk sang to him. When he stopped, the song lingered for a few more moments.

"That is... fascinating, Keeper." He finally said, once more looking over the blade of the tomahawk. Feeling the strange holes, he looked up at the Keeper again. "I assume the holes are what make the music?"

The Keeper nodded gently and chuckled before speaking. "That is not *all* there is to this weapon, but I shall not cheat you of learning that yourself."

Karos nodded and dropped Windsong back into his axe frog. Then he began looking around for something to replace his precious hunting knife, his seax, which he'd had since childhood.

"Keeper?" He asked a moment later. "Is there any way to repair this?" Pulling the seax's sheath from his pack, he pulled the handle out and dumped the blade next to it. Moving over, the Keeper raised an eyebrow and prodded the metal. Making a few odd noises here and there, the Keeper inspected the weapon. Finally, they shook their head.

"The weapon is irreparable. The metal spirit is gone from the weapon; it gave its last to..." The Keeper touched the weapon once more and closed their eyes. "Stop a man from harming a woman."

"Indeed. It broke when I stabbed it into the arm of Magus Kefarion after getting his attention away from the woman he was assaulting." Karos replied. Giving a gentle sniff, he placed a hand on the weapon. "Perhaps it can be remade, Keeper?" But the Keeper shook their head.

"Again, Warden Ranger. The metal spirit is gone. You could reforge the weapon, but it would not have the will to hold itself together. It would only strike once and then break again. The will holding it together came from... your mother." The Keeper finally said. Karos nodded sadly.

"My mother blessed this weapon to forever strike true, and I received it from Calem Bloodstone, the Dragonsmith of my childhood." He said, finishing up his thought.

"It gave its all. Let it rest, Warden Ranger. I will keep it here and give it a place of honor. Now, come." The Keeper said, pulling Karos along to the racks and racks of weapons throughout the armory cave. "Look through these and tell me what calls out to you."

Nodding at the instruction, Karos looked at each weapon, his mind searching through the various daggers, knives, and other tools. In the back of his mind, he knew he wasn't just seeking to replace a *weapon,* but a *tool* as well. As he moved along, Karos noted the different weapons until his eyes stopped on one. Blinking, he examined it for a moment as it sat on the rack, its scabbard next to it.

Odd looking weapon, he thought to himself as he reached for the handle. At first, he wasn't sure exactly what to make of it. A handle made of what looked to be ox horn, wrapped with leather. A blade that came out straight for a short distance, before curving sharply downward, giving the leaf-shaped blade a rather humped appearance. Then, from the tip, a wider portion coming back and narrowing down to meet the handle.

"Hm." Was all Karos said as he grasped the handle of the weapon. Picking it up and testing the way it felt in his hand, he looked it over a few more times. There was a deep fuller running along the spine of the blade, and it looked; well, *fascinating* to the Nolvern man. "Keeper?" He finally asked. "What is this?"

"That is a khukari, the type of blade used by the nomadic Farlanders. It serves as weapon and tool of many uses. I think... " Grabbing Karos' hand, the Keeper adjusted the man's grip slightly. "There." Then they stepped back to look the man over. "Yes. I think that fits you, Warden Ranger." Nodding, Karos belted the scabbard on where it felt right, and slid the weapon into it.

Once he'd finished gearing back up, Karos looked around for a moment, wondering if anything was missing. A casual glance picked something up on one of the armor racks. A hat. Specifically, a teardrop shaped hat of green suede, with brown wings on either side and a single falcon tailfeather poking out of a pocket on the right side of the hat. On the left, Karos found as he approached and inspected the hat, there was a pocket which, upon trying, he realized fit his whetstone securely. Raising an eyebrow, Karos had a thought. *Perhaps this was made for my use?* He wasn't sure, but the Keeper hadn't said anything so far, so with a glance back at them, he picked up the hat and settled it on his head. For no reason he could fathom, the hat just felt... *right.*

"That was crafted based on the hat of the First Warden Ranger. Elkin Thuraen." The Keeper said quietly. "I have been waiting for centuries for a Warden Ranger to notice it, let alone wear it. Wear it proudly, Karos." With that, the Keeper bowed and excused themself while Karos adjusted the hat until he was comfortable with how it sat on his head.

There, he thought to himself; *I feel like a proper Ranger again.*

15

15: The Skies Above Westerspring, Dragonmoor

Sighing, Thäoldr looked out over the world as he flew on Namryll's back. Already he was feeling stronger, though the terrible taste in his mouth persisted. Grinning, he patted Namryll's neck affectionately.

"To Ormere Keep. If this plague sickened the Paragon of Healing, we must hasten to bring the cure to him, as well as the others of the Council. They think me mad, but it is I who will save them."

Aye, Thäoldr, and they shall look ever the fool.

The great dragon's wings pushed massive drafts of air below her as they took to the sky- higher and higher until they were at their maximum flight height. Then, she winged to the south and east to carry them home.

At my best speed, it will be at least a week of travel. But if I maintain my best speed, I will need to rest. And we must land at least twice to not risk your health.

"Aye, I know right well the challenge. I cannot ask you to push yourself further than you feel capable. I can only remind you of how critical our task is. I will also be watchful of my condition, I assure you."

Good.

The finality in the dragon's tone told him she would accept no dissent and that conversation was ended. More would come up, he knew, and he would deal with them in time. As the landscape shot by below them, the Rider reflected upon the events of the past few days. A terrible thought came to his head- would the Council even recognize him at this point? They were used to seeing him with his metal arm, scars, and tattoos. They would be hard-pressed to recognize the blonde youth he had become.

It is likely they will challenge you to prove who you are.

"That is a good point, Namryll. Hopefully, they do a challenge rather than dismiss me."

It will be their deaths if they do.

That was also a good point. They had nothing to gain by disbelieving him and their lives to protect by trusting the elf. He hoped they would see common sense. But in his heart, he knew it would not be that easy. They had always found it hard to trust him, given that he had bonded with a black dragon, but when Vaelyn had taken an interest in him, that had worried them further. The Council had done their best to separate the two painlessly, but the damage had already been done. Thäoldr had already been taught of Mirror, or Void Magic, though he did not pursue it further- until now. But there had been bad blood with how they treated him until he became the Paragon of Knowledge and had proven his use to them. In their eyes, he was still that unstable youth and he knew it was going to be even more difficult to change that now.

Sighing, Thäoldr ran his fingers through his hair. The

gesture felt strange to him and he wondered if it would not be better to shave his head bald. That was the more comfortable state for his head, though the beard was acceptable. His mind was a whirlwind of thoughts and he knew that to be an after-effect of the massive amounts of energy he had pushed through his body. In a dark corner of his mind, he wondered how much time he had left and when he would end up like Vaelyn. A mad floating energy being incapable of remembering friend or foe and incapable of feeling or interacting with the world. *After this plague business is done, we must focus all resources on learning to stave off that end.* That was the only thought running through his mind that made sense at the current moment. The rest were snippets of information, both old and new, and had little bearing on his situation. Idly, he wondered how the Rangers dealt with this problem. He had talked to Karos about it for a short time, hardly enough to glean anything useful, but at least he knew what it would be like.

Karos, the elf thought, *an interesting man.* He admired the man for his tenacity and often wondered just how he had survived the magical onslaught that Vaelyn had put him through. It appeared that the man could wade through magical attacks with little ill effects, though when he collapsed to the ground, it took quite some time for him to recover. He felt for the man, as most of his weapons had been broken and his body tortured in such a way, but somehow, he'd come through it all and after time to gather himself, had seemed stronger for it. That type of resilience was fascinating to watch, and he wondered if all Rangers shared it. *I would hate to face the Rangers in open combat,* he pondered, *for they do not seem to know or care when they are best. Truth be, this entire ordeal has been one massive battle, and it seems to be nowhere near an end.* He knew the legends, that the Rangers could run to the ends of the world and back without rest, but he wondered just how much truth those held. His own Riders indeed may face the same issue. They may command the sky, but they were mere mortals- and their lives were fleeting.

Hours passed, and Thäoldr crossed the border into Nevian. Below, the groves and swamplands flashed by and he reveled in the view. Be it his first flight or his thousandth, he never ceased to be amazed by how incredible Seran looked from above. The landscape was breathtaking even as it flashed by and Thäoldr tired. He realized that not counting the time he'd spent unconscious from the cure; he'd not slept in a few days. Shifting his belts and part of the saddle, he lay back and got comfortable. Trusting in his dragon to continue the way, he closed his eyes and drifted off to sleep.

Waking to the feeling of descent, Thäoldr felt a momentary panic. Was something wrong? Had his dragon been injured? Shifting, he glanced to the sky and got a read on the day. It was just after midday and they were flying through clouds, giving the black dragon some refreshment as she flew. She dropped further, before beginning a full descent towards the ground. They were on the Dragonmoor side of the Wyrmspine Range and in safe enough territory to land.

Touching down in a large open field, the dragon paced for a moment until she found a comfortable spot. Once she was content, she curled up for a nap, while doing her best to not disturb her rider. Closing her multifaceted eyes, she let out a great huff.

Laying on Namryll's back, Thäoldr stared up into the sky. They had made significant progress today, but still had much to do and far to go. In the back of his mind, the Sage of Wind wondered if all his work would make a difference in the end. What would follow these events? *I feel there is a storm on the horizon, and we have only seen the lightning from afar.*

The thought was from far away, and at first, Thäoldr wondered who it was. Glancing down at his dragon, he realized it could not be her– she was off and away in the skies of dreams. The voice sounded maddeningly familiar, but only just.

"Who speaks?"

The query Thäoldr whispered to no-one sounded strange, even to him. He was not really expecting an answer, though it would do much to calm his nerves. Closing his eyes for but a moment, he felt everything shift. Everything changed around him and when his eyes opened, he recognized nothing, apart from the fact that he was no longer laying upon Namryll's back. Slowly, he rose to his feet and looked around. *This is not my world.* The sky was a brilliant rainbow, and Kjetta was nowhere to be seen. Flecks of gold hung in the air as if frozen in place. Everywhere he looked, a blue ground beneath him stretched off into oblivion. Closing his eyes once more, he tried to mentally force himself away from this alien landscape, but when he opened his eyes, it was still there. If he focused, he found he could hear whispering– so much whispering it nearly maddened him. *Where am I?*

"You are with me, child."

Whirling, Thäoldr looked for the source of the voice– the same voice who had whispered in his mind earlier– and found nothing. His mind grew more and more disconcerted and disquieted by the moment, when all at once, the whispering stopped. For a moment, there was no sound, no thought, just stillness and the vision of the endless landscape. The elf closed his eyes once more and once more he opened them, this time to find a woman standing before him. *Is she truly there?* She stood a little taller than him, with a skin of gray scales and a face he had only seen in dreams. Graceful horns adorned her head, growing from her temples to curve back in the manner of a dragon's horns and hung from the bony spikes were rings of gold. She was clad in battle armor of scaled mail and fine make and Thäoldr wondered if she was perhaps a Rider from a time long forgotten. She looked more regal and more dangerous than any of the paintings he had seen of the Kingmages and somehow felt familiar- and comfortable, but he could not recognize her, no matter how he tried. It was quickly becoming maddening, and he felt foolish.

The woman reached out and touched his shoulder and suddenly he could see much more than just her. Around them both walked hundreds, nay, thousands of Riders. Thäoldr recognized some, both great names from history, and some of his own that had passed on over his years. One approached to silently regard Thäoldr and the woman before speaking in a sad bass voice. At first, the elf could not see the face, as the shadow of a hood obscured it.

"Sage of Wind, Mother of Dragons. We stand upon the precipice of an unprecedented cataclysm. The work of Vaelyn has consequences that reach much further than this plague alone. Far worse events have been set in motion. You recognized the works of Vaelyn as Mirror Magic, but it is known by another name- Void Magic. Something from beyond our realm entirely."

Thäoldr nodded slowly. This shade was saying nothing he did not already know, apart from the other name for Mirror Magic. Sighing, the Sage of Wind looked between the two nearest him. He was unsure of what was happening, and it was annoying him. He was about to speak when the woman raised a hand.

"In the annals of the Riders and the histories of the Rangers, there is a record of beings almost beyond mortal comprehension. They have only been seen thrice before in the history of Seran, and each time they have brought changes that nearly destroyed the world."

The woman's voice held more power than Thäoldr had ever known. He suddenly felt tiny, unsure of himself. The voice was terrifying and comforting at the same time. Despite that, he could not place it. In the back of his mind, he wondered if this was a ruse and they were keeping his attention.

The woman's eyes flashed dangerously as the thought crossed his mind. She spoke again, her magisterial voice making Thäoldr want to hide away.

"You know better than any to doubt, not the evidence of your eyes and mind, Thäoldr Sagewind. You question who I am, who my friend is. Perhaps this will remind you."

With a motion of her hand, the woman pushed the man's hood away, revealing his face. The violet eyes caught Thäoldr's attention first, and they reminded him of Vaelyn at first- then he realized. The dark hair, the graceful physique. He was in the presence of the First Rider, Gelvrentael himself. Immediately, Thäoldr cast his eyes downward and dropped to one knee, to the amusement of the woman.

"He recognizes you, Gelvrentael, but not me."

"Give him a moment. Remember that I had trouble recognizing you when you first appeared to me."

As if emboldened by Gelvrentael's words, Thäoldr's eyes shot up suddenly. His mind had made the leap, but he could still not quite believe it. The name was on his tongue, but he dared not speak it. Instead, he murmured her title, scarcely believing who was addressing him.

"Dragon-mother."

"Indeed. I am dal'Kiyr and this is my true form. You realize that your trouble recognizing me comes from my nature. I am a deity and unless I... minimize myself, your mortal mind cannot understand me well. It takes a powerful mind to come to terms with what they are seeing. Now rise, Thäoldr. I so hate seeing folk grovel."

Shakily, Thäoldr took to his feet, before looking between the two legends. One a literal goddess, speaking to him almost as an equal. The other, the one who the Order of Gelvrentael was named for. The First Rider, the one who walked the lands to find his way. Being around them was intoxicating- and terrifying. He felt smaller than he had ever felt in his life, but somehow equal.

"Now listen carefully, Thäoldr. Things are in motion that cannot be easily stopped- but you must gather your allies to mitigate the effects and try to stop what is coming. It is hard to describe because even I cannot truly see what it is."

Thäoldr arched an eyebrow curiously. This was not much to go on and if he were to rally both the Riders and the Rangers, he would need a much better lead. In his haste to move things along, he asked a single question- and felt he would immediately regret the answer.

"Gelvrentael, what say you about the alliance between the Order and the Rangers?"

Gelvrentael regarded Thäoldr severely for a time as he sifted through old memories- painful ones, ones he had hoped never to relive.

"When I was much younger, there were no Rangers or Riders. There was a single entity- The Snow Guard, serving the First Kingmage, Ywelin Nachtvolk. When I was born, they were already legendary, with names among them that have been lost to time for many thousands of years. I could go on for some time, but what is important to know is that both the Riders and the Rangers descend from the Snow Guard. There was a great calamity, and the Guard fell before a foe of incredible power. Elkin Thuraen and I were among the only survivors. He would create the Rangers and you know well where I traveled. Look in your records and convince the Rangers to do the same. You will see the truth in my words, Thäoldr."

"You have solved one problem, my child. But more tasks await. But all is not lost, for you have allies that number among the ablest in Seran. They will light your way when all seems darkest."

In a flash, it was all gone. Thäoldr's eyes flew open, and he was back in the field, on his back, atop Namryll. He puzzled over what these last few minutes could have meant, and he did not like the options. Sighing, he lay there, feeling Namryll breathing beneath him. He felt a random twitch and a spark of lightning jumped from his fingers. He knew what it meant- he was running out of time. Soon enough, he would weaken, his body consuming itself in a desperate bid to maintain the energy he had already pushed through it. He had studied what had happened to Vaelyn, for it had happened to more than a few Riders over his years. The final form was called a *lok'vi*, a name the Rangers had coined. It meant Spirit of Magic, and the path to becoming one was not pleasant.

That event is far, and away, Thäoldr and it may not happen. You worry too much. The voice was much nearer than before and quite sleepy. Looking down, he saw that one of Namryll's jewellike eyes was open and regarding him with care and affection. *Sleep. Nothing will risk attacking a black dragon, even one that is sleeping.*

Thäoldr heeded the sage advice and soon drifted back into the darkness of rest.

When Thäoldr next awoke, the night was pitch-dark. Blearily, the elf roused himself and went to touch one of his tattoos and ignite a mage-light. When he hit bare skin, the Sage of Wind cursed again and again. *Vaelyn! You bastard!* Sighing, he reached up to his shoulder, touched his fingers to his skin, and traced the pathway nerves down to his wrist. Then, focusing on pushing the needed energy out of his body and into the shape he wanted, Thäoldr manifested a glowing blue orb. At first, it was barely visible, but after a few moments, it flared to life, glowing brilliantly enough that the entire area was illuminated in the comforting light. Namryll was nowhere to be seen at first.

Namryll? He thought apprehensively, thinking she was absent for fell reasons.

I am nearby. Just hunting. You are safe, came the thought, sounding rather like his wife's voice down a long stone corridor. Nodding, the elf went to work putting up a small fire and preparing a meal. The fuel didn't take long to find, and he still had ample supplies in his saddlebags, thoughtfully left next to him by Namryll. As he unpacked them, he happened to glance at the larger pack sitting next to the saddlebags.

The cure. Sighing, he almost packed his things back up. *Must not waste time when so many lives are at stake.* But instead of approval, there was instead a mental pressure that came from Namryll. Blinking as the weight of the suggestion nearly caused him to fall to his knees, Thäoldr looked up. *What is it, Namryll?*

You will be useless for your tasks if you are delirious from hunger. Eat. She commanded with a note of finality that shocked the elf. It was rare for a dragon to show such defiance, but Thäoldr couldn't fight against it. Every time he tried to put things back in the pack, the pressure would increase. Finally, he relented, unpacking his mess kit and rations. A cooking pan with a folding handle and a small pot nestled on it. A plate made of steel. Utensils of iron. Finally, his rations. As he looked over what he had, the Sage of Wind sighed gently. *Amrilyn packed the best she could provide.* Said Namryll gently.

When? The elf asked.

While you were asleep during the cure-making. She responded.

Nodding, Thäoldr unpacked the first of the ration bags and peered in, taking stock of what it contained. *Smoked pascha salmon, always pleasant. Looks like... Delranael Spring Cheese. Must have cost a few Aureim to get from the Islands. Travel bread, of course, good enough. Honeycomb, what am I, a wood elf?* He allowed himself a chuckle. There was no end to his gratitude for the woman for packing the rations, and the very look of it all made his stomach rumble louder than it had for many a day. As he laid the ration bag out in front of him and reached for his belt knife, the elf noticed something else in the pack. *What is this?* Grabbing the item, he lifted it. The moment he saw it, he realized what it was. A wineskin. *Praises be!* Uncorking it, he took a sniff of the wine. He wasn't a connoisseur by any means, but he knew *good* wine, and this? *This smells incredible. From the smell alone, this must be something impressively expensive.* Blinking, he grabbed his travel cup and poured some of the wine in. A pale white wine, giving Thäoldr the impression that the rest of the ration packs contained, probably, fish or poultry, which suited him just fine. Chuckling, he corked the wineskin and took a sip of the wine. It was crisp and tart, and tasted like it was right off the vine. Nodding appreciatively, Thäoldr made a note to save the wineskin for later, and only sample from it when resting. The cup though? He drank that as he ate his meal, reveling in the tastes of the meat, cheese, bread, and wine as they mixed together.

It was more than enough to lift his spirits.

About an hour and a full adventurer's meal later, Thäoldr was ready to set out again. As he packed his bags once more, he took a glance around. *Dawn is likely still far away*, he thought. Stretching out as one always did before getting back up in the saddle, he pondered what to do next. Certainly, he had to make for Ormere Keep, and as soon as possible. But where from there? Should he try to meet back up with Karos, Sardra, and Khula? *Or should I...* He stopped that line of thought short with a wave. The Vault was an absolute last resort. Besides, the danger was already past, or so he hoped.

Time would tell how wrong he was.

Glancing up as a shadow passed, barely visible, across the ground, Thäoldr caught sight of the whirling, jeweled eyes of a dragon. Namryll had returned, and when she landed delicately next to him, he reached up and scratched one of her eye ridges. Then she dropped her neck and angled her shoulder far enough down that he could climb aboard, watching as he secured the satchel containing the precious cure in front of him and tightened his belts around it and himself. "Secure!" He roared with more life than he'd had the past few days.

Secure, she echoed before arranging herself. She sat back on her haunches, causing Thäoldr to tilt backwards. Then she bunched her formidable leg muscles up, took a breath, and a heartbeat later, the two were propelled into the sky. At the apex of the mighty leap, Namryll unfolded her wings and began beating the air to push herself higher and higher. When they reached flight altitude, the dragon opened her wings to their full width, soaring on currents and heading once more toward Dragonmoor's Wyrmspine Mountains, heading on a southern path to Ormere Keep, the stronghold of the Order of Gelvrentael.

A few hours on, with the relaxing feeling of air on his skin and in his hair, Thäoldr found his eyes struggling to stay open. His hands slid from the belts a few times, his head drooped. *Thäoldr!* Came the voice in his head, jerking him awake.

Aye! He replied, trying to shake himself back into full wakefulness. Glancing around, he saw the comforting bulk of Namryll, the wisps of clouds, the stars above, and the four moons drifting lazily overhead. Blinking away some of the sleepiness, he shifted in the saddle and sighed. *Namryll, we may need to land so I can sleep.* The dragon rumbled gently but continued flying on.

No, we can afford no delays. Tighten your flight belts and sleep in the saddle, dear Thäoldr.

Within moments, the old elf was following the instruction, his belts tightened enough to press into his flesh. His eyes were closed, and he was arranged straight up in his saddle, to look like he was fully alert. But he was snoring, his chest rising and falling slowly and gently, his hands limp at his sides.

16: ???, Westerspring

Fae awoke with a start. At first, she couldn't tell what was around her, but her senses told her it certainly wasn't the hostel. Blinking away the darkness from her eyes as best she could, the woman glanced around as things began to realize around her. She was... *somewhere, that is certain.* Sighing, she grabbed her gear and got herself together. Belt, rapier, pouches, pack. Boots. As soon as she stood, the bed vanished, which was altogether strange, but given that Fae *knew* she was dreaming, it could be forgiven.

I am dreaming, yes? She wondered, looking around. Stepping away from everything that seemed to wobble as she looked at it, the wood elf shook her head. *This is a dream.*

Oh, but it is much worse. A voice boomed in her head, trying to cow her. Wincing at the volume against her slight hangover, the woman looked for the source of the voice. It was then she realized she wasn't on Seran. In fact, she wasn't anywhere she recognized. The landscape looked completely wrong. Spires from the sky. She was standing on air. Or at least, what looked like air; but was it? Taking a few tentative steps, she nearly fell out of the eye of an impossibly large creature; only her reflexes, honed by many decades adventuring, saved her. Gripping the iris of the monstrosity, she blinked–

–and so did the monster. Glancing at the iris, she saw the coloration; the coloration of the skin as well. *What in the fuck?* She'd nearly fallen from her own eye. Blinking, she narrowly avoided her own eyelid and looked at the ground below. *Somewhere* below. *Fuck it.* Taking a leap of faith, she let go of the iris and fell.

And continued falling for what felt like an eternity. When she landed, it was a hard landing, slamming down into the cold stone floor of a gaol cell. *What?* Her gear was still on her. Her clothes were still there. But she was in a gaol cell, one that smelled faintly of urine, despair, and childbirth. *This is your future,* said a voice. *Denounce Karos, and you may get another chance.* That was odd enough, and Fae knew the voice was lying. Things would have to change *massively* and for the worse if she, an adventuring captain, were to be gaoled for supporting a *Ranger.* Shifting herself, the woman closed her eyes for a moment.

This is a dream. She repeated again. Little by little, she exerted control over her own mind, even as a foreign influence attempted to dig in. *I am Fae Cos'Criux, Adventurer. Captain of Dire Company, Krygan–Shawv Adventuring Guild. I know not who nor what you are...* she took a breath, massed her mind and strengthened her resolve, *but you can fuck right off.* In all directions, she sent a blast of mental fire. Fire hotter than she had ever mustered. Her response was a cacophony of screams, and the mental pressure dropped away instantly–

–and then she saw the creature plain. Unable to hide from her, the Void–Sleeper stood there, a strange, smoky being in her world. Sickly green teeth. Yellow eyes. A shroud of smoke surrounding it, but with immense effort, Fae was able to lay the creature bare. Immediately, she began committing details to memory. *Eighty spearlengths tall. Made of the night sky, but perverted. Smoke and hate. It reeks of decay, and it burns my skin.*

Pushing back will do nothing. But Fae was beyond such a creature's capabilities, it realized as she doubled back on its mind with crushing force. This was no scared child, as it had expected. This was a woman who'd seen the worst that mortals could offer, and then some. Like the *other*, she was something stronger than it expected. It recoiled, trying to goad her into advancing into a trap. But she dropped back mentally, gathering her strength. But when she expected it to attack again?

It was gone, as if something else had drawn its attention. And there she was, standing in the middle of Wolf River's town square, staring at a bewildered Ranger. "Are you well?" They shouted at her, and suddenly, Fae was aware of many Rangers standing around, armed and ready.

"I saw it." She said grimly. "I saw the face of the greatest enemy we could ever know." She snarled. "And I made. It. Flinch." A cheer went up from the assemblage as they realized that there was indeed hope for their world if such an enemy as they'd seen could feel fear. And feel fear it did. Not just from Fae, but from a Ranger, trapped in its world, rampaging through and burning everything they could to dust.

As Fae set out upon the road once more, a pair of eyes watched from afar. Hidden even from the wood elf's formidable senses. Hidden from her view. They stalked her, watching her actions with interest as she made her way toward Hollyhead along the

Grand Road. Other tasks called them away at times, but for the most part, they marked her progress with interest.

Fae, on the other hand, was hoofing it as fast as she could. The encounter with the Void-Sleeper had given new urgency to her steps. New speed, to the point she'd considered commissioning a horse. Or a carriage, perhaps, if she wanted to ride in style. But in her own way, she pushed herself to her limits, jogging across the verdant, gentle lands of Westerspring at her own pace.

A week out from Wolf River, she stopped short, thinking she'd seen something ahead. Towns aplenty, of course, but this was different. Dropping low, the woman took a breath and shifted along, crawling along the ground until she was in a position she could see with her telescope. Extending the brass tube, she peered through it and took a breath, stabilizing herself. Then, her stomach dropped.

The dal'Korin forces, what looked like a small strike force of skvath-trapa, or 'storm troops.' Young dal'Korin who were so eager to die for the cause of the Scala'Dun that they would throw themselves *beyond* the front lines in order to cause havoc where and when they could. They were hardy, tough, and fast. A few were experienced fighters, but by her reckoning, none were over the age of sixty.

Which meant she had the advantage in experience. Grinning, she pocketed her telescope and took off at a dead sprint. As she ran, Fae drew upon her affinity for the world around her and offered some of her life in exchange for the power to do a devastating blow. Sprinting, she could hear her heartbeat in her ears, feel the thudding right up to the tips. Her lungs burned, her heart pounded, and the dal'Korin noticed her; their mistake, for they knew then they were doomed. Turning from their slaughter of a gah'Drin caravan, they readied themselves to receive the obviously suicidal wood elf.

As she sprinted toward the enemy force, Fae charged energy through herself into her left hand. Her right grasped the hilt of her rapier, and the moment was upon her. Knocking a blade away, she slammed her hand into the ground, unleashing an explosion from her body outwards. All around her, the skvath'trapa were flung away by the sheer ferocity of the blast, and their clothes ignited from the heat. The screams were immediate, and Fae went to work.

Clearly, they have ne'er faced a spellsword. With a grin, she twisted and delivered a one-two punch into one foe. A firebolt to the face, scorching him, searing his skin and eyes. And less than a heartbeat later, she slashed his throat from ear-hole to ear-hole, leaving him to bleed out from the gaping laceration in his neck. Without missing a beat, she turned and kicked out, knocking another foe backward before firing off a quick succession of three overcharged firebolts to his center mass. The first impacted, blasting his leather armor apart. The second seared his skin, and the third punched a hole through him, and he fell.

One of the skvath'trapa rounded on her, clearly a more skilled one than she'd expected. As her rapier came toward him, he parried the slash and went for a stab himself. However, she was able to outmaneuver the relatively clumsier broadsword, drawing a laceration up his sword arm. He switched arms, trusting on his natural healing abilities to close the wound, and brought his broadsword in once more for a thrust, this time rewarded with a yelp of pain. His reward, apart from seeing the wood elf's blood splatter on the ground, was her grabbing his throat and blasting fire through his scales until his head disconnected from his body. *Three of five.*

Spinning, Fae turned to face the other two. A firebolt barely missed her, skimming off into the distance, and Fae snarled, responding with a spell she'd created. Touching her pathway nerves, she launched a ball of fire that landed near the foes and sprayed out liquid flames around itself as it exploded. The hapless dal'Korin, being nowhere near ready to deal with the multiple attacks, shrieked as the liquid fire clung to them, searing through their armor and tough scales, their flesh, and into their bones.

Standing victorious, Fae looked upon the destruction she'd wrought, and what the skvath'trapa had done. The town was all but obliterated, the evidence of a proud, if doomed, resistance plain as day. Walking through the burning hamlet, Fae did her best to marshal survivors to save their homes, their friends and family. Rangers that'd been en route flocked in and came to help, but the message was clear; the Scala'Dun was making their moves. *Time is of the essence,* Fae realized, and after informing a Ranger what had transpired, took off once more. Time was against her; against everyone. So she knew she couldn't dally.

So off she took, heading into the distance and doing her best to keep her spirits up. The farther she got from the burned town, the happier she found herself. At least, until her thoughts returned to the oncoming war. To Karos, wondering what he had up his sleeve. To Dire Company, and where they might be able to meet up with her. There were other Rangers she knew and wished to catch up with, hoping they were still breathing.

Eventually, her thoughts drifted to Karos once more. When would she meet the man again? What would that meeting be like, and would it lead anywhere important? Would it lead anywhere useful? Thoughts collided and swam around, and soon enough, she found herself walking through the night. Exhaustion was nowhere to be found, and instead, Fae just found herself wishing for *answers*. Answers she hoped would come in time, but there were still too many unknowns. Too much going on for her liking. Too little time to deal with all of it.

Brushing back her locs, the woman popped her neck and kept rolling along the road. By moonlight, by magelight, she kept up her pace until her legs screamed for mercy. Until her sweat threatened to freeze to her face even in the warm summer night. Shifting off the road, Fae dug a quick firehole, lit a fire more for warmth than cooking, and bundled up to sleep. Box, ever present but oft unseen, patrolled nearby to keep her safe, communicating with other foxes to ensure they had constant watch.

Fae's sleep was uncomfortable, plagued not only by restlessness, but also by strange dreams. A forest of shadows, people she couldn't identify. Whispers she could barely hear. It was enough to drive her back to wakefulness, and when her eyes snapped open, her hand, grasping her rapier, drew it in an instant.

"Easy now, friend." A kindly voice said from next to her. Hardly daring to breathe, Fae looked over to find a haggard old man stoking the fire in the firehole. "I mean you no harm, you can put that away." Forcibly steadying her breathing, the woman sheathed her rapier and nodded, as if she weren't absolutely terrified.

"Well met, friend. I apologize for the sword. Restless night and bad dreams." She said a moment later, though she kept her left hand charged, mentally pushing energy through her pathway nerves. *Just in case.* "How can I aid you? Your hood and garb are worn and ragged, though a keen eye could tell they once were fine as could be."

The man gave a chuckle somewhere between mirth and sadness. She was right, though, that his garb was nearly threadbare. Caked in mud and dust. And in truth, they *had* once been fine.

"Well, 'tis a sad tale. I am a knight of the Empire, but my son was held to ransom, and I have little coin to my name. My wealth is in my land; in people. I live the way the Rangers ask, and ask little of those I protect, save for food and aid when needed." The man said gently. "I have been trying to build up my gold to get him back, and when a priest offered to front the Aureim, I took him for his word. However, he has now demanded payment, before my harvest could sell, and within the week, I must pay three Sereim, or I lose everything." The knight said. In the flickering firelight, Fae could easily see the tears trickling down his face. "My wife, beset by grief, passed some time ago."

"Fear not, my friend. These things have a way of working themselves out." With a sly wink, the woman shifted herself and quietly dispelled the energy she'd built up. There was no need to slaughter this man, who was clearly broken to the point of being unable to lie. "Get some rest. I have little supplies, but what I have, I can and will gladly share." Quickly, Fae threw together her cooking supplies and soon had a hearty venison jerky stew cooking. In the firelight, she could see the man hungrily staring at the pot, and chuckled gently. "A watched pot never boils, friend. I am Fae Cos'Criux, by the by, and you?"

"Corvain. I am Corvain of Dunverio." The knight replied gently. Taking a breath, the man shifted and watched as Fae cooked the stew. Carefully, the woman reached into her coin pouch and felt through her coins. She'd amassed a bit of a fortune over her years, and though she stored what she could back home, the woman knew to always carry a few precious coins. In this case, she had a Sereim, one of the platinum coins of the realm, the most wanted. Just one, the rest was gold, silver, or coin, but she wagered it would help. Once Corvain had eaten his fill and fallen asleep, she tucked the coin in his hand. All too well, she knew the feeling. Destitute and desperate in a strange land. Watching over the man, she waited until morning to protect him.

Sometime during the night, a Ranger had visited and deposited two more Sereim, having heard the tale from Box, Fae's ever-faithful companion. And then?

Then the Ranger had gone on a hunt to find and confront the crooked priest. Trotting alongside him was an overly large rodent, and if one's ears were keen, they could pick up the faint squeaking of arguing rats.

V

Dragon's Mooring

17: Wyrmspine Mountains, Dragonmoor

When Helve awoke, she was still in the giant's home, though pleasantly enough, he'd deposited her on a normal-sized bed. *Normal.* That was a strange concept in and of itself. To the giant, she must seem absurdly small. *Unimportant,* even.

But nothing could be further from the truth. Hovar and Uiuth were still chattering away, so the woman slipped out quietly to stand in the brisk morning breeze. It was approaching winter on the continent, and though Dragonmoor was in the southerly reaches, it was still decently chilly. With a yawn she'd not thought herself capable of, Helve stretched and wriggled until she felt more normal. More herself. Then, she slipped back into the house, wanting to thank her hosts. *Though,* she wondered, *would captors be a better word?* A moment later, though, she chastised herself for such thoughts. She'd allowed herself to come along.

"Ahh, good morning, good morning. I trust you slept well? I do hope Hovar and I were not too chatty for your comfort."

The Sendweln asked, quirking a rocky eyebrow at the woman.

"Nay, good Uiuth. I was quite comforted by your voices, though I fear Viktor will be quite lost without me." She replied with a kindly smile.

"Then, may I suggest we be away before good Hovar decides upon a new topic?" The Sendweln said with a smirk. Nodding, Helve and Uiuth made their farewells to the giant, who was sad to see them go. It wasn't often that people addressed a giant, fearing the worst about them. But already, Helve had learned so much more than what she'd planned to. So much more than what she'd needed to, even. With a heavier pack than she expected, the woman made her way up Uiuth's arm and onto their shoulder.

Then, the two were off.

A few hours later, as Kjetta crested the eastern horizon, Helve and Uiuth had ambled down the mountain enough to see Alvarath and Vu'Locav. Both dragons lazily regarded the two approaching, as if expecting them; or finding them overly late. After saying her farewell to the mountain guardian, Helve settled herself, dusted her clothes, and did her best to arrange her hair. Then, she stepped to the cave mouth.

He has been worried, but convinced you would be upset if he came after you. A draconic voice echoed in her mind.

"He would have been right last night." Helve growled slightly, though she was trying to calm herself. "Viktor Bludstyn!" She shouted into the cave, receiving a startled yell as a response.

"*Nel ca'e armä*, Helve. I thought you had decided to walk the rest of the way to Starwatch. Are you hurt? Are you well?" Viktor said, evidently beside himself with worry as he ran towards the muscular, short woman.

"Calm yourself, Viktor, I am fine. Now," she said, making a show of dusting herself off, "shall we take to the sky once more?" If she still had any feelings for the man, they weren't showing right now. *If.* She knew she did, that much was certain. But how blunted the tip of those arrows had become after the foolishness he'd shown? That much she wasn't sure about. She *wanted* the man. Beyond anything else, she wanted to be seen as more than just a Forge-Second and colleague. She wanted to be a *companion,* in far deeper ways than he seemed capable of seeing her.

Nodding, Viktor didn't even feel the gust of air as the obvious hint flew over his head. "Aye, I suppose we should." Glancing up to the dragons, he quirked his head as he heard a mirthful rumble coming from both of them. "Something amusing, my friends?"

Neither dragon was willing to betray Helve's instructions. He would either figure it out himself; or not at all. She'd taken the time to clean herself up. To lace flowers in her hair. Ancestors, she'd even tied her bodice in such a way to accentuate her breasts. *And he still does not get it.* Rolling her eyes, the woman shrugged a moment later. *In due time, I can hope.* Taking a breath, Helve clambered up Alvarath's shoulder to the saddle and settled herself in. Looping the flight belts where she needed to, the woman glanced over at Viktor as he arranged his bulk on Vu'Locav, and a moment later, the two were skyward.

You must realize he is not going to take the hint, Helve. Alvarath said gently, his voice echoing in the woman's mind.

I can hope, can I not? She replied.

With a gentle shrug, the dragon beat his hefty wings and

carried her onward, heading to the east. Toward Karnost and Starwatch-In-Karnost. It would be another few day's ride, but Helve knew she was reaching the point where she would just accept that Viktor would never see her as anything but a friend and workmate.

When the two dragons landed, Kjetta was hanging high in the center of the sky- midday, and both beasts knew it was time for a break. Circling lower and lower, they spotted a Ranger from above and bellowed a greeting. In response, the Ranger shot up a flare of green fire, indicating that they wished to speak.

"Hail!" The Ranger bellowed a moment later as the dragons and their riders reached conversational distance. "I have news and protection from plague! Land quickly that I might inoculate your riders!"

When the dragons landed and the two dismounted, the Ranger sprinted over, carrying a strange basket-like contraption. From it, the Ranger, face fully visible, withdrew two vials of a strange black liquid. Handing one to Helve and one to Viktor, he spoke a moment later. "I carry news. This will cure the plague and prevent its return. However, do not let it touch your tongue, or you will vomit."

"What?"

"It is the most foul-tasting shit concoction I have ever tasted," complained the Ranger, "but it is necessary."

"Cracked steel, man, slow down and explain." Viktor demanded a moment later, utterly confused. "Plague? Inoculate?"

"Viktor, just drink the stuff and I will explain as I can." The Ranger shot back a moment later. Rolling his eyes, the mastersmith examined the liquid in the vial, uncorked it, and took a mighty swig-

-and had never regretted anything more in his life. True to the Ranger's word, it was the most foul, pestilent sludge he'd ever drank. Even doing his best, Viktor still had the unfortunate luck of having the stuff touch his tongue, and immediately doubled over. The Ranger threw a hand over the man's mouth and issued a single, powerful command. "Swallow."

With a shaky gulp, Viktor managed to hold down his vomit and swallow the concoction. To his endless chagrin, Helve looked none the worse for wear, though her vial was empty. Shuddering, the man pulled himself upright and grabbed a wineskin, uncapped it, and started drinking desperately. When the taste finally left his memory, the wineskin was empty. Helve shuddered slightly and smacked her lips before grabbing her own wineskin and draining half of it.

"Now! Ta! I must be off!" The Ranger crowed before sprinting into the distance, leaving the two utterly confused.

"You promised an explanation!" Viktor called after him.

"Plague hit hard. Many dead. This stuff will protect you. Farewell!" The Ranger shouted as he loped away.

"Are they normally so brusque and rushed?" Helve asked Viktor as they settled to let the dragons hunt for lunch and stretch their wings. Her rump hurt from the saddle, and she could only imagine the discomfort the half-giant man was in. Doing her best to avoid giving away her annoyance at his obtuseness, Helve instead focused on making a quick meal for the two of them.

Humming to herself, the stout, short woman watched as Viktor checked his pack, checked that the cargo they were carrying hadn't been damaged in transit so far, and did his best to stretch out. Grunting, he shifted his shoulders back and forth, as if trying to tease a muscle into relaxing. When he couldn't, though, Viktor turned his back to a large stone and dropped against it. Once. Twice. Three times he struck the stone with his back, grunting again and again as he tried to use force to knead his muscle.

It was then that Helve saw her opening. "Sit, you fool. Before you break your back." She commanded the half-giant, and obediently, he dropped to his rump and arranged himself comfortably. Grabbing her forge-gloves for additional grip, the woman slipped up behind Viktor, using the rock to give her much-needed height. Then, reaching for his shoulders, she started kneading the muscle as roughly as she could, knowing the man needed it to get the knots and kinks out of his steely muscles.

"*Nel ca'e armä*, Viktor. Have you not bothered using that salve I got you?" She grunted at the man, doing her best to work out a particularly massive knot in his left shoulder. "Keep this up, and you will be crippled far before your time." Shifting her position, Helve used her elbow and what weight she could muster to knead deeper into the man's shoulder, trying desperately to get the muscle to release. When it finally did, there was no mistaking the sound of relief Viktor made.

Smiling sweetly, Helve spoke up. "Where else?" When Viktor indicated, there she was, kneading, massaging, and doing her best to get the man's body to respond to her touch. Even as she felt the wiry, steely muscles under her hands, Helve wondered what they'd feel like actually holding her. *Embracing* her. Sighing, she leaned against the man for a moment, letting him feel her breath on his skin as she worked over each and every aching, knotted muscle and moved on.

As Helve teased relaxation out of a particularly bunched and cramping calf muscle, Viktor let out a groan. "You are a miracle worker, Helve." The woman allowed herself a small smile, and wondered just what she could get away with, working her hands upward under the pretense of kneading out the pain. When she reached his thigh, he didn't react at all. In fact, he seemed as if he were reluctant to even mention her positioning. How she'd arranged herself before him. A moment later, though, when one of her hands gently pressed against his manhood, he blinked. "Helve?"

When he looked down and caught her gaze, he didn't see his Forge-Second there. He didn't see someone wishing to work with him. He saw the amorous, needy gaze of someone who'd put their passions and desires away for so long that it must hurt. For the first time, Viktor *saw* Helve. Saw what she desired, but had been too afraid to ask for. Saw, in her eyes, what *he* needed. He had pined over Seldred for decades. *But now? Here?* Was the time right to take another lover? And *Helve?* Certainly he enjoyed her company. He loved her in his own way, but did he wish to take her as his lover? The questions swam around in his mind. But the question he asked belied his intent and what *he* wanted.

"Are you certain?"

It didn't take the man long to realize just how certain Helve was. When she nearly threw herself into his arms, the relief on her face plain as the day was bright, he *knew.* When she nearly tangled herself in her clothing while attempting to remove it. Remove it for *him.* He *knew.* To his utter discredit, though, the man never asked one important question. He never asked how long she'd been waiting for this.

Waiting for him to see her as she *wanted* him to. As she *needed him to.* But for the moment, those thoughts melted away and were gone like the morning mists. Because right now, she needed him more than anything. Needed his touch. His embrace.

And by the Ancestors, now that he recognized the need written across her face, he was more than willing to provide. More than willing to give Helve the love she'd been silently screaming for, all these years. And so, with only Kjetta and the plants around them to witness, the two fell into a desperate embrace. Both knew that with the way of the world, they may not live to see tomorrow. So they had to make today as special as they could.

When they awoke hours later, tangled in each other and fiercely satisfied, Viktor and Helve didn't speak at first. What could be said in the wake of such an event? Such radical change in the both of them had happened that neither was ready to breach the subject yet. For the moment, the two just wanted to bask in the feelings washing over them. Though they knew duty should come first, both Forgemasters knew there was no harm in resting now and then.

Though they didn't speak at first, both knew that their bond, already steelsure, was more than unbreakable. Both had shared not only each other's physical form with the other, but also their most vulnerable moments. Their deepest secrets and wishes. Their desires, their spirits, and everything they were. For now, they just wanted to enjoy each other's presence. The feeling of the other against them. The surety of their skin–

to-skin contact. But when a bandit clan happened across them, the two were forced back to the reality of their world.

"Oi. Wussatwegotere?" Said one voice, snarling as they spoke. Viktor flinched as a spearhead prodded his back.

"Get gone, lest you awaken the sleeping giant." He muttered, trying to sound intimidating. Trying to sound less asleep and more annoyed.

"Youfinkdatgonwork?" The voice said again, and the prodding happened again. Rolling his eyes, Viktor readied himself to shift.

"The fuck do you even want?" Viktor shot back, grumbling as he turned his head just enough to see the source of the voice. A centaur stood a few feet away, and a faerie stood over Viktor, spear at the ready.

"All yer goods are ours." The centaur shouted.

Helve hissed ever so gently, letting Viktor know she was plotting something. He could feel the crackling of energy through her body. Nodding ever so slightly, the half giant rolled one way. Helve rolled the other and lobbed a fireball at the centaur while Viktor simply grabbed the faerie by the neck and squeezed.

Shrieking, the centaur tried calling out for his allies. One tried to respond despite paralyzing fear, just before he was grabbed by a dragon winging down from the sky. A moment later, the dragon threw the centaur into the distance, while another dragon came down and blasted the survivors with frosty breath. Letting out a titanic roar, the two dragons circled and alternated blasting frost and fire until the bandits were annihilated or had fled.

Shaking her head, Helve pulled on her clothing, watching as Viktor disposed of the unfortunate faerie in his grasp. Then, he too got dressed, and the two waited for their dragons to wing down and land. One after the other, the dragons touched down gently, glanced around, and shifted their bulk. Alvarath bowed low, one shoulder barely off the ground, wing splayed out to let Helve clamber up into her saddle. Viktor, being the bigger by far, simply vaulted to Vu'Locav's neck. Then, clearing each other's wingspaces, the dragons took to the sky once more.

Circling upwards, the dragons each caught updrafts to carry themselves higher into the sky. Beaming over at Viktor, Helve let out an ecstatic whoop as Alvarath carried her higher and higher. Once they'd reached flight altitude, the two dragons resumed their path to Karnost. They still had a day or so of flight ahead of them, but the woman didn't care. Finally, Viktor and her had shared a bed. Shared each other's bodies. Together, they'd shared a day of passion for the first time in their knowing each other.

By the time the passengers were once again saddle-sore, Starwatch Mountain's bulk was dimly in sight, perhaps a half-day's flight. Circling in to land, the two dragons deposited their cargo on the ground and took off a moment later to stretch and reconnoiter the area. This time, Viktor and Helve had the good sense to set up a tent before retiring within to once again enjoy each other's company. As night fell, their arousal could be heard by creatures near, and felt by creatures far.

A lone Ranger, happening by on a quest, a hunt, or some other task, stopped in sight of the tent and perched curiously to listen to the two as they talked. They weren't prying, of course, just listening to the tones of voice. The hushed, loving tones. With a chuckle, the Ranger prepped a firepit and gathered branches. They could tell the two were in the depths of love and needed time together. *But, that does not mean they need surrender the comforts of warmth.* With a chuckle, the Ranger extracted their firekit from one of their pouches. Fluffing out their jute cord and putting flint to steel, they struck sparks until one took in the nest of fiber. Gently, they blew on the nest to coax the embers into a flame, and deposited the flaming ball into the kindling they'd arranged.

Within moments, a happy, crackling fire was birthed, and the Ranger hung a kettle from a pot holder. High above, four dragon eyes watched over the Ranger, the camp, and the area. Only one pair of said eyes regarded the Ranger with interest, but said nothing, knowing the man was safe. Far safer, in fact, than many of the people their passengers had dealt with recently.

It was around midnight when Helve and Viktor realized someone was there as the Ranger started humming an old tune to themself. Poking his head out of the tent, the half-giant glanced over at the Ranger. "Ah!" He said with a chuckle. "Well met, friend. I apologize, you caught us at an awkward time."

The Ranger simply nodded and chuckled before pointing to the pot bubbling gently on the tripod over the fire. Then, he seemed to go back into his own mind, scratching his white beard as his dandelion-yellow eyes scanned for any sign of danger nearby. Softly, he whispered something that neither Viktor nor Helve could catch, though both could hear the faint beating of wings. "Can you not speak, Ranger?" Helve asked a moment later. The man simply shook his head, his onyx skin glowing in the firelight.

"What aid can we give?" Asked Viktor, now fully clothed

and stepping out of the tent. If the Ranger were intimidated by his height, he didn't show it. Instead, the man simply looked up and at Viktor, seeming to be the same height for a few moments. Raising his hands, the Ranger communicated his desire via sign-language.

"Just companionship for the night. I am on a quest to Karnost." His hands said quickly.

"Karnost, eh? We are bound there likewise to deliver things to the Kingmage and his sister." Viktor said gently. With a nod, the Ranger indicated he knew their quest already. "If our dragons are willing, would you like help to Karnost, Mysterious Ranger?" In response, the Ranger simply angled his head, as if to say that he was thankful, but had no need. Raising his hands once more, he signed.

"I can get there just as fast, friend. But you have my thanks." With a smile, the man shifted himself slightly, as if to invite the two to sit next to him. Then, confirming the invitation with his hands, the man posed a question. "What news have you? I am afraid I have been rather absent from things lately."

"Apparently, so have we. There is a plague running the rounds, and your Rangers are now working with the Order to distribute a cure. Whispers of war, strife, and hatred all around. And that is just what I have gleaned from chance encounters with wandering folk." Viktor said. "Apart from that, I am as lost as you."

Nodding, the Ranger said nothing and stirred the pot of soup. Then, reaching into one of his pouches, he removed a crimson-colored honeycomb and took a bite. Chewing quietly, he stared into the flames and pondered the happenings and the goings-on. It was clear he had more to ask. More that he needed to know. But right now, he couldn't suss out the words he needed. After a moment, he shrugged and let the two lovers arrange themselves comfortably before dishing them up some of the stew he'd made.

When dawn came, the Ranger parted ways with the two, and they clambered back to their saddles. Alvarath and Vu'Locav looked none the worse for wear after a week or so on the wing, but it wasn't hard to tell that they longed for the end of the journey. So, making their final push to Karnost, the four friends arrived just after midday. There, laying before them as a jewel in the endless seas of farmland, was Karnost and the magnificent spire of Starwatch Mountain, one of the highest mountains in all Seran.

Winging in toward the dragon platform high up on the mountain, Alvarath was the first to answer the challenging cry of the watch dragon. Vu'Locav answered after, both giving their throaty, bellowing clarion calls. The watch dragon answered again, and the two landed daintily on the platform. Immediately, three soldiers rushed to each dragon. Two unloaded the cargo for the Mastersmiths riding there, and one assisted the passengers to the ground. In accordance with the law of the Mountain, they were offered a magic device to aid their breathing at the high altitude. Viktor, being half-giant, had no need. But Helve, strong though she was, made sure to take the device and strap it to her face to breathe easier.

"Once you are within the Keep, you can remove it," the soldier said, "as you will be under the protection of the Kingmage." Nodding, Helve adjusted the mask to make it as comfortable as she could, before following Viktor and the procession of soldiers into the halls. Once she was safely within the walls of the Keep, she pulled off the mask and took a deep breath of the warm, abundant air. Viktor nodded and kept stride with her, making sure she didn't have to run after him.

When they arrived at the door to the Great Hall, Viktor and Helve paused. Just for a moment, glancing back at the tunnel where their dear dragons awaited. Unknown to them, both were being pampered and treated with the highest of honor. "Right." Said Viktor, turning to the soldiers. "You two have the greatsword known as the Script Blade. On my word, you will present it to Kingmage Harthos."

Helve followed after with the two soldiers near her. "And you two carry the Moon Spear, crafted with expert hand for High Counselor Hillevi. On my word, you will open the case and present it to her." With a nod, the soldiers readied themselves. Raising a singly massive hand, Viktor pounded on the door to the Great Hall. It swung open.

A herald sounded a trumpet as the procession entered. Another herald opened a scroll and spoke, a stentorian voice echoing through the Great Hall. "I present Mastersmiths Viktor Ulfricson Bludstyn and Helve Uhfalo of the Dragonsmith of Coldforge!"

Making their way to the throne, Viktor and Helve stopped at the respectful and appropriate seven paces. Viktor bowed and Helve curtsied, and the massive Nolvern Kingmage and his surprisingly small sister answered both in kind.

"Welcome, Viktor son of Ulfric, Son of Calem, of Clan Bludstyn-of-the-Mountains." Said Harthos in his grave, yet energetic voice. "And to you, Helve, Daughter of Lanai, Daughter of Selai." He said with a smile. There was a pause while the four people stared at each other, wondering who would break out of the frankly *insufferable* formality demanded by their stations.

"Right, fuck this. Viktor, it is damned good to see you again." Harthos. Smirking to himself, Viktor made a mental note to remember who won that little engagement. Stepping from the throne and making his way to the half-giant, the Nolvern Kingmage, who stood only three feet beneath the other man, reached up and slapped him on the shoulder. "I presume you have them?" Viktor nodded and grinned. Snapping his fingers, he motioned for the soldiers to bring the massive case containing the Script Blade.

It was presented to Harthos, who opened the case reverently. Quietly. At the same time, his sister, Hillevi, had greeted Helve warmly, and was opening her own case in turn.

"By the Ancestors..." Harthos whispered as he beheld the grandeur of the massive blade. Nearly as long as Helve was tall. About as wide as an executioner's sword, and with runes that Harthos could *feel* from the moment he opened the case. "Never have mine eyes beheld a work as fine as this." He whispered.

"It would do well to test the grip, my liege." Viktor said gently. Nodding, the burly man gripped the handle of the sword. Bringing it up to his face, he examined the weapons with a master's eye. Stepping out of the way, Viktor ushered the two soldiers to a safe distance.

Harthos, ever the master-at-arms, went through sword drills to test the weight. The grip. Everything. With a smile, he realized the sword *felt* as if it weighed only a few pounds. "Weight?" He asked Viktor.

"2 Stone."

Grinning, Harthos threw the sword this way and that while testing his grip. It felt *perfect*, as should be expected from a master of the craft. Hillevi, likewise, was running through the manual of arms for spears, and nodded with each precise movement.

"It feels as if the weapon itself *tells* me when to stop." She mused, looking at Helve. "No doubt this is your doing?"

Helve nodded. "Aye, milady. I know the stories of you and Kingmage Harthos right well, and know that you prefer precision and grace while he prefers strength and power."

"Making me sound like an ass," Harthos muttered, to a chuckle from his sister.

"It is true, though." Viktor said. "You *did* manage to break that hammer."

"Not my fault!" Harthos complained. A moment later, everyone broke into chuckles.

When they'd gathered themselves, the Mastersmiths and Nobles said their farewells to each other, promising to visit soon. Then, they were off, none knowing what the next day would hold, let alone the next years.

But they were Seranese, and for the Seranese, sacrifice was a way of life.

18

18: The Wilds of Dragonmoor

When Karos finally gave the word to stop, Khula felt like she was going to fall over right there. Her legs were barely responding, and her body was crying out in pain. She had pushed through the distance as best she could and refused to let either of the Rangers see that she was having difficulties keeping up. Quickly, she shifted her pack from her shoulders to the ground and dropped before massaging her legs as they attempted to cramp up. Breathing deeply, the woman focused her mind on other things, trying to will the pain away. Her shoulders were sore from the pack straps, her legs were aching and cramping, and she was convinced she had blisters starting on her feet.

Quickly checking over herself, Sardra tightened the sword belt she was wearing. Thanking the stars they stopped at the *tengjäv*, she grabbed one of her waterskins, offering it to Khula. The woman took it, quickly making the sign for 'thank you' before uncorking the skin and taking a long pull. When she pulled the skin away from her lips and swallowed, Sardra noticed that color almost immediately came back to her face.

"Poor dear. We have run you ragged. Come, get those boots off. Let me see your feet."

Khula was hesitant to take off her boots, being afraid that her feet would come off with them. Taking over quickly, Sardra unlaced Khula's boots and had them off in a moment, to reveal that she had wrapped her feet. Nodding slightly, the dokk unwrapped the woman's feet, pausing only when she saw the telltale signs of broken blisters. As she finished removing the woman's footwraps, she cursed as she saw how raw Khula's feet were. The poor woman sucked in a breath of pain as the air stung her abused feet. Sardra growled out a command to her Warden Ranger, obviously less than impressed.

"Damn you, Karos, you have run her off her feet and her feet off her! Get over here and help me!"

Karos bounced over quickly, looking for the trouble. When he saw the condition of Khula's feet, he paled slightly and dropped to one knee to work on the other leg. Quickly dropping his pack next to him, he unwrapped Khula's foot and looked it over. It was not quite as bad as Sardra was making it out to be, but it was still quite raw and blistered in different places. Unpacking a few packs of bandages he had wrapped around poultices, the Ranger began working. Quickly applying the healing bandages to the injured flesh, the man tenderly wrapped Khula's feet with the bandages first, followed by fresh footwraps.

"Now perhaps you will listen when I suggest we stop, Karos."

"Sardra, we hardly have time."

"Time, time. It is always about time. Karos, I am certain that the Kingmage would not send for us without expecting that it would take some time for us to get to him. So, ease up.

I can take it, but her feet are nearly gone."

Karos put his hands up in a gesture of surrender. It was clear that Sardra was going to take up the motherly mantle left vacant by Kiri. That thought stung him slightly as he reopened that wound in his mind. Shaking his head, he looked around to gauge their location. Sadly, there were no useful landmarks and though the area was familiar, its location escaped him now. They were a mere ten spear lengths from the road, far enough that they could safely relax. Leaving Khula in Sardra's care, he ventured out to find enough fuel for a fire while they rested.

Back at the small camp, the two women sat near each other, talking. Sardra watched intently as Khula posed a question with her hands and pondered it for a moment.

"I do not suppose Karos *has* anyone. Of course, he has the Rangers to lean on for support- not that he ever *does*," she growled slightly. Karos' inability to tell others his problems was becoming not only legendary among the Rangers, but a subject of much debate and mirth. "But I do not think he considers anyone close enough to trust them. Even I have had limited success getting the man to open up to me and I've drawn his blood before in sparring."

Another question was posed, and Sardra shook her head vehemently.

"Nay, I do not wish to take him as a lover and husband. I see him too much as a father to ever feel comfortable with, even thinking about such things."

Both women nodded their concurrence to that statement, but in the back of her mind, Khula toyed with the idea. A moment later, she came back to reality, knowing that she could never love a man who would not open to her. *Perhaps in time, he will, and my mind will change.*

Sardra spoke, her own question forming in her head.

"What of you? What will you do now that you are mostly free?"

Khula grinned, but Sardra could see there was pain behind the cheery face. She had only heard snippets of what things had befallen her over her years, especially at Magus' and her parents' hands. It hurt her deep, for she knew what it was like to be treated and traded as a *thing* rather than a sentient being.

The woman's hands worked quickly as she came up with her answer.

"I will travel. If Karos will have me as a companion, I would like to travel with him. He is quite fascinating from what I have seen."

Sardra chuckled gently and realized that it was the first time she had been able to laugh about anything in many a day.

"That he is. Has he ever looked at you and left you wondering if you had just drooled on yourself?"

Khula nodded and let out a silent laugh. Then she moved her hands quickly, posing another question.

"Has he ever tried to explain things but wandered off into six different tales at once?"

"All the time, my dear, all the time."

Both women were laughing heartily, with Sardra sounding like water running over rocks and Khula silently bouncing, when Karos returned. His arms were full of sticks and dead-fallen wood and he quickly began piling them and readying kindling for a fire. Once he felt the site adequately prepared, he motioned to Sardra, giving her an unspoken request to light the fire.

Rolling her eyes as she realized what Karos was asking,

the woman traced a line along her arm. Her pathway nerves glowed brightly, and a gout of flame erupted from her hand to strike at the kindling and fuel. Once the fuel caught fire, Sardra closed her hand, cutting off the pathway from realizing more flames.

With the fire crackling happily, the trio seated themselves comfortably. Karos looked to his companions for a moment before reaching into a pouch and extracting a quantity of a sand-like substance. Casting this sand into the fire, he waited and watched for their reactions.

Sardra had seen this trick before and even used it herself. It was most often a way to contact the Ancestors, but she felt that this was not Karos' intent today. The flames turned a bright blue and Sardra smiled- blue was Kiri's favorite color, specifically the blue of the skies. Nodding approvingly, she glanced to Khula.

Khula, on the other hand, had never seen someone change the coloration of flames before. She gasped when the flames turned from their usual reddish orange to a bright blue and watched with wide eyes. The flames shifted their color once more as different chemicals caught fire and soon the flames were burning with a jewel-like purple color. It was quite a sight to behold, and the woman glanced at Karos.

Karos smiled as the woman looked at him. When she asked what he had made happen, he thought about it for a moment.

Using color-sands is usually reserved for times of great import to contact the Ancestors and Ancestresses, or as a method of tribute to the dead. Each Ranger carries a pouch of sand which is made from shavings of different metals and a little bit of magic; when that sand is cast into the fire, it changes the color of the flames. I first saw it used when I was a Tenderfoot, back after the Coldforge Massacre. The Rangers took me, as my parents had taken to The Path and they showed me the death-rites. We-"

He stopped as he realized both women were laughing at him. He could feel that there was no ill will in the laughter, though, but it still gave him pause. Sardra looked over to Khula and smiled, before looking back to Karos.

"Karos, continue, but I challenge you- stick to one topic."

Karos blinked, trying to zero in on one specific topic, and nodded slowly.

"I used the sands to make a small tribute to Kiri. She will forever be in our hearts and we shall write her memory in the stars."

Khula nodded, and Sardra reached across to pat Karos on the shoulder. He was not crying, for he'd seen loss often enough that it hardly caused him to cry anymore. *But damned if it does not sting,* he thought to himself. Khula interrupted his musings with more questions in the sign language.

"Do the Ancestors truly speak to you? I was always told that they work in far too mysterious ways to actually speak to mortals."

"Aye, Khula. In fact, if they so choose, the Ancestors may walk Seran. Many times, have I encountered Veldan as an old man in ragged robes. Kindness, company and stories is all he desires from us mortals. Veljra and Ybril often walk with the Rangers, sometimes guiding us, other times simply giving company. I have been to many funerals where Veljra stood next to me or others and sang the Deathsong with us. I have talked with Indeka, though he prefers the company of Elves and I have had dinner with Enkar and dal'Kiyr as we sat around a fire discussing the happenings of the world."

Khula nodded, impressed. Evidently, the Ancestors worked in more direct ways than they had taught her. Her parents had always told her to be skeptical of those preaching of the Ancestors and that true happiness would come from submission to Magus. Oh, the things they would say if they could see her now. Something told her they would see her before too much longer and she knew there would be a reckoning. Even more so, she found she did not care. They had to answer for the things they had done, for the monster they'd set loose upon her.

Looking at Khula, Karos found the inner turmoil written on her face. Arching an eyebrow, he asked her what was wrong, his hands moving quickly and precisely as he spoke. He was curious about what was bothering her and found that he wanted her to be calm and happy, if possible. The thought of her smiling ran a thrill through his mind, as it did with Sardra. Seeing his Rangers happy never failed to make Karos feel accomplished.

Khula's response was a shake of the head at first. Then, after a few moments, she brought her hands up and signed a genuine answer. As it turned out, the shake of the head was not only to clear her mind but also to give voice to the ridiculousness of the situation she had been in.

"When I was born, my parents had already promised my hand to Magus. I am their only child and their agreement was that at first, I would wed him upon reaching 'the age of consent.' I doubt I need to remind you what that is."

Karos barely held back a surge of vomit. She was 30 currently, which meant that they had expected her to wed Magus at the tender age of 14. *Unacceptable*, thought Karos, *though that is sadly the norm. Powerful men like Magus have their pick of girls and women.* Nodding, he allowed the woman to continue, though in the back of his head, he calculated how old Magus would have been, and the answer only made him more ill. He would have been 50.

"My parents only asked my opinion when I had reached the age. Of course, I begged and pleaded with them to stave off the marriage until I was at least an adult and they did- only after forcing me to promise Magus that my dowry would be that much larger and my submission that much sweeter."

Khula shook her head sadly. Something in her eyes made Karos glad that the bastard was dead- though the ramifications of that fact had yet to be seen. Inwardly, he hoped that the next General of the Red Lance would be a kinder man. *Perhaps I must lean on my resources.* Nodding, the Ranger motioned for Khula to continue with her story.

"To make me "realize my love" for the man, my parents made me spend as much time with him as would be acceptable to society. He was a bastard, treating me as if I were property rather than a person. I am quite surprised though that he never attempted to force himself on me before..."

She clenched and unclenched her fists a few times. *These are the hands that took the life of Magus Kefarion.* Somehow, that thought alone gave much more comfort than she had felt for some time. It was almost intoxicating to think about.

"When his closest friends were with us, they would expect me to serve them food and drink and if I failed to be as quick as he wished, he would strike me. They would throw drinks in my face and other such things. If I dared speak in the presence of him or his men, I was immediately struck and sent away. I could not walk outside unless he could see me and, for whatever reason, I was forbidden to look at the night sky."

That was an odd one for sure. Why would one be forbidden to look to the stars, unless someone thought it would give them ideas of freedom? Khula took a moment and shook her head. That part of her life was over now, and she would never go back to her parents.

"But now I am free and Magus' life ended at my hands and I worry because the feeling was... addictive."

Karos arched an eyebrow as the words formed on Khula's hands. That in and of itself was worrying to him, but he could understand where it came from.

"When I cast stones, it feels different- impartial, as if I am merely dealing out justice. But killing him with a blade felt like I was being set free. Like thirty years of pain and hate were released in one moment."

That was a little more comforting to think about. After all, if one lived under oppression for most of their life and suddenly had the chance to change that. *How many would? How many stories would be like Sardra or Khula, given the chance?* Looking over to Sardra, he saw the woman nodding with a new appreciation for the Lady sitting near her.

"Your story, Khula, is not that dissimilar from mine. It ends almost the same way, too."

Sardra's voice sounded distant, as if she were trying to recollect some memory- and the recollection caused her pain. The pain was born from something different, though. Not from resenting her parents and the place they decided for her, but from loss.

"My family- my *entire clan* was captured and were taken as chattel. For weeks, they starved us, beat us, tore away who we were to make us submissive. I watched as they reduced childhood friends to selling each other out. They forced us to watch as they took others to bed. They passed us from owner to owner and by the time I escaped, I was the only one who had kept my mind whole."

Khula looked absolutely horrified. Never had she heard of such things, and it made her sick to her stomach.

"My point is- both of us were promised for someone else. Both of us seized our chance to end our tormentors. You with the broken sword of a friend, me by tooth and claw."

To emphasize her point, Sardra bared her teeth and claws, giving Khula a chance to see the cruel weapons. The woman nodded at the dokk's story and took a breath.

"And we were both given a chance at something new by the Rangers. Time will tell if you make the same choice as I."

Sardra grinned slightly, and Khula nodded. Karos chuckled and shifted in his seat, before pulling a bedroll off his pack and laying it near the fire. Then he gestured to Khula, indicating that she should get some rest.

"We continue on at first light. Get some rest while you can."

Khula had her own bedroll, so she looked to Karos with some concern. Finally, she had had enough of wondering. Moving her hands quickly, she posed a question to him; her face demanding an answer.

"Nay. I have not slept in many years. I will sometimes enter a meditative trance to refresh myself and rest, but I cannot sleep anymore. My mind wanders back to painful events and they infest whatever dreams I would normally have. As a result, I wake up drenched in sweat and often screaming."

Khula looked quite horrified at that revelation and nodded as she crawled into the bedroll that had been prepared for her. Getting comfortable, she closed her eyes, intending for just a moment to clear her head. Instead, she fell into a deep slumber, hardly moving as her mind filtered out all nightly noises.

Karos watched the woman for a moment, at least until he was sure she was asleep. Then, he glanced up at Sardra. Waving her over, he angled his neck, stretching it out until it popped. Then he repeated the motion in reverse and sighed. Concern was written on his face, as plain as the night and Sardra became worried.

"What is it, Karos?"

"My *litik'röka* aches. It is as if a great storm is building and I have only just become aware of it. Things are in motion, terrible things."

He shook his head and placed a palm against his *litik'röka*, feeling the silver threading and the jagged scar. There was energy thrumming through the metal and into his head, giving him a headache unlike anything he had had before. He sighed gently and looked at Sardra once more.

"I have no doubts that the Red Lance has been informed by now, for their eagles fly faster than our feet. We must make ready to deal with any knights we see on the road. Damn, how I wish Sir Caldred were still alive. We could lean on him and influence the next General."

"Aye, but would it be safe to affect that much change? The Knights are not as dim as you still think them. They know when one of their own speaks with us."

"Indeed, but they respected Caldred enough to not try anything foolish. I fear that Sir Elgrave is nowhere near as powerful."

"It is because he is new. Give it time before you lean on him, else we may lose him as a contact."

Nodding at the advice given, the Warden Ranger stared into the fire for a few minutes, uncaring that it would impair his night vision. His mind was racing, especially now that the *dra'la'thel* had worn off. Looking into his pouch, he realized he was nearly out of the stuff and glanced up to Sardra.

"Am I going mad, or have we just been smoking that much?"

"Let me think... We have partaken of the *thel* at least three times since leaving the *tengjäv*. So yes, we have been smoking that much."

Karos blinked, his eyes wide. Never had he so depended on the drug– *yes, it is a drug*; he thought. Was he addicted? Could one get addicted to something that evened out their mind? Or was he just growing increasingly stressed as the days went by?

Cursing silently, he looked at his hands for the telltale signs of withdrawal and dependency– quaking fingers, a slight blue tinge to the tips. He saw nothing, but the thought remained, plaguing him.

"Come, Karos. I will take watch. You need rest. I doubt you've tranced since this whole affair began."

Karos shook his head– whether in a denial of needing to trance or in an affirmation that he had not, only he knew. But her wisdom was sound, and he knew she was dependable. She would wake him upon the first signs of trouble. Nodding finally, the Warden Ranger arranged himself, his legs crossed beneath him and his hands on his knees. Slowly, he focused his thoughts out of his head– except for the thoughts of what was to come. For it was a use he had not divulged to Khula– the Trance would often, if one's mind was clear and calm, allow them to see glimpses of the future. Just enough to warn them of what was to come. As he focused, more and more thoughts vanished, until only the pertinent ones remained. He felt the manic energy he had been running off of slowly dissolve from his body and he realized just how weary he was. *Surely this has added age to my body*, he pondered, before pushing the thought away. As he felt the energy leave him, a thought dawned in his mind. The Rangers rarely, if ever, became *lok'vi*. In fact, he had only seen one in his years. Reaching out with that branch of thought, he explored it as much as he could. Perhaps the grounding of the Trance aided in one not becoming a *lok'vi*?

That thought entertained him for quite some time as he considered the ramifications. Of course, he had had no one to begin down that path, so he had nothing to go on. *Perhaps, though, it would be useful to teach to Thäoldr the method of the Trance.* When he had finally exhausted that line of thought, he pushed it from his mind and finally relaxed. Time sped up and his mind fought to process all the stimuli that had happened over the past weeks. As his mind relaxed, it became easier to focus on each thing, processing them through his mind and pushing them away.

At length, he felt his stamina return, his throat healed and even his *þrúnsaal* seemed to quiet. He felt ready to face the challenges of the day and let his eyes open. At first, they saw nothing but black, but light quickly came through and the images realized before his eyes. There was Sardra, already cooking breakfast for the three of them. She seemed ready enough to face the day, but then again, she was always ready. Glancing to the side, he saw Khula, still sound asleep. *She needs it,* thought Karos, *but I feel we must be ready to move on.* Kjetta was just peeking his head over the eastern horizon and there was a beautiful stillness to the world. As he stood, the Ranger stretched himself out, shifting this way and that.

"Good, you have returned. What can you tell me about the

journey ahead, or were you not able to find enough focus?"

"I was, Sardra, worry not. What I found was not good. I fear trouble is in the air and it will find us sooner rather than later. My *litik'röka* still aches, but not as bad as before."

Clicking her tongue, Sardra finished cooking- it was not enough to feed all three, Karos realized, and the man nodded quickly. It was enough to keep Khula going- the two Rangers had had more than enough food for a week of travel. Leaning over, he grabbed Khula's leg gently and shook her.

Her reaction was immediate. She screamed, a terrifying wail fit to raise the dead and sprung the knife she had chosen from the *tengjäv* in her hand. It took her a moment to realize she was not among Magus and his friends, and she heaved a sigh, sheepishly sheathing the blade. Expecting admonition, she quickly signed an apology, only to find that the faces regarding her held no judgment. Her surprise mounted when Karos spoke to her, his tone gentle.

"I trust you now understand why I do not sleep. I apologize. I should have found a better way to wake you."

Khula nodded slowly, either at his apology or at the under-standing of why he did not sleep. Another moment passed, and she was back to her usual self. A smile crept over her face as Sardra presented her with food and she signed a quick 'thank you' before eating. She ate quickly, unafraid of someone interrupting her or getting angry at her lack of manners. When she finished, Sardra swiftly took the plate and cleaned it with a bit of water from a skin and placed it next to the fire to dry. Kjetta brought himself over the horizon and the day began. Shortly, they had packed up their small camp and made their way back to the road to continue on to Dragonmoor.

They had been on the road for hours and Karos was readying

himself to give the command to halt when he stopped. Dropping to the ground, he unsheathed his knife and plunged it into the dirt before placing his ear to the pommel. Closing his eyes and slowing his breaths, he listened for a few moments before yanking the knife up, sheathing it and waving his companions off the road.

"Twelve horses, laden heavy- possibly war-horses."

"How far out?"

"A minute, perhaps less. They are traveling at great speed."

The group slipped into the tall grass a few spear lengths from the road and laid themselves low to watch as twelve knights, bearing the standard of the Red Lance, rode up. Karos cursed under his breath and signed a question to Sardra.

"Flame it. How did they find us so fast?"

"I would assume they have hawks watching our every step, Karos."

The Warden Ranger merely nodded and began reaching for his bow. His movements were slow and practiced as he tried to recognize each Knight by their stature. Sadly, he had not kept close enough tabs on the Red Lance to see most of them, but they were more than some of the simple hedge knights that filled their ranks. Staying low, the trio watched as the men drew closer.

The leader of the group dismounted and slid to the ground, his armored boots gently clanking as they struck the dirt road. He drew his sword, obviously preparing for combat, and shouted.

"I know you are here. Come out and we can end this amicably."

Karos chuckled gently as he stood, his hands in full view. He did not doubt that he could draw steel quickly enough to ward off an attack, but one had to always be careful around The Red Lance.

"Amicably, you say, and yet you draw steel."

"'Tis just insurance. One never knows just how *unpredictable* your kind is."

"Rich, coming from the ally of one of the most lascivious knights in Seranese history. Did you even know the man? Or did you just follow him because he promised riches?"

"Speak with respect when you speak of Magus, *peasant*, or we will kill you where you stand! We know your tricks, Ranger; and you are no threat to us."

Karos could not help but grin at the man's confidence. His sword flashed from its sheath and he focused his mind on a powerful Sk'av'A phrase. His eyes began to glow and his hair flashed a different color- just for a moment.

"You seem to think you still face the same meek man your Red Lance looked upon before. But certainly, if you wish to try the lives of you and your men, advance."

As he spoke, the Ranger used the toe of his boot to draw a line upon the road. His sword was gripped carefully in his hand, though it still felt off- it did not have the same weight as Northrage. Neither was it an enchanted blade, but it would do. It was a tapered blade, as opposed to the Nolvern blade he was accustomed to, with a ring on the handle separating the two halves. The pommel itself looked like an acorn and the sword tapered naturally to a sharp point. The fuller ran nearly the full length of the blade and the crossguard went straight, rather than curved as he was. The only defining feature was a small leaf of silver placed in the middle of the crossguard. But it was a weapon, and the Way-Watcher had told him the story of that specific blade. It was a noble enough blade and had been waiting its chance to serve again for over two centuries.

"This is the sword wielded by a great Ranger. He served on the Kingmage's Guard for many years until he was called to face down a knight that spent his days pillaging and raping. Perhaps you have heard of that knight. His name was Elrayv, and he was the founder of your order. He died a coward's death at the end of this very blade."

That was enough to anger the knight into action. He stepped over the line and snarled at Karos.

"How dare you insult Elrayv the Great! I will have your head, peasant!"

He swung his sword, but the blow never came down, even though Karos was ready for it. The man abruptly began clutching at his head for a moment before falling to the ground. When Karos glanced at his foe, he saw that the man's helmet had gained a sudden grave indentation and split, revealing a rock that was dug into the man's skull. He was obviously dead before he hit the ground and that turn of events surprised Karos. Glancing to the obvious source of the rock, he arched an eyebrow.

"He can launch rocks without picking them up!"

Eleven horrified knights turned tail and ran back to their horses, quickly mounting up and riding past Karos with the speed of a terrified rabbit. The dead man's horse looked at its former master with a mix of pity and sorrow, before Karos made his way over, sheathing his sword. The horse regarded him coolly, before realizing that the man was no threat to him. When Karos spoke to the horse, his tone was even and calm and his words were in the primal tongue, the Lifesong.

"You are your own master. Be free of all bonds."

His knife flashed out and cut the saddle and bridle away from the horse's body and a gentle slap sent the creature off into the distance. It would have a time rediscovering its old spirit, but Karos felt it was a better life than living under a knight. When that messy business was over, the Ranger waved to his companions and they continued upon the road.

When they next stopped, the sun was descending toward the western horizon, and it was time to change the bandages on Khula's feet. This task was done quickly so that the Rangers could focus on other things that needed to be done to prepare for the night. Karos once again went to gather firewood, leaving Sardra and Khula to talk once more.

"How deep-seated is your hatred for the Red Lance? You did not even give that man time to talk before you struck him down. It was impressive, for his helmet was heavy steel. Where did you learn to throw like that?"

Khula's response came quickly as her hands worked into the various signs.

"A friend taught me. Halfling. I cannot remember his name that well, but he was a wonderful teacher."

Sardra nodded and flexed her fingers, feeling a slight twinge. She was still hiding the injuries she had earned at Vaelyn's hands, but she'd already taken more than a few healing potions. She was healing, at least, but she would be uncomfortable for quite some time. Arching an eyebrow, Sardra posed another question.

Khula's answer came quickly and emphatically.

"No. I had no friends growing up, though I tried to be kind to the house-servants."

No friends, thought Sardra, no one to turn to or confide in. It makes sense, cut someone off from everyone else and they should develop the way you choose. It is not unlike the way the Rangers train. She chuckled gently, remembering her own years as a Tenderfoot. A few of the scars she wore proudly had happened then and a few of the ones she wished to forget had as well.

Sighing gently, Khula leaned back against her pack to look to the sky.

"Ara be blessed. Today was quite kind to us."

The voice was Karos' and both women nodded their assent to his assessment. It had been a wonderful day, despite the interruption of the Red Lance. Even that had ended in a far more interesting manner than any of them had expected. Khula was quite proud of herself for rendering aid when least expected and knew it was a sign. She was growing stronger, more confident with every day traveling with the Rangers. Her skin was burning, but her companions took care of her and she knew that when they arrived at Starwatch-in-Karnost, her family would scarcely recognize her. That thought suited her just fine.

As Karos brought the kindling and fuel to a happy blaze, the trio sat around it and talked about their lives. At least, most of them did. Beyond talking about what had already been revealed, Karos refused to open further. It was as if he were trying to consciously shut them out. Finally, Khula could bear no more and nearly shouted, her hands working feverishly.

"Why do you act as if opening up to someone will cause the end of days? We are your friends, Karos. Not your foes."

Karos glanced up sheepishly and scratched at the back of his neck. It was difficult to say why he did such things, but he figured he must try his best. Opening his mouth to speak, he closed it after a moment, realizing he did not quite have his words ironed out. Sardra looked amused that the girl had taken him to task, and she was quite curious as well.

"There are many reasons I wish to keep myself aloof. The first is a feeling of being a burden with my problems. As if I am causing grief for everyone when I tell them what is bothering me or what is on my mind."

Khula worked quickly to deliver a retort, her eyes rolling.

"It is more of a burden to have you suffer in silence."

Karos put his hands up in apology, and the girl shook her head.

"No. You do not get to act as if you have done something wrong. You do not get to act a victim when I ask you questions."

"Then what am I to do? I constantly question myself and feel I must either defend my actions or apologize for them. I have opened to folk before and lost close friends. It seems that when I open myself up, pain only follows."

He sighed and shook his head gently. Taking a deep breath, he drifted back in his memories.

"I am afraid that if I open myself up to someone, I will cause their doom. I know it to be unfounded, that such things are not predictable by mortals, but the feeling persists." The Ranger shook his head sadly and took a breath. The ferocity of Khula's words took taken off-guard and he could not help but continue to be amazed at the amount of fire the girl had in her body. She was a fierce ally already, and he hoped to never draw her ire.

"One must admit there is a problem before they can correct it."

Sage words, thought Sardra as she regarded Khula. *Surely Karos had heard them before, but had he ever heeded them?* That was the troublesome question. He seemed to earnestly want to improve himself, but he reluctantly took the steps to aid his own mind. It was ironic that the man who always went to the aid of others had such trouble giving himself the same care.

Rolling out his bedroll once more, Karos waved to Khula to get some sleep. Then, he glanced to Sardra, giving her an unspoken instruction to go into the Trance. It was her turn to rest. Arching an eyebrow, the woman asked a question with her eyes.

"I am fine, Sardra. I will take watch- you rest."

Shrugging, the dokk took a seated position and placed her hands on her knees. Three breaths later, her eyes closed, and she emptied her thoughts. She focused on one tangible thought- the road ahead. What she thought they would encounter, especially considering that they had now killed two important knights bearing the standard of the Red Lance. Surely, this was going to come back on their heads eventually. *Hopefully, though, we will have the Kingmage to mediate.* After all, the Kingmage's word was law and not even The Red Lance were foolish enough to challenge such a person.

Karos looked at the two people resting under his protection and sighed gently. *Hopefully, we can do better than with Kiri.* The thoughts were coming again, and he had nothing to keep them away. Clenching and unclenching his fists, he focused on his breathing. Drawing a deep breath in, he focused on the thoughts plaguing him most. How he had failed his Rangers by letting Kiri die. How he had failed Khula by letting Magus make off with her. How he had failed everyone by not making a true cure. When he exhaled, he shifted the focus of those thoughts. *Kiri had gone to her death willingly to give us time to come up with a plan of attack.* It was a hollow thought, but it bolstered him. He had been unconscious and insensate when Magus took the girl, as had Sardra, and Thäoldr was half-blinded. Another hollow thought. He tried to forgive himself for that one, but even though he knew there was nothing he could have done- unless he could miraculously have taken magical blasts better, it still stung. Finally, his thoughts turned to the cure- *how could we have created a true cure without knowing the true nature of the plague?* The thoughts boiled away impotently as his *prúnsaal* attempted in vain to build itself back up. It would take quite a lot more to derail such thoughts, but Karos knew it would come in time. In the meantime, he would sing to keep it at bay overnight.

"Come far and away, the road to me is calling
Calling me astray, even as my home is in sight.
Ere break of day, I know I must go wand'ring,
'til once again a camp I make at night."

The Wandering-Song had always been a favorite of his and especially now he felt it appropriate. The night wore on around him as he kept vigil over his friends, his eyes ceaselessly moving from point to point to seek out any potential foe.

As the night wore on, Karos could feel his *prúnsaal* readying another attack on his mind. He was growing bored with song, though he could tell that his companions were enjoying it in their rest states. Khula was smiling softly in her sleep and Sardra looked like she was more relaxed than before. Searching his memory, he found a different song to sing- one more upbeat and fast-paced.

"There was a bog, 'twas a rare bog and a rattling bog and 'twas down in the valley-o. Oh, roh, the rattling bog, the bog down in the valley-o..."

Slapping his hands against his legs to the rhythm of the song, he sang, quietly at first, though growing in intensity. The song was an old traveler's song, meant to distract them from the toil of the road. It grew longer with each repetition and soon enough Karos was singing at a ridiculous pace, unaware of the stares of his companions. Then, he heard another voice join in as Sardra picked up the song.

"Now in that bog, there was a hole, the hole in the bog and the bog down in the valley-oh!"

Karos chuckled and continued the song, picking up speed as a challenge to his ally. As they started the second verse, Karos realized a new sound- someone drumming on a pot, giving a hollow tapping sound. Glancing over, he saw that Khula had awoken and was tapping a small pot she had upturned. Evidently, this was a song she enjoyed.

The song continued long into the night and when it was done, Khula implored the Ranger to continue singing, as she listened to the sad voice, showing cheer for what she guessed was the first time in a long while. Smiling, she brushed a lock of hair back behind her ear and spelled out the song she wished to hear him sing.

Nodding, Karos sang the ancient song. It was about the great and rare Nightmare, a horse of noble bearing, that seemed to be made of onyx and fire. Khula smiled and arranged herself to comfortably listen to the song and was soon back asleep. Out of deference, the Ranger finished the song before looking up to Sardra. She was regarding him with kind eyes as she sat there, serene and calm.

"What is it, Sardra?"

"I have rarely seen you smile without it being a short-lived thing."

"What of it? Am I supposed to walk around grinning like a jester?"

"Nay. And do not turn this into a negative thing, Karos Waking-Fire. This is a side of you most of us never get to see."

"You know my reasons, Sardra."

"Better than most. But that does not mean I cannot hope to see you smile more often."

"Why should I? With the things I have seen, I doubt happiness is possible."

"Karos, resilience of heart is a necessary trait of a Ranger. We have both seen far more than we let on. Done more than most will know in defense of the peace. We cannot undo that, but we can be happy despite it."

Arching an eyebrow, Karos regarded the woman. She, if anyone, had rights to claim a harder life than he had had. But here she was, singing along, smiling. She had recently been beaten within inches of her life and she'd come back- though not without injury, he could tell. She hid it well, but he knew her better than most.

As she sucked in a breath, Sardra felt a tightness in her chest- just for a moment and not nearly painful enough to be alarmed about, but enough to remind her of her injuries. She needed more rest to recuperate, but that would not be possible for some time.

"Come then. Let us have a cheery song from you, Wood-Strider."

When Sardra began singing, it seemed as if all care drained away from the world. It was a cheerful song; one meant to lift the spirits and give hope. It was a refreshing song to hear and Karos soon tapped along to the beat.

19

19: Dragonmoor

When Thäoldr awoke next, he was in the air, upon the back of his magnificent beast. She had taken the time she needed to rest and then, without waking her rider, had taken to the skies once more, as she knew the way to Ormere Keep by heart. Thäoldr was refreshed and ready to face the challenges the day held, and his eyes were keen as ever. As he searched above and below his dragon for any threat, he became keenly aware of the cries of a griffon. At first, the creature sounded distressed, but as Thäoldr listened, he realized the beast was calling to *him*.

"Hail, Paragon of Knowledge!"

A woman's voice tore through the open air as a griffon winged up next to Namryll.

"What crisis begs your attention today, Thäoldr? Perhaps the calling of the Council? Or perhaps you have a message from the Kingmage that is being ferried by a certain dashing griffon rider?"

Thäoldr whirled to regard the woman as she grabbed a small letter off her belt. Touching one of her tattoos, she slung the

297

letter towards him, using magic to ensure it would land in his lap. The man still fumbled a little, as he was still getting used to his flesh arm.

"Did you not have an artifice arm when last we spoke?"

"That is a very long story, Wyria. It involves much pain."

"Well, open your letter and then you can tell me while we are on the way to Ormere."

Thäoldr shook his head at the girl's impertinence. She was intelligent, for sure and a hard worker, but damned if she was not a smartass. Quickly flipping the letter over in his hands to reveal the wax seal of the Kingmage, the Sage nodded and broke it open. Unfolding the letter quickly, he began reading—oddly enough; they did not dictate the letter. It was written in the Kingmage's own hurried hand and was barely legible, but Thäoldr knew that to be a quirk of the Kingmage's own writing. It was a summons and seemed important at that. He began reading the letter to himself to confirm its contents and ensure he was reading it correctly.

"To my lord Thäoldr Sagewind. I request your presence as soon as possible, on grave matters regarding the future of Seran. I realize you are currently a-wing on important matters and I give you time for that. But your presence is important, and I wish you to arrive and be present at the time the Warden Ranger is here."

Interesting, thought the Rider. Shrugging, he folded the letter back up and jammed it into his belt to stay. Then he glanced over at the other rider. She grinned back and her mount ducked precariously close to Namryll's wing. Immediately, Thäoldr put up a warning hand. The girl rolled her eyes and dropped back into the proper position.

Just because you do not know how to enjoy yourself, the girl growled mentally. *Does not mean that others cannot.* Shifting her focus to her mount, the girl issued reassuring thoughts, radiating warmth and love. The beast responded in kind, issuing a challenging cry to Namryll. Then, her wings beat hard, pushing the beast forward faster and faster.

It would seem Eyfa would like a race. The dragon rumbled, amused. Then, her great wings beat harder, and she pushed forward, trying to catch the smaller, lighter griffon. Eyfa stayed ahead of the dragon, though, using her lighter weight and faster wings to her advantage.

At first, Thäoldr was annoyed- they were on a mission and had no time to play in such a fashion. Then, he glanced down and checked their position- they were closing in on the 250-mile landmarks, a pair of great stone pillars that marked the distance from Ormere. He had not even realized that they'd passed the 500-mile markers some time ago. Evidently, their game had taken the distance down quite a bit.

When the massive castle was in sight, both Riders breathed a sigh of relief. Reluctantly, Wyria reined Eyfa in, knowing it would not end well if she tried to land at high speed. As Eyfa backwinged to kill her momentum, Wyria noticed Namryll was doing the same. Both creatures slowed significantly down and began circling downwards as they came to land.

When Thäoldr dismounted and removed his flight helm, Wyria was struck dumb by how much younger he looked. Gone were the scars older than her, gone was the silvery beard. His head and beard were full of bright blond hair, and she realized she had only seen him like this in the old paintings. Sucking a breath in, she realized she was having dirty thoughts about the elf. Turning red, she realized she was glad her flight helm was still on and he could not see her face.

It would not do to let such thoughts slip, she thought to herself and slipped her helmet off. Waves of red hair cascaded down her shoulders and she shook her head until she was sure she left no hair clinging inside the helmet. Then she ran to catch up to her elder, playfully striking his elbow.

"Come on then, you told me nothing on the wing. What happened to your artifice arm?"

Thäoldr shook his head and sighed. It was best for her to learn of the evils that faced them, but did she have to be so inquisitive? Then he realized who he was in the company of. Wyria, one of the most irritatingly inquisitive Riders he had dealt with in an age. If she could learn patience, she would make a wonderful Paragon of Knowledge once he passed. He did not like to think in such terms, but with the way he was feeling, he knew it was coming. He knew he could not nail down the day, but he knew it would be his time before long. He took a breath, feeling the energy crackling within him cause his heart to skip a couple of beats. Just a moment was all he took and then he continued.

"I have seen much, Wyria. But believe me, when I say I have never thought possible that I could replace an artifice arm with a flesh arm that had been lost for over ten centuries."

Wyria nodded slowly and motioned for him to continue.

"But this I learned at my expense- all things are possible in Seran. My foe was using a form of magic I have almost never seen before. I could feel my body changing- my precious scars, even my tattoos- are all gone. My arm has been restored and... it is strange. It is clumsier than I remember, but perhaps all is not lost. I possess more vital energy than I ever have."

He was not keen to let on all that had happened- the Rangers putting their energy into him, the massive outburst of energy he had caused with the abryx shard. Those were things that others did not need to know- at least until he had learned how they may be of use to others. It would not do to give out that information yet.

"You are leaving out more than you let on, Thäoldr. Tell me the plain tru-"

Thäoldr held up a warning hand. She had a keen enough mind to guess that he had hidden something, but now was not the time.

"This is not the time. The Council still sees the Rangers as enemies. To tell them what I have learned would be to incite a war upon them- and that would neither go well for us nor for the folk of Seran."

Wyria nodded slowly and sucked in a breath. As they approached the great door into the Main Hall of the Keep, she ran ahead to open it. Touching one of the crystals next to the door, she focused her mind on the door opening. Slowly, the massive portal began to swing wide, creaking as it did. *How much does that door weigh?* The woman wondered to herself. She pitied the folk who had to open it without magic- *surely it weighs at least a ton. The assembled knights of Seran would be hard-pressed to breach it.* Her comments continued in her mind as she surveyed the thickness of the door. It was about ten inches thick, wrought with wood and steel. She ran her hand over the door for a moment, before nodding and waving at Thäoldr to follow her. It had been some time since she'd been in the Council's presence and she wondered what it would be like? Would they even allow her in? Or would they prefer secrecy while speaking with Thäoldr? An impatient tap on her shoulder reminded the woman that the older elf was still in her company.

"We are not going to the Council Chambers."

"Then where are we going? And what are those vials you are carrying, Sage?"

"We must hasten to the Hospitallers' wing."

All the color left Wyria's face as she realized the gravity of the situation. He was carrying vials of unknown material and rushing to the hospital wing; surely something was gravely wrong. Pursuing him, she plucked a vial from the many he was carrying and examined it.

"What sort of liquid is th–"

He rounded on her with a look somewhere between pity and anger in his face. At first, she thought the anger directed at her– but then she realized– it was focused far and away. The pity, though, that was reserved for her– *and whoever drinks of these vials*, thought the woman.

"Drink. Quickly and try not to let the liquid touch your tongue. Do it now that you recover faster and sicken not. For your safety, I must press on alone. We will meet again when this task is over, and you will fly with me to Starwatch-in-Karnost."

Something struck Wyria after a moment and she realized what it was– there was *no one* about. It was midday. There should be activity everywhere! But the Keep was silent as a tomb. In the back of her mind, the woman thought that something must be terribly wrong. Taking a breath, Wyria nodded slowly and uncorked the vial she held. A moment later, she nearly gagged and looked at Thäoldr's retreating form warily. Heeding his advice, she downed the vial in one go. It took all her willpower to not vomit right there, and she nearly blacked out. But in a testament to her indomitable spirit, the woman held firm, even as her body tried to force the terrible mixture back up her throat.

"What manner of evil drink is this?" The woman asked to no-one at all.

Thäoldr pressed his hand against the sturdy door to the hospital wing and took in a breath, readying himself for the things he may see. Reaching out, he activated the crystal that held the door shut and commanded the portal to open. It swung wide, and the smell struck Thäoldr, nearly doubling him over. It was worse than the potion he had made, and that was saying something. He picked up the scent of rotted flesh, burned bodies and more. Shaking his head, he pressed on through the stench and made his way in before his eyes widened in horror- *every single bed is filled. Every rider in Ormere must be here*, he thought to himself. *I pray I have enough of the cure.* Moving quickly, he picked out the Council members, one by one. His heart sank as he realized he was too late for at least two of them. He could barely recognize them, as their faces had all but rotted away- but the color of their garb, though stained heavily with blood and bile, told him their identities. *Elgariin, rider of Kazalok. Kal'Umrul, rider of Struun.* He fought back the sorrow he felt, realizing that there were more important matters to attend to- like the five other Council Members that still survived.

The first was Ryva, Rider of Griffon Lyarn. She was in dire straits and he could see that she did not have long to live- so he moved to her quickly. Uncorking a vial of the cure, he forced it into the woman's mouth and down her throat- holding a hand over her mouth to ensure she would not spit it out. As her eyes turned to him, begging to know why he was torturing her so, Thäoldr mouthed an apology. Right now, his only focus was ensuring she would survive. When he finally felt her swallow the potion, he nodded. Almost immediately, the woman's fighting spirit came back, and she weakly batted his hands away from her mouth. Then, Thäoldr was off- whether to his next rescue or victim, he was not sure.

Approaching the next member of the council, Thäoldr had a moment of being struck dumb as he realized something else that was wrong. *Where are the healers?* A glance around told him the grim news- they numbered among those still clinging to life- and to those who were unmoving in death. Cursing his luck, the Sage tilted the next head up and looked into the eyes. They were glassy, but not yet dead. The rider was still there- but did not have long left. He knew he had to work quickly.

"Councilor Tyrwyn. I know you can hear me, that you are still fighting. You must drink this, no matter what."

It was hard to tell if the man would survive the potion, let alone if he would heal from the plague, but damn it all, it had to be tried. Gently tipping Tyrwyn's head back, Thäoldr poured the potion down the man's throat. He sputtered and coughed, trying to fight the awful tasting fluid- but as soon as it worked through his system, his breathing ceased to be audible. Thäoldr had a moment of terror and fumbled around to feel for Tyrwyn's pulse, thinking he had killed the man- and found that it was growing stronger by the second. Confident that the man would recover, Thäoldr patted his shoulder and hurried on.

The next member of the council was a horrific sight- barely alive, their flesh pooling in an oily puddle beneath them and on the ground. Their organs were exposed and with each breath, Thäoldr could see the movement of what muscles had not melted away. A single eye was left, darting desperately in the socket. The only thing that allowed the elf to recognize the unfortunate soul was the blood- and gore-soaked ribbon proclaiming their deeds. *Everyn.* To see the Paragon of Skill reduced to such a state- it nearly caused Thäoldr's stomach to empty itself. Resolutely, he held onto his lunch and leaned close, noticing that the woman's mouth was trying to form words. She was much worse off than the other two had been, so even her voice was nearly silent. The lonely eye that was left focused sharply on him and as he leaned, he heard the woman's plea.

"Kill... me... end... my... misery."

With each word, her body heaved, and she used more vital energy to speak and breathe. She was in agony, but something was keeping her from being able to just die. His eyes watered as he realized that the woman would not survive, no matter the interventions he made. Reaching for his belt knife, he growled as he remembered where it was- destroyed with his sword. So, his hand moved and sought hers, finding it quickly. The blade came into his hand and a quick search told him where her heart was. *One quick thrust- and she is free.* He took a breath and looked her in the eyes.

"I am sorry, Councilor Everyn. I failed you."

With those words, he plunged the dagger into the woman's heart. She took one more breath, as if to shriek in pain, but her voice was gone. She exhaled one last time and was still- mercy had taken her. Thäoldr growled and his hand released the blade.

"No more!" He cried out, running to the next councilor. They were at least better off- muscle still protected their organs. Sighing in relief, he took another vial and looked the councilor in the eyes.

"Yldrayd. Drink this- it will help. Try not to let it touch your tongue."

Grabbing the woman's hands, he wrapped them around the vial and brought it to her lips. Pouring it into her mouth, he readied himself to cup his hand over her lips. To her everlasting credit, Yldrayd took the draught without complaint or fight. She took a steadier breath and her eyes darted around with more energy. Her mouth worked and soon enough, she spoke.

"That... was the worst... thing I have ever drank."

Blinking, Thäoldr laughed at the woman's statement- not because it was humorous, but because of how true it rang. Nodding to her, he passed a wave of healing energy over her to give the woman's body a boost in rebuilding itself. Then he was away.

Finally, he came to councilor Ergyrn. He was holding on well and was still talkative- just what Thäoldr expected from the Paragon of Healing. Judging by the bottles strewn around, Ergyrn had all but used the entire supply of healing herbs in the storerooms to keep himself and his staff alive. But it was not enough- there were the telltale signs of death in more than a few of his healers, but some still clung to life.

"Come then, Thäoldr. Whatever evil drink you have, it cannot be worse than this sickness."

Ergyrn shook his head and took the vial as soon as the elf offered it. Uncorking it, he waved the potion under his nose and sighed. *Such an evil smell, and yet it has restored most of the council. Thank the stars for that.* Downing the mixture as quick as he could, he tried not to think of what he was putting into his body. Gagging heavily, he grabbed for Thäoldr's waterskin, which the elf quickly handed over. After a long draught to calm his stomach, Ergyrn spoke.

"Damned if that was not terrible. Hurry! Take to the healers- what ones still breathe- and get them back on their feet. From there, we will have aid for the others."

Nodding, Thäoldr left the dwarf with half his remaining potions to distribute. Then, he moved to healing the healers- or at least saving their lives. The various herbs gave him some measure of hope, but he knew the recipe for the cure by heart at this point. Regardless, it was going to be a long day.

Within a few hours, the least-damaged survivors were back on their feet. The others still faced a long road to recovery, but they were at stable. Meeting around the councilors that were still bedridden, the elders of the Riders spoke to one another.

"Thäoldr, we owe you our lives. How can we repay you?"

"First, formally declare the Order keeping us at odds with the Rangers void. Old hatreds are just that- old. They have been ingrained for so long that I doubt any of you remember what started them."

That was a tall order, but in the death's face they had just witnessed him curing, they didn't care. Ergyrn, in fact, seemed excited.

"Perhaps the Rangers can teach us of their medicines. Long have I wished to learn some of what they know, though trained in the arts by the Masterhealer himself I be."

Thäoldr smiled at Ergyrn's readiness to accept change, though he knew not all riders would be as accepting.

"Aid all you can and know this- Gelvrentael has spoken to me and he showed that our alliance with the Rangers has precedence- and that we may even be descended from one common force."

The Elders looked to each other in shock. Could it be that the Riders and Rangers once counted as one army? Surely, they would have been unstoppable!

"You said you learned this... from Gelvrentael?"

"Aye. He and dal'Kiyr appeared to me in something that felt too real to be a dream."

One elder scoffed and shook their head, only to be growled at by the others. It would not do to anger Thäoldr, they thought, especially when they owed him their lives.

"Then I look forward to your report on the matter, esteemed Paragon of Knowledge. I assume you have contacted the archivist. Asked him to search the records?"

"Not yet, considering that he was near death five minutes ago."

"Too right."

When the elders finished their conversation, Thäoldr bade his goodbyes and made his way out of the Hall of Healing. Back in the great hall, he met up with Wyria, who had procured some food.

"Wyria, we mus–"

"Eat. One, I must get that taste out of my mouth; that was the absolute most evil thing I have ever drank in my lifetime and I have had Urok Ale. Two, if I know what your daughter says is true, you fly for at least a day without eating and I have yet to see you break your fast. Sit. And. Eat."

She pointed emphatically at the stone table. Sheepishly, Thäoldr sank his rump onto the bench next to it and Wyria placed food before him.

"We are not like those foolish Rangers who only eat once a week. We cannot draw energy from Seran. Which means you must have a good meal before we fly for Karnost."

She waggled a finger threateningly, and the elf rolled his eyes.

"Come then, sit and eat, Wyria."

The woman chuckled and joined him, quickly digging into her own food. The Order held manners as important, but the woman felt that right now, none would judge her- least of all Thäoldr. The bread was stale and the stew cold, but it was food. Sighing, Thäoldr realized it would be some time before things were normal here. *Too many dead,* he thought, *too many lives cut short.* Taking a moment to steady his mind, he forced himself to slow down, considering each bite as he ate. As he did, though, he realized how much the thought of food nauseated him- and how little taste it had.

Sighing, Thäoldr resigned himself to finish the meal, meager as it was. It would serve its purpose for now and fuel him for the journey to come. When he had finished, he looked to Wyria, who immediately shot to her feet and retrieved the pottery and silverware.

"Wyria, I am perfectly capa-"

"No time. To your dragon. I will be with you shortly. We have solved the crisis here and must away."

Thäoldr opened his mouth to argue and thought better of it when he saw the woman's face. She would give no quarter in this matter. Turning on his heel, he took a jogging pace and made his way out to where Namryll was sunning herself. She saw him coming, though, and flipped herself over and readied herself to take off. Angling downward slightly to allow him access, the great dragon rumbled as he climbed into his saddle.

"To the skies, Namryll! To the skies!"

The great dragon braced herself for a moment, wings folded. For a heartbeat, they looked as if they were a well-detailed statue. Then the dragon kicked off, powerful legs propelling her and her rider into the bright blue sky. Her wings unfurled and pushed them higher and higher as she caught an updraft. Focusing on the distance to close, she aligned herself with the direction she needed to travel. Then she was off, gliding for as long as she could before her great wings pumped.

Taking in the view as he left Ormere, Thäoldr wondered what he would find in Karnost, before realizing thoughts closer to him. Turning in his saddle and craning his neck, he looked to see what he could see of Lenara- if Ormere was in the state it was, surely Lenara was worse.

"Namryll," he began, his thoughts racing once more, "did we send a batch of the cure to Lenara? Please, tell me yes."

Fear not. Yrblaith, Rider of Ernyll, took to that task with as a much cure as she could carry. The dragon seemed unconcerned, which gave Thäoldr a small measure of comfort. Taking a breath, he shifted back in his saddle and focused his mind on the ride ahead, piercing through the fog caused by his racing thoughts. Idly, he wondered when Wyria would join him, as she had planned to.

Abruptly, that question was answered as the scream of a griffon sounded, chased by the beast itself. The girl let out a whoop, both hands raised to the sky. She loved flying as much as she loved life, and it showed to the elf. Angling his head this way and that, he popped his neck, trying to work out a kink that had been there since the battle with Vaelyn. *Ancestors, that felt like a lifetime and it already feels so far off.*

A song made its way into his conscious mind and he caught himself humming it for just a moment. His focus shifted back to the skies ahead, and he felt his hand twitch as magical energy rippled through his body. There was no pain to the feeling, but a feeling of near serenity. That alone was cause for concern to the elf, and he quickly tried to shake it off. *Perhaps we should abstain from magic for a time. I feel as if using our powers– such as they are since our tattoos are erased– would hasten our demise.*

At length, his thoughts turned to family– at least, the family he had left. *Cirahael.* Was she alive? Sighing, he reached out with his thoughts, trying to bridge whatever distance separated them. He leaned on Namryll's mind, begging her to speak with Briem. *I must know if Cirahael is still drawing breath.*

Calm yourself. I will speak to The Beacon. Thäoldr had nearly forgotten about that device. The dragons spoke through it, using the massive crystal of Ancestorsheart to communicate across vast distances. Should Briem still be drawing breath, they would be in contact shortly.

Thäoldr trusted in his dragon and tried to relax, though his breath became shallow and fast as his mind focused, attempting to mentally bridge whatever distance he could. He sighed after a moment and resigned himself to the distance ahead. It would not do to lose focus right now, and he felt as though his mind were working faster than normal. He wondered where Karos was for a time and realized that he must make his way to Karnost as well. It would take time for him to arrive, as he was on foot– though Karos was full of surprises, so Thäoldr knew to expect the unexpected.

A few hours passed, and Cúledan came into view. At first, Thäoldr could hardly see the city and he wondered if they had been too late to save anyone. But as they approached, he saw at least five dragons landed there. Namryll quickly spoke to each beast and gathered their reports before touching Thäoldr's mind once more.

Kelthryll reports maybe fifteen hundred survivors in the city proper. This report comes from her rider, Olvik. Ykaryll reports nearly five-hundred in Castle Vigilance, but not among them is King Dalviin or his wife. Of course, most of the nobility survives, sequestered away from the trouble. Namryll sounded bitter about that, and Thäoldr felt the same way. The nobility could not care less if people are dying if it does not inconvenience them. Smirking, he half wondered if the folk hiding away in Castle Vigilance were basically using the events as a chance to throw a party.

Ykaryll says her rider believes that is the case. The voice sounded even more bitter, and the elf patted her neck. *No surprise there,* he thought to himself. Never miss a chance to socialize.

As they passed over the city, an odd sight- folk gathered in the town square struck Thäoldr. At first, Thäoldr thought they were rioting as two Riders worked to distribute the cure- then he realized they were cheering. They were singing the praises of the Riders and chanting their gratitude. The sight warmed the old elf's heart, and he leaned on Namryll, who let out a call in defiance of evil. Idly, Thäoldr wondered why Wyria was being so silent. A casual glance brought the realization that she was nowhere to be seen.

He was about to speak to Namryll when he saw a shadow overhead and a shrill cry pierced the flight-winds. Eyfa dropped from above playfully, and Wyria called out to Thäoldr.

"Come on then, Sagewind! Surely you know better than to let a potential foe sneak up on you!"

Casually, the elder Rider raised a hand, stretching his pointer and ring fingers out in a commonly accepted gesture showing where Wyria could put that line of thought. Chuckling, the girl returned the gesture with a smile and dropped back into proper formation.

Sometime around first watch, the two spotted the twinkling light of Karnost ahead of them. Grinning, Thäoldr motioned for Wyria to fly for the landing platforms that had been erected high on Mount Starwatch. These had been crafted long ago to allow the Order of Gelvrentael easy access to the Great Hall- and to report directly to the Kingmage without having to make the slog up the Mountain. Wyria nodded, though they were still a long way off- but they were flying high enough that they could see through the many leagues between them and the city.

Within a few minutes, they had landed gently on the stone platforms and dismounted their beasts one at a time. The elder Rider looked at his younger counterpart, nodding at her to take the lead. After all, she no longer reported to any Rider- instead, she was directly under the supervision and at the disposal of the Kingmage. Thus, it was only right that she be the first to get his attention. In the back of his mind, he wondered how long he had been at his current tasks. It had to have been at least a few days that he had been working.

Wyria was excited- then again, she was always giddy when she came back to Starwatch Keep. The Kingmage was always friendly enough and there was always plenty to be done. Reaching the great stone door, she closed her eyes for a moment and thought of the command for the door. Reaching out with her right hand, she traced her pathway nerves to express the magic. In response, the great door swung open silently. She regarded the darkness within for just a moment and nodded before crossing the breach. As soon as she had entered the Great Hall, she saw the Kingmage and his sister, sitting in their thrones at the far end, as well as three forms she didn't recognize.

"My greetings to you, Kingmage Harthos Harrolsen and to you, Lady Hillevi Harroldottir!"

The woman bowed respectfully before continuing to speak.

"I present Thäoldr Sagewind, Paragon of Knowledge of the Order of Gelvrentael, retrieved as requested by your eminence."

The rather burly Nolvern on the throne nodded slowly and waved his hand, indicating that the woman should allow the elf to approach. Wyria bowed once more and motioned at Thäoldr to advance. As he did, she fell into step with him. They stopped roughly ten paces from the throne and Thäoldr threw a crisp salute, crossing his hands over his heart and bowing. The man on the throne regarded him for a moment before speaking.

"Thäoldr Sage of Wind. When last I saw you, you were bald, scarred, and tattooed. What has transpired to transform you in such a way?"

"My lord, much has happened. We discovered the source of the fell plague gripping Seran."

"Aye, Karos has informed me of this. He also states that you faced an old mentor- Mulrah Vaelyn."

Thäoldr shot a surprised glance to Karos- how had the man retained that information while he was being beaten into the ground? He *was* a Ranger and *the* Warden Ranger at that, but he had taken one damned impressive beating. Chuckling, Thäoldr nodded, confirming the report.

"Aye. He was behind the plague and my transformation. He has become a magic-shade, a path I fear I have begun to walk down. I have, however, formulated a cure for the plague- while I trust in Karos' work, this plague is not of Seran, or the Ancestors. It is of Mirror Magic, called by many Void Magic. I am told an attack with this claimed the lives of a Rider, Porrik and his mount Tyfa. I saw o–"

"A vision, you say. The Ancestors spoke to you, Thäoldr?" *Karos. Of course.* On the bright side, he could chastise Karos without fear of being wiped from existence.

"Aye, Karos. And if you allow me to finish, I will explain it."

Karos looked acceptably deflated, while Harthos looked as if he was holding back a laugh. Sighing, the old elf continued.

"In this vision, dal'Kiyr herself, along with Elder Gelvrentael, appeared and told me of terrible things to come. They speak of an evil that Seran has only seen a few times before– they call it a Void Sleeper."

Karos visibly paled, Harthos looked quite concerned, and even Hillevi seemed disquieted. Thäoldr had heard of great evil things, but had never heard that name. Looking from one to the other, the question on his mind flowed from his lips. If both were worried, surely it was something terrible indeed.

"What is this creature? What is a Void Sleeper?"

Karos went to speak before he noticed Harthos opening his mouth. The Ranger's mouth snapped shut as he allowed the Kingmage to give the word.

"The Void Sleeper is a creature of incredible evil– and near limitless power. They appear in our world as a massive smoke-creature with the most terrible yellowed grin and eyes shining with hate. How many Dragonriders still live?"

"It will take me some time to gather those numbers, my Kingmage. Why do you ask?"

"The last time a Void Sleeper came into our world, an adventuring company led by then-Warden Ranger Erkosa the Adamant followed it as it burned a path of destruction the likes of which we have yet to see in modern days. It is said that when they could bear watching its assault no longer, they rallied

1500 of the greatest knights, mages and Rangers of their time-even the Order of Gelvrentael, in a rare move, aided them with 300 of their best."

Thäoldr *had* heard of that incident, just not the names or the name of the beast. Slowly, he understood the gravity of the situation.

"Five of them survived. Dragons were rent in twain. The army was crushed, burned, annihilated. But they killed the creature. And where it died, it is said nothing will ever grow again."

The story made sense to the elf now, and he nodded gravely.

"Karos, if this demon awakes, Seran may not survive. I want word sent out to every Ranger. Give each the description of the beast and tell them to be on guard."

Karos slapped his bracers together and turned to Sardra. She nodded quickly and took off running, but not toward the exits; She was bound for the aviary, to select the birds that would spread instructions to as many Rangers as possible. This was dire news indeed, and she hoped it was an unnecessary precaution.

Thäoldr looked between the two men and gauged their responses to each other's company. Karos seemed relaxed to the point of looking insolent, and Harthos seemed as if he cared not.

"Well, Harthos, it seems the time will come when you *and* Hillevi must prove your station." There seemed to be unmitigated cheek in Karos' voice, and it shocked Thäoldr. He turned to take the younger man to task- after all, he was speaking to the Kingmage- not only the most powerful Mage in Seran but also its ruler. Respect was always to be given. He was even more surprised when Harthos answered, as if he didn't care about Karos' insolent words.

"Aye. I trust we can put faith in your abilities, Karos? You were injured right well, if Sardra's words ring true."

"Believe me, child. They do, but I stand ready. I know, though, that is not the only reason you have summoned me- and it is obviously not the reason you sent for Khula."

Sighing, Harthos shifted in his seat and gestured to Hillevi. The slimmer woman regarded them through ice-blue eyes before speaking.

"It has come to our attention that you both were responsible for the death of General Magus Kefarion."

The tattoos over her eyes gave Hillevi the look of being quite angry; and Karos could feel Khula quailing. He opened his mouth to protest, but a hand raised from Hillevi stopped him short.

"Khula Tallam- you suffered much at his hands- as well as at the hands of your parents."

On the word 'parents', one of the great doors leading into the Great Hall was opened- in came ten knights, clad in full armor and the regalia of the Red Lance- and they were escorting her mother and father. Khula went white and nearly fainted, while Karos drew his sword, rounding angrily upon Khula's family and the knights escorting them. He growled, moving into a protective position, with the borrowed sword flashing dangerously in the light of the many torches.

"Karos! *Siðik!*"

Harthos was on his feet, hands in position to cast what would probably be a devastating spell. Energy rippled around his body, his pathway nerves glowing from his hands up to his neck. Hillevi stood as well, her spear in her hands, angled dangerously as she called out to the Ranger.

"*Lläs etja! Sunget krevik!* Harthos, damnit. These men have been chasing us across Seran! I will not let them attack Khula!"

"Karos! Obey your Kingmage and sheathe your damned sword! *Hav'a!*"

Growling, the Warden Ranger reluctantly tipped his sword to the ground in a gesture of compliance, before sheathing the blade. He half expected the knights of the Red Lance to make an arrogant comment, but they were oddly silent. One tapped the side of his leg in a gesture that everyone but Karos missed- and it was a Ranger hand-sign.

"Report, Ser Hythwain."

Hillevi leaned against her spear idly, eyeing Karos as if she expected him to make another play at engaging the knights. If necessary, she would pin him to the flagstones with her magic- or worse. The Warden Ranger flinched when he realized how brash he had been- and how close he'd gotten to revealing something he wasn't sure he was ready to. He had felt the Phrase in his throat- it had nearly erupted from his lips to bring the whole damned Great Hall down around them. But something had stopped him. Turning his head ever so slightly, he caught Harthos' eye and realized that the man had some goal already in mind- and had probably been the one to suppress his use of the Sk'av'A.

"I fetched Sywerd and Juri of Tallam as requested, my liege. Word has been passed of Magus' death as instructed, not just to them, but also to the leaders of the Red Lance. It has not gone as well as planned, Kingmage."

"Then send for them, Hythwain. I will explain why they are to stand to my words."

"Aye, my liege."

The knight Harthos had been speaking to gave a swift salute

before making his way out of the Great Hall. Quickly enough, another knight took his place in the formation, obviously meant not to protect the Tallam parents- but to forcibly guide them. It slowly dawned on Karos that they were not here in any power- they were here under arrest and in duress.

"Sywerd... It has been some time since last I was in your company. Never would I imagine you would betray the law in such a way- and hide it for three decades." Sywerd shifted uncomfortably, his ratlike face scrunching up in discomfort. He averted his eyes from the powerful trio in front of him and focused on his daughter. *Damn her*, he thought, *we will punish her for this!*

You cannot hide your thoughts from me, Sywerd. The voice wasn't that of Harthos'- it was Hillevi's, echoing in his mind with the force of a boulder striking a still lake. Sywerd had to choke back a scream, lest he reveal his absolute terror. *She will not be punished- for she is no longer your concern.*

"Khula of Tallam. Step forward."

The stentorian voice of Harthos echoed through the Great Hall, shaking the torches in their sconces. The woman addressed quailed for a moment, before Karos gently jogged her elbow, reminding her he was there. Taking a deep breath, Khula stepped toward the throne, watching with terror as Harthos rose to his feet. Karos felt quite small when watching him, though he had enjoyed the other's company many times before. Watching everyone around him, the brawny man unsheathed his great sword, the Script Blade. It was a massive weapon, patterned on the great claymore of the ancient Morians. In the Kingmage's hands, Karos knew it could serve as either a two-handed sword when Harthos wished for powerful strikes, but he was just as capable of using it one-handed. It had a massive blade running roughly four feet, nearly five; and it was adorned with Sk'av'A runes and Indekari script, both intertwining and forming phrases that Karos knew to be terrifyingly powerful enchantments. This was a sword meant for channeling enough power to destroy armies. In the back of his mind, Karos realized he recognized that handiwork- as well as the mark of the maker. The sword came from Coldforge, from the very fires of the Dragonforge itself, and was likely forged by the half-giant Forgemaster. Searching his memory for a moment, Karos sought to remember the man's name- only to come back to reality with a sudden feeling of being miniscule.

Suddenly, all the assembled folk felt quite powerless in the face of the Kingmage. But Karos knew it to be foolish-Harthos was kind to a fault and was one like Karos, in that his blade would never leave its sheath without a purpose. He resigned himself to watch as Harthos strode down the steps of the Throne, towering over Khula's meager form. It was a comical juxtaposition, with Khula standing a quarter spearlength under Harthos, who stood over a spearlength tall. Even Hillevi, the younger sibling by mere minutes, only came to the middle of his chest, though she stood as tall as Karos. Harthos was an enigma and absolutely terrifying to the unready.

Khula felt faint as Harthos beckoned her forward. When he unsheathed the great sword, she felt the urge to run- after all, what purpose could he have for that but to punish her for what she had done? She closed her eyes for a moment and forced those thoughts from her head. If she were to die for what she had done to Magus and his knights, so be it- she would die free. Opening her eyes, she stared upward, her gaze locking with Harthos' in a gesture of defiance that shook the larger man.

Harthos regarded the young woman as she stared up at him. He could sense many things in her mind and could see it in her eyes. She was willing to die just to escape what her parents had done to her. She was willing to risk her life for friends she had made over a few weeks' time. He could see the Ranger blade on her side, showing that not only was she ready to defend herself, she was throwing her lot in with the Rangers- whether she joined them was her choice. After a moment, he smirked.

"Lady Khula of Tallam. You have suffered much at the hands of your parents and husband, and have been a victim of customs that are prohibited by modern law."

Hillevi abruptly joined in, her voice echoing through the room.

"You have shown mettle of the highest degree and interfered in affairs that could have cost your life a thousand times over, all without fear."

Harthos spoke again, bringing the sword around and focusing his eyes on the blade, turning the flat to face him and Khula. As he spoke, the sword crackled with energy and the very air seemed to hum. Thäoldr's eyes widened- he had had massive amounts of energy pushed through him during the fight with Vaelyn, but this was on a whole different level. His skin tingled, and he glanced over at Wyria, who looked rather excited.

"In the name of the Ancestors and Ancestresses, I charge you to be wise and learn all you can." As the first line of the incantation issued forth, the great blade dropped gently to touch Khula's left shoulder. "In the name of the Ancestors, I charge you to carry yourself and your chosen name with pride."

The sword arced up and over Khula's head to drop and touch her right shoulder. "In the name of the fathers, I charge you to stand strong against any storm." Again, the sword arced, this time back to the left, again tapping her shoulder. "In the name of the mothers, I charge you to protect all you are able." Once more, the sword arced over to touch her right shoulder. "In the law's name, I charge you to be just in all dealings." He brought the sword up in front of his face, the flat of the blade obscuring his visage.

"By the power vested in me by the Ancestors and the Council and in the eyes of all witnesses here, I dub thee Knight Khula Frelas. Forever are you free from your parents- no longer do they hold any authority in your life, and their name dies with them- though I doubt I needed to confirm that. You are free to explore our lands, to come and go as you wish, without expectation of any man or woman being sent to fetch you. I dub you freewoman and Knight of Seran."

Khula's parents began to raise a ruckus, shouting and carrying on as they realized he stripped their power.

"You- you *dare-*"

Sywerd's words were cut short as a throwing stone collided with his nose, causing an audible crack. He fell backwards, blood streaming from his face and he shrieked. Khula turned to face him, her arm still outstretched from casting the stone. Harthos was impressed- she had not even looked away from him and had still found the stone in one of her pouches and cast it with perfect accuracy. Evidently, there was more to her than a delicate flower. Nodding, Harthos turned to regard Khula's parents.

"And you. Knight Khula, I ask you to recount their crimes as readily as you can bear to. I ask you to be truthful, in the name of Enkar, with bearing witness."

Khula nodded and prepared to sign, and Harthos shot a glance at Karos.

"Karos. You will perform the duty of Truthspeaker. Give voice to Khula's words and on pain of death, be truthful."

The Warden Ranger nodded solemnly and Khula turned to face him. As she spoke, her hands shaky with emotion as she recounted her earliest abuses, the Ranger's rage only grew.

"This witness I bear in the name of the Ancestors and the Truthlight. I, Khula Frelas, formerly of Tallam, was treated as chattel for a period not less than twenty-three years. From the time I was seven years old, my only education was how to be an amicable and subservient housewife; to where I was not taught The Charges, The Virtues, and *barely* taught of the Ancestors and Ancestresses. My freedoms were restricted, and I could not go outside without the man my parents intended for me. My room was windowless, and I was forbidden to look to the night sky. I was treated worse than house servants, made to dress in a manner arousing to Magus Kefarion from the time I first menstruated."

Harthos and Hillevi exchanged glances. Between them, their thoughts in sync, they wondered if it would be better to simply slay Sywerd and Juri right there. But a harsher crime was becoming clear in their minds and they silently agreed.

"I was promised to Magus Kefarion as wife and subservient from the time I was born. Upon reaching the age of consent, I was to be given to him in exchange for enormous sums of money, protection of the Red Lance upon my family and for favor in local politics, to include the removal of opponents of their ideals. I was able to convince them to spare me until adulthood and thus married; I was bearing his heir and...

" she sighed gently, hanging her head as if the knowledge was shameful "...miscarried. He blamed a friend of mine, Sir Crelsthan of Sendes, and murdered him. I was made to promise Magus my body whenever he wished for it, so that I would conceive anew, and I broke that oath many times and was severely beaten and even branded for my trouble."

She flexed her wrist gently, trying to get her mind to settle before continuing to speak through Karos.

"When I finally reached adulthood and was married to Magus, I took every chance I had to avoid being in the company of either my parents or him, but they always seemed to find me. They assigned a Voice to me, but they instructed her to speak what they wished me to say, rather than be a voice for me. They silenced my will until the Plague began and I escaped with the aid of a Ranger. Events prevailed, and it led me into the company of Karos and made aware of just how deep my abuse went."

Once more, the Kingmage and his sister exchanged glances, speaking to each other through their deep mental connection. *What say you to* ket'rak, *Hillevi,* thought Harthos at his sister, examining her responses silently.

We must carefully consider this. Declaring ket'rak would have repercussions, the Tallam family is enormously powerful. We would potentially make many enemies.

Enemies be damned, we must mete justice upon them. Both Kingmage and kin nearly jumped from their skin. The voice belonged to no one in the room and had an authority beyond what they could question. It was the voice of the First Judge, Enkar himself. Though they knew him to be nowhere in the room, the nobles looked around, almost as if trying to see if anyone else had heard the demand.

Karos was still reeling when they looked at him, the voice having caused an intense headache to flare up. He blinked hard, trying to regain his senses, and looked up, bleary-eyed. When his eyes finally focused, he saw Khula standing before him, evidently unfazed. Incredulous, he pulled himself to his feet and looked her over before speaking a single word.

"How?"

She smirked and shook her head. Her hands worked quick, telling him all he needed to know.

"I am no stranger to that voice."

"Nor am I, but it was loud enough to cripple everyone."

"Oh? Perhaps Enkar did not wish to cripple me."

Karos glanced around and was amazed to realize that he and Khula were the only ones that had recovered so far. Harthos and Hillevi were still clutching their heads and the guards surrounding Juri and Sywerd had all but collapsed. The two had evidently been affected as well, but seemed to try to make a run for freedom. Then, just as suddenly as the pain came on, it was gone from everyone. Karos felt the pressure in his head subside and raised an eyebrow.

"Now! Attack!"

The voice was Sywerd's, and as soon as it had left his lips, the knights of the Red Lance readied weapons. All but one who broke ranks and ran to Karos. All could feel the tension of the situation grow, and it gave the Kingmage pause because of the outright audacity of the Tallam family. The knight who had approached Karos turned and readied his blade against his own comrades, and Karos' sword likewise flashed into his hands. Khula grabbed for a throwing rock from one of her pouches and it set the stage.

Sywerd began charging his energy, readying some spells

that he had been learning in secret. Energy crackled from his fingertips for a moment, before the Kingmage decided enough was enough.

From above came a great gust of wind, smashing downwards into the Tallam troops, slamming them to the floor. Every time they tried to crawl back to their feet, the wind would gust again and dissipate within a few feet of them. The source was obvious; Harthos was on his feet, hands outstretched and pathway nerves glowing bright. He had entertained this nonsense quite long enough, and he knew Hillevi felt the same way.

As Hillevi stood, she charged her own pathway nerves, straightened her left arm and closed her fist, aiming her hand towards the crowd of people her brother was keeping flat on the floor. Mentally, she searched through the hundreds of spells she had learned and the countless more she was practicing and selected one. Her pathway nerves glowed, and she traced them down to her hand, causing a circle of flame to form around her wrist.

Sywerd pushed his knees under him and throw his hands upward. It took most of his energy, but he dispelled the downdrafts flattening his entourage. He stood first and tried to ready another spell, just as Hillevi unleashed a bolt of flames. It struck him in the center of his chest and launched him backwards, slamming him into a wall and he fell to the ground, insensate. His guards scrambled to their feet and one readied himself to throw a spear, but never got that far. A dagger appeared in his chest and he fell to the stones, dead. All eyes turned to the source of the dagger– Thäoldr, who had been content to stand silent and watchful until now.

"You *dare* attempt a coup against the Kingmage?" His voice

echoed into the great hall as he took an up position near Karos and began charging his own pathway nerves. If this was to be a coup attempt, it would be the shortest in Seran's history.

"Enough!" Came the call from Harthos' throat. The knights attempted to rally, but at a single flick of the Kingmage's hand, they were scattered in every direction, their armor rent and crumpled by some spell only the Kingmage knew. Karos glanced up to see that Harthos' pathway nerves had become a fiery red and his hair, which he normally kept contained, had become wild and somewhat unsettling. None of the knights moved and Karos wagered them to be unconscious or dead. In the back of his head, the Warden Ranger admitted pride in the younger man; evidently, he was making good on his duty to constantly push the boundaries of spell–casting. When he next spoke, he directly addressed Khula, including her new title.

"Knight Khula, I know right well you know your way around Starwatch Keep. I ask that you fetch my Masterhealer and the Kingspell. Be swift about it, please."

Khula snapped to and nodded quickly, before dropping her stone back in a pouch and darting out. As soon as she was gone, Harthos looked to Karos, before indicating with his head that the Ranger should retrieve Jurl and Sywerd. Nodding, the Ranger made his way first to the man slumped against the wall. He did not react, which prompted Karos to check his neck for a pulse, before pinching one of his neck muscles roughly. The man groaned weakly and slapped at his hand, but reacted little more than that, causing Karos to shake his head gently.

"Milady Hillevi, you have knocked him nearly insensate. He is responding only to pain."

"Oh. No. Anything but that."

Karos did not miss the sarcasm in her voice as he grabbed a small ampule of *paktimoni* and a piece of cloth. Breaking the ampule open and lightly drenching the cloth with the liquid inside, he brought it up under Sywerd's nose. Immediately, the man's eyes shot open and a dark stain spread on his trousers. Scoffing, Karos picked himself up and kicked the man in the side.

"On your feet, Sywerd."

Sywerd, who was just conscious enough to act without question, scrambled to his feet and stood with all the steadiness of a drunkard. He nearly fell a few times, only to be seized by Karos. Finally, the Warden Ranger dragged the man over to the throne and dropped him to the stones. Then, he did the same with Juri, who struggled more.

"Unhand me! Fucking peasant!"

"Be silent, lest I cut your damned tongue from your foolish mouth, wench."

"You would not dare, Ranger. You need me alive."

"*Te kintaris*, Tallam whore. I have no need of you."

When the last words left Karos' mouth, Juri realized just how dire her situation was. At a single word from the Kingmage, her entire line could end in dishonor and ruin. *What would mother think of me now?* She thought to herself, her terror rising. A few yards away, a door opened to reveal Khula, returning with the Starwatch Keep Masterhealer, a tall urok by the name Ornash Ge'Varn. Behind them trailed the Kingspell, a young gah'Drin lass called Lyrwyna. She carried with her a rather strange looking metal instrument and looked rightly annoyed.

"My liege, I really must protest this summons. I was in the middle of transcribing your notes on–"

The girl went silent as the Kingmage held up a warning hand, both to stop her from mentioning what she was working on and to focus her attention. At an unspoken command, she charged her pathway nerves and expressed a bright blue flame in her hand, before placing one end of the metal instrument above the flame to heat.

"Sywerd and Juri Tallam. For your crimes against the sapient, the crime of slavery, the abuse of a child, the attempt of treason and other crimes, it is with the utmost solemnity that I strip you of nobility, rank, name, possessions and station."

At a hand motion from Harthos, Karos and Thäoldr moved quickly, cutting away belt favors and any signs of station that Sywerd and Juri were wearing. They then cast them at the foot of the throne, where they were incinerated by a spell from Hillevi.

"By the justice of Enkar and the laws of Seran, in the eyes of all the witnesses here. I declare you both *ket'rak*, forgotten by Ancestors and Ancestresses. You will be exiled from all cities, towns, hamlets, and hovels, to receive aid from none of the good folk of Seran."

At another hand motion, Karos and Thäoldr brought their daggers to Juri and Sywerd's tunics. Both were sliced open to bare their chests and Karos also sliced the fascia protecting Juri's breasts. They exposed fully her before the Kingmage and his friends and she struggled. She had heard stories of being declared *ket'rak*, but never thought it would happen to her. This was a new low, and it was all Khula's fault! *Damn her and her spirit and damn those "friends" she has made!* As she spat curses against her only daughter and the friends who had uplifted her, Juri failed to notice the white-hot brand approaching her.

"May the Ancestors close their eyes to you forever more and cast you off The Path when you find your end."

Juri let out a shriek as the brand touched her flesh. She attempted to pull away, but Karos held her secure. Her scream echoed through the Great Hall many times over, becoming a deafening cacophony of anguish. But still Karos held her firm until it seared fully the brand onto her skin. Then, as quickly as they pressed it against her, the brand was removed, leaving a seared diamond with two curves, two bars and a tear inside upon her chest. The wound bubbled and sizzled, the burn having gone straight to her sternum. Juri was hyperventilating. She could not catch her breath and the world was spinning around and around, while her vision tunneled into darkness.

Moments later, she was unconscious in Karos' arms. The Masterhealer stepped over to her and checked for a pulse. It was still there, though quite rapid. Quickly, he placed a square of gauze soaked in healing potions over the three-inch-high wound. It sizzled slightly more, and he worked to secure the gauze in place. Then, trading off with Lywyrna, he took up the brand and approached Sywerd, who was now pale and terrified. Lywyrna unrolled a scroll and was about to begin an incantation when Harthos interrupted her.

"I will perform the rite, Lyrwyna."

"Aye, your majesty."

Nodding, the girl stepped out of the man's way and stood at the ready as Harthos traced complex patterns in the air. This resulted in the air becoming charged and active, with lines of lightning connecting all points and forming a strange design. Then, he reached through the middle of the design and placed his hand on the brand on Juri's chest. Energy flowed down his arm and out of his hand, sealing the brand to the woman. A faint green glow in the brand's shape emanated from Juri's chest, visible even through the cloth that had been wrapped around her. The glow grew stronger until it was clear to all around and Harthos stepped back.

"Please, I beg you. I will give you anything you wish; money, power, whoever you desire."

Sywerd was a babbling mess trying to ply Ornash with treasures that he no longer had access to, but the orc was unfazed. Bringing the brand around, he pressed it to Sywerd's chest without a single word. The skin sizzled and burned, cracking under the intense heat, and soon the brand had burnt through the first few layers of flesh. Sywerd had tried to hold it back, but the instant the brand met his skin, he began screaming. But that was not enough. The brand had to go deeper; deep enough that no matter what he tried, it would be there until the end of his days. *Or until he earns reinda*, thought the orc, *but that is not damned likely.* He added more pressure to the brand, letting it burn its way into the damned man's flesh.

The screaming stirred Juri from her unconsciousness and when she came to, she could still barely breathe. Every movement of her chest made it ache like she had never known, so she quickly began taking smaller breaths. Her eyes were wild as she looked around, trying to gauge where she was, and it took quite a moment for the realization to dawn on her she was still in the Great Hall, being held by the Warden Ranger. She attempted to jerk away to no avail and glanced over as Ornash finished branding Sywerd.

Sywerd gasped for air as the brand was pulled away from his body and instantly regretted doing so. As his chest expanded outward, the skin that had been seared and traumatized stretched and tore. He began coughing as Ornash handed off the brand to Lywyrna and began preparing a dressing and bandage for the wound. Harthos stepped over and began the incantation he'd performed at Juri, with the same result; the brand was sealed and glowed through the coverings Ornash put on them and when it was finished, Thäoldr released his prisoner, allowing the man to fall to his knees. Karos released Juri, before quickly putting his boot behind her leg to bend her knees as well. When both were kneeling, Harthos spoke once more.

"Henceforth, you are banished from all cities and towns of Seran. Even the gah'Drin and tal-Edröhel clans will recognize you as *ket'rak* and shun you. You are welcome nowhere. Now!"

Harthos snapped his fingers and twelve of the Kingmage's Own snapped to attention, their armor clattering. With a wave of his hand, they were summoned over and came at a trot. When he next spoke, there was no trace of the emotion he had delivered the Tallam their sentence with, no trace of kindness or pity.

"Get these *ket'rak* out of my sight."

"*Aya*, your majesty!"

Immediately, two of the Kingmage's Own seized each prisoner and dragged them out. It would be a hard road for them for sure, not only because of the sentence handed down, but because of the descent from Starwatch Keep itself. It was nestled about halfway up Mount Starwatch, which placed it at just under a league above the city, and it took weeks for folk to safely ascend, save for the Riders, who could operate at nearly any altitude thanks to the intense training they undergo.

Harthos and Hillevi regarded Karos and his entourage once more. Sardra had come back into the Great Hall some time ago and watched the ritual silently, but now spoke.

"Kingmage, your will is done. I have sent every bird in your aviary out to carry messages to the Rangers spread across Seran."

Thäoldr spoke next, angling his eyes up to the ruler and his advisor. He weighed each word and took a few breaths.

"Kingmage Harthos, High Advisor Hillevi. With your permission, I will return to Ormere Keep and see that preparations are made for the upcoming troubles."

Harthos nodded solemnly. When he spoke, the voice came less as an order and more as a request, as if Thäoldr was a friend rather than a subject.

"Master Thäoldr, I ask you to take this to heart and prepare how you may but realize this; your time is running out. A timeglass has been placed and the grains are in motion. You may have realized this already, but your time will end. You may find it wiser to enjoy what is left."

Thäoldr grimaced; he had hoped to keep that a secret from Karos, lest the young man try to come up with some way to stave off the inevitable. Such seemed to be the way with him, and the Paragon of Knowledge had already been sorting through his vast stores of information to learn what was happening. It annoyed him when Karos turned to him.

"On that note, Thäoldr. The Rangers have a-"

"The Kingmage is speaking, Karos."

"Thäoldr, heed to Karos' words. They may prove handy."

"I- very well, your eminence, Karos, continue."

"As you may or may not know, the Rangers do not sleep. We do not sleep because when doing so, we face the dark things we have done in service to Seran. We face the evils done to us, the things that led us to become Rangers. These memories mass against us and we wake up in short order, screaming and clutching weapons. We do not get rest this way. But some time ago, the Moot and past Warden Rangers put their minds to solving the problem and discovered that there is a way to rest, to give energy back to the world; to ground oneself without sleeping. We call it the Trance. The Archivist here has records and teachings, but you may find it useful to request a *saal'kwen* to teach you the Trance. The Change may be inevitable, but we may stave it off for a time."

Thäoldr nodded, hugely impressed. *If what he says is true, this could be invaluable.*

"Indeed. Khula Frelas!"

The woman looked up when addressed, blinking and raising a hand to point at herself. Harthos nodded and grinned.

"You must now realize. You are the bride of the late Magus Kefarion, who had an extensive property in Dragonmoor. As well, you are the only honorable and non-exiled member of your former family. Which means, dear Khula, that you are now *quite* wealthy. Use it wisely."

Khula was nothing short of shocked at this revelation. Certainly, she had known it to be a potential outcome, but to have it confirmed was something else entirely. Blinking again, she looked up to the Kingmage and simply bowed.

Then, together with Karos, Sardra, and the knight who had joined them against the Red Lance, she made her way out of the Great Hall. As they left, the Kingmage called out to them, one final parting request.

"Now then, defenders of Seran. Take to your tasks and keep hope in your hearts. The night is darkening, but no night lasts forever. If by blood must the light return, then so shall it be."

Sardra grinned for a moment before speaking up. She echoed

the very words that had given her strength in dark times, this time for all to hear.

"We are Seranese and some of the hardiest of our kind. Already we have sacrificed much. However, your majesty, your grace, we know life is never without sacrifice."

Seranese Names and their Pronunciation

1. Artlur - Art-lure
2. Tirian - Tee-ree-uhn
3. Pehin (Species) - Peh-heen
4. Delvoranth (Species) - Dehl-vore-anth
5. Rúwia - Roo-yah
6. Alador - Awl-ah-door
7. Jerut - Jeh-root
8. Magus - May-Goos
9. Vaelyn - Vie-linn
10. Elras - Ell-rahs
11. Ywelin - Ew-ell-inn
12. Mara-gith - Mah-Rah-Gihth
13. Mojhannar - Moh-hah-nahr
14. Ulivar - Ooh-lih-var
15. Berram - Burr-uhm
16. Lorvin - Lowr-veen
17. Havlai (Species) - Half-lie
18. Lillia - Lill-ee-uh
19. Govlim (Species) - Gohv-lihm
20. Gwendlyn - Gwehn-d-lihn
21. Klurgan - Kloor-gahn

22. Errol - Err-ole
23. Treshkin - Trehsh-kin
24. Hes-Fal-Garan - Hess-Fall-Gah-Rahn
25. Helvaraith - Hehl-vuh-writh
26. Haldwygg - Hahl-dwigg
27. Earlaine - Earl-aine
28. Llornywn - Lorne-yewn
29. Eldyg - Ell-dig
30. Salrin - Sawl-Rihn
31. Knost - Kuh-nost
32. Kyrgin - Keer-Geen
33. Ulzi - Ool-zhee
34. Tazka - Tahzh-kah
35. Ni'La - Nee-Lah
36. Amrilyn Sarthon - Am-rill-ehn Sawr-tawn
37. Searla - Seer-luh
38. Sonorus (Species) - Sow-no-roohs
39. Ku'Sao'Raan - Koo-Sow-Rahn
40. Algord - Awl-Gourd
41. Oskin - Osk-in
42. Pohgrak - Poh-grack
43. Alhan Tu'Garyig - Al-an Too-Gar-yeeg
44. Galrajh - Gall-rajj
45. Dularin - Dooh-law-rihn
46. Elkin Thuraen - Elk-een Thoo-ray-en
47. Corvain - Core-vain
48. Dunverio - Duhn-veh-ree-oh
49. Hovar - Hoh-vahr
50. Uiuth - Ooh-youth
51. Tyrwyn - Teer-win
52. Everyn - eve-rin

53. Yldrayd - Eel-dray-duh
54. Ergyrn - Err-gear-nuh
55. Ykaryll - ee-kar-eel
56. Olvik - owl-veek
57. Yrblaith - Eer-blade
58. Ernyll - Err-neel
59. Kelthryll - Kehl-thrill
60. Sywerd - Sew-ahrd
61. Juri - Joo-Ree
62. Ornash Ge'Varn - or-nahsh geh-vahrn
63. Lyrwyna - leer-wee-nuh
64. Harthos - Harr-toss
65. Hillevi - Hill-eh-vee
66. Spintki (species) - speent-kee
67. Ormere - Oar-meer

Pronunciation and Meaning of Terms

1. Shkali - sh-kah-lee (Victory!)
2. Iyz'keð seltri - eyes-ked sehll-tree (lit. Cold War)
3. Anegidara - ah-neh-(hard)gee-dah-rah (pansexual)
4. Sadja - Sahd-yah (Head Scout)
5. Laghe - La-hey (Lake)
6. Valoria - Vah-low-ree-uh (Valor)
7. Kuksa - kuk-sah (drinking vessel)
8. Katryg - kah-triig (my truest)
9. Teljt - tel-yet (friend)
10. litik'röka - lee-teek ruck-ah (honor's kiss)
11. Sarashal - Sah-rah-shall (plant)
12. Talthras - Towl-thruss (plant)
13. Calcanna - call-cahn-nuh (food)
14. Seax - see-axe (weapon)
15. Khukari - khoo-kah-ree (weapon)
16. Skvath-trapa - Skvatt-trah-puh (storm/shock trooper)
17. Edja - (Edge)
18. Ket'rak - Keht-rack (exile, branding used as punishment)
19. Siðik - seeth (soft th)-eek (Halt!)
20. Lläs etja! Sunget krevik! - les eht-yah soon-geht kreh-viik (Battle cry. Blade Bite! Wound Fester!)
21. Hav'a - hah-vah (Now!)

22. Te kintaris - teh ken-tahr-iss (On the contrary)